TITANS
RISING
THE CALLING

BY
D.E. VARNI

ISBN-10: 0615566952
EAN-13: 9780615566955

PROLOGUE:

HOMECOMING

The Earth was an immaculate blue with white clouds rolling over the landmasses below. From the depths of space, a fleet of massive starships jumped into orbit. It was the 453rd fleet, on time. Aboard the flagship, the USS Excelsior, the Admiral called out commands to the helm.

"Steady as she goes."

"Aye sir," answered the helmsman.

"Take us to our new home. San Diego shipyard should be a pleasant sight."

The ship slowed and crept closer toward the Earth and the rest of the 453rd followed the flagship. The crew walked casually across the many decks, with a spring in their step. Soon the Excelsior would land on Earth. Soon they would be home.

On the flight deck, the pilots boarded their fighters to guide the fleet in with a heroes salute. They launched out of the hangar on the EM rails and quickly corrected their course to fly alongside the fleet, standing as sentries while the parade made its way into the upper atmosphere above the Western Hemisphere, and slowly descended. In the Insertion/Extraction hold, dozens of Alpha/Beta Model-4 [AB-4] transports waited to launch their battle weary soldiers to the Earth.

Inside one AB, unofficial master sergeant, private first class Daniel Henry Rooke sat in full kit, his helmet in place with the visor up. He gripped a long rifle that looked like a naginata at his side with the butt resting on the floor as he eyed the bayonet in silence. Around him, the cabin buzzed with activity. Men and women talked boisterously about what they were planning to do when they finally reached the ground. A number of men and women were in agreement that the first thing they would do is find a restaurant and have real eggs.

Next to him, a man sat down and didn't bother to pull down the harness into a locking position. Rather, he reclined and groaned, laying his head against the headrest, like a weary commuter. He was an oddity to the battle hardened soldiers in the cabin. Dressed in Bermuda shorts and a Hawaiian print button down shirt, he looked like he was waiting to hit the beach, except he wore knee and ankle braces and his shoulder was in a sling. Then, as if just noticing Daniel, the man smiled and winked.

"You mind if I sit here, soldier?" said the man.

"No." replied Daniel, uncaringly.

Daniel said nothing else, but returned to fix his eyes on the blade in front of him. The Hawaiian print man rolled his eyes.

"Well, you're a talker." he announced. "Could I have picked a less talkative person to sit next to?"

The warmth in the man's voice was unmistakable and Daniel found he could not suppress a smile for the man.

"Sorry, sir." said Daniel. "I'm just not in the mood to be talkative right now."

The man studied him with knowing eyes and nodded.

"You have the look of a man who lost everything."

"Almost," replied Daniel with a wan smile.

"I've been there."

This irked Daniel. The man sitting next to him had the decided look of a man who lived in luxury for the duration of the war. Probably a senator's son, kept far in the back, or more likely, a starship crewman. They were renowned for their soft beds, their steak dinners and their real eggs and milk. Nothing powdered. Nothing with nourishment supplements in it. No intravenous nutrient intake ports in their uniform mobile armor for longer durations between supply drops.

"I beg your pardon, sir," replied Daniel. "But I doubt it."

"Well," roused the man, "I'm not going to go into it, but I've literally seen hundreds of good men go up in flames. And I knew them all."

Daniel looked up at the man and read his face. Behind the easy smile and the reckless glare in his eyes was a pain that matched his own. There was only one other kind of soldier in the war with a right to be battle weary, in Daniel's estimation, and he now had the strong feeling he was talking to one.

"You're a pilot."

"I'm a pilot."

"What do you fly?" asked Daniel, unnecessarily aggressive. The man smiled at the challenge.

"I fly a Roman." answered the man, smiling.

Daniel eyed the man and nodded.

"That's a nice bird."

"Yeah, they can do a hell of a lot of tricks," replied the man conversationally as he unconsciously rubbed his affected shoulder with his good hand, "I'll personally attest to that."

"Daniel Rooke," said Daniel, offering his free hand.

"Daniel," taking his hand, wincing a little as they shook. "I'm Tom. Tom Harris."

Daniel blinked.

"Not Captain Thomas Harris."

Captain Thomas Harris? It couldn't be. The very man who piloted *Chariot of the Gods*—the most advanced Roman starfighter in the fleet. Surely this was just a man with the same name and rank. After all, Harris was a fairly common name. And Daniel had met hundreds of Toms.

"Yeah, that's me." said the man.

Daniel blinked again looking at him in an entirely new light of awe.

"Sir, it's an honor."

Harris smiled. Just then, a grunt's voice broke the long buzz from the other soldiers and took dominance in the cabin.

"Excuse me," said the grunt, his voice dripping with sarcasm. "Did I just hear you right? You're Captain Thomas Harris?"

The cabin fell silent as three dozen soldiers turned and stared at Harris.

"Yup."

"Zeus?" challenged another grunt.

"That's me," smiled Harris.

The silent eyes pored over him, studying him in a silent, awed reverence. Harris seemed to shift uncomfortably, recognizing the hero worship and unconsciously rubbed his leg as though he were trying to straighten his shinbone. Finally, a bold woman undid her harness, set her helmet down and walked over to Harris, extending her hand to him.

"Sir, it's a real honor." The rest of the grunts nodded in agreement, and a few close by patted their fists on his shoulder, or offered their hands to him, which he shook, somberly. The bold woman eyed Harris curiously. "Why are you down here with the grunts?"

"I felt like going for a walk in the sunshine," smiled Harris, visibly glad the staring was over and conversation had opened again. "I hear we're landing in San Diego. Maybe I'll walk across the border and blow my backpay on cheap alcohol and expensive girls."

There was an eruption of laughter from the men, while the female grunts blushed or frowned.

"You're really Zeus?" asked another grunt, "I mean, wow, *the* Zeus!"

"Look," chuckled Harris, "it's not that big of a deal."

"You were the one who covered the AB advance during the taking of Gliese 876 d."

"I had that honor," replied Harris with a solemn nod.

"I heard you were ordered back to the fleet because they didn't want to lose you in that turkey-shoot. You really led a team into the upper atmosphere against orders?"

"It was only against orders until I got commendated for it. Then it was all a part of the Admiral's plan."

The others laughed at hearing this and began slapping him on the back or merely touching him as if to one day be able to say: *"I touched Thomas Harris. I touched Zeus."*

Just then, a soldier flung himself into the AB cabin with excited eyes.

"Hey, I just heard there are Specials on the Excelsior."

The cabin changed on the turn of a dime from awe and respect to nervousness and excitement, depending on whose eyes and conversation you kept up with.

"Specials?" demanded the female grunt who had shaken Harris' hand, "Really?"

Harris nodded to her, acknowledging it was indeed true. Several teams of Specials were indeed on board the Excelsior.

"There's no such thing as Specials," scoffed the sarcastic grunt across from Daniel.

"What do you mean, 'no such thing?'" challenged another soldier.

"They're just comic book serial stories for the kids back home."

"I hear they're real," insisted one of the female soldiers.

"You believe in the Tooth Fairy too?" challenged the sarcastic grunt across from Daniel. Something in him seemed on edge. He took it personal that someone would smear the Specials teams and he found his voice.

"Hey," called Daniel across to the sarcastic grunt. "I got saved by a Special, once. Big guy who didn't even need a rebreather. He was one tough mother. No. Specials are real."

"Was it Maximus?" asked a watery-eyed soldier excitedly.

"No," replied Daniel, "I've never seen Maximus, except from war footage feeds to the rec-room."

"Man," sighed the watery eyed soldier, pushing on his neighbor's shoulders, "can you believe a guy can do all that stuff?"

"Not really," answered Daniel with a shrug. "I've seen a lot of men do extraordinary things on the front. I've just never seen anybody fly before."

"I don't know much about the Specials," said Harris, instantly commanding everyone's attention with an easy smile. "Back when I was doing AB runs I had a few in my cabin, but I didn't talk to them. I just did my job and deployed them planet-side."

"You met Specials?" asked the watery-eyed grunt with awe in his voice.

"No, I didn't *meet* them." corrected Harris. "I transported them toward the middle of the war. That was all before I got promoted. Afterward, I didn't hear much about 'em. They were kept away from the general population."

"Yeah," scoffed a soldier toward the back of the cabin darkly. "I'll bet."

"What's that supposed to mean?" challenged Daniel, eyeing him critically.

"You don't know?" scoffed the grunt. "They're not like us. I heard they turned on us during the war. Fought their own men."

"Bullshit," scoffed Harris. "No one would turn against the Earth."

Daniel felt a growing respect for Harris, and turned to him for an answer that made sense of the war and the Specials, painting either in a good light.

"I don't know about that," replied the grunt, menacingly.

"I've seen a lot of things," answered Harris. "But I'm telling you, there's nothing that has ever unified the Earth more than this war. Ideologies, religions, ethnic groups, they all got along together perfectly fine once they all had a common enemy. The Quill unified us in a way that's unprecedented. No one is going to turn away from their own planet."

"Maybe they don't want to join the Quill," surmised the soldier across from Daniel, "Maybe they want to rule Earth. You ever thought about that?"

"Let an ignorant person talk," replied Harris, "you'll hear a lot of stupid things."

There was a smattering of chuckles following this statement and the soldier across from Daniel went red-faced.

"Hey," scoffed the soldier, "freedom of speech."

"You're in the military, now," retorted Harris. "I'm ordering you to change the topic."

The soldier went silent and glowered at Harris. The silence was shared by the rest of the grunts for several moments, as though the command were universal for the soldiers aboard the AB. Finally, the watery-eyed soldier broke the silence: "I wonder if Maximus is on the Excelsior. That would be so cool."

"Maybe I can get a picture of him for my kids," added a female grunt.

The trivial conversation did not include any harsh criticism of Specials or talk of treason, so Daniel felt no need to be a part of it and withdrew back against the back of his seat.

Daniel turned to Harris.

"Anyway," sighed Daniel as Harris met his eyes, "that's what it was like on the planets. Isolation breeds gossip. Without contradicting points, gossip becomes unassailable fact. Try to break a grunt's opinion. I dare you."

"Well, the pilot's not cut off from the flow of information." replied Harris. "He gets it every day. The good and the bad."

"So you know how the war ended?" inquired Daniel, excitedly.

"No." Harris' answer was emphatic.

"Seriously?"

"Seriously. I was on sortie and the fight was pretty heavy, then two fleets jumped in at the same time. The 553rd and a Quill fleet composed of starships that made this ship look tiny. I thought we were going to lose. Against those kinds of numbers? The math just runs out. And I'm real good at long equations."

"So what happened?"

"The Quill fleet rolled right past us and took position surrounding the space station we were trying and dying to just get close to. Next thing I knew the Quill pilots went into full retreat. Then the Excelsior made the call commanding all operable fighters to stand down and land in her hangar bay. There weren't many fighters left, so we didn't take up much room. Then the Quill sent out drones to collect the escape pods and lifeboats and brought them back to us.

Next thing we know, the Admiral of the fleet is telling us the war's over."

"But what happened?"

Harris shrugged.

"Beats me. All I know is my job's over. No need to train newbies, or beat myself up in a cockpit anymore. The war's over. It's a new world, kid. You worked hard for it. Be proud."

On the viewing monitor, they watched as the starlit black canopy was pushed back to welcome the familiar blue and rolling white. Harris smiled at the viewscreen.

"Momma, I'm home."

As they descended into the atmosphere, the turquoise skies became their ceiling and they all watched, mesmerized, as clouds reached up and rose above the viewscreen. On they travelled, cutting the mist, passing along the rolling California coastline, hugging on a southeasterly course toward San Diego. As they pushed on, they reached the bluffs of Santa Monica adorned with a pier with a Ferris wheel and a rollercoaster filled with people, rushing about like ants, so far below.

Suddenly the sound of proximity claxons began ringing and every grunt in the cabin was alert and keenly aware that something was wrong. They eyed the viewscreen watching for signs of attack, but nothing interrupted their view of the Santa Monica Pier. Seagulls danced on the wind, venturing closer to the viewscreens. The grunts stared out at the familiar sight and every eye welled up with tears. They were really home. They were being welcomed home by the scavenging birds of the ocean. Bold birds who seemed to fear nothing came in close and rode the currents outside the hull of the USS Excelsior. Just then, Harris let out a groan. Daniel turned to him and saw him collapse in slow motion. It was as if his body turned into a ball and rolled him flat on the cabin floor. Grunts began shouting up to the AB pilot to

order medics and a crash cart to be brought to their AB—
and that is when they saw it…

Dancing in the sky, a boy with wings darting about, rising and falling on the wind's currents waved at the ship with
a broad smile. They watched in disbelief, as the boy danced
higher and seemed to cheer their progress across the sky,
mingling in with the seagulls that had moments ago inspired
such a warm feeling within them, now to be left stunned as
the boy darted this way and that, like a feather on the wind.

Daniel stared at the boy in utter shock, his mind awash
with data he was handed on his first day of boot camp,
when a stern soldier stepped forward and told them all he
was honored by their bravery and selflessness in light of
the coming battles they would face. He then glossed over
theory of space-time and how there was a real possibility that the travel to another planet might take place in a
matter of months for them but the time on earth may be in
the years. The understanding was that—regardless of the
war's outcome or whether they survived their tour of duty
or not—they may never see their loved ones alive again.
Daniel, being an only son with his parents dead already,
had not given the speech much thought. But at the sight of
the winged boy flying effortlessly on the breeze he glanced
around and saw all the faces of the hardened grunts grow
long and full of dread; fearing their parents had died, and
they had traveled for thousands of years, only to return to a
world of bird people.

The world might as well have perished.

Daniel glanced down at Harris' body sprawled out on
the cabin floor, twitching and frothing at the mouth in the fit
of a seizure. He stared at the oddity for a moment, vaguely
aware he should do something, but the boy on the viewscreen was such a powerful pull he turned away to stare at
the wild winged boy smiling and waving at them in all the
joy of summer. And the proximity alert claxon pressed in on

him as he felt himself drifting into a dreamlike state, praying the vision would evaporate altogether to the return of the seagulls. The uncomplicated seagulls.

The claxon changed in pitch and urgency as his world blurred until all was blackness and Daniel recognized his alarm clock was ringing.

CHAPTER 1

UNSEEN SIGNS

D aniel awoke in a cold sweat and studied the oddity of the alarm clock next to him as it blared 2:30 pm. With a grunt and a swat, the snooze button turned the alarm off and Daniel lay on his back as the high humid chill of the New York winter warred with his heater venting seventy-two degrees. Cold one day, blistering the next, the New York weather was another *climate change* reminder that infuriated the residents who never knew whether to bundle up or go out in shorts and t-shirts. All you could count on was the humidity to compound whatever weather you were experiencing at the moment.

Daniel laid there for with an unmistakable sensation of dread. Both the problem and asset is, as a veteran, one grows accustomed to dread and suppresses it. With a shrug, he rose and proceeded with his day. Showering was a wonder of tactile experience as the cold water hit the skin and warred with the room temperature, to his thrill. He took his time in the shower, long after he was clean, just to feel the sensation against his skin as he turned to let the water pulse against his face and chest.

The day began like any other. He woke, he groomed, he dressed and stepped out into his living room feeling the quiet press in on him. She was gone. The furniture stood there in his living room wholly reminding him he was alone. Across his couch, his jacket lay haphazardly discarded. When she lived here, he would always tear the townhome apart looking for it only to have her pull it out of the closet. He always marveled at the idea of hanging his jacket up as novel. He picked up his jacket and ran his hand across the fabric, efforting to press out the wrinkles that may have accumulated over the night and sighed. It had been hard on him to find himself in a relationship, somewhere between freedom and commitment.

He had reveled in the freedom to come and go as he pleased. To work well into the night and return at dawn to crawl into his lover's arms and sleep until noon. To wake and find he was alone was nothing new. To wake and realize she was not coming back was something Daniel would have to grow accustomed to.

His lifestyle had pushed her away. His work took up the rest of the space. There was no room left for her, and Daniel was still too young in mind to realize he had to compromise. Her absence bit into the morning, tearing at the walls and pressed in on him. He felt her absence like a malignancy inside him.

He did not have the will or patience for mourning the loss of her. All he had was the frustration that she had left. What was he supposed to do? Daniel was a New York

Detective. A relationship should be about more than the petty arguments over lost time. He had a job that took its toll on his soul and necessitated him to walk a rigid tightrope throughout the day requiring a maximum effort to remain on the good side of office politics and the rest of his energy to weather the civilian population's aversion to anything related to Law Enforcement.

Afterwards he required silence. He would stop by a diner, have a cup of coffee, and read over his notes from the day's traumatic events, divided into crime scene footage and documentation of events from witnesses, if there were any. He would study the case file and pored through for any insights he might have missed at work.

After he put away his case files, he sipped his coffee and would read anything that removed himself from his identity as a cop. He read *Thus Spoke Zarathustra*, and pondered the possibility that his role was to make room for the ubermench to take his place. In this day's society, there was a clear population that fit the bill. They were called Specials. A community of super humans that existed scattered across the globe. They were here. And Daniel found new meaning in Nietzsche's diatribe on the superman as he encountered case files dedicated to "Special attacks" or eyewitness accounts of Special "disruptions" in the course of his daily police work. He read *Man's Search for Meaning* and let himself consider the world through the eyes of a man surviving in the darkest of circumstances. He too, had survived in the darkest of circumstances, and suffered flashbacks to this period in his life where nightmares walked on planets under distant suns, toward the edge of the map where monsters lived. He read *Malcolm X* and wondered what it would be like to die just when the light bulb went off and a new path of insight opened before him. This troubled him the most. As a young man in his mid thirties, he had the world open to him. The thought of some elusive insight being robbed from him by a bullet just when the light hit him was just too much to process. But mostly, he read about the Sol War and studied it voraciously.

Somewhere deep inside, Daniel longed to find that one book that would explain the war clearly enough that he would at last understand what role he played in the overall campaign he had enlisted in so long ago. Being a veteran of the war, he enlisted through passion and patriotism to his country and his planet. But the war was fought so far away from Earth, it didn't make sense when you thought about it too long.

Why did an alien race pick a fight with a planet that didn't even have a decent space program? It took a spacecraft six months to reach Mars. It took the Quill twelve seconds. This was a well documented fact. And still, they felt like picking a fight with humans. It didn't make sense. And with so little information coming out about the end of the war—just that it had ended—the entire affair, and all the deaths seemed nothing more than a shouting match before the politicians could meet across a boardroom table. Now the Quill were talked about as business partners with the nations of the Earth.

Occasionally a story appeared on the nightly news that a Quill starship was in orbit at a space station meeting dignitaries, or, even more surprising, landing on the Earth itself and entering into business negotiations with emirs in Dubai, or one of the mega corporations in Japan. It seemed the war ended with an opening of business talks. Daniel would scoff at this. Thinking of all the men and women who sacrificed their lives for their planet and now the enemy was entertained by the elite of every nation for access to the miraculous technology they had. *We sacrificed our lives for flying cars...* he would think.

This is what he did with his days after work. He worked some more, he let his mind wander new topics or studied itching obsessions and finally, from fatigue, made his way home to be with his girlfriend.

It wasn't like I was cheating or anything, he would protest when she would let her disapproval have a voice. But it was not enough to be in a committed relationship. It was not enough to live together. She wanted to be with him. Not what was left of him, when he came home incoherent, his head aching from the day's thinking and needing a decent home cooked meal and a bed to lie in. She argued that his apartment was just a place to sleep for him, and that she hardly saw him unless he climbed into bed and ran his hands across her body, restless for the possibility of intimacy.

Daniel replayed all the arguments in his head, how she provoked him. How she berated him in her anger and infuriated him. But he could not let go of the good times of being close to her. Being inside her. And afterward, lying there talking until he fell asleep in her arms. He would miss her.

Finally, when the apartment yielded the last of its visions and ghosts of the dead relationship that haunted him, he turned, dressed in uniform slacks with a military fit, a dress shirt, and a sports coat, tucking a military sweater and a heavy coat into a duffel bag along with his side arm. Just before leaving the apartment, he picked up his badge and walked out the door. He made his way down to the diner and ate, and then made his way toward the police station.

Yet today was to be entirely different from his usual undertakings. Yes, there would be the chase and the arrest. There would be the joking in the locker room. There would even be the tension in meeting the public that did not trust him based entirely on the acts of some of his peers, but by the end of the day, Daniel Henry Rooke would be a different man.

He just didn't know it, yet.

CHAPTER 2

THE CALLING

The 81st Precinct was located in the area known as the Bedford Stuyvesant or Bed-Stuy, which was in the north central area of the borough of Brooklyn. It was an older building, with parking on the first floor beneath stilted columns supporting the second floor where the offices were located.

Daniel walked past the patrol cars haphazardly parked on the sidewalk, into the lobby on 30 Ralph Avenue and jumped onto the elevator just as the doors were closing, causing the officers and secretarial staff to jump as he appeared in their midst and shot him annoyed glances— for slowing their progress down—as they now had to wait for the elevator doors to slide all the way back open, pause for an additional five seconds before slowly crawling shut again.

The elevator was slow as it climbed, leaving them to listen to the grunting sighs and deafening silence interrupted by the dreadful Muzak pumped dimly from unseen speakers. Heaven forbid the elevator breaks down in mid-flight between floors…this tomb of surly expressions and disgruntled nasal exhalations underscoring their discontentment would have made for an uncomfortable, albeit amusing catastrophe.

Jumping on the elevator was not really necessary for any of them, however, most of their offices were located on the second floor anyway. When the elevator doors opened again, Daniel stepped off leaving the frustrated people behind him—their eyes burning into the back of his head—and walked into a small room choked with cubicles surrounded by offices where sergeants and supervisors peered out at the floor with cold authority.

As Daniel walked past Commander James McGuiness' office, the door opened and McGuiness darted out with his arms folded with a cool authority, a Panasonic notebook in his hand.

"You're late," said McGuiness.

"I'm early," corrected Daniel with a smile.

"You missed roll call," snapped McGuiness.

"I'm a Detective now, Jim." replied Daniel.

"Look," pressed McGuiness, "We've got a situation brewing in Boerum Hill. We think a group of people took over a project and that they're setting up a drug refining facility in plain view. The neighborhood's so hot I can't put bodies in there without sending out coroners for pick up."

"Well," replied Daniel, "we're talking about Boerum Hill, here."

"The point is," snapped McGuiness, "I need someone to take the case."

Daniel extended his hand to receive the notebook.

"I'll poke around and see what I can do." said Daniel.

McGuiness withdrew the notebook outside of Daniel's reach, a stipulation in the air.

"I can't offer you any backup." warned McGuiness.

"I haven't had backup since I made Officer Third Class," scoffed Daniel, snapping his fingers for the notebook.

"So I can count on you?"

"Just give me the file, Jim."

McGuiness handed a wafer thin pad with a lit display scrolling with everything Daniel would need down to the 911 calls that first put his district on alert and followed up by eyewitness accounts from neighborhood snitches and patrol car video/audio in the area. All this data contained in the memory of a computer no thicker than a sheet of paper, but made durable by the plastic housing that encased it. Daniel looked down at the viewscreen and scrolled through the data absently as McGuiness patted him on the back.

"You're a good man, Rooke," said McGuiness with a sly grin as though he had just released a hot potato from his hand and turned to walk back into his office adding, "Don't think I don't remember favors."

Daniel had heard this before. McGuiness had doled out many "favors" like this before and never paid anyone back for their working a task he had asked them to fill.

"Yeah, right." scoffed Daniel, absently as he sat down at his cubicle.

Daniel pressed his hand on the touch screen of the file. It blinked and the word AUTHORIZED appeared across the screen. Daniel stared at the footage from an ATM across the street of 69 Boerum Place, showing two teams of men rushing into the apartment complex well armed and moving with military efficiency.

Daniel watched them sweep the rooms on the interior security feed before they shot out the cameras. These men were definitely ex-military. Probably Sol War veterans.

A lot of veterans had it hard coming home to find no jobs, and with no need to keep such a healthy military now that the war was over they were awarded honorable discharge and a quarter of their backpay, which was all the UN could afford without bankrupting the World Bank. The veterans were left fumbling blindly. The only ones who could find work were the smart ones who took work as soon as they disembarked from their ships, or the lucky few with connections, either through a comrade-in-arms or by the happy accident of birth into the right kind of families.

For the rest, there was the downward spiraling depression as the alienation of society set in after the parades, when the Sol War became yesterday's news and soldiers became little more than someone to buy a drink for, and then turn away, back into your previous conversation.

There were still veterans who wore their decorations to get free drinks at bars. It had become an embarrassment, and people quickly turned away from them, leaving them to deal with the traumas of war on their own.

What was becoming increasingly more common was for veterans to turn to criminal activity. There was the kidnapping/ransom and bank robberies that had grown so sophisticated the police needed veterans like Daniel to train them on how to deal with the new threats. People who had no problem firing into an open and busy street. Who understood face recognition software and disguised themselves by hiding the shapes of their features. Who were equipped to be tactical and technologically savvy. People who moved with boldness on the urban landscape.

They understood how to control a street and how to adapt to an environment—meaning they could command a city block and vanish into the wilderness of the urban jungle. These were dangerous men. Probably the greatest threat to a civilian population is a disenfranchised veteran with special operations training.

This was going to be tricky. Daniel only hoped he wouldn't come up against someone who he knew from the campaign, or worse, someone who saved his life.

Daniel continued to flip through the media feeds, watching the men systematically take over the entire project, entrenching themselves in key apartments, using the residents as human shields against Law Enforcement. One could not storm into a project undetected. The eyes watching the coming and going into the neighborhood would start a mile out. They would be sophisticated. They would have their own monitor feeds. And more importantly, the eyes of the community watching the infiltrating Law Enforcement personnel.

Any new face would be checked. Any recognized face as Law Enforcement would receive either the cold shoulder, or the show of force, depending on how cocky these people were.

Daniel was inclined to think they would be extremely cocky and hostile. He would survey the perimeter of their stronghold. Look for the sign of being watched, and then watch the watchers. He would shake them down for information on the security of the neighborhood. But where to begin?

Daniel sat at a diner down the block from the project, sipping his coffee and studying the faces outside the window. The winter weather had decided to set in, and the temperature plummeted outside as prostitutes shivered in the chill wind and nearly dove into cars for the warmth of the interior of the cabs. Dealers bundled up and buried their faces into their jackets up to their noses, eyeing the streets above the brim of their coats.

Durfee Diner was a hotspot for illicit activity. Drug dealers and pimps ran their operations from the comfort of the pleather booths and kept to themselves.

They knew Daniel. Each had been arrested by him at one point or another, and now gave him a wide berth, the pimps comfortable in the fact that getting money from a girl who quickly left the diner and headed back out for the Boulevard was not enough to arrest him over.

Besides, they all knew what Daniel was after. And with the grins they wore it was obvious they both knew nothing helpful and were happy they didn't have enough even for a shakedown. They were working the outskirts of the neighborhood for a reason. They didn't want to be shaken down for their profits.

Daniel kept his eyes out the window, studying the building across the street. A "Big Brother" surveillance camera dominated the view. It was obvious it had been shot at before, but the bulletproof plastic protected the camera inside. It had become a standing joke to watch a young turk take out his gun, fire a shot at the camera and within seconds, a police cruiser would pull up and arrest the turk for criminal trespass, illegal possession of a firearm and destruction of city property. Three years, and this turk would come out of prison like a college graduate.

It had been six hours since he arrived in the diner, sitting, reading over the case file, occasionally glancing out the window at the street's activity. He glanced again at the camera hovering over the intersection and studied it curiously. His eyes trailed the rooftops across the street for any sign of movement. Nothing. If anything was changing in the neighborhood, it remained hidden.

The only thing that stood out was what the city had installed. A camera network that surrounded and penetrated the city streets, keeping watchful eye over the day's street commerce. It was allowed activity, so long as it was kept quiet. No loud shootings or elaborate deals—just the passing of cars and the simple handshakes exchanging money for drugs, or the prostitutes who used motel rooms or private parking lots for their business transactions.

Daniel knew every girl working the street, having arrested many himself. He knew every man standing close by, and he even knew a few of the buyers, whatever business they sought.

The diner was like an office for the petty drug dealers and pimps. It was lucrative, but slow. Which is why these non-affiliated businessmen did their business outside the neighborhood. Anyone seeking their business would have to venture out and seek them out at the diner. And these men sat there casually, waiting for the shakedown—knowing it would come soon.

Daniel knew if this was a *new jack* operation, it was only a matter of time before a hand reached out here. And he was not surprised when the entrance opened to permit three strangers to the diner. They walked in with a cold authority, as if the diner belonged to them already and approached the drug dealers and pimps.

Daniel slid his credit card across the card reader strip embedded in the table, got up and made his way closer to the confrontation, tucking his notebook into his inside jacket pocket. He merely watched, waiting to see how far the men went to making their presence known. If they claimed territory in the burrow, he would be on them in seconds.

"Look at these fools," said the smallest gangster, gesturing toward the pimps and dealers. "Don't they know who runs these streets?"

Daniel watched as the pimps and dealers rose and squared off with the three gangsters. Grabbing his shoulder holster beneath his coat he depressed the panic button hidden there. Within minutes, the place would be crawling with cruisers.

"Looks like you're in the wrong place," said a dealer with a dismissive wave. "Your territory ends a block from here."

The smallest gangster reached inside his coat and pulled out a 9mm Glock and aimed it at the dealer, shooting him in the abdomen. The dealer fell to the ground in pain, clutching at his belly while the other dealers and pimps backed away a fraction of a step—yet not far enough—in an effort not to appear weak.

"Who else got something to say?" demanded the gangster, while his associates pulled out their guns and aimed down on the dealers and pimps.

Behind them, Daniel pulled out his sidearm and aimed at the backs of the three men cowing the pimps and dealers.

"NYPD! Freeze!" shouted Daniel.

The gangsters turned and blindly opened fire on Daniel.

Daniel knelt down and let the bullets passed over his head, instinctively firing back and hitting one of the gangsters in the spine, who fell to the ground and did not move while the other two retreated out through the entrance and ran into the street.

Daniel pulled out his cell phone as he ran out the door with a glancing look back at the two shot men on the diner floor.

"This is Detective Daniel Rooke, badge number 9-9-0-8-4-1. I have a shooting at the Durfee Diner located on the corner of Atlantic and 4th. I need two paramedic busses at that location to treat two black males with gunshot wounds to the abdomen and spine for cart off. I'm currently in pursuit of two black male suspects ranging from late teens to mid twenties travelling down Pacific. Will need assistance."

Daniel ran to his car and flung the trunk open, stripping off his jacket and pulling on his heavy Kevlar flak jacket on. Then slammed the trunk shut and eyed the direction the gangsters were running. They were going into the protection of their turf. What local Law Enforcement had recently rechristened The Hurt Locker.

"Roger, Detective Rooke, back up is twelve minutes out."

Daniel had heard it all before. The point was, he was a problem in the department and not many wanted to work with him. He was on his own.

Daniel raced after the two suspects down Pacific, gaining on them as he ran. The two gangsters, realizing how close he was, began to throw trashcans over to block him, which he easily hurtled. Then they ducked down a corner and he momentarily lost view of them. He pushed harder around the turn and found a deserted street. Behind him, he heard the distinctive sound of a door latching. Daniel doubled back and found, as often was the case, an apartment access doorway stashed between two businesses. He looked up to the second floor and saw the two suspects racing up the stairs toward the third floor. Daniel checked the door and found it secure. On the wall was a series of buttons followed by the names of the tenants. He slammed his fist on the button labeled "manager." After several rings, an elderly voice grumbled through the speaker.

"Sir, this is New York Police in pursuit of suspects in your building. Buzz me in, please!"

His plea was answered with a buzz and Daniel yanked the door open, racing up the steps three at a time. As he reached the third floor landing he saw the gun before it fired. Ducking back down the staircase, he returned fire as the two suspects raced up the remaining stairs to the rooftop access. Daniel heard the slam of the fire escape door and raced after them, bursting through the roof access fire escape to see the two gangsters hurtling onto the rooftop of the adjacent building, racing off like deer.

Running across the rooftops, his brown flak jacket pulled and buttoned tight to keep the extra trauma plates in place, Daniel grit his teeth as his cheeks seemed to stretch and harden against the New York evening's winter chill while the pops of sparks and the cuts of the ricocheting bullets pelted his legs and face. The two gangsters had found a ladder and laid it across the gap between the building and the next and were walking it like a tightrope. Daniel crept out from behind his shield point and aimed at one of the gangster's back. It would be a simple thing to fire, but it was not his way to shoot a man in the back. With a groan he raced up to the ladder just as the last gangster crossed, and they pulled the ladder across to their side, letting it tumble down into shadow where it crashed loudly in the alley below, hitting concrete and trashcans.

On the far side of the gap between the two buildings, the gangsters laughed at Daniel and taunted him.

With a smirk, he holstered his weapon and stepped back several yards—the gangsters watching him, now curiously. With a deep exhale, Daniel raced toward the edge of the building as fast as he could, doubled over from his effort. Jumping to the façade at the rooftop corner, he used the six-inch thick embattlement to push himself a few more inches higher in his leap and subsequent arch in the hopes of reaching the next rooftop across the long abysmal yawn of the alleyway.

Without even the time to calculate, Daniel held his breath as the shadow below seemed to move from the still bottom to the wall of the building he had leapt from as if calculating the energy required to pounce and seize him to the wintry tomb below.

On the far end, he landed on the tips of his toes, his heels suspended precariously over the widening mouth of the shadows. Daniel fought the air in front of him pleading with angels to take his hands, demanding a mere finger-hold on the falling snow flakes on the air—reckoning if he moved quick enough and pulled on the snow flake hard enough, he might be able to push off of it and correct himself. Two shots fired and bullets rushed past his ears with a crack. Somewhere between the spiritual and the illogic state of the defiant at death's doorway, his salvation came in the form of a .45 shell slamming into his back trauma plate, sending him forward, face down into the snow of the far roof.

"I got chu!" bellowed the suspect.

"You got him?" heckled the other, "He was gonna fall! Now we killed a cop!"

"What'chu worried about?"

"I wanted him to die down there, you ignorant motherfucker!"

Across the yawning chasm, a figure in a long grey trench coat stood resting his wingtip shoe on the façade, leaning over the abyss with a casual demeanor suggesting both an easy superiority and a wry disappointment. His white hair and bristly mustache blew in the winter wind and his voice was rough and grizzly, yet held a blueblood's air to it.

"And I would prefer he didn't die," said the man. "At least until after he had heard my proposal."

In their fright, the two men stood straight as rods for a long moment. As usual, the first effort was in daring themselves to acknowledge a threat for what it was and then to deal with that threat—whether it be it by subjugation to it or a display of superiority. Within a moment, it was clear which of the two they had chosen as they aimed their pistols at the figure.

With the flickering puffs of fire and smoke from the barrels of their pistols, the two men answered the threat with cold action. The return fire was instantaneous and overlapped their own shots and the two men fell over the facade and tumbled into the abyss.

"Figures," grunted the harsh voice in a mutter. "Rooke! You okay?"

Daniel stirred with a groan and craned his head back toward the man in the trench coat.

"Who wants to know?"

The stranger leaned over the edge of the abyss and grinned at Daniel, who instantly recognized the enigmatic Agent Lawrence Boatman, formerly General Boatman, of the United Nations Interstellar Armed Forces.

"Your lifeline." replied Boatman, fastening his pistol into his shoulder holster. "Unless you want to go back to being shot at by drug dealers, pimps, gang bangers and junkies without backup on a daily basis."

"Hey, it's a gig." retorted Daniel as he rose, dusting off his pant legs.

"Not one for knuckleheads like us."

"Where'd my suspects go?"

"Down there."

Daniel looked down and noticed the scuffled prints in the snow on the rooftop and the scuff marks at the edge of the building and leaned over nervously, peering down into the abyss.

"Shit," spat Daniel as he dug in his pockets for his cell phone. "I'd better call this in. They could still be alive down there. Either way, they're going to feel that fall in the morning."

"My men can just as easily facilitate the handling of the bodies as your men could. In fact, I have five men down there handling it as we speak."

Daniel eyed Boatman closely for a moment, weighing his words and realizing that a visit from the legendary General Boatman was a rare gift.

"I'm assuming this is something that shouldn't be discussed in a shouting match across rooftops?"

"Not exactly, no."

"Meet me downstairs. We'll talk it up at the diner down the street."

"You read my mind."

Twenty minutes later, Daniel and Boatman were sitting comfortably in their booth at Durfee Diner. The paramedic busses had just pulled away with their cargo of gunshot wounds and the patrol cars who had finally answered Daniel's summons quickly retreated from the block without so much as a word to him as though he were something undesirable and unwanted.

Daniel and Boatman sat patiently as the waitress laid down their plates. The waitress was silent and uncomfortable in serving the two men and her hands shook as she set down the ketchup bottle, glancing nervously at Daniel's badge at the end of his necklace.

Daniel realized her discomfort, tucked the badge into his flak jacket and smiled to her politely.

Unsure what to do, the waitress turned and quickly hurried away.

"A little skittish, wasn't she?" observed Laurence.

"This diner is a local hang out for dealers and their buyers," replied Daniel with a reassuring wave of indifference. "We get a lot of pimps in here with their girls too. I'm pretty well known here."

"Are we in danger?"

"Not any more than anywhere else in the burrow, the way I figure it. At least they know me well enough to keep their distance. Besides, I don't need to bust them. This Diner's been under surveillance for six months."

"Yes, I know." replied Boatman, "Which is why I'm curious as to why you chose this place to have our little talk."

"Well," said Daniel thoughtfully, "let's just say if I don't like what you have to say, at least I know it'll be on record that I did not agree to your request."

"You must know me better than that," chided Boatman. "I have men over there commandeering the surveillance post as we speak. There is no one listening that is not already in the know."

"Well, the second reason I chose this place is the club sandwich is good, and they have free refills on sodas."

Boatman looked down at his undercooked eggs and then back up at Daniel with a trace of annoyance.

"I wish you would have told me that before I ordered the breakfast platter and coffee."

"Sorry about that."

"So I hope you don't mind if I go over some particulars in your background before I begin."

Boatman pushed aside the breakfast platter and without ceremony produced a thin sheet of plastic with an illuminated touch screen, laying it out before him as he fetched his glasses from his suit's breast pocket. Daniel merely shrugged.

"I got nothing to hide."

Boatman pressed his finger to the screen and scrolled down the list of documents until he reached a file entitled RookeFile_1 and began to gloss over the dozens of documents with a look of critical boredom as he scrolled through the dossier. His nasal muttered tone seemed to be somewhere between boredom and sleep.

"You are Detective-First Class Daniel Henry Rooke of the NYPD. You started out this illustrious career of yours with 'New York's finest' as a beat cop working the Midtown West area." Boatman took off his glasses and looked up at Daniel with curiosity. "That's the area that used to be called Hell's Kitchen, isn't it?"

"Yeah," replied Daniel. "Some residents still call it that, for old time's sake. Unfortunately, it's a boring shift working that area. Mostly, we just break up bar fights and arrest the homophobes when they started getting a little too biblical and began beating up the locals in the gay community, there. Other than that, being a beat cop in Hell's

Kitchen is just an excuse to take long walks and draw a paycheck."

"Not really your cup of tea, I take it?" concluded Boatman with a grin.

"No, not really."

Boatman donned his reading glasses again and turned back to the file and scrolled a few pages down.

"Within thirteen months you'd been promoted to Police Officer Second Grade and transferred into the Emergency Service Unit. Impressive—but only stayed there for ten months. Why?"

"ESU sounds exciting. Kinda like the stories about S.W.A.T. We trained really hard, too. Unfortunately, when you're actually doing it, you find yourself standing around a lot."

Boatman nodded drowsily as if the answer was sufficient enough for him and returned to the file in front of him.

"Jacket shows you've been decorated numerous times. Often receiving promotions in accompaniment with the medals—received the Excellent Police Duty medal as well as one for Meritorious Police Duty for pulling wounded officers and civilians out of a danger zone, under fire from gunmen who had just robbed a bank. This raised you to Police Officer Third Grade. A Commendation Community Service medal a year later for pushing a woman and her child out of the path of a taxicab, which had in turn, ran you over. The hospital report shows you had burns across your body from being dragged under the car for fifty yards and a dislocated shoulder."

"Yeah," scoffed Daniel. "It still pops out from time to time."

"That incident raised you to Police Officer Fourth Grade," ignoring Daniel's response out of hand. "You took the Detective's Exam, passing with the bare minimum, three points above failing. You then received the rank of Detective-Investigator. And finally you received the Police Combat Cross, which also gave you the added push you needed to make Detective-Second Grade. All within four years of your joining the force." Boatman took off his glasses and added "You are a regular commendation whore."

"I just show up and do the job," replied Daniels. "They can decorate me or let me get to work. It really doesn't matter to me."

"But you apparently had no problems with the fast track promotions."

"With promotion comes a bigger paycheck, and a greater chance of being able to implement change in the department and the community. I won't deny being a little bit ambitious."

"And you no doubt made a lot of enemies as a result of those changes, I'm sure."

"Making enemies doesn't concern me." replied Daniel, matter-of-factly. "When they've got the balls to deal with me, we'll see how it turns out."

"Now Detective-First Class and very near making Sergeant. Currently working jointly with the narcotics and gang departments of the Organized Crime Control Division, and you have a reservist standing in both the Special Operations and Task Force Divisions as an alternate. Busy boy. You are currently assigned to the 81st Precinct for the Bedford-Stuyvesant sector of the Brooklyn borough."

"No place for a veteran to call home but the Bed-Stuy."

"Yes, a veteran." said Boatman, as if they had finally come to the point of their meeting. "Formerly of the UNIAF where you held the rank of Private First Class, though there is evidence to support you were to be awarded with an unheard of bump up in pay grade to master chief due to the death of so many officers, if not for the death of your superior officer, one Lieutenant Colonel Chord Forrester."

"Yeah, Colonel Forrester was a good man."

"Lieutenant Colonel Chord Gerard Forrester was killed in action during the battle for Valley 862 on Gliese 876 d."

Daniel bowed his head somberly.

"The Valley of the Wolves broke a lot of hearts, that day."

"Yes, it did at that," replied Boatman solemnly.

Valley 862 was situated on an earth-sized planet in the Gliese 876 system called d[1]. The region was designated a battlefield where tens of thousands of soldiers were dropped onto the planet's surface to take control of the valley away from alien forces in an assault codenamed Operation La Revanche des Loups [Revenge of the Wolves]. Most of the soldiers did not walk out of the valley. The battlefield became known by survivors as the "Valley of the Wolves." And a silence stretched out between them that neither seemed willing to break, Daniel for fear of disrespecting the dead, Boatman with an unnerving patience as if waiting for Daniel to speak. Eventually, Daniel grew uncomfortable and leaned back in an effort to return to the point at hand.

"So," began Daniel, "I guess the million dollar question is; to what do I owe the honor of the presence of the great Lawrence Boatman?"

Boatman sat with his cup of coffee, swirling his half-and-half into the black and watching it transform to a creamy brown. Daniel became transfixed on the swirling war of brown, white and black mixing into darker browns, and the image of a gas giant planet rose in his mind's eye.

When Daniel looked up, he caught Boatman's eyes on his. Piercing blue over his spectacles, as the twitch of his white mustache gave him a critical expression. Daniel met Boatman's eyes, which seemed to peel back the layers of his mind, and Daniel realized both he and Boatman had been lost in the same thought.

Boatman glanced back down at the coffee and pushed the mug away from his line of sight and leaned forward, his eyes fixed once more on Daniel's.

"Let me begin by putting a question to *you*," replied Boatman, "Do you always pack the spare trauma plates under your flak jacket for the work out, or is it more of a security blanket for you?"

"A little of both, I'd say." replied Daniel with an easy scoff. "So what are you trying to sell me, Lawrence?"

Boatman propped his elbows on the table, adjusted his posture on the firm booth cushion and folded his hands methodically.

"I can't offer you a better paycheck than local PD. It's just not in my budgetary means."

"How little?"

"Unfortunately, a little less than a teacher makes."

"Please tell me you're talking about a tenured college professor's income."

"Try less than a high school teacher without a license or a college degree."

"That bad, huh?"

"I'm afraid so."

"So what are you offering me then?"

"Elevated entry into a new department of law enforcement not yet brought out into the public, but technically on the books."

"Elevated?"

"These are Specials teams we're working with," continued Boatman, with a glowering stare that told Daniel they had finally arrived at the point of the meeting. "No one will work with them. Which is fine with them, but the powers that be want them on a tight leash. I think you can put on a good show of it while you take down collars in the field."

"So how much of it is acting?"

"No acting. You'll have cameras on you most of the time when you step out on assignment, cameras on you some of the time when you're not. The rest of the time, you'll be on damage control."

"Damage control?"

"One of your boys mouths off in earshot of a journalist," clarified Boatman, "I want you there to plug the leak quick. Our DC department will have heads up on all stories out of Associated Press and the right to bury whichever story we choose. Unfortunately, the high risk of the potential for leaks from your department has made it of great necessity for a large sum of the project's funding to go to the damage control department."

"So basically, they'll be paid well to cover our reputation, but we'll be paid shit to do the actual work."

"Unfortunately," concluded Boatman, with a surly grimace that brought the appetizing nature of the job offer to a brutal finality. "However, I think you'll be very good at minimizing the spread; which means more money to be allocated to other means, like say, a better salary."

"I think you've got way too much faith in my abilities, Lawrence."

"Really? I don't think so."

"I do."

"You don't think I should have so much faith in your abilities? That's fine. But I'll tell you two things I do have faith in. One is your performing abilities. They're Olympian to say the least. Plus, I've never known a man to jump across an alley from one three story rooftop to the next...especially when you can't see the ground. That alone, would make you desirable. These guys aren't easily impressed."

"I'm not here as a show pony act, Lawrence. No sale."

"The other is the word of one of our subordinates who vouches for you in battle; someone who witnessed your performance under pressure personally in the last real engagement of the war."

"Considering how bad the losses were in the Valley of the Wolves, that leaves only three men out of fifty. How are they?"

"None of them made it back to earth. Davis and Grey were both KIA due to landmines and Lennox has been MIA since the last engagement. He's been upped to full K, just to clear the books. I'm sorry to break it to you, Daniel. You're the last surviving man from your division."

The words hit Daniel like a punch in the stomach, and unconsciously pulled at his chest as though feeling for the telltale signs of a heart attack. Boatman sat there for a moment, realizing Daniel was troubled.

"You okay, Dan?"

"Lennox too?" scoffed Daniel, and he pushed his club sandwich away from him. He had lost his appetite with the news.

"Come on, son." said Boatman. "I'll brief you on your new job on the fly."

Boatman rose, swiping his credit card through the reader embedded in the dining table, and made his way toward the exit. Daniel followed with numbly shaking steps behind him.

CHAPTER 3

THE POST

The C-47 roared high and hard in the frigid evening sky at such speeds to set the farthest tips of the craft ablaze with the sparking of frost to mist leaving long trailing plumes of warmer air newly introduced in a horizontal tornado effect behind.

Inside the cabin, Boatman stared ahead at an overhead light, playing with the tip of his finger along the ridge of his gum line, picking at his teeth. Daniel, who had been typing on his notebook, inputting his suspicions—about the big brother towers being used to probe the neighborhood for possible threats—into the new jack file, jumped with a start and lurched forward, kicking his legs free like a top unwinding.

"So who's speaking so highly of me?" demanded Daniel, at last.

"What's that?" replied Boatman, still picking his teeth.

"You said someone put in for me."

"Maybe I misled you," said Boatman at last, and leaned over to speak in hushed tones, demanding confidence. "This guy wasn't in your platoon or your division or even the legion. But trust me; he was in the mix right along with you. He's a real tough son of a bitch. Not the type of guy you'd forget."

"If he wasn't in my unit, or even the legion, then who could possibly vouch for me?"

Boatman looked around the cabin casually, noting the soldiers and agents on board the flight—bending their ears toward them for something to hear to break up the monotony of the drab, colorless existence they had been enduring in the C-47—and patted Daniel's hand.

"I hope you understand I can't really talk about it right now. You'll see him soon enough. And trust me, when you see him, you'll remember him. Of that I have no doubt."

Daniel did not approve of the cloak and dagger tactics. The hints of government secrecy only compounding his annoyance in being brought from New York with Washington DC as their destination being the only thing he knew for sure, with hardly a word to relieve him of his concerns, and the references to Specials involvement did not ease his worries. Many of the Specials, it had been rumored, since their return from the front lines had taken to mercenary lifestyles at best and lives of crime at worst.

Daniel could hardly blame them after the way they were ostracized by the government and the populations upon their return. Many of them had successful careers of their own before they were drafted to contribute their considerable talents to the war. Upon their return, they received no military grants for college or loans for purchasing property.

Their former careers were, for many Specials, barred from them.

Being a Special, to many human resources interviewers had become the equivalent of having a felony on your record. Many Specials now worked at minimum wage positions performing menial or grunt tasks for pennies on the dollar.

It was as if the government closed the doors on their citizenship in every way but the demand that taxes be paid. In many ways, this point of view was actually very accurate. Surely there must be some hard feelings toward the normal human community.

How could he be expected to lead a team of Specials who felt that normal human citizens had ostracized them in almost every way that mattered when he himself was a normal human? To be expected to lead men who resented him based on the fact that he was considered more acceptable than them? It seemed an impossible task. Boatman seemed to read his expression and leaned in toward him.

"How you holding up, son?"

"What you are asking of me is harder than you're making it seem," said Daniel, studiously. "There's the matter of how these people are going to handle being forced to take orders from me. I don't see this happening."

"You're going to have to win their trust, son."

"How?"

"I found a way." said Boatman, rather cryptically. "You will too."

"What do you mean you found a way?"

"Once upon a time, I commanded the whole damned battalion. It was meant as a punishment for me being such a damned hardhead. But I soon began to feel privileged. To be a part of their duties, and see what they could do on a daily basis. To watch them give their all each time out through that hole. It was inspiring. I was damned proud of the lot of them. If a disgraced general could win their respect and trust, I see no reason why a roughneck who survived all the engagements of the entire war couldn't earn it with greater ease and style."

"What's the hole?"

"That's classified, son. Shouldn't have said it. You'd be better off forgetting I said it."

"Alright." said Daniel, with no small amount of annoyance.

He looked away toward the window and watched the cyclones forming off the wingtips with a mesmerized gaze and tried to focus on the patterns they made in an effort to forget how annoyed he was at how he could have an elevated position and not the same level of clearance as his subordinates. This would battle in his mind the rest of the way to his destination.

Washington D.C.

Daniel stared out the limousine's window and watched the foot traffic fly past his window in a blur that his eyes hardly bothered to keep in focus as the restaurants, barbershops and pool halls streaked by. They had passed monuments and sites that many tourists from around the world had traveled continents just to see and the limousine had not slowed for anything save traffic and the occasional pedestrian before speeding off again down the avenue, taking turns through some neighborhoods with beautiful architecture, from modern to landmark to dilapidated and still the car kept going. The only thing that was clear to Daniel was that wherever this base of operations was, it was far from Georgetown.

Lawrence Boatman was extremely tightlipped about the location they were headed. He would not betray the slightest bit of information, informing him that, government vehicles, like everything the government owns, has eyes and ears. All he knew was that wherever they were headed, the destination had been designated "the Post." This did little to assuage his desire for more information about the location before they arrived. For all he knew, the Post was under water in the Atlantic.

He had grown tired of trying to pump Lawrence for information and now contented himself with watching the demographics change as they moved speedily from neighborhood to neighborhood. They were at present, in a rough part of town. Ironically, it reminded him of the Bedford-Stuyvesant—only the Bed-Stuy was much better off in terms of crime and city renewal projects—The Bed-Stuy had a bad reputation that had followed it for years. But even though the subsection of the Brooklyn borough had its quirks, including a still large drug and gang problem due to the low income the many inhabitants still suffered in, it was far more elegant and inviting than the neighborhood Daniel currently found himself in.

Finally, the view slowed and came to a stop in front of a brownstone-type building on 3830 Georgia Avenue, right on the border of the rough and gritty Georgia Avenue and Shepherd Street Districts of northwestern Washington DC. Georgia Avenue and Shepherd Street Districts were famed for being resistant to gentrification, and battled with itself, eating itself alive as gangs and Metro police patrols seemingly took turns tearing at the community, both sides oppressing the neighborhood's law abiding citizenry, instead of aggressively attacking each other. Local citizenry were hardened and street savvy, lashing out violently at new faces. The faces peering at the limousine's tinted windows with skeptical glares seemed to be anticipating a need to be violent toward its occupants. Boatman recognized the stances the pedestrians were taking toward them and with a frown, unsnapped his shoulder holster as if anticipating having to shoot someone. Boatman then turned and smiled at Daniel as if nothing were out of the ordinary, his hand on the door latch.

"We're here, son," said Boatman. Then added, "You ready?"

Daniel's eyes bulged and he glared at Boatman.

"This is bullshit," gasped Daniel.

"Like I said," replied Boatman indifferently. "the Specials' program is on a tight budget. You were expecting a view of the Washington Monument? Not even spooks get that lucky." Boatman opened the limousine door and turned back to Daniel, adding "You coming?"

Boatman stepped out into the DC street and made his way through the crowd of hostile onlookers toward the Post's main entrance.

Daniel stepped out of the car and closed the door behind him. The limousine barely waited for the door to shut before the wheels chirped and the long car darted down the street and quickly around the corner. He stared in surprise as the limousine vanished from view and cursed himself for not listening to the voice that had been screaming in the back of his mind all day.

"I knew I should've stayed in New York," muttered Daniel.

He turned and faced the crowd of onlookers who seemed to be determining whether to attack him or let him pass unmolested, depending on whether or not he was considered by them to be a threat. It was clear that the onlookers had made their determination and finding him wanting. Daniel scoffed again, and walked through the crowd of hard stares with a mounting annoyance at what he predicted would follow shortly.

I'm going to have to drop one of these men if I want to get some neighborhood respect, thought Daniel grimly. *Otherwise, I'll be ducking and dodging fists and bullets for the remainder of my time here.*

Daniel did not look forward to this. Although he was a capable man, quite accustomed to violence in his life, he did not seek it out, and certainly did not revel in the acts of combat he was far too proficient in. His grim demeanor soon possessed him, and his face and mannerisms altered his appearance. And very soon, he appeared the most dangerous man on the block.

The crowd almost jumped out of his way—a few heckles from the braver men at a very safe distance from him underscored the hostility of the surrounding neighborhood and confirmed Daniel's opinion. He would definitely be left no other choice than to fight for his right to walk these streets unmolested.

Daniel counted the number of fights a white man would generally have to win before a predominately black community would finally allow him to be there without undue threats of violence. He figured about five should do: One or two against one adversary, and an additional three or four against groups of men in the subsequent retaliatory fights for winning the first two man to man. If he was very lucky, he would not be placed in a situation where he would have to shoot a man for attempting to gun him down.

It was the retaliatory fights that always gave Daniel concern.

He followed Boatman into the main lobby with stained wallpaper on the walls suggesting water damage from leaking pipes. The carpet was hard and crackled when he stepped on it. The varnished wood around the borders of the wall appeared in need of a second coat and the elevator doors appeared to be smeared in some kind of dried grease that dust had clung to, giving the doors a furry appearance.

"Nice place," scoffed Daniel.

"Again, you fail to remember; budget."

"Right, let's just get moving."

Boatman took out two handkerchiefs, extending one to Daniel. Daniel took the handkerchief and looked at him incredulously. Boatman covered his mouth and nose and gave a slight cough as the elevator doors opened and a rancid smell of urine wafted at them. Daniel instantly covered his mouth and nose and hesitantly followed Boatman onto the elevator. The elevator doors closed slowly, and the lift then hummed as it strained to crawl on an unbearably slow ascent.

"This just gets better and better, doesn't it?"

"Budget," replied Boatman.

"How did you even find this place?"

"Metro PD had a surveillance post here for a few months. With this location, they were able to gather evidence of several of their more high profile drug dealing and white slavery operations and made arrests that gave the police department a great degree of fanfare. You might

remember a few from the news." Boatman began to enu-
merate the many cases in a wry, matter-of-fact tone, "There
was the Terrell Arawak arrest and that Russian Mafia family running the brothels. That raid was actually two blocks
from here.

"They arrested Malik White at the diner off of Warder
Street, right around the corner from here. And there were
a few dozen very unspectacular cases that this surveillance
outpost aided in making cases for. Mostly by accident.
Someone mugged a girl at the ATM right across the street
while twenty cops were watching it on a big screen set up
in the flat. Or a prostitute takes a john onto a side street
right in line of sight with the camera and videotapes the
enraptured look on the man's face as the ponytail appears
and disappears, reappears and disappears. There were a lot
of other comical arrests like that made because of his place.

"However, due in part to the Department's increasing
boldness in the neighborhood, what with them walking in
and out of here at all hours, and the cruisers that would
park here and bring up Chinese takeout, it soon became
clear what was going on, and the community finally found
out about this place and grew so hostile about the police
presence in the building that was both disrupting the community's status quo and arresting so many black men and
women—regardless of the fact they were caught committing felonies and misdemeanors on recorded feed—that the
officers that would routinely use this base of operations for
stake-outs started getting attacked by the locals.

"The most popular incident in the media was the beating
of Detective Miles Dennam who ran the surveillance operation. You might have heard of it. It made national news. A
group of seventeen African American youths beat him to
the point of near death. He was rendered paralyzed and
declared brain dead two weeks later. As a direct result of
the attack, the police, expectedly, flooded the neighborhood

with riot gear, leading to the arrest and injury of several dozen young men and women in the neighborhood. And, of course, the NAACP started making claims of racism and declarations of the existence of a police state in the greater DC area. This location became so vilified in the community, that the police department couldn't *give* it away fast enough."

Boatman smirked and chuckled to himself, glancing back at Daniel's pale face.

"We got this location at a steal," added Boatman, with a Cheshire smile.

"They were attacking police officers?"

"Yes," replied Boatman, as though they had reached an important area for discussion. "It would be a good idea if you refrained from producing your badge to any of the locals. Not that it should matter."

"Why wouldn't it matter?"

"You're no longer a civil servant." replied Boatman, matter-of-factly, "at least not for New York City.

"What's that supposed to mean?"

Boatman turned and scrutinized Daniel with the barest trace of empathy in his tone.

"You couldn't expect this meeting to be only an interview, could you? As soon as I explained the function I sought you out for, you knew too much. There is no return to your old life, now. You are now the Assistant Director and Team Commander of the United States Specials Investigations Task Force...or SITF. Welcome to the team, Agent Rooke."

The elevator doors opened revealing a barren room with fold out tables and ancient computers plugged into frayed wire outlets. The walls were similarly stained to the water damaged walls in the main lobby and only the carpet seemed relatively new, though it was clearly bleached from sunlight, and there were several unaccountable stains on it throughout the room.

There, before him stood impressive physical specimens all dressed in plainclothes. They walked about the room in boredom with cynical faces, or leaned against the fold out tables or walls with their arms folded. They hardly seemed to notice him, or care that he were there.

Against the wall, one of the men sat up and smiled from his seat in an old squeaky chiropractic office chair. He sprang up and grinned from ear to ear. Daniel was dumbfounded. The bald, muscular grinning man stood at full height, easily clearing six foot three inches, and walked across the room with a gregarious demeanor toward him. Despite the last time he saw him he was in head to foot exoskeletal body armor, Daniel would have recognized Leonard Stonebreaker anywhere. His size and face gave him away.

"Leonard?" breathed Daniel, "Is that you?"

"Guilty as charged," replied the tall hulking bald man.

"I thought you were dead," scoffed Daniel, a grin starting to stretch across his face.

"Not yet," beamed Leonard. "So I take it you got the full briefing, ah? Glad to have you aboard." Leonard turned to Boatman and growing instantly rigid, saluted him. Boatman returned the salute casually, and Leonard spoke casually again. "Didn't I tell you this son of a bitch was tough? He'll do just fine."

"So I take it you referred me?"

"Don't look at me," replied Leonard, throwing his arms up playfully, "I just said if I had to take orders from norm-hume, I wanted it to be someone I'd fought alongside in the war. I might've told 'em about how you handled yourself on Gliese 876 d, that day." The term norm-hume was a slang for Normal Human that the Special community adopted during the war. Because the Special community had been so segregated, they have developed their own slang to passive aggressively combat the spite that normal human populations use when they mention "Specials." Daniel recognized the slur and pursed his lips.

Leonard put his arm around Daniel and redirected him so that they both faced the others in the room in an attempt to include them in the conversation. "Ol' Rooke over here, is a war hero. He's one of only fifty three soldiers to make it out of that little suicide run in Valley 862."

Daniel nearly grinned out of embarrassment, a discomfiture that was greatly compounded by the fact that no one else was smiling, but Stonebreaker.

Daniel tried to change the subject to something that did not include the disinterested others when a young and handsome dark haired man in the corner came forward with an easy smile that was quite disarming. His piercing blue eyes seemed to offer a warmth and eerie captivating quality and stood pronounced, flashing from behind thick dark brown hair that had seemed black, at the far end of the room.

"I remember that engagement," said the handsome young man, "Valley of the Wolves, if I'm not mistaken. The heads put every body from seven armadas they could find into that valley. Terrible tragedy. Such a waste of lives for a rock without the slightest strategic value."

"Yeah, it was." replied Daniel. "I lost a lot of good men in that valley."

"Daniel," said Leonard, "this is Bradley Overman. Call sign: Maximus."

Daniel was stunned. The legendary Maximus had a mythos as great as a comic book character. And there he was. Young, vibrant, powerful and beautiful. It was no wonder he was given so much press time. The poster boy of the Specials Battalion in the flesh. He was easy and personable, with a silent charm and very easy to like.

Bradley did not seem easily impressed, but gave credit to Daniel solely for surviving the engagement and appeared pleased at the prospect of his leading them. However, it was also obvious that he, like the rest in the room, with the exception of Leonard and Boatman, was reserving his judgment.

A beautiful raven haired Asian woman stirred from the corner, her figure was firm and shapely, but her voice was filled with mockingly dry sarcasm.

"You were at the Valley of the Wolves?" said the woman, "I didn't think any officers made it out of that engagement."

"None did." replied Daniel, matter of fact.

It was at that moment that every man in the room went rigid and she grinned as if she had proven her point. Every jaw tightened. Daniel noted this, and was taken aback. A wiry olive skinned man in the back of the room stepped forward with a critical eye and a harsh tone.

"And you're not an officer?" demanded the man coldly.

Leonard hazarded a smile and appealed to Daniel.

"Mr. Rooke, I'd like you to meet Stephen Giordano. Callsign: Kiloton. He'll be your offensive player in the field. Trust me, when he goes off, you want some yardage between you and him. And the girl who's acting like it's *that time of the month* is Elizabeth Meng. Callsign: Burn."

"Nice to meet you," said Daniel with an easy smile and extended his hand.

Stephen did not take the hand.

"What was your rank," demanded Stephen, then seeing the expressions on Stonebreaker and Boatman's faces, he quickly added, "if you don't mind my asking?"

"I was an enlisted man. Private-First Class."

The others looked up and scoffed, glancing over at Boatman. The only black man in the room, a six foot seven, four hundred pound man, kicked off the wall and glared down at Daniel.

"And this man is going to lead us?" spat the man. "A private?"

Leonard stepped in between Daniel and the towering figure of a man with a look of warning, but it was Boatman who restored order.

"Stand down, Henry." replied Boatman coolly, "That's an order."

"No disrespect General, but this is bullshit!" railed Donovan Henry.

"Donovan's right," said the man in the back.

He spoke softly, but his words were immediately registered by everyone in the room, as if they reverberated in their skulls.

"Daniel, may I introduce Tobias McCormack. Also known as Paladin."

"I've heard of you," said Daniel, impressed by the man he never met before.

"Don't take this the wrong way Daniel," said McCormack disgustedly, "But I haven't heard of you. And that means something to me." McCormack turned to face Boatman addressing him. "General, we all signed on to serve under you, but when you informed us we were going to have to serve under a field commander who was a normal human, we had hopes that at the very least, it was someone credible. I don't see how you expect us to follow someone this green."

"That's right!" chimed Donovan, and glared down at Daniel, jabbing his fat finger into his forehead. "We don't care how badly you want to walk with the Specials and say you were one of us. This little dream you got of playing with the big boys ain't going to happen. Your little fantasies of rolling with the top dogs is going to get one of us killed."

In one deft move, Daniel gripped the long thick finger and wrenched hard, causing a spasm throughout the massive frame of Donovan, followed by a kick to the back of his knee, sending the giant form crashing to his knees, as he twisted the bent arm behind his powerful back. The other

Specials rushed forward with every intention of attacking Daniel. Leonard and McCormack raised their hands in warning, and the others stopped dead in their tracks. Donovan yelped in agony, as Daniel continued to twist and reposition his grip so Donovan had no chance to discern how to break free of the hold.

"Okay, listen up," shouted Daniel in annoyance. "One, I don't like being judged. Two, I don't appreciate being poked by fingers. What is this, high school? I did my time. I proved my merit. I could give a fuck what you think. I've been working as a New York City cop in Bed-Stuy for the past five years since I got back from the war and cut loose from my mandatory eighteen month Veteran's Societal Rehabilitation training program. And I was happy with that. I was just informed last night that I was being drafted into a job that pays less than what I was making. I am not happy. But I've been given the job, and I'll do it the best way I can. As team leader, I need to know that you will follow my orders to the letter and trust my decisions. If that can only happen putting me to the test to see if I can keep up; then name the test already. I was given a job, and I took the job. And I don't like these games of who's the alpha male, so get used to me. Because I'm not going anywhere."

Daniel released Donovan, sending him forward with a kick to the back to collapse to the floor. Donovan gripped his finger and glared back at Daniel in a rage, seeming to billow and expand.

McCormack raised his hand and everyone in the room cringed as he spoke the word *"Stop."* Daniel was intrigued, as McCormack had not so much as opened his mouth, yet the powerful man who seemed to be a veritable wall cringed as if he had screamed at him.

Donovan began to decrease in mass to his original height and musculature, though still not taking his eyes off Daniel.

McCormack walked up to Daniel and with a slight grin, nodded his approval.

"Alright," said McCormack, "A test."

The others nodded their agreement.

CHAPTER 4

THE TEST

A half hour later, Daniel and the Specials were climbing out of an old primer colored van with tinted windows in front of Duke's Olympian Gym, an abandoned boxing gym located off of the 1300 block on Randall Street. Graffiti covered the walls of the building and seemed to stand out from the white paint on the exterior.

Daniel assumed it was the new spray paint that all the kids in Bed-Stuy were using—the paint so resilient to attempts to cover it over, that would show through up to twenty coats of paint as if it were sprayed on just an hour ago. The edifice had crumbled from deep holes, apparently from being used for target practice by the gangs in the area. It was clear from the spread of the holes it was caused by

automatic weapons fire. Wood panels covered with adver-
tisements for inner city music releases and liquor brands
covered the glass doors.

Leonard led them to the doors covered with heavy
chains, unlocked the padlock, removed the chain and pushed
in the doors, revealing a dust covered floor that opened into
a lobby.

The Specials poured in and Daniel followed them into
the main gym. They gathered around in a wide circle surrounding the dilapidated ring and they traded glances with
each other in amused interest, waiting for Daniel to enter
the ring.

"Remember son, you can walk away at any time," whispered Leonard with some concern. "There's no harm in it."

"Yeah there is," replied Daniel dryly.

Daniel stripped off his flak jacket and shirt, revealing his swimmer's physique and with the expulsion of a
heavy sigh through his nostrils, climbed into the ring with a
bored and annoyed expression. Upon entering the ring, he
stretched his back and contorted his neck until a series of
loud pops escaped.

Meng grinned and glanced at the wiry young man, Chad
Beach, known as Crimson.

"Looks like the norm-hume thinks he can win," snig-
gered Meng to Chad.

"Remember Elisabeth," replied Chad, "in a real fight,
the other guy wouldn't allow you the time to stretch."

Donovan chuckled and glared with anticipation at
Daniel.

"You got that right," muttered Donovan. "All I see is a
lot of posturing. We'll see how this white bitch acts when
the chips are down."

"Donovan," scoffed Beach, "you realize most of us here
are white, right?"

"Yeah, but I've seen you fight, Chad." replied Donovan. "And you fight like a nigger. Don't get it all twisted, man. I don't see color in y'all. We cool. This pasty mother fucker's going down, though."

"Just don't get too tall on us, Mammoth." chided Chad. "The roof is not that high."

Donovan glanced up at the ceiling and pursed his lips considering Chad's assessment.

"True," replied Donovan. "Good looking out."

"Gentlemen!" barked McCormack. Meng quickly turned to him and glared hotly. "Lady" McCormack added, "Are we done yet?"

"Yes sir!" they said in unison.

"Good," concluded McCormack, and then took a judicial tone bordering on drill sergeant. "Daniel Henry Rooke, you have elected to enter into a trial by fire of your own free will. This will be a fight that will last until you have been pinned three times, or until you tap out."

"We're wrestling?" scoffed Daniel.

"Not exactly," replied McCormack. "You want to lead us into battle. This team has been organized solely for the purpose of subduing and arresting Specials who are breaking the law. Since you wish to lead, it is only fair that you prove you are even remotely capable of going up against a Special. We are asking you to go up against the team. Since this is a test, and you are only a normal human, we will not use extreme measures. This means no third-degree burns, Elisabeth. No growing taller than a truck and trying to stomp on Rooke, Donovan. No use of telepathy in order to halt Daniel's progress, Brad. That goes for me too. Telekinesis only. Other than that, the match is fair game with the only exception of match rules, which are no hitting a man while he's down, unless he is still an active threat. Which means if he is in TKO or KO, you return to your corner and wait until he is revived to determine whether or not he can continue."

"This is going to be fun," snickered Stephen. "I'll try to leave a little bit of him left for you guys."

"You're sitting this one out, Giordano."

"What?" railed Stephen indignantly.

"You heard me," responded McCormack.

Stephen waved his hands in disgust and walked away, propping himself up against the wall, letting his eyes bore into Daniel.

Chad brushed his long brown hair out of his eyes and raised his hand.

"What about me, sir?" asked Chad.

"Have fun, Mr. Beach." replied McCormack.

Donovan tapped Chad on the shoulder with his fist as a show of support and they shared a smirk as they turned and eyed Daniel as a prize. Donovan's face then contorted.

"Wait a minute," said Donovan, "So if we knock him out, you can still wake him up and he can go again?"

"He is only a normal human," replied Meng.

"All of us have been downed in combat, and we returned to the fray with renewed vigor," answered McCormack. "It stands to reason that we should give Rooke the same chance we've all had."

"What if we accidentally kill him?" asked Chad.

"General Boatman has already made arrangements with cleanup crews in the eventuality that comes to pass."

"Great," scoffed Daniel, "I feel better already."

"You can step down out of that ring any time you like, Rooke." retorted McCormack. "No one's keeping you."

"Let's just get this over with," snapped Daniel contemptuously. "I'm getting bored up here all by myself."

"You heard the man," said McCormack. "Mammoth's first up."

Donovan grinned and stretched his leg over the ropes, as he entered the ring. Daniel seemed puzzled for an instant. He did not remember Donovan being so tall. An instant later, Donovan had grown an additional five feet, and glowered down at Daniel.

"Time to bring the pain, white boy."

Daniel scoffed and his heart sank. How was he ever going to bring down a man who could add to his size and—quit possibly—strength at will?

Mammoth scattered the thought by bringing his foot down so hard, it went through the decaying ring leaving his knee at an even level with Daniel's hips.

Daniel sidestepped and kicked hard against the side of the knee and Donovan roared in pain.

With a powerful wide arch of his arm, Daniel was blown out of the ring and he bounced off the far wall, crashing to the ground.

Daniel laid on the ground and did not stir.

"It's over," concluded Meng.

Donovan finally pulled his leg out of the hole in the center of the ring and stood on his pensively, testing his knee gingerly. A moment later, Daniel rose to his knees and spat blood, wiping blood from his nose and flicking it off his fingers disgustedly. He rose and cracked his back, letting out a groan. Then walked shakily back to the ring and just cleared the ropes where Donovan stood even taller than before.

"You thought that was cute, didn't you, bitch?" spat Donovan. "Kicking me in the knee?"

"I kinda liked it, yeah." replied Daniel with a grin.

Donovan swatted Daniel again, and he bounced off the ropes, rolling in between Donovan's legs and jumping upward, punching Donovan in the groin as hard as he could. Donovan doubled over and hit the mat wide eyed and gasping.

"That little bitch cheated!" railed Donovan and rolled onto his back with his hands between his legs, cupping his groin.

"There are rules in this street fight?" spat Daniel. "Sorry, I didn't get the memo."

"Actually, there are rules," retorted McCormack. "The sparring rules that any boxer, wrestler or martial artist abides by. Even in Muay Thai, there is no below the belt punches or kicks."

"First of all; if I make it through and end up leading this team, I'm going to have to pull some pretty dirty rabbits out of my hat to hold my own against our collars in the field. Secondly; I'm in here going up against seasoned Specials without a weapon, so I'd appreciate a little leeway."

"Alright, fine." replied McCormack. "Mammoth, you're out. Take a break. Crimson, Burn, you're in."

Chad and Meng grinned as they congratulated each other with a slap of their hands while Donovan's eyes burned into Daniel. Finally, Donovan climbed out of the ring pointing to Daniel, silently promising their personal fight was not, by a long shot, finished and then slowly turned and stepped over the ropes and returned to the wall, crashing hard onto the ground next to Stephen and took to nursing his knee. Daniel frowned as Meng and Chad eagerly jostled up through the ropes and hopped in place anxiously awaiting the go ahead as they cockily glared back at him.

"If I'm going up against two," scoffed Daniel, "and one of them is an energy emitter, I'd appreciate a weapon."

"You pull a weapon on me, this get's ugly." spat Meng.

"What," replied McCormack, "makes you think one of them is an energy emitter?"

"The chick's name is 'Burn,'" scoffed Daniel. "I don't think she got the call sign for her sunny disposition."

"You got that right, *private*," spat Meng, and with a flick of her hand, a flame billowed between her fingers.

Daniel gestured to McCormack, silently informing him his point was confirmed for him. McCormack chuckled and shook his head.

"How about a bo staff?" suggested Leonard with a wink to Daniel.

Daniel looked over at Meng skeptically.

"You got one made of carbon with a fire-resistant coating?"

"No, just the bamboo." replied McCormack. "But I'll make it a rule that we can take away the weapon and use it against you, but we can't destroy the weapon through energy projection or telekinesis."

"You got a deal."

"Give it to him," barked McCormack over his shoulder to Leonard.

Leonard tossed it to Bradley, who tossed it into the ring to Daniel. Leonard gave a grin to McCormack and Bradley.

"Watch this," said Leonard.

"Are we ready yet?" scolded Chad.

"Baby needs a security blanket," chided Meng.

Daniel took a defensive position and waited with his bo staff at the ready position. Daniel surmised that Meng would have to be taken down fast, suspecting Chad to be a greater physical threat in close quarters combat and his mind raced with possible assaults, discerning how he could be neutralized and studied the harder road of combat, where the soldier takes the role of an athletic chess player, studying moves, probing for weaknesses, praying he is still conscious by the time he finds the Achilles heel.

His scenarios shattered amid the booming call for war that shook down his spine to his knees and continued down to his heels.

"Begin!" shouted McCormack.

Daniel quickly launched at Meng. Within an instant, her fists glowed and seemed to transform into billowing balls of flame. The heat was so intense; Daniel instantly re-coiled, feeling his skin burn within five feet of her. Raising her fists, she launched the balls of fire repeatedly at Daniel, singing his hair and scalding his skin where the balls passed.

Daniel was lucky. It seemed pretty obvious by her call sign that her abilities would be related to radiating energy of some kind, but he had not expected her abilities to include the projecting of fireballs.

Meng laid down a suppressing fire while Chad launched overhead with an aerial display of kicks and punches with the dexterity of a chimpanzee in a tree, equally using both his arms and legs to press his attack, while scarcely ever touching the ground; using Daniel's own chest, shoulders, arms and head to propel himself upward again. And with seemingly incalculable spins, leveling several punches and kicks to his head, Chad seemed to dance around the fireballs as if he had them timed perfectly.

Fighting Chad was unlike anything Daniel had ever an-ticipated. Chad was easily faster and far more powerful and he proceeded to fight him with a bored and lazy expression that impressed upon Daniel that he was holding back—an interpretation that angered him.

The bo staff snapped and spun violently, almost keep-ing up with Chad, and many of his blows were blocked as Chad became more and more annoyed at his inability to land a solid strike.

Every time Chad attacked, the heat from Meng dissipated and the field of fire quickly diminished to almost nothing. Daniel began to see their strategy in taking turns in keeping him off balance while the other laid down an assault to sup-press his attacks and keep him on the defensive. He began to appreciate their teamwork and solidarity of mind. It was clear by their joint assaults and their apparent boredom they had performed these maneuvers hundreds of times.

"Time for something new," said Daniel with a smile.

Chad was frustrated by Daniel's grinning and began to fight harder. Temporarily overwhelmed by the assault, it was all Daniel could do to merely block, and no attack was made until Chad had leapt back, and Meng continued to press her assault.

Daniel recoiled from Meng and when Chad launched at him, tossed the bo staff into Chad's midsection and with his foot, propped up the other end of the staff against the mat, causing Chad to pole vault over him.

Daniel darted into the space the bo staff opened between Chad and the mat, and rushed Meng; punching her in the forehead, knocked her to the floor as Chad landed on his back, roiling on the ground in agony a short distance from where Meng laid staring at the ceiling, unable to move.

McCormack seemed surprised, but only for a moment.

"Maximus," called McCormack, "You're up."

Chad and Meng rose shakily and glared back at Daniel with disgust, then smiled when they noted Bradley climbing into the ring.

"Looks like I just graduated," smiled Daniel.

"I don't know what you're smiling for," said Bradley, "you're not going to win this match."

"You'd be surprised," said Daniel, with a scoff, "how many times I've been underestimated."

"I'm sure," replied Bradley. "But the point is you're now facing a telekinetic. Do you have a strategy?"

"Not really," replied Daniel. "In situations this fluid, I kind of have to come up with a battle plan on the fly."

"Well," replied Bradley, "I hope you don't mind if I don't give you time to form one, then." With that, Bradley's fists balled, and Daniel was stunned by an impact to his nose and mouth from out of nowhere. Daniel wiped blood from his nose and looked perplexed at Bradley for an instant.

Bradley stood ten feet away from him, and appeared not to have moved so much as an inch toward him.

Daniel then charged Bradley and a series of blows propelled Daniel backwards landing hard onto his back.

"Like I said, I'm not going to give you the chance to form a battle strategy."

Daniel rose slowly and stared perplexed at Bradley. The next blow came hard across his chin, bending his head back hard in a snap and Daniel fell to the floor again, his bo staff rolling out of his grip. He laid their stunned for several moments.

"If you get up, I'm going to keep going." said Bradley, matter of fact. "Tap out, Agent Rooke. There's no shame in it. You just aren't up to the task."

Daniel rose to his knees, and Bradley did not wait for him to rise. The assault sent him back to the mat.

Daniel rolled over onto his stomach and pushed himself to his knees again, taking up the bo staff.

Bradley merely sighed, and with a nod of approval, took a defensive stance.

Daniel then charged Bradley and held his bo staff firmly in front of him. In an instant, he felt the force like solid air or invisible concrete pressing against his fist and bo staff, bending it, as another force came right up the middle and propelled him backwards, crashing against the matt again.

"I'm impressed," said Bradley with approval. "You made three feet on me. But playtime's over."

Daniel rose and took his bo staff up again.

"You'd be right about that."

Daniel charged on Bradley again.

Bradley seemed to frown as if he did not prefer to lash out at him. This only flashed across his face for an instant.

The next instant, Bradley's eyes grew wide and focused and Daniel felt the brick wall pressing against his bo staff and right arm again. Using the staff, he felt the field and discerned that the force was no more than a few inches in diameter and rolled away from it, discarding the bo staff as it bounced off another projection leaving Daniel only three feet from Bradley.

Daniel leaped up and kicked Bradley directly in the face, sending his head back with a snap that brought him to his knees.

Bradley put his hands on the mat and fought to regain focus quickly.

Daniel brought his leg back for a kick to the back of the skull when a sudden pain affected his skull and sent him back a step.

Perplexed, Daniel stood still for an instant and quickly recovered, fearing Bradley would regain momentum.

Daniel grabbed Bradley's wrist, yanked it hard and dug his fingernails into the nerve between his index fingers, pinching the nerve hidden there. Bradley yelped and his arm went limp allowing Daniel with a hard wrench to twist his arm behind his back, forcing Bradley to lay flat on the mat.

For a brief moment, Bradley seemed to resist, and Daniel felt the concrete force begin to stretch out and press against him, almost enveloping him.

With a hard yank, Daniel threatened to dislocate Bradley's shoulder.

An instant later, Bradley, frustrated and in agony, tapped the mat three times.

Daniel recognized this as the sign of submission, which ended the match and released Bradley, who laid perfectly still, groaning as he gripped his arm gingerly.

Meng, Chad, Stephen and Donovan each took steps collectively toward the ring, but Leonard, McCormack and Bradley waved them off, and the four stopped in their tracks, with silent annoyance.

Bradley heaved backward onto his knees, and gingerly felt his arm, massaging the muscles from his shoulder down to his wrist. McCormack seemed momentarily awestruck, but quickly reverted to the blank expressioned wall.

"That was an interesting tactic." concluded McCormack coolly. "Tell me, why did you grapple Brad? It seems a threat as powerful as Maximus should have deserved a more direct physical assault."

"Mr. Overman is a powerful threat," agreed Daniel, with a nod to the now rising Bradley. "But he underestimated his opponent, which can get you killed in the field. As far as why I chose to grapple him, I gotta say, kicking him was a tempting alternative. But I had a feeling a man as seasoned as he is would probably recuperate fast and be prepared for such an assault. And then I figured out that what I really needed to do was scatter his thoughts and make it hard for him to focus."

"And how did you come to that conclusion?"

"I don't know. Something occurred to me and I decided to change my strategy."

"Can you tell me what occurred to you?"

"I don't know. It was like all of a sudden my mind flooded with hundreds of facts that I never considered before. The primary fact I ended up focusing on was that telekinesis, like telepathy, was a focusing of will, which the agent forces into reality against or onto a selected subject. That that will can be broken through distraction. And pain was a perfect distracter. I can't explain it. It just sort of popped into my head. It gave me a little bit of a headache, too."

"Interesting," muttered McCormack.

"Well you made the right choice," chimed Bradley with a gregarious slap on Daniel's back. "I was augmenting my telekinesis into a shield. If you had attacked me with a blow, it would have redirected back at you. But manipulation of the joints and pressure points! That I wasn't expecting."

"How's your arm?" asked Daniel, mainly out of concern, but also to remind Bradley of the pain he had just inflicted on him. Bradley grinned and rubbed his shoulder.

"Nothing a pack of ice couldn't cure," replied Bradley with a smirk. "Trust me; I've had worse during the war."

"Glad to hear it, Mr. Overman."

"Brad," chimed Bradley, offering his hand.

"Daniel."

"Welcome to the SITF."

Donovan, Meng and Stephen grew instantly indignant, while Chad seemed accepting of the decision.

"He didn't even get to fight me," spat Stephen.

"Stephen," replied McCormack, "You've caused serious injury to your own team members by detonating too close to them in simulated combat. *My* shields have trouble blocking your explosions. I'm not going to pit you against a normal human just to make a point. To many *Specials*, that'd be suicide."

"Yeah, well," pressed Stephen belligerently, "If he can't hold his own in a safe environment, how's he going to hold up in the real thing?"

"Stand down, Stephen."

"No!" demanded Stephen defiantly, "This is important! I'm not going to put my life in the hands of a norm-hume."

"Giordano," bellowed Leonard, and Stephen instantly jumped to attention under the commanding voice of Leonard and remained at attention until Leonard dismissed him with a jut of his chin. "Stand down!"

Stephen skulked away back to Donovan and Meng.

"So that's it?" said Daniel in disbelief. "I'm in?"

"No," answered McCormack "not yet."

"So what next?"

"You and me are going to have a little talk," concluded McCormack, and glanced at the others "alone."

"Back at the Post. One hour."

McCormack then turned to leave and the others followed. Leonard pulled Daniel into an expressive one-armed hug that displayed both his comradic feelings for

Daniel and his desire to keep the others from assaulting Daniel from behind.

"There," cooed Leonard, gregariously, "that wasn't so hard, was it?"

"Oh, piece of cake." scoffed Daniel, and they chuckled out to the van while Bradley and Chad kept pace between Daniel and the mutinous three.

"So," said Daniels as he and Leonard climbed into the van, "this meeting between me and Tobias, anything I should be worried about?"

"Nah," sang Leonard. "He's just going to give you the run down. Don't sweat it."

"I trust you."

Back at the Post, Daniel walked down the long hallway to the last door on the right hand side and opened the door, leading him into the small converted office. McCormack had just taken a seat behind the desk and was putting files back into the desk drawer when he noticed Daniel standing there.

"Have a seat," said McCormack politely.

Daniel sat in the old office chair delicately nursing his injuries and sighed.

"So what now?"

"You and me are going to have a test of wills, first."

"How?"

"I'm going to try to enter your mind," began McCormack matter of fact, "and you're going to try to stop me."

"You've got to be kidding," scoffed Daniel.

"This is the only way you're going to be able to stay on the team."

"I just proved myself back there on your own test," spat Daniel hotly, "now you want to change the rules?"

"You can think what you like," spat McCormack, glaring at him with a cold authority, "I don't give a damn what you think. But when we get out there, we'll need to be able to trust you. Do you think Bradley and me are the only telepaths out there? There are some who are even more powerful than we are." McCormack studied Daniel for a moment, as though choosing his words very carefully. Finally he returned to speaking. "There are three reasons why the powers that be usually trained telepaths to provide strategy in combat. One, they could save money on communications devices, and two, a telepath could orchestrate the battle from a very safe distance."

"What's the third?"

"There was a darker side to our presence on the battlefield. It was called the DC Protocol. It stood for Divide and Conquer. These were protocols for psi talents to affect enemy troop movements during battles where enemy forces had control of the battlefield through a form of psychic infiltration, forcing hostile combatants to turn on their own forces and sow discord among the enemy. In several engagements we received these protocols which gave us permission to affect enemy troop movements directly, by entering their minds and turning their own forces against them."

Daniel's face grew long as the implications of what McCormack had just told him set in.

"Jesus," he gasped.

McCormack continued, seemingly indifferent to Daniel's discomfort.

"It required a great deal of skill, and more often than not, the horror of it drove a great many Specials insane due to the fact they were under orders to murder so many so callously. They called it *bomber's guilt*. In effect, they said it was the same as pilots dropping bombs at a distance killing so many unknown faces. To a telepath, it was far worse. We experienced their thoughts and dreams. Flashes of their lives. And then turned them on their comrades, in some cases relatives, and forced them to pull the trigger.

The best of us could affect nearly entire battlefields, turning a great threat into powerful allies. They were aware of the fact they were murdering their own men and were screaming and weeping in horror. When their own men finally killed them, the psychic blowback was almost the same as killing us as well. We felt ourselves die and then our consciousness would snap back into our own bodies. The second most powerful of us was a young man I'll never forget. Errol Polls. Errol was a good kid. But he was a powerful psi talent. He had the ability to possess multiple targets at once and force them to lash out violently at their own men, turning entire legions against the remaining forces."

"What happened to him?"

"This is just conjecture, but in one engagement, when the protocol was activated, he spread his consciousness too thin. There were thousands of them, that day. He began weeping but he turned the tide. Saved us all. After the enemy troops were decimated, though, something happened. The next thing we knew we were fighting each other. I was also swept away in the madness until I realized I was not in control of my actions. Then I looked up and Errol was on the hill screaming. He'd lost control of his own abilities. Me and a handful of Specials had to go up that hill and kill Errol. I can still see his eyes."

Daniel was horrified. *"To kill a comrade in arms,"* he thought. He could never have done it.

"I think you could have," replied McCormack with a sad smile. Daniel pulled away with anger at having his mind read. "You're a soldier. If one of your own was killing your other men, I think you could have done the exact same thing. That's why I let you take the test. If you couldn't do it, I would have told the General to take you away immediately."

"Why are you telling me this?"

"Partly to lower your defenses so I could get a good reading on you," replied McCormack, matter of fact.

Daniel was mortified, and a deep sense of betrayal overtook him.

"So all that was one big lie?" he spat as an indignant rage began to build within him. "Just to break into my mind?"

McCormack merely sat there, silently indulging in a reminiscent smile.

"Riot was a good kid. He was very real," concluded McCormack. The next moment, his eyes became hard and regretful. "—all the way up until I killed him."

There was a long pause that seemed to stretch out between them. One that McCormack did not intrude upon. Daniel began to squirm in the silence. His anger had subsided a great deal, but he could not take the snapping bite out of his question.

"What's the point of the story, other than so you could peek into my mind?"

Daniel was instantly apologetic for having spoken too harshly when McCormack smiled, and seemed to wave off his silent self-rebuke.

"You have to understand how dangerous this task is going to be. Every time we go out, we could run into a Special that was a part of the psi program. One that could have been subject to the DC Protocols. That's a high level psi talent. I need to know you won't be compromised so if you do end up leading us into battle, you won't become a liability to us."

"So how do we fix that?"

"Look at me."

"What is this, some kind of mind meld?" chided Daniel with a scoff.

"Do I look like Mr. Spock to you?" scolded McCormack, "Just shut up and look into my eyes."

McCormack leaned close, peering into Daniel's eyes. Daniel was instantly uncomfortable, fully aware how this would seem if someone had merely opened the door to see the two men leaning toward each other, gazing intently into each other's eyes.

"If you kiss me, I swear to God…"

"Shut up, please."

Daniel sat uncomfortably and tried to breathe calmly.

"This may hurt," said McCormack.

"Great," scoffed Daniel.

Then his world went white. There was an almost audible pop and a sensation of pain in his skull that almost brought him to screaming out loud. It felt as if a cool gel had begun to creep across the space between his brain and his skull, and he was aware that something was filling up his skull, causing the sensation as if his head was ripe for bursting. Then the gel seemed to form needles, and began to penetrate his brain.

He could feel the movement of the liquid deeper into his brain, down past his eyes, and he gasped as he felt an electrical current travel through his skull, as if the gel had caught fire inside his brain. Then the world went black, and all he could hear was his heart beat pounding as though it were threatening to rip out of his chest and his own breathing racing, labored near the point of panting.

When Daniel opened his eyes, he was shuddering and his heart was racing. He was drenched in sweat and he fought to control his breathing. He felt like he had run ten consecutive one minute miles and his muscles ached from tense spasms.

"What the hell did you do?" panted Daniel.

"Made it difficult for a psi talent to read you," replied McCormack. "If someone tries, it will prove extremely painful. Like all predators, the hunter prefers the weaker prey. This should remove you from being a target by all but the most powerful or persistently curious psi talents."

"What happens then?"

"If a psi talent is that powerful and determined enough to see inside you despite the pain and risk to him or herself, there's ultimately nothing that can be done."

"Why?"

"Because if they're powerful enough to get through your mental defenses," replied McCormack grimly, "They're also powerful enough to compromise everyone on the team."

"I was afraid of that."

"There's nothing more I can do for you," concluded McCormack with a wave of his hand. "Your defenses could block both Bradley and myself quite effectively. Less so, with Brad."

"How do I know what your saying is true?"

McCormack dabbed his ears and held it up to the light in front of Daniel to show the droplets of blood on it.

"Because," replied McCormack, "after I taught your brain how to defend itself, I then attacked you. Trust me. There's no way a high level psi talent could invade your thoughts or affect your actions without paying a dear cost."

Daniel sat and weighed McCormack's words of reassurance, and was far from reassured. He had received a valuable gift from Paladin —a thick and powerful wall that prevented him from being read or controlled—but his words made him feel that all the defense in the world was just so much tissue paper compared to the real threat of the highest level psi talent. Daniel felt sick to his stomach, and his strength left him, finally, leaving him only the pain his body felt from the traumas he had received only a few hours earlier.

"You need rest," concluded McCormack. "I suggest you get some sleep to recover. You've had a busy day."

Daniel nodded, and rose slowly, walking over to the door and held onto the knob as a thought occurred to him. An annoying question that began to weigh heavily in light of all he had undergone and learned from McCormack. Especially in regard to the Divide and Conquer Protocols.

"Who was the strongest?"

"What?" said McCormack, looking up.

"You said Riot was the second most powerful psi talent in the Specials Battalion. Who was the first?"

McCormack seemed to recoil into his chair, as if the subject was one he would have rather avoided.

"Simon Kolinsky," said McCormack with concern, as if the mere mentioning of his name was the same as being in his presence. "Call sign: Ark. The most amoral man I ever met. Messing with people's minds was like a game to him. All any of us were to him were pieces on the board to be moved on a whim. He was so powerful, he not only mastered the DC Protocols against the enemies he controlled friendly troop movements as well. Both sides. At the same time. We kept him in a stasis chamber that was carried into battle like the Ark of the fucking Covenant and opened only at the utmost need. Last I heard, after the war they took that box to the deepest, darkest hole they could find, hooked it up to a life support system and kept it shut. I don't think anyone'd be stupid enough to free him. Ever."

"And if someone did let him out?"

"There's a reason he liked to call himself Pandora. Trust me, if we ever go up against him, there will be no hope."

Daniel nodded silently. It was not the answer he would have liked to hear, but the truth had often worked that way with him. A heavy sigh escaped him, and his eyes nearly shut. His head bobbed and he had to shake his head to remain alert.

"Do I have a room here? Or do I need to check into a hotel somewhere? Preferably in the Northwest section of the city."

"You can always go check in at the Courtyard Washington Northwest; it's got some incredible views of the landmarks. Unfortunately, it's a little pricy and you'll be responsible for the bill and transportation costs. Didn't the General tell you? No one gives a shit about us."

Daniel nodded as if he had expected that answer and scoffed.

"Any place here?"

McCormack laughed, and pointed down the hall toward his left.

"Your bags and weapons were delivered while we were at the gym. They're in room 406, down the hall and to the left. We tried to clean it up a little, but don't expect miracles. This place is a shit hole."

"Right," muttered Daniel. "Thanks."

"Have a good night, sir. We'll work on your strategies for us first thing in the morning."

Daniel waved McCormack off half caring and walked out of the room, feeling his mind growing heavy and the need to lie down becoming a paramount necessity. Daniel did not even care that federal agents had been in his apartment, going through his things. He knew they probably bugged his place to ensure he would not be a leak for information. After all, it's what he would have done if he were assigning someone else to a sensitive job like his.

Daniel reached room 406 to find Donovan standing against the wall next to the door. He looked down at Daniel disgustedly.

"So you think you're big shit now that you're on the team, huh?" scoffed Donovan coldly. "Well let me tell you something. There ain't no way I'm going to take orders from some pasty faced white assed norm-hume bitch like you. You heard me? I don't know when, but sooner or later, you an' me are going to finish what we started back there. You feel me?"

Daniel nodded uncaringly and pushed the door open weakly and left Donovan standing there frustrated as the door closed behind him. Daniel stripped off his clothes and let them fall wherever they would without a care.

The room was musty and stale and the aroma of mold and old decay battled with the smell of Lemon Pledge and air fresheners. In short, it smelled like a new used car with a dead rodent in it. Daniel did not care. He fell on the starched sheets and did not bother to wrap himself in them or climb under them. He buried his face in the pillow and smelled the only thing that smelled truly fresh in the entire room—the smell of new pillows.

"Probably the most expensive thing in the room," he thought as the lights went out and he drifted into the darkness.

Within the count of three breaths, he was snoring.

Back in McCormack's office, Bradley entered and sat down as his friend stared out the window in deep thought, wholly disinterested in the distant and nearing sounds of police sirens wailing.

"You felt it too?" said McCormack, unsurprised.

"Yeah," replied Bradley.

"I'm not wholly concerned with my decision to train Rooke. He would have found a way to overcome you eventually. But it probably would have taken him a half hour or so. Maybe he would have lasted that long, I don't know."

"He's pretty tough," replied Bradley, "He just might have lasted that long." McCormack chuckled, nodded his agreement, and then trailed off again, staring out the window again. Bradley was equally as frustrated. "Who do you think it was?"

"I don't know," said McCormack. "I haven't the foggiest idea who. But what worries me, is how strong he was."

"Yeah, it wasn't even subtle. It was like whoever it was didn't care that we heard."

"Whoever it was, it's clear they want Rooke on our team," concluded McCormack. "This either makes him an asset in keeping him close, or a liability in keeping him too close."

"So what do we do?"

"I've already done the best I could to keep that from happening again," replied McCormack. "If they're that powerful, it won't matter much."

"So what about Rooke, then?"

"He'll sleep off the trauma I put him through. He'll feel like he got hit by a bus in the morning. Then we'll work with him on implementing strategies for combat scenarios. Make a playbook and get the team to memorize it."

"You know, not everybody's happy about you appointing Agent Rooke."

"I know. It can't be helped."

"I think we're going to lose some of the team."

"Not Chad," replied McCormack. "And he has more reason than any of us to leave."

"Yeah," replied Bradley. "It's a shame about Sophia."

"A Greek tragedy," replied McCormack.

"Do you think we can even get him a visitor's pass to the AbSpec Facility?"

AbSpec stood for Abnormal Special. An Abnormal Special was a class of Specials who were visibly different and have no ability to blend in with the normal human populations. They are viewed as alien or animalistic.

"Are you kidding me? With everything they've put her through she's nothing more than what they think of her, at this point."

"Someone should burn that place to the ground."

"Don't even think about it," growled McCormack. "Don't even nurse that thought. Just let it go. The sooner Chad forgets about Sophia, the better off all of us will be."

"I guess you're right."

"The only way we can function in this job working for the government, is if we forget how much they've wronged the entire Specials community. That's the only way."

"Right," said Bradley. "I'll let you alone to think. Good night, Toby."

"Brad," said McCormack, his tone rooted Bradley to the ground. "Don't ever mention The Zoo again, especially to Chad. It wouldn't take much to find the facility's location, with our level of clearance. And the last thing we need is him going off in some misguided attempt to break out those prisoners. That's the last thing we need."

The AbSpec Facility was nicknamed "The Zoo" because of all the "animals" and "freaks" caged there. It is described as a science facility in some federal grants, a prison in others and rehabilitation and reintegration facility for abnormally mutated Specials on closed congress file. No matter where the funding came from, all denied such a program had ever existed. Bradley swallowed at the thought of a mass breakout and the harm it would do to normal human/ Special relations and knew McCormack was right. He did not like it much, but he had no choice.

"Right," replied Bradley, grimly. "Good night, Toby."

"Night, Brad."

McCormack sat introspectively for a few moments, listening to the sound of Bradley Overman's footsteps growing fainter down the hall until he could no longer hear anything but the sirens wailing in the distance and the occasional shouting match down the street.

When he was sure he was alone, he opened the drawer on the side of his desk, and began to rummage through the numerous books and field manuals within, until he found one marked *Psi Talents [A two volume manual]: Unlocking their Abilities & How to Neutralize Them.*

Across the front cover were bold letter words stating CELESTIAL CLEARANCE EYES ONLY.

Paladin flipped through the manual's appendix, passing chapters with odd titles like Chapter 1: The PreCog: Myth Or Asset? Chapter 2: The Psi Ball: A Psi Talent's First Steps, or Chapter 4: The Remote Viewer: From PROJECT STARGATE to Now. The second section of the manual was filled with chapters far more ominous. It was entitled PSI TALENT: Neutralizing The Threat. In the second volume of the manual the chapters had titles less dedicated toward the training of the psi talents, but more focused on the breaking of them. This was evident in chapter titles such as Chapter 12: Sensory Assault: The Use Of Techniques Formulated by First Earth Battalion and PsiOps And Tested In Gitmo And Abu Ghraib For Use Against The Psi Talent or Chapter 14: Penetrating And Nullifying The Psi Ball. Finally he found the chapter he was looking for. Chapter 17: How To Cancel Out The Psi's Talent, Pg 373. Halfway down on page 375, McCormack found what he was looking for:

"As we touched upon in Chapter 12, we now revisit the Psi Talent's ability to maintain their phenomena under stressful conditions. Telekinesis, like telepathy, is a focusing of will, which the agent forces into reality against/onto a selected target/ subject. The Psi talent's mind is the cause of the phenomenon. However, it is also the source of the Psi talent's downfall. The will of the Psi Talent can be broken through distraction. One primary distracter, using a wider classification, is pain. Through the introduction of pain into the controlled environment, Psi talents become disoriented, unable to maintain the focus necessary to continue to capitalize on the phenomenon they themselves

manifest. Thus, through distraction, i.e. pain, the
Psi talent is neutralized with greater ease."

McCormack closed the training manual and returned it to his drawer, then returned to staring out the dust and oil stained glass in quiet contemplation pouring over Daniel's words and scrutinized the similarity between his new insights and the research manual. There was no doubt that the text had been fed directly into Daniel's mind by an unknown party. The one thought returning again and again to McCormack was:

Who are you?

CHAPTER 5

THE LINE IN THE SAND

D aniel laid in his bed in a contorted angle with his arms extended straight between his thighs and his neck arched in an odd way. A long low snore drew out of him and he moved his head subtly, in an unconscious attempt to wipe the drool on his cheek and chin onto the pillow without moving his arms. He did not open his eyes, though he was so very near to being awake. He made every attempt to resist the waking world, as was evident from his head constantly turning away from the morning sun light pouring in from the stained windows. He lay there motionless for quite some time, until a fist pounded on the door.

"Daniel, up an' at 'em!" shouted the commanding voice, "You got ten minutes until your meeting with McCormack and Overman. Shake a leg!"

Daniel attempted to jump up, only to grow rigid and still, his eyes opened wide in surprise. He let out a soft labored groan and remained perfectly still as he slowly took inventory over every sore joint, muscle and bone. The cartilage in his nose throbbed and he could not prevent the single tear from trickling out of his eye to maddeningly tickle his cheek. He did not bother brushing it off for fear of the wrenching, seizure causing pain he fully expected to feel.

"My God," muttered Daniel, "I think I'm dying."

Another pound on the door shook him, and he unconsciously turned his head to the door, sending another jolt of pain down his spine. He winced and grit his teeth.

"Come on, Rooke!" shouted the now clear voice, easily distinct as Leonard's "We're burning daylight, here!"

"Gimme a minute, will you?" shouted Daniel.

"What," inquired Leonard with mock concern, "do you want time to finish jerking off?"

"I can't move my arms to jerk off, asshole!"

"Toughen up!" bellowed Leonard critically, and he pounded on the door.

"Hey, I'm your superior officer, now! Do what I say and get me a gallon of ICY/HOT!"

There was a long pause and when Leonard's voice intruded on Daniel again, it was with some sincere concern.

"Are you okay?"

"I think I got a little more hurt yesterday than I realized. Just give me a few minutes to stretch out, will you?"

"Sure," replied Leonard with some nervous concern. "Take your time."

"Right," muttered Daniel, and with a sigh, rolled off the bed to collapse onto the floor with a thud. His cheek pressed against the hard-crusted carpet, Daniel felt a tickling sensation all over, as if he were laying on soft fiberglass.

He quickly rose to end the odd sensation and brushed his arms, legs and face with disgust, trying to brave the waves of severe pain he felt with every motion. After the pain had passed, he took long moments to stretch to ease pain in his muscles, though it did nothing for the pain to his bones and nose.

Finally, he opened his duffel bag and dressed and within a minute, he was walking down the hallway toward the common room. Donovan sat with his arms folded on the chiropractic office chair, leaning back against the wall.

"You still here?" spat Donovan with disgust.

"Obviously," scoffed Daniel. "Where's the kitchen in this place?"

"Find it your damn self," spat Donovan, a wanton malice in his eyes.

"Thanks for your help," replied Daniel in frustrated annoyance, and cringed at the loud voice that echoed explosively through the common room and reverberated down the hall.

"Fuck you!"

Daniel muttered to himself as he walked down the hallway toward McCormack's office as Leonard appeared out of a side room with a grin.

"Seems like you're up and about."

"Only in body," scoffed Daniel. "Where's the kitchen in this place? I'm starving."

"We don't really have a kitchen. But breakfast was brought in an hour ago. It's in here."

Leonard stepped out of the way to allow Daniel into the makeshift commissary. Daniel was surprised. There was no stove, no microwave or even a refrigerator, but the room was clean, with white and black tiles on the floor and countertop shining back at him in the soft illumination of the overhead fluorescent light.

"This place is so clean," gasped Daniel.

"Well, we gotta eat somewhere," scoffed Leonard. "Hurry up with chow; you got a meeting in five."

"Right," replied Daniel, and he sat down at the table, and began to fumble through the take out containers and empty scrambled eggs, bacon and toast onto a paper plate. Daniel was so content with the notion of eating the first solid meal he had had in nearly forty-eight hours that he did not even care when he noted there were no forks or spoons anywhere. Soon, he was shoveling handfuls of eggs and bacon onto the toast slices and forcing the piles into his mouth and licking his fingers. Within a few minutes, he had finished his meal with great satisfaction despite the inconvenience of not having silverware and he tossed the paper plate into the trash bin in the corner of the room and walked down the hallway toward McCormack's office, still licking the excess egg off his fingers.

When Daniel reached McCormack's office, he found McCormack and Bradley sitting idly, discussing potential strategies for the next training exercise.

"Morning," said Daniel.

"Agent Rooke," chimed McCormack, "Leonard informed me you were in pain. I trust all is well?"

"I'm fine. I've actually had worse, if you could believe it. But it's been a long time since I've had it at all."

"Well," concluded McCormack, dryly, "it's better your body remember and grow accustomed to pain. There's going to be a lot of it in your future."

"That's comforting," scoffed Daniel.

"Have you had time to think about how you intend to use us?" asked Bradley.

"Beg your pardon?"

"Did you learn anything about our strategy," he pressed, "and how to fix the problems in our protocols from what you saw in the scrimmage, yesterday?"

Daniel sat back in his chair thoughtfully and focused on Bradley and McCormack.

"I learned that Beach spends too much time in aerial attacks, and though he's faster than anything I've seen and he hits like a mule, he still has to come down. And when he comes down, he's open to attack."

"Good," said McCormack, "What would you do about that?"

"I'd like to see him stay more grounded. Has he had training in martial arts?"

"He's been versed in all the important forms of hand to hand combat."

"What are the important ones?" inquired Daniel.

"Did you recognize any of the styles?" pressed McCormack, ignoring Daniel's question.

"It looked like a cross of Tae Kwon Do and Regional Capoeira, though some of the grappling and pressure point maneuvers he attempted suggest Krav Magda."

"That's a good assessment," congratulated Bradley, "How would you handle Crimson?"

"I'd take his legs out from under him when he came down before he could get proper footing. He can press a powerful and intimidating attack in the air, but he also doesn't have the power he would have from a grounded assault. He can't pivot off the heel to give a greater whipping effect to his punches or kicks that he would be able to do if he stayed on the ground. In the air he's vulnerable. If he's going to keep jumping, he's got to do it faster and hit harder. A seasoned fighter could dodge an air attack and hit him hard before he touches the ground, sending him flipping through the air. And after yesterday, I confirmed a suspicion I long had about jump kicks. They give up power for an intimidating show of force. That intimidation doesn't work on seasoned fighters. I'd like to teach him how to pivot on the balls of his toes to add a little extra power to his punches and kicks. Plus, I'd like to see how he handles himself against a bladed weapon or an opponent with speed and strength more on par with him. I find that when one uses a martial style and they fight another opponent who uses another style, it can be problematic for the fighters. His problem is not everyone knows how to fight. I figure that despite his obvious skills, he's just been getting lucky and getting by."

McCormack and Bradley turned to each other and traded looks of approval that clearly demonstrated what Daniel said had confirmed their suspicions and beliefs and then returned intently to Daniel.

"What about Elisabeth?" said McCormack clinically.

"Who?"

"Elisabeth Meng," corrected Bradley.

Daniel seemed perplexed for a moment.

"Burn...the Asian girl!" added McCormack irritated, then sighed. "Don't worry. I'll get you dossiers on all team members after we're done, here. You can study them at your leisure."

"Okay," said Daniel, and then pursed his lips. "As a strategy, projecting the fireballs as a form of suppressing firepower is a solid formula, but she has a problem in that she can only release them in bursts, and you can figure out the timing of her bursts as well as the speed of the fireballs."

"How fast are the fireballs traveling, then?"

"I'd say about thirty-five miles per hour."

"Interesting."

"What, am I wrong?"

"Not really," replied McCormack. "The fireballs travel at thirty-four, actually."

"So why are you breaking my balls?" snapped Daniel, with annoyance.

McCormack just glared back at him with a reserved annoyance.

"Get on with it, Agent Rooke."

"Right," scoffed Daniel. "Anyways, like I said, it's a good strategy, but her bursts can be timed. I assume her rapid fire bursts was her full capacity?"

"That's her top speed as far as delivery of her payloads," answered McCormack. "but she has a few other tricks up her sleeve."

"Like what?" demanded Daniel.

"I'll leave that to your research when I give you the dossiers."

Daniel scratched his head.

"You're not really helping me, here."

McCormack grew visibly perturbed and studied Daniel for a moment.

"We're not here to help you, Daniel." snapped McCormack. "We're here to train you so you can help us. All the information you're requiring of us can be found in the dossiers. You'll find they're quite thorough when documenting the abilities and endurance levels of Specials. You're doing fine so far. Just get on with it."

"Fine," scoffed Daniel, more than a little put off. "Because Burn's bursts can be timed, they can be avoided, putting her and the rest of the team at risk. I would like to have her train to vary her pulses into random patterns, so that the enemy can't get a good timing on her pulses."

"What kind of patterns?"

"One pulse per second one barrage, three pulse per second another barrage—that sort of thing. Make the enemy gun shy by making her assaults unpredictable. I would like the enemy to worry that every attempt they make to move from one cover to another could be the one attempt they get nailed in. If we can pin them down, we can easily create a strategy that doesn't result in risking injury to members of our team."

"Setting aside the whole Special/Norm-Hume prob-lem," interjected Leonard, "I'd like to offer that a cornered man is a dangerous man. What's your solution to a pinned down Special, then?"

"That's what grenades are for," concluded Daniel, as if the answer was obvious. "Problem solved. No one on our team gets hurt."

Bradley and McCormack traded looks of concern, but then returned to the role of the stone-faced audience.

"And what about Henry?" inquired McCormack.

Daniels thought for a moment. Donovan Henry was a physical threat from the beginning, and there was not much he could say against the man's strategies, other than the fact that he was such a big target, he was likely to draw the majority of enemy fire. That was a concern.

"Donovan's abilities are obviously to change height and mass, but I also suspect to change density and strength."

"Go on."

"Donovan's problem is ego," Daniel concluded. "He gets cocky, and he thinks that by being bigger and stronger is enough to turn the tables on the situation. Setting aside the fact that he's a big target in a firefight, and the fact that as far as I can discern, he's not bulletproof, my problem is with his physical structure when he grows. It seems to me that his bones lose their density in the change. It's my contention that if he were to grow bigger than a house, his bones would become brittle. Kind of like those spindly tall basketball players. They're always falling down and get-ting injured for the season."

"Okay, I'm still with you," said Bradley, "Go on."

"Well, if he can also augment his density, he could harden before he grows then harden again and grow some more. It seems he just plain grows, leaving himself need-lessly open to injury."

"Harden?" asked said McCormack skeptically, and traded an exasperated look with Bradley.

"I figure they're two separate things," replied Daniel, "Pushing up to grow, and pulling in to harden. By pulling in, he increases his mass. Like shrinking."

"I don't think you understand his abilities all that well."

"Really? Then tell me something; why does Donovan have a changing waistline?" "What are you talking about?"

"Yesterday I saw his waistline change three times," pressed Daniel against the disbelieving audience's glare of disagreement. "It seems to me, he has the ability to increase his strength and density by shrinking or pulling inward. He may not even be conscious about it, and just sucking in so he doesn't look so fat."

"Wait," scoffed McCormack, "you're telling me that you've discovered something that the Camp Gamma Specials Medical Staff, in over five years of study did not detect?"

"Camp Gamma Specials Medical Staff?"

"The Base Science/Medical Facility for Specials Base Camp Gamma. They were—on paper—a Mobile Military Hospital unit only stationed at Base Camp Gamma to moni-tor the military personnel's health and perform surgery on the wounded returning from the front lines. However, they were also the mad scientists who experimented on the weaker powered Specials, in order to encourage their use-fulness in combat through DNA splicing, drugs and radia-tion exposure. The desired result was a powerful Special with a high endurance and survivability level. As a result of the experimentation, the scientists were responsible for the creation of 98% of all Abnormal Specials. And you think you've learned something new that wasn't first documented by them?"

"When you put it that way," chided Bradley, "it sounds a little farfetched."

"Maybe you should just read the dossiers and we can continue this after dinner," said McCormack, ignoring Daniel's hypothesis out of hand.

"Fine," snapped Daniel, "You want me to prove I'm right? I'll be back."

Daniel stormed down the hallway into the main living room and spotted Donovan still propped against the wall in the rickety chiropractic office chair.

"Mammoth," snapped Daniel "I need you."

"Bitch, fuck you," spat Donovan, "I don't give a damn about you."

Leonard appeared over Daniel's shoulder and glared at Donovan.

"Staff Sergeant Henry," barked Leonard, "You are disobeying a direct order from a superior officer."

"This ain't the military no more, Leonard." scoffed Donovan. "I respect you, man. But don't bark at me like you can handle me. The only man I'll take an order from is the General or Paladin. Shit, Paladin should be leading us anyway. Not some norm-hume bitch like this, here."

Leonard took a step forward and Daniel put his hand on his shoulder bringing him to an immediate halt.

"I got this," said Daniel.

"You want to go?" spat Donovan, and he kicked the chair out of the way and clenched his fist. "Come on."

"You want to get embarrassed again?"

"Man you got lucky yesterday and you cheated, too."

McCormack and Bradley raced into the room to separate them, but Daniel warded them off with a wave of his hand.

"I cheated?" spat Daniel, "I guess that's the best explanation you can come up with, since I beat your fat ass fair and square."

Donovan seemed to billow, and then shrink, his stomach pulling in and forming near rock hard abdominal muscles under a layer of considerable body fat. His arms became more defined and his thighs and ankles took on a powerful body builder's physique as he began to stretch outward and upward to nearly the ceiling.

"Bitch, I'm gonna kill you," bellowed Donovan.

Daniel merely smiled and raised his hand to Donovan in pause.

"Hang on a second, Mr. Henry." said Daniel, and turned back to McCormack and Bradley. "See? He can do it."

Donovan stood up straight and was instantly frustrated. He had been waiting to fight Daniel ever since he first arrived, and now Daniel was not even facing him, but talking with McCormack and Bradley.

"Do what?" spat Donovan, "What the fuck is that white motherfucker talking about?"

Daniel walked out of the room and McCormack and Bradley followed him back to the office leaving Donovan to stand there in growing mortification and contempt.

Back in the office, Daniel sat down as McCormack and Bradley entered.

"That was crude," said McCormack with a wry smile. "But you made your point."

Bradley however, did not seem pleased at all.

"I hope you know," said Bradley, "you just alienated a team member who was already thinking about dropping from the team. This is not at all the way you should be leading us."

"I understand your being displeased with how I got my results back there, Overman," replied Daniel, "but as far as Mammoth's concerned, I don't think he's going to want to be on the team much longer as long as I'm here. And I refuse to have my orders questioned or overridden in the field, so as far as I'm concerned, unless we have a meeting of the minds and overcome this little power play he's committing me to against him, me and him are at an impasse."

The three of them sat in silence staring at each other for a long minute until McCormack broke the silence with a stern nod.

"Understood," replied McCormack.

"But Toby," began Bradley critically, "you saw what happened back there. He baited him into a fight. Donovan's livid. I haven't seen him this upset since he found out Mirage was a former Crip."

"Your discomfort with how Daniel achieved his results is noted, Brad. But we both knew it was a gamble taking Henry on the team in the first place. His racism and belief in conspiracies committed by white people against the black community was bound to become an issue when we went public."

"So he's already fired?" scoffed Bradley in disbelief, "Just like that?"

"No," replied McCormack coolly. "It's up to him. But judging from how he's actively seeking to undermine Daniel's authority, and his encouraging of others to take sides with him in protest of Daniel's appointment as field commander, it seems like he's taking himself out."

"I don't believe what I'm hearing," declared Bradley with a building annoyance that began to affect the desk between him and McCormack with a vibration. "He's our team mate. We went through the whole war together."

"Can you control him?" replied McCormack critically, "Can you keep his mouth shut? Can you keep him from exploding whenever Rooke gives an order in the field?"

"What do you want me to do," spat Bradley, "rewrite his thinking?"

Daniel sat there for a moment dazed, quickly recovering and whirling on Bradley.

"You can do that?" gasped Daniel.

"Not now, Daniel." spat McCormack, and returned his critical glare to Bradley. "If Donovan is out, it's because Donovan can't figure out how to overcome his own racism to be a team player."

"I can't be a racist," said the deep voice from the hall-way, and Daniel turned around to see Donovan, who now filled the doorway glowering down at them. "I'm black. Racism was invented by white people. Y'all motherfuckers are racists. But I love you guys because of what we went through together, and I know you two got my back. But don't expect me to follow this white racist motherfucker right there. You want me to go, I'll go. I don't want to be ordered around by no bitch-ass cracker who doesn't know the first thing about fighting a real fight. I'll be gone to-night. And I promise you, Lizzie and Stephen don't want none of this white motherfucker, here, either. I won't be going alone."

"That's fine," replied McCormack. "We need a team that's going to act like a team. If you can't get with the pro-gram, then thank you for letting us know now, and no hard feelings, Donovan."

"So you keeping this bitch?"

"The bitch stays," replied McCormack.

Donovan stood in the doorway staring in utter disbelief for a moment. He was so confident his protest would have won McCormack over. Now, Donovan realized he had just fired himself.

"Fine," scoffed Donovan, "I'm out."

"You can stay till the cargo plane leaves in the morning, if you'd like." said Bradley, despondently.

"No, I'm cool." replied Donovan. "I don't want to even eat anywhere with that motherfucker right there."

"Whatever," replied McCormack and he turned to the window, fuming.

"Donovan, think this through," urged Bradley, "What are you going to do if you quit? Do you even have a job lined up?"

"I'm sorry, man," replied Donovan, "You guys and the General are my heart, but I don't like the way this is headed. It's better if I leave."

"You always got a place here, Don." said Bradley, kindheartedly. "You know that, right?"

"I know, man." said Donovan softly. "And I appreciate that. I really do. But I don't think I'll be coming back to this team, especially with the direction it's going down. This politics is bullshit."

"If you turn your back on us," warned McCormack, "just don't fuck up out there. I don't want to have to meet you on the opposing side of a battlefield. Can you do me that?"

"Oh, I'll keep my nose out of trouble, for sure, man." replied Donovan, dismissing the concern out of hand. "I don't want to be playing around and give these motherfuckers an excuse to lock us all up in concentration camps or something."

"Remember you said that, Don."

"Right," said Donovan, fully aware of the threat McCormack had just made and nervously shifted in his stance. "Look, I'll tell you what. I'm going to walk the straight and narrow, and I'm done with the whole adventure thing, but if you guys need me, holler at me. I'll come running. You got my word on that."

"We just might do that, Donovan." replied McCormack. "Knowing the road we got ahead of us, we just might do that."

"Right, well, I'm out."

And with that, Donovan Henry shot a glare at Daniel, and disappeared around the corner and all there was to prove he was still even in the Post, was the heavy footed plodding sounds the floorboards made as he walked back and forth in his room as he put his belongings into his duffel bags.

"So what now?" said Daniel, breaking the silence.

"We tell the others at lunch," replied McCormack, "if Donovan doesn't tell them first. Then we got to find out how many people want to follow him, and take what's left to form the team around."

"This just got difficult." muttered Daniel.

Daniel sat with his head down in quiet frustration and he reflected on the first days in office that Abraham Lincoln had when the South—feared he would be an abolitionist President, who would bring the federal government firmly over the people to dictate state policy, and in a preemptive decision to negate his potential future policies regarding the loss of state sovereignty—seceded from the union.

Here, Daniel sat facing the certainty that the Special team he was appointed to lead would disband before he even gave his first order. He sat in silence and stewed over his likely return to the Bed-Stuy in defeat and neither Bradley nor McCormack even dared to dismiss his fears. It was almost certain that the Specials Investigations program was over before it even had a chance of beginning.

Daniel walked down the hallway to the kitchen with a grim sense of purpose. The dominating thought on his mind was that somehow, he would have to counter the fears and contempt of his subordinates in order to even begin to hope to make a case for the possibility of salvaging the team. He could hear the muffled voices on the other side of the kitchen door rise and lower followed by occasional bursts of dry laughter as he reached the end of the hallway. He pushed the door open to find that he did not need to bring his grim mood with him. It had been waiting for him in the kitchen.

"Well, look who's here," scoffed Elisabeth with a dry laugh.

"Hello, Private." spat Stephen.

Chad sat at the far end of the table, saying nothing. He had at least, remained neutral, though it was clear he was aware of Donovan Henry's departure, and was not pleased. He busied himself with his ham sandwich and kept his head down. Elisabeth narrowed her eyes at Daniel and smirked.

"So, what are your *orders, sir*?" she snickered.

"You don't have to call the private *sir*, Elisabeth." joined Stephen.

Leonard kicked the table, sending it crashing against the far wall and both Elisabeth and Stephen fell silent. He did not say a word. He merely stared at them as if he had visions of devouring their flesh while their hearts still beat in his hands. They both squirmed under Leonard's glare and traded nervous glances to each other like errant children under a heavy handed father's watch. Finally Leonard turned and smiled at Daniel.

"Sorry, sir." said Leonard, at last. "Won't happen again."

"Yeah, it will," gainsaid Daniel. "It'll keep on happening until they learn who's in charge."

"And who is that—" spat Elisabeth, too angry to care of Leonard's disposition any longer. "—You? It takes more than an infantry man to get me excited. You can't handle me. No man can."

"And if you think I'm going to let you throw your weight around over me just because you happen to be a normal human, you can forget it." railed Stephen. "The only reason you're here is because Congress and Homeland Security don't feel comfortable letting a Special lead Specials. They want a normal human in the role of the slave driver. And I'm too powerful to be your whipping boy. Besides, I outrank you, *private*."

"That's fine," concluded Daniel. "You don't want me leading you? That's fine. But as you've stated, the government isn't going to let this little team form unless there's a *norm-hume* at the helm. Without me, you've got no job. No job means no paycheck. Where are you going to go, if you're not here?"

"I'll find work," replied Stephen, dryly. "Believe me."

"At minimum wage?" replied Daniel. "The truth is, for a Special, there are only three lines of work left: There's government work, there's minimum wage brute work, and there's mercenary work. And that's it. If you take mercenary work, the pay is good, but you'll be going up against the government team that does get formed and taken down by us."

"I'll take my chances." spat Elisabeth. Stephen grunted his agreement.

"That's fine," replied Daniel. "I wish you well. I really do. But you won't do well for long. Why do you think Specials can't get jobs that pay well? Why do you think Specials are rejected from higher paying jobs? Why do you think that Specials with United States citizenship can't leave the country? Because the State Department had declared you as either being an asset or a threat. That's why you're all labeled, not by tattoos, but by your credit reports. A job does a background check on you and a word with big capitol letters flashes over your report saying SPECIAL. I should know. My buddy does Human Resources for the New York City Police Department. He's always complaining about how nervous he was when the word flashed across his screen. Your kind is so vilified in this day's society, it's virtually impossible for you to have normal lives outside the government. The government is making it impossible for Specials to get work outside the military and government branches because they want control over you. It's a fact of life and it's unavoidable. If you work for the government, you're an asset, and they'll throw you a bone. It doesn't taste good, but it's better than minimum wage. And the mercenary job will pay you well, but like I said, the government will find some reason to bring you in on charges and process you. Most likely, for leaving the country without proper visas. Listen to me very carefully, because this is the greatest bit of wisdom you were ever offered, and I ask you to consider it. You are now in the eye of the hurricane. If you step outside of it, just an inch, you'll risk getting swept away. And you'll find it is very hard to find your way back. If you quit, you can easily be replaced. Those on the outside looking in want in. You'll just delay the team's debut by a month, maybe three. But it will happen, with or without you. I've seen most of you perform, and I see potential for growth that I'm interested in working with. But if you want out, I won't try to stop you. It's your life. It's your choice. I just think if you're going to make a choice it should be with all the facts."

Daniel looked at each set of eyes and all of them appeared appalled by what they had heard. Chad had set his sandwich down and pushed the plate away and was now staring out the window. Stephen looked as if he had been punched in between the eyes, and his eyes burned bloodshot as his mind worked through the logic in Daniel's words. But Elisabeth looked murderous; she kicked her chair back and glared at Daniel with disgust.

"Any place is better than being in front of you, *private*." spat Elisabeth, and she stormed out of the room, down the hall, and slammed the door to her room.

"Sir," muttered Leonard, "could I have a word outside?"

"Right behind you."

Leonard walked out into the hallway in a daze, and as soon as the door closed behind them, grabbed Daniel's arm in an unbelievably powerful grip and virtually dragged him to McCormack's empty office, closing the door behind him.

"Are you out of your mind?" whispered Leonard harshly.

"Leonard, they were about to walk out en masse. This way, we get to keep about fifty percent."

"I could have seen Donovan and Giordano being lost causes, but you just drove Elisabeth out with that little speech. Do you have any idea where that leaves us?"

"Burn is a powerful asset, to be sure, but from what I've read Kiloton is also an energy projector with far more firepower."

"You want to talk about firepower? What you've read was misinterpreted. Giordano has no control over his abilities. He just explodes. He destroys more than he preserves, and he's a liability to the team because he sometimes goes off when there is no threat at all. He's a hothead with literal explosions."

"What do you want me to say?" replied Daniel, heatedly. "Burn walked, and Kiloton might actually stay. I can work with whoever wants to stay but I'm not going to beg to keep someone from leaving."

"We need Elisabeth," retorted Leonard, "She has precision control. Her ability to maintain an almost continuous rapid fire with her energy projection is an asset to the team. You just traded a known asset for an unknown variable."

"I can deal with that," replied Daniel. "After all, I am an unknown variable. If Stephen is willing to get over himself and let himself be led into battle by a private, then I can show him a thing or two about his abilities."

"What do you know about his abilities?"

"Nothing," replied Daniel, matter-of-fact. "But it seems to me, that he was allowed to train this way because of the impact he would have on frontline enemy movements on the battlefield. I think his abilities can be focused in different ways, if he commits to training."

"That's a big risk you're taking."

"No more a risk than the Camp Gamma Specials Medical Staff underwent when they encouraged the talents of the Specials on the frontlines."

"They did that through drugs and radiation exposure and tortured and perverted more people than they helped." spat Leonard. "In the end, the Specials Battalion was a shadow of its former strength because we lost more soldiers to the Camp Gamma Medical Staff than we ever did to the enemy. And I'm not even going to mention what happened in SMD 552nd."

"What's that?"

"Science Medical Division 552nd was a program designed to research and implement DNA manipulation in Specials to capitalize on their abnormalities and produce more durable and effective abilities for use against the enemy. SMD 552nd is the cause of most of the degenerative conditions resulting in Specials being reclassified as Abnormal Specials."

Daniel stood there momentarily taken aback at the horrors and atrocities that first McCormack and now Leonard were explaining to him about the war effort to make better more efficient soldiers. It seemed the Specials community had an even more raw deal than he had initially known from his limited contact with the community in his former life as a New York Detective. At the same time, he could not allow himself to be sidetracked from his original point in this argument with Leonard, but he took a more somber tone in going about it.

"Look, I don't expect to have an ideal situation by having the men I want under me. No officer has the pick of the litter. They take what they have and mold it to the best of their abilities. I'm going to have to be part team leader, part mad scientist. And I need you to back up my plays to keep me from killing my men during their training. I don't know how much they can take. I've never even considered what it would take to train a Special. I don't want to work without a safety net here. I want you to be my back up. I can't do this alone. I trust you, more than anyone else."

"I'm a Special, Daniel." replied Leonard. "I'm one of them and I'm on their side. How can you trust me?"

"Same reason you trust me," replied Daniel with a grin. "We fought in battle together, and when everyone else ran, we were standing our ground fighting right alongside each other. I've got your back. I need you to have mine, and save me from making the huge mistakes I'm bound to make."

Leonard shook his head and sighed hard, rubbing his bald head in thought for a long moment before responding.

"I can do that," replied Leonard. "And I've got your back. But I need something from you."

"Anything."

"The next time you feel the need to lecture the men on something, check with me first. That was too much reality for them."

"I'm sorry about that. I wasn't thinking. I just wanted to contain the threat of the team disbanding."

"By pointing out they're third class citizens who can't get a real job outside the government? That the shit pay they're getting is the best they can get without risking prison time? That the government is out to get them? Do you honestly think the men will be able to fight for a government that does this to their own kind?"

"I honestly don't know," replied Daniel, "But I'd rather have them know, than have them make rash decisions and regret it."

"Do you honestly believe the government is out to get us?"

"No," replied Daniel, "I believe that there are individuals in the higher echelons of the government with an axe to grind or a policy to enforce, or both, and that the persecution of Specials is being largely affected by these individuals. I also believe that these individuals will eventually need to be dealt with, in some manner, if there's ever going to be a state without persecution of any minority group. Until we can find a legal way to do it, we're bound by those policies and we're going to have to enforce them."

Leonard nodded, critically staring at the ground weighing every word Daniel said before finally craning his head up to him and staring directly into his eyes.

"I think I'm looking down the road the same way as you, but I don't like how you're going about it."

"You're not going to like every decision I come up with. But those I come up with in the heat of the moment, you'll have to back up. I promise you, I'll do everything I can to brief you on my decisions before I implement them from now on, but you're going to have to take into account the occasions where there is no time to second guess and immediate action is called for. In those moments, I'll rely on your support."

"It's a start," replied Leonard, not entirely happy with Daniel's stipulations. "When I don't agree with your decisions made in those moments when immediate action is called upon, I'll try to pull you aside or at least get my disagreements publicly on the record."

"I can appreciate that for now," replied Daniel, not pleased with the implications in Leonard's choice of words.

"In that case," concluded Leonard, "if you don't mind, I'll go check on the men and make sure they're not all packing their duffel bags."

"Good call," replied Daniel apologetically. "And thanks."

"Yes sir," replied Leonard. And with that, he turned and left Daniel alone in McCormack's office.

Daniel stood silent for a long moment, then crashed down onto the chair facing McCormack's desk and buried his face in his hands as a long sigh escaped him.

"I've heard you've been busy," said the voice from the door.

Daniel looked up to see McCormack leaning against the doorframe with a grin meant to offset his mocking tone and critical glare.

"Please don't start," begged Daniel, "I've just went toe to toe with Leonard, and I don't think I could handle another bout with you.

"Fair enough," replied McCormack, taking his seat at the desk. "You couldn't have expected anything you said to go well, could you?"

"Was there something better I could have said?"

"Not really," replied McCormack, "No. They needed to hear it. But it was rough coming from a normal human, and came off condescending and belittling."

"How?"

"Kind of like a white cop peaceably preaching common sense to a black man; it may in fact be accurate, correct and proper, but it just sounds belligerent and patronizing to the listener and grates the nerves. In the end, the listener feels as if the authority figure is using another tactic to place himself firmly in a position above them. No proud man is going to allow another man to be anything more than an equal with respect ideally going both ways. I'm surprised no one attacked you."

"I'm sure they thought about it."

"I'm sure they did," chided McCormack. "Look, I'm sure you're tired of having this pointed out to you, but you're a normal human. And being normal, you have no idea what it's like to be a Special. You can't hope to relate to them. It's just an impossible undertaking.

"Going back to the Special/black comparison, I want you to appreciate the state of the average Special a little better. A Special is mistrusted as soon as he enters a room. A Special is viewed with suspicion and assumed to be of malicious intention before they even introduce themselves. That is where the similarity between the two ends, though, because a large number Specials were not born black, so the whole persecution based on what you are is relatively new to us.

"Those that are black, like Mammoth, have a different outlook. Nothing's really changed, for them. They just have a lot more power and street smarts. But they expect their civil rights to be violated anyway. They already had contempt for government and law enforcement because they fought hard for equality and civil rights and learned that even though it is in law now, government and law enforcement can choose to ignore it when it suits them.

"This is new for the rest of us. We're upset because we knew what we had and have now lost it. We had civil rights, as well as the right to go where we pleased and do what we liked as long as it did not infract laws. Now there is a policing state within the state. Did you know that Specials had to carry 'special' licenses? The licenses tell where we are from, and we can be arrested for going outside our zones. For a Special, we might as well be a farmer in China. And if we want to move to a new area, for work or a change of scene, we need to check in with the government to plea for authorization allowing for the move, and they notify the neighborhood we're moving into beforehand that we're coming. One of the key differences between us and the black society in America is that for the majority of Specials these days, they can simply blend in with society and avoid all suspicions."

Daniel blinked in astonishment.

"How?" demanded Daniel. Such a thing was not possible with the background checks following the Specials.

McCormack smiled grimly.

"They were the lucky ones who were able to avoid detection by the government for the draft. Or they attained their abilities in one of the dozens of wave events that hit the earth after the Specials Battalion had been formed and the draft had been stopped. Or they were simply too young at the time to be considered for the draft so the government didn't even bother to examine their cases with greater scrutiny. It's easier to get accepted into a good university and find good work without that damnable label following you on a background check."

The picture McCormack painted was bleak and Daniel could empathize, but he was being told it was unacceptable to try to relate to them. In frustration, he ran his fingers through his hair and scratched his scalp.

"Look," said Daniel, "I may not be able to relate to a Special as far as having abilities that appear at least paradoxical to normal humans, but I can relate to them as one human being to another. Nothing's stopping me in that regard."

"Except yourself," replied McCormack. "Let's set aside the fact that they see you as different and don't trust you because they don't know you and don't want to know you. Do you really expect to reach them by reminding them they are different, and underscoring their isolation and alienation from society?"

"I was letting them know their options," replied Daniel hotly. "If I didn't tell them, I'd be doing the men a disservice and letting them loose into society no better than sheep."

"And in doing them a service, you put the nails in your own coffin. To the Special, what you'd said merely reinforces their persecution complexes and gives them the option of either submitting to a slave state of existence or the life of a hunted fugitive."

McCormack's argument was unassailable and Daniel sank lower into the springy old leather chair in defeat.

"I wasn't thinking while I was saying it. I was just telling them." Daniel sighed and buried his head into his hands. "I really fucked up, didn't I?"

McCormack sat on the edge of the desk over Daniel and patted him on the shoulder. "Buck up," said McCormack, "It wasn't that bad. It's salvageable. Just watch what you say, next time."

"And what happens the next time there's a mutiny?"

"It might very well happen. But that little stunt of yours won't work twice, anyways. They're all angry now. If you reinforced your position at this point, they'd really turn on you. And you would have to explain to your superiors how your entire Specials team became fugitives."

"Even you?" stammered Daniel, in disbelief. "And Bradley?"

"We're Specials, Agent Rooke." replied McCormack, matter of fact. "We may be patriots, but we won't turn a blind eye to this persecution forever. The government knows this. That's why they're creating as positive a spin about our organization as possible in order to create a symbol of what can happen when Specials loyal to the United States dedicate their lives to the safety and security of our nation and its states.

"One of their hopes is that other Specials will want to join up and put themselves more directly under government control. The media spin will make it desirable for Specials to enlist in the Specials Investigations Task Force through a *hero campaign*. And with the desired and eventual influx in ranks they'll be able to document more Specials who might have avoided detection. In doing this, the government will be taking potential dissidents—due to their own machinations against our kind—and turning them into loyal soldiers.

"As far as if we'll turn rogue at some point, it depends entirely on the direction the government policies against us leans towards. If it bridges gaps the government made in the first place, and makes at least the smallest form of reparation, like fixing the background check reports so we can get out from under the *Teflon ceiling*, we'll remain good soldiers to the cause."

"And if not?"

McCormack's smile was foreboding.

"Then it was a pleasure serving under you, Agent Rooke."

Daniel blinked in astonishment.

"So this could still blow up in my face at any time, then?"

"Most likely," replied McCormack, matter of fact. "But it won't be your fault. Even though, in all eventuality the blame will be passed onto you regardless."

"Great," sulked Daniel, "Just perfect. Is there anything else you want to tell me?"

"Not right now," he replied "no."

"I need to think."

"That's fine," replied McCormack, "Just remember, dinner should be at six."

"Right."

Daniel rose in a daze and walked out of the room, down the hallway and past the main room where several sulking eyes burned him before returning silently to the floor, ceiling and walls.

He hopped over a barricade and walked down the steps next to the elevator, through the stale moldy air, past the stained and weathered wallpapered walls as he wound his way down to the lobby, walked out the door, and onto the sidewalk of Georgia Avenue. The neighbors walked around him with hard stares to which Daniel was oblivious, and he walked down the street past the restaurants, pool halls and barbershops until he found himself at a small restaurant at the end of the block on the corner of Quincy Street.

Without even caring, he pushed the door open and entered the establishment, his feet finding the way on autopilot while his mind swam with the precarious position he found himself in. He was a soldier once, with the greatest fighting force the world had ever seen, quickly overshadowed by the Specials Battalion that they quickly grew to rely on, and now found himself working with Specials on an *"elite"* government project only to learn that the Specials were only conditional employees with political policies playing the major role in their conditions as to whether or not they would continue working for the federal government.

It seemed that he had been dealing with the Specials/ normal human politics for years—as if the strife developing between the two branches of society had been warring for all his life. It was all too much for him, and Daniel was extremely frustrated in that he had only dealt with such political and social issues as long as he had held the position of team commander, which had now totaled four long days. It felt much, much longer.

He sat down at an empty table amid the staring faces without noticing. Even the waitress's tone was threatening.

"You lost or something?"

Daniel looked up at the woman and took her in. She was tall and frail, her skin was soft and dark, and her hair was beautifully shaped, yet wild and free and accentuated her beautiful face. If not for the cold expression on her face, Daniel would have been very pleased with seeing such an attractive woman. Her dark almond eyes bored into him. Because of her cold demeanor and judgmental tone, he confirmed that today was definitely *one of those days* and could not help but chuckle.

"You have no idea," sighed Daniel, and shook his head.

"You want some coffee?"

"Yes, please."

The waitress studied him critically for a moment, and then turned and walked back to the counter to pour him a cup and then returned and set it unceremoniously on the table.

"You want anything to eat?"

"What do you have?"

"Soul Food," she said with a cold challenge in her eyes.

"Do you have ox tails?"

"You want ox tails?" replied the waitress with an astonished blink.

"And greens, if it's not too much trouble."

"You eat soul food?" she asked with a dumbfounded expression, plainly finding Daniel to be an oddity.

"Ma'am," said Daniel with a wry smile, "I'm from Bedford-Stuyvesant in New York. Even the Chinese food is Soul Food."

"You're from Bed-Stuy?" scoffed the waitress. She then leaned over her shoulder and yelled back into the kitchen. "Hey, Tremell. This white boy says he's from Bed-Stuy."

"Probably," shouted the man from the kitchen. "There's a lot of everything there, now."

"What part of Bed-Stuy you from?"

"I'm off of Amity Street in Cobble Hill."

"Hey Tremell," shouted the waitress over her shoulder with an amused smile. "This white boy is claiming BoCoCa."

"Damn," exclaimed Tremell from the kitchen. "Tell him I'm from Boerum Hill."

"I'm very familiar with Boerum Hill," said Daniel with an easy smile.

The waitress seemed to suppress a mirthful curl of her lips and her eyes seemed to diminish in hardness.

"Can I get you anything else to drink?"

"I'd like a beer if I could."

"No beer here," she replied, and leaned toward him with a lowered tone as if offering him a secret pleasure. "But I could get you some wine cooler in a coffee mug."

"Maybe I'll just stick with the coffee."

"You sure?" smiled the waitress. "We take care of our own, here."

"I appreciate that, but I shouldn't be drinking anyway."

With that, the waitress' eyes narrowed and grew cold.

"You a cop?"

"No."

"You sure?" pressed the waitress critically. "You look like a cop."

"I'm sure," replied Daniel, fully aware how critical it was that he answer correctly. "I do government work, but it's not really cop work."

"You're not one of those stakeout fools are you?"

"No."

"Because we don't want no white people watching us, here."

"Ma'am," said Daniel, slightly annoyed, "I used to be a cop in New York. I quit. I now work for the government. Last time I checked, Homeland Security was for the protection of the United States from terrorist activities inside the U.S. or against U.S. embassies or U.S. interests around the world. Discovering terrorist plots and putting an end to them before they happen. Now, are you a terrorist?"

"No," blinked the waitress, nervously.

"Then I'm obviously not here for you or your neighborhood," concluded Daniel. "Which I might add, I now live in."

"You live here?"

"Yes."

"Where?"

"Down the street," he replied. "The brownstone down the block, just shy of Warder Street."

The knowledge that a government operative was now operating out of that particular building instantly registered to her as a dangerous element being injected into the neighborhood.

"What is Homeland Security doing in *that* place?"

"City PD sold it," replied Daniel, matter of fact. "And the government got it at a good price."

"There's a lot of people in the neighborhood that don't like white people and hate cops taking up in the neighborhood. You may want to move before you get rushed."

"Trust me, if they rush that place, they'll wish they hadn't."

"You a cocky white boy," replied the waitress disapprovingly.

"No," replied Daniels. "Not cocky. I just know who I'm living with, and they're far more efficient than any DC SWAT team. If the locals decide they want to rush my flat, they'll be in a firefight they have never imagined."

"So you living with cops," concluded the waitress, coolly.

"No cops," he replied as he took a sip of his coffee, "just some special friends."

"How special?"

"—Forces. Let's just say they can handle themselves as well as I can, if not better." The waitress stared, unsure whether or not to take Daniel at his word. "Trust me," he concluded. "No one wants to go up to that flat. They'd be taking their lives into their hands and handing it over to my boys. And the last thing this neighborhood needs is another killing."

The waitress put the check down and backed away from Daniel.

"That's six-fifty for the coffee."

"What about my ox tails?"

"We don't need your business."

"Ma'am, I meant no offense."

"I don't care. No. Get out."

An old man rose from the corner and immediately took an authoritative role in the room. The others instantly returned to their coffee and food and tried to shut out the scene the waitress was making as the old man grabbed her arm and pulled her around.

"Tamika," demanded the old man. "What are you doing?"

"This white motherfucker is not going to come onto this block and talk shit. No. I want him gone. I want you out of here."

"Tamika, go take a break."

"But grandpa, this white boy's a cop."

Several of the patrons turned and glared at Daniel. He ignored them. The old man was incensed.

"So?" replied the old man, authoritatively. "Cops get police discounts, around here."

"Do you realize how much trouble we could get in from helping him? Kick him out, grandpa. Please. Do it before Jonas finds out."

"I'm not afraid of that thug. He can kiss my ass. Him and his gang."

Realizing the depth of the situation and the implication for the restaurant if he stayed, Daniel grew instantly compliant.

"Sir," interjected Daniel appeasingly, "if it's a problem for you, I can leave. It's alright."

"Well, it's not alright with me," growled the old man. With a wave of the hand, he dismissed the waitress. Instantly and indignantly, Tamika obeyed as the old man sat down at Daniel's table. The others in the restaurant returned to their meals and did not look up again.

"So much gang trouble in the neighborhood with all the drugs and turning girls out to tricking and all the protection pay offs, people start getting so they afraid to even be kind to each other. It's enough to make you sick.

"See, when I was a kid, we had racial tension, but we could still play basketball and football with the white boys and the El Salvadorians and the Chinese, and it was all good. My granddaughter is so young; she doesn't know that this neighborhood was gentrified a few decades ago. But then the riots came around again, like they always do, and after that, the gangs started attacking the white people and the yellow people and the brown people and then everyone who wasn't black moved almost overnight. It was so bad the cops couldn't do a damn thing. And then the black on black crimes started up. And the cops *wouldn't* do a damn thing. Now, this neighborhood is so closed off now, it's eating itself alive."

Daniel didn't know what to say. He merely sat there and listened to the old man rattle on, and actually began to enjoy himself with the old man's easy smile.

"Yeah," replied Daniel, "New York's not much different."

"No," replied the old man, "I wouldn't think so. Brooklyn, Harlem, The Bronx, they got the same problems we got. It's just the cops seem to actually care, around there. Over here, the police are just interested in keeping us from moving too close to the White House. After that, they leave us alone to just kill each other."

"It's that bad, here?"

"You live in the neighborhood. You telling me you don't know?"

"To tell you the truth, we just keep to ourselves."

"You just here for a place to sleep, then?"

"Pretty much," replied Daniel uncomfortably. "To be quite honest, I could have thought of a few better places to lay my head at night."

"True that," replied the old man. "Thank you for the honesty, by the way. Not many white folks want to let it all out like that."

"Well, since I can't get too much into what's going on with my situation, I figure I gotta be honest about the rest."

"Fair enough," replied the old man cagily. "You saying you got no issues or agendas with the district, that's cool with me. But my granddaughter's right. There are a lot of brothers and sisters who don't really care what you're here for. They just want you out."

"Really?"

"There's already talk about it," replied the old man, as casually as a conversation about who the real father of a baby could be. "They think the police rolled back up in there. Seeing too many white faces walking into our neighborhood. Getting out of limousines and strolling around. Tell me you weren't stupid enough to come up in here with a limousine."

"Don't look at me, I didn't order the damn thing. My new boss took me in his car."

"Well, everyone's talking about the white boy who rolled up in here in a limousine, and strolled right through a bunch of brothers and sisters and made his way through like he owned the block. If that was you, I'd suggest you keep your ears sharp. Because a lot of ignorant niggers already know about you."

Tamika dropped a plate and it shattered on the ground. Her body was rigid and straight with shock.

"Grandpa!" she hissed scornfully with a look of reproach.

The old man leaned over his shoulder and barked back at her, craning his head around the room with authority, challenging with his eyes anyone to criticize him or tell him he was wrong.

"That's right, I said it," he shouted. "They're a bunch of ignorant niggers. What do I care? I'm an old man and I stopped being afraid of ignorant niggers years ago. They want to fight me, as old as I am, I may die pretty quick, but they're gonna have the fight of their lives before I go down."

Most turned their attention back to their plates, as if these momentary explosions were an all too common occurrence while others laughed to themselves at his courage. Daniel was impressed by the fearlessness of the old man.

"Sir,"

"Charlie, please. Same as the restaurant." said the old man. "And you are?"

"Daniel," replied Daniel.

"Nice to meet you, Daniel."

"Pleasure," he responded with a wry smile.

"So what do you have to say?" inquired Charlie, gregariously, a glimmer in his eye. "Go on, spit."

"What's with this Jonas I'm hearing about?"

"No," shouted Tamika resolutely. "We're not talking about them. Grandpa, please!"

Charlie waved her off and returned to Daniel with a plain expression drawn with lines of frustrated worry.

"Chris Young has got a gang down the block called Princeton Place Kings. Back when I was a kid, the Kings had a different name, back when they were Bloods. But that fell apart years ago. Princeton Place Kings used to be Princeton Place Parus or 3P, until the Bloods organized into a national family to more effectively fight Mexican Mafia and the Salvadorian Gangs. Then the DC Bloods rebelled to continue business relations with the Salvadorians. Now Kings fight against local black gangs Quincy Street Crips and Sheperd Street Mafia."

"Why?"

"They had dealings with a Salvadorian gang that sprung up out of Los Angeles, years ago. Called themselves Salvatruchas, or something else that makes you trip over the word. Anyway, the Salvies brought the drugs in, and the brothers bought it, packaged and nickel and dimed it. It was a pretty sweet deal, until the Bloods unified into their own right little black mafia to branch into interstate crime, that is. Once that happened, the Salvies became a threat. They controlled a lot of the drug and skin pipeline out of Central and South America, and ran it straight up to a few blocks from here. The Bloods couldn't have that. So they told 3P's to hit them and close the pipeline down. 3P's made some serious green off that pipeline, though. So they told the mafia to go fuck. So bloods started driving up into the neighborhood and paying off the local Crips to take 'em out. The mafia called 3P's traitors, and rats, telling everyone they could they weren't really bloods. 3P's didn't give a shit. They just changed their names and told 'em 'fuck you.' There was some serious gunplay in the neighborhood for a while. The Kings sided with the Salvies, and every time Bloods came on the block claiming, they got dealt. Eventually, the mafia just decided they'd stop at Virginia and then skip DC and Maryland and move straight on up to New York." Charlie leaned back in the chair and sighed, thinking about how far back his memory traveled, still keeping his eyes on Daniel's, and the sparks swimming around the corneas danced a little as he drank in Daniel deeply. "These days, they're always fighting with another gang a few blocks up. The Quincy Street Crips. And don't even get me started on Shepherd Street Mafia."

"What do they fight over?"

"Territory to run their businesses, mostly. They got their drugs, their girls, their protection. Not much has changed since I was a kid, son. Gangs always fight over the same reasons. But you know this. You're a cop."

"Ex-cop," Daniel corrected, "I retired last week."

With that, Charlie gave a loud laugh and ended in a snicker, shaking his finger at Daniel as if he had just told a good joke.

"Man, cops don't retire. They just get killed. It may be a heart attack or cancer that does them in, but that's just a bullet of a different kind."

"I heard that," agreed Daniel, and he gave an easy smile back to the grinning old man.

"So anyway, let's get serious. What's really going on?"

With all Charlie's gregarity, it was difficult to spot, but Daniel instantly realized he had been buttered up for the better part of ten minutes just to come to this question and he was fully aware of every ear bending toward him—every sense on alert to their conversation.

Daniel had to grin. He had to appreciate the man. Charlie was good at cracking tough nuts. Still, aside the fact that the public was not supposed to know yet, telling a room full of battle weary strangers that a team of Specials working for the government had just moved in down the block would have set the neighborhood into a tailspin for sure, and Daniel had no interest in dealing with an angry mob.

"Well, the government bought a property off Metro PD and we're using it as a halfway house for veterans until we get a real location."

"Veterans, huh?" pressed Charlie, disbelievingly. A skeptical glare took his eyes, the pinwheels of sparks swimming the edges of the corneas. "I was in the Marines. What about you?"

"Honestly?" said Daniel and a wry grin took his face as he swelled with pride. "UNIAF infantry."

"And the others?" pressed Charlie.

"Mainly infantry and special operations."

Charlie's face instantly contorted and he rubbed his head as if he had an itch.

"All these new fangled militaries," scoffed Charlie, seemingly meandering into new dialogue, though somehow, Daniel doubted they would stay derailed for long. "I liked it when it was just the Army, Navy, Air Force and the Marines. It was just simpler. Now we got the space army or whatever. Anyway, I'm just too old to really care about space. There's such a rush to get there and be in it and just too much of it. And then you want to go places; this planet and that planet around this star or that star. And it doesn't do any good, because it's not like you can breathe on the damn planet anyway. No. They have to bring their space suits and their breathing chambers and tents and things. And then the new tax system to cover the expenses the government is spending to pay for the whole thing. And all it means is less money for me, but the government gets to do new cool shit. It just gives me a headache."

Charlie leaned in and sighed, folding his arms on the table, visibly exhausted. Daniel studied the old man as an oddity, and waited for the train to find the tracks again. Charlie chuckled and looked back at Daniel—the sparks swirling the cornea again.

"Listen to me. Just yammering on and on. Enough of me. So the government's taking good care of you then?"

"I'm in the Georgia Avenue District in between gang lines, and you're the first local face I've seen that's actually smiling at me. I don't know about taking good care of us."

"Yeah, this neighborhood's not real keen on strange faces."

"Yeah," agreed Daniel, efforting to steer the conversation farther away from employment. "I heard about the cops that got beat down."

Charlie seemed instantly ashamed and shook his head wearily.

"That was terrible. It really gets me. We called the police and told them what was going on and asked for help. The cops gave us the help in cleaning up the streets, then everyone started hating the cops for doing their jobs and then the neighborhood started attacking cops. Then the cops came back like an army in riot gear and went door to door. Plain insanity."

"I've seen that before."

"I'm sure you have," replied Charlie and gave him a funny look that made Daniel aware Charlie was referencing his background as a police officer. This only lasted for the briefest of moments, before he changed the subject. The sparks circled and danced around the cornea, and two pin-points of red light seemed to laser into him. "So why the long face, son?"

Daniel stared at the sweet old man's face and felt himself fighting himself to steer away from sensitive information. At long last, he compromised, picking through sensitive information, and placed a larger degree of emotion and frustration into the events of the morning than he actually had.

"I had an argument with my flat mates. I guess I stepped on a racial landmine and I ruffled some feathers."

For the briefest of instants, the old man grimaced, and the pin lights in the center of his corneas faltered. The very next instant, Charlie had recovered, and it seemed as though he had merely empathized with Daniel's pain and offered a shoulder.

"That can happen," began Charlie, "believe me, I know. You want to talk about it?"

Daniel studied Charlie for a moment and had the striking feeling that the old man had failed in some task, and had either from frustration or interest in Daniel's problem given up trying, for the sake of the conversation. Normally, Daniel did not play with people he felt were trying to hustle him, but a part of him that was curious if the old man was actually trying to turn him, or if he had misinterpreted the situation altogether. Regardless, he knew he liked Charlie, and that there was some mystery about the old man that drew him closer, seeking some prize to be gained. Some skill to be sharpened.

Daniel smiled sociably and chose his words carefully, occasionally stalling for time, and subconsciously, allowing himself to play a part of a more submissive individual, waiting to see if the spider is attempting to seduce the fly into its parlor, or to teach the fly to be a better spider.

"Well, I can't really talk about it. But basically, I tried to relate with them and empathize with where they were coming from. They wanted to remain segregated, and I pushed the issue. That's when the bomb went off."

"Damn, son." snickered Charlie with a wry look as if he had figured Daniel out. "You're like one of those utopians—idealistic white boys trying to heal race relations. I've seen it before. The problem is they either get killed quick or get cynical and quit. And it's a damn shame, because they usually got a point, but the folks they're talking to are just plain ignorant or too full of hate to let a white boy help. You can't help them. They either want to know you or they don't. You gotta let the ones who don't want to be your friend go."

"Yeah, I guess." scoffed Daniel. "It's just such a waste. I really don't know what I'm doing here."

"Shit, you're trying," exclaimed Charlie. "It's better than most. Keep on trying, and forget them if they don't have the sense to do the same."

Daniel suppressed a grin.

"Do you always take strangers under your wing like this?"

Charlie smiled and stretched his arms out as if he were declaring himself the lord over all he surveyed.

"That's why they call me 'pops.' I help who I can, when I can."

"I appreciate it, Charlie. I really do."

"Don't think on it, Daniel. Now let me see what's taking them ox tails so long. You wanted some greens too, right?"

"Only if you got them."

"We do soul food here," declared Charlie as if the answer was obvious. "Of *course* we got greens."

Within a few minutes, Daniel was hunched over his plate of ox tails and greens eating the first meal he could call *home cooked* in a long time. And as his belly filled, a deep sense of contentment overtook him as he remembered the soul food restaurant down the street from his flat in Brooklyn, and his ex girlfriend's meals she would easily throw together, whenever he had the slightest notion for soul food.

After his meal Daniel put down his money, but Charlie wouldn't hear of it and was so adamant on Daniel feeling at home and not isolated from the community that he offered that he come back any time, and invited his "friends" to join him for "the best ox tails this side of New Orleans."

Daniel thanked Charlie gratefully and left a twenty-dollar bill as a tip, which led to another confrontation with Charlie, until they finally agreed that the money would go to his granddaughter for her *kind attention* to his needs.

When Daniel finally stepped out onto Georgia Avenue, he quickly made a right, and made his way back past the pool halls, restaurants and barbershops, until he was walking into the brownstone lobby, up the foul elevator and out into the flat to be greeted by none other than Laurence Boatman himself.

Daniel could tell from the silence of the flat that the Specials had gone. Boatman stood before Daniel leaning on a cane with a disappointed glare of annoyance in his eye, and his white bushy moustache picked up at the corner of his mouth and almost gave him the look of a sneer. There was no mirth in his tone. He was immovable, and his voice ground like stones.

"Good afternoon, Daniel Henry Rooke. I'm glad you're finally here. I believe we have an appointment. If you'll be so kind as to follow me we can begin."

And so fell all hope.

CHAPTER 6

IMPLEMENTING STRATEGIES

Daniel sat down in the rickety leather chair facing McCormack's desk and was instantly uneasy. The desk seemed cleaner than before.

"Had it been straightened up, or had Paladin decided that enough was enough and took the team with him?"

Daniel did not have time to nurse the thought, as Boatman manned McCormack's leather chair and folded his hands on the desk.

"It seems you've had an interesting day, Daniel." said Boatman, his voice damning.

"Yeah," scoffed Daniel, "you could say that."

"You're not going to waste my time by denying anything, I take it?" said Boatman, examining his cuticles with a severe expression.

"I don't see the point, considering the flat is bugged."

"And what gives you that notion?"

"You told me."

Boatman's face contorted and he pursed his lips as his cheeks turned red.

"I'm getting old," concluded Boatman, "I used to lead men into battle and could remember the name of every man and woman under me as well as their dossiers in their entirety, adding the updates to their jackets oftentimes myself. Now, I have trouble remembering what I said and to whom." He brooded for a moment and then discarded the thought out of hand adding "What to do?"

"I believe you were about to drill me a new one, General?"

"No," replied Boatman. "I should. You've been negligent in your role as team leader, allowing two to quit."

Daniel sighed. Only two had quit. This gave him hope.

"Elisabeth Meng I take it?"

"Yes. Meng." muttered Boatman scornfully. "A beta class energy projector with the potential of reaching alpha under the proper stress environment, supervision and training. A potential alpha class on the team is a considerable asset. And you let her walk."

"She was going to walk regardless, Lawrence."

"So was Donovan Henry, I know. You will still be blamed for their leaving the team and it will appear on your jacket. After the first outburst where Henry left, you were under scrutiny. Then only a handful of hours later, you have a second outburst. This second one is monumentally more grave. It is graver because of what you said in an effort to create a more manageable environment for yourself. It suited your purposes to make them more docile, but you gave them a new target for their hostility in order to achieve your goals. What you said paints their employer in a bad light, to say the least."

"You aren't honestly going to sit there and tell me it's not true."

With a flash of the eye, Daniel was aware how thin the ice was where he tread and instantly grew silent. Boatman's eyes bored into him, and he leaned toward Daniel, seeming to tower over him from his seat. Boatman's eyes dared Daniel to say but one more word. Daniel knew better than to anger him.

"But it's *not* true," growled Boatman, murderously. "And you would do well to *remember* that. It's not true because my *superiors* wish it to not be true. And if *I* have to say it's not true, I am sure as hell not going to let my *subordinates* say any different. Do you understand me?"

"Lawrence," began Daniel, trying to inject reason into the dangerously volatile conversation.

"Mr. Boatman, at this point," replied Boatman, with a cold smile.

"Mr. Boatman," began Daniel, passively. "I don't see how I could have handled that situation any differently."

"Neither do I," replied Boatman. "But that is why I'm not the team's field commander. Your job is to think of new and innovative ways to accomplish this government's desired outcomes. Not new and innovative ways to fuck up. I think two is quite enough, don't you?"

"Yes, sir."

"There will not be a third."

"No, sir."

"Remember you said that," warned Boatman and held his stare for an uncomfortably long moment, only to be broken by his pressing on. "All in all, you did better than I thought you were going to do. But in all honesty, that little speech you gave could have gone either way. Still, you managed to save sixty percent of the team. Mammoth and Burn are fine soldiers, but their loss is no great one. In all actuality, their absence offers us a greater ability to contain loose ends. Henry and Meng are highly volatile individuals and they both have problems with both authority and respecting their oaths to keep state secrets a secret. There were bound to be problems with them in the media anyways, so their 'not being here' any longer actually ties that problem up nicely. Filling their slots should be no great problem, and you were quite right; it should only take us between one and three months to fill them. The problem is who? And what are their capabilities? What we need is an energy projector with a greater degree of control."

"We still have Kiloton."

"Yes, and I heard what you had to say about Giordano. And it's good to hear you so optimistic. But I am a pessimist. In that way, I am hardly ever disappointed. Stephen has no control over his abilities, as formidable as they are. He is a wrecking ball, while Meng was a laser beam. You see the problem?

"The other problem is that your optimism does not sit well with me, and it does not sit well with my superiors or our funders. It does not sit well because you are not an expert. You are not an expert on leading men into battle. You are not an expert on Specials abilities and you are not an expert on the human genome. Given that, I cannot put much stock into what your gut tells you, what your feelings are, or what your opinion about a given subject is. The only thing you did get right is that you are 'an unknown variable.' If Giordano does succeed in controlling and manipulating his abilities to the teams advantage, that's fine. But I'm not putting stock in it. I'm going to find another energy projector with control and skill. And you're going to be nice to them. I don't care if he tries to kill you. Do we understand each other?"

"Yes, sir."

"I did not start this project to see it fail at the whim of a man without experience, capability or intellect. I've watched you scrape by since you've gotten here. Mostly on dumb luck and force of will. I put you with McCormack and Overman so you could be trained in strategy and battle-field logistics, not so you could bond with Stonebreaker or trade stories over highly classified protocols or incidents—that never happened—that are way above your pay grade. I don't care about your feelings or your level of comfort with Specials. What I do care about is seeing this project make it out into the public and the results we will get once the program picks up steam. And I cannot do that with dead Specials by bad leadership. You've had four days, and I want results. Now your strategy session this morning was insightful, I'll give you that, and it's clear you have a degree of insight that would allow you to take these soldiers and get them to a state battle readiness. But you are not battle ready. You can fight, of that I'm sure. And you can certainly take a punch. But you can't implement strategies to the men yet—not because you aren't quick enough or smart enough, I haven't seen you perform yet to make that call, but—because they don't trust you. I need them to rely on your decisions. I need to see the men enact your orders in the field."

"And how is that going to happen? You want me to take them down to the street and run a scrimmage for the locals to see?"

"I did not give you permission to speak, Rooke." snapped Boatman. Daniel began to burn inside with the way Boatman had lectured him and bit his tongue, returning to a reclined position, his eyes burning into him. Boatman did not give the slightest inclination that he cared. He pressed on. "Don't worry about the training. I'm taking you to the James J Rowley Training Center for that."

"We're going to the Secret Service training facility?"

"You're talking, Daniel. See to that, will you?"

Daniel grew silent and looked forward again.

"I'm going to put the men through the training course, and give them a good stretch. They've been cooped up here for too long, and it's starting to affect them. They need a good run. Afterwards, they will have time at the academy to look over the playbooks and memorize their tasks. Do you have any idea how you're going to use the team yet?"

"Yes, sir. But do you think it's wise to set up a strategy if the team's not assembled yet?"

"They're two short. In battle, that happens. I need strategies from you covering attacks from single combat for all the team members all the way up to battalion strength."

"For the enemy?"

"Both sides."

"That's a lot of strategy."

"They will memorize it, and then we'll put them through the paces to see how quick they can implement your strategies. You'll have the remainder of the day to work on it. I suggest you use their expertise in this to help formulate your methods more effectively. McCormack, Overman and Stonebreaker especially."

"I'll put something together."

With that, Boatman smiled and rose from his chair, notifying Daniel that the meeting was now over. Daniel sighed with relief and put his head down feeling utterly defeated.

At the door, Boatman stopped and turned.

"Oh, before I forget," he began. "Your little romp to that soul food café on the corner of Rock Creek Church and Georgia? I suggest you refrain from giving out information on the goings on here. I don't want a repeat of what happened to the local police happening with us. The last thing we need is a group of Specials injuring and killing residents in a neighborhood such as this. Especially considering there is now no black man on the team. You nearly cost yourself your third strike with that reference to your '*special friends.*' Nearly."

"Yes, sir." replied Daniel, too mentally exhausted to reply in any other way.

"However, we did like your cover story you came up with in your conversation with that Charlie character. We can use that."

"How?"

"We'll simply leak to the press that there is a halfway house located in the Georgia Avenue district of the metropolitan District of Columbia area for veterans who returned from the war and upon being discharged, found themselves homeless and jobless. We can easily spin it to the media as a reward from a grateful nation for their heroes in uniform who have returned home to unnecessary hardships. We can even add that we are also actually assisting them with work placement, and explain that in the military, each soldier was educated in a trade. Why not? There are programs like that for veterans anyway. Any information the Associated Press digs up regarding the use of the location and any job assistance for Sol War veterans can only support our claims. There. The people now know about you and the others and we have control over how and how much they know."

Boatman seemed pleased that he had resolved the dilemma in his own mind and was resolute in his planning and it seemed it had been as much for his own benefit as for the hidden microphones scattered somewhere throughout the flat. It was as if Boatman had dictated his scheme to an invisible secretary taking notes and Daniel knew that somewhere, there was a tech crew rushing about trying to process everything he said and send it up the chain of command for implementation at the soonest possible timetable. Daniel could not suppress a grin of utter awe.

"You're enjoying this."

"Daniel," answered Boatman. "I used to affect grand changes to the battlefield from troop movements and logistics at a whim. These subtle manipulations are for men with far more political ambitions. And I am not a politician. However, playing the game is unavoidable and I am beginning to take to it." then added, "Though in retrospect, if I played the game years ago, I would already have my pension and be enjoying my early retirement with full honors as a high ranking officer, who served his country and planet honorably and with distinction, should."

"And now?"

Boatman's eyes focused on Daniel and locked him in a severe gaze.

"Now I will play the game," he replied. "And you had better start playing it too, if you don't want to end up going back to Bedford-Stuyvesant and the low rank of Deputy Inspector."

"At least I had respect and the pay was better."

"Well, there's nothing I can do about your pay grade. But I will tell you this—Respect is something earned. It's not going to come to you because you survived so many engagements and lived to tell about it. Your men can claim the same thing. You're going to have to give them something more."

"Like what?"

"I garnered their respect through being a hard disciplinarian who worked them to the point they either produced excellence or died. My implementation of battle strategies made them an unbeatable fighting force, and allowed them to have pride in themselves and each other for their accomplishments. Most importantly, I encouraged them to consider themselves as soldiers as being part of a brotherhood—an ancient fraternity of comrades in arms that encouraged fealty and fidelity to each other— in creating this unity among the men it left me no place to stand due to my rank and leadership than the position of a surrogate father. The men will look to you as a leader in similar ways and you must encourage the bond between them."

"Something tells me they won't take too well to viewing me as their father."

"Maybe not," granted Boatman, "But considering you were from the 423rd, you have some notion of what it is to lead through example. *'First one onto the battlefield, last to leave.'* That is the truest way to forge a bond between yourself and the men. If you are willing to put yourself in harm's way as much as they are, you may not be viewed paternally, but you will have their respect and they will follow you anywhere."

"I've got no problem with being in the middle of it. In all honesty, the main problem I have with being team leader is that I have to hang back to give the orders necessary to make the battle turn in our favor."

"Your main role is to lead the men to victory and if at all possible, bring the men back safe and sound. Your role as strategic advisor is crucial to the success or demise of the team. You're going to have to compromise with your ethics and hold a safe position and leave the grunts to handle the demolition and assaults. That is your role. They know theirs. Know your own."

Daniel put his head down and mulled over Boatman's advice to him critically reexamining his own position as team leader.

As Boatman left the flat Daniel could not help but reflect on his own commanding officer's ethics in leading the men into battle. An ethic that in all likelihood contributed to his being killed. Daniel knew his own infantry commander, Lieutenant Colonel Forrest, would have grit his teeth at such a command. As the late afternoon sun began to poke through the kitchen window, Daniel turned his back to the glare and used the light to write his strategies out by.

His mind poured over the different kinds of battlefields he had fought on. He considered the rocky to liquid terrain, temperature, thinness of air. Whether the battle would be in mountainous, jungle, swamp or desert terrain, and after an hour had passed, began writing up strategies for urban assaults. A chill went down his spine as he calculated his worst fear scenarios. A heavily populated area with an enemy using the terrain, architecture and populations as cover to fire from behind, limiting and choking the possibility for return fire. Daniel began to work up a model of attack plans for these contingencies and found himself devoting most of his time to developing rules of engagement.

Daniel's Insights

Daniel leaned over McCormack's desk furiously writing in the dark when all of a sudden the lights blinked on, temporarily blinding him. He sat there cringing in a daze as the prismic flashes of light danced in front of him.

"You know," chided McCormack, "you could go blind like that."

"I could go blind from *this*," railed Daniel, pointing back at McCormack with one arm and shielding his eyes with the other. McCormack just laughed and walked over to his desk, picking up Daniel's strategic formulas and glossing through them. Daniel was instantly self-conscious.

"Come on Daniel," said McCormack, "Let's see what you've got."

"It's not ready yet," warned Daniel, self-consciously.

"War strategies never are," replied McCormack, "Even when they're being implemented."

McCormack stood quite still as he flipped through the pages with a critical look that frustrated Daniel and his heart sunk at the thought that his attempts at designing a proper battle strategy had just met with utter failure.

"So how bad is it?"

"It's a start," replied McCormack. "Your strategies on Air/Land Battle scenarios bear promise. I'm not sure we can stick to all your rules of engagement, though."

"The rules of engagement for urban assault are kind of mandatory," insisted Daniel hoarsely.

"It can be expounded on," replied McCormack, unconcerned. "We need to ensure the public's safety as a first objective, of course, but most of them will have been running for cover long before we ever arrive. Mostly, the only worries we will have are news cameramen and journalists getting in our way, trying to get the perfect shot or the more gung-ho police officers jumping into the middle of it. Still, your mock up on how to deal with hostage situations is promising. I can't think of anything to add to it, actually. Good job."

"And the other contingencies?"

"We're mainly going to be employed in an urban setting, so we won't work too much with your other contingencies. Besides, most of your insights into jungle warfare seem to match up with insights drawn up in the *Vietnamprimer* report."

"Oh," replied Daniel with a defeated sigh, "you've read that."

"That was standard reading for officers in training when I was in basic," replied McCormack, dryly. "You know what they say: *Those who forget history*... It was informative."

"And what about the other environments?" inquired Daniel embarrassed.

"The mountain terrain scenario sounds like you read it out of *Kargil War: Battle Plans & Logistics Revisited*. Don't get me wrong, it was an enlightening manual, and any soldier would take the lessons learned in that text to heart. But you're not giving us anything new. Everyone on your team has considered these scenarios because as Specials, we were all trained in every environment our drill instructors and the scientists could think up. We even took a unit consisting of the most durable of us and were ordered to perform a five-minute battle scenario halfway down the Marianas Trench—and you haven't lived until you try just moving with those kinds of pressures. And by the way— rainforests and forests are not classified as jungles, no matter how thick the canopy. They would be separate envi- ronmental classifications."

"So I just wasted seven hours for nothing then," scoffed Daniel and he kicked McCormack desk in frustration.

"Actually, you put your head in the game for the first time. I'm being critical because you'll need to be. You turn in this to your superiors; they will laugh you out of the office and make you a punch line at the committee hearing. But as far as your Fighting in Fortified Objectives section is concerned—you've listed bunkers, forts, projects, strategically contained neighborhoods and cul-de-sacs. I think that about covers the urban element to fortified objectives. And I wouldn't touch your highlighted sections pointing out the watch points. Especially the sniper points. That's the part that's worrying me. Going into an area where we're on the ground, and they're on the rooftops pinning us down and picking us off. We'll have to put that scenario up in our drills as a top priority. And I agree with your assessment. It's vital that before the team goes into any area, we will need a complete layout of the region from streets to architectural blueprints, to sewer, electrical and subway tunnels. Walking into another man's territory means they know where all the hidden areas are and how best to exploit them. We would be at a disadvantage without those schematics. How would you train us in this?"

"I'd take you to an urban warfare center," responded Daniel. "Give everyone a layout of the area and give us five to fifteen minutes to memorize them as best we can. Then I'd get us dropped smack in it and we'd have to overcome resistance and reach our objective in say, five or ten minutes?"

"Let's try to do it in five," replied McCormack, approvingly. "Resistance?"

"I'd like there to at least be a twenty to forty man team against us. If we can make it out of that, I think we'll be good in the real thing."

McCormack was visibly worried and eyed Daniel skeptically.

"Twenty to forty what?"

"Forty infantrymen or twenty special ops," replied Daniel, more confidently. "Or ten Specials."

"And where do you expect to pull in ten Specials from?" scoffed McCormack. "It's going to take us months to replace the two we just lost."

Daniel eyed McCormack for a long moment.

"Does he honestly think I'm that stupid?" thought Daniels as he glared at him. "Boatman virtually pulled me in off the street to field a highly visible team to take down collars in the field," he replied coldly. "I may not be the sharpest tool in the shed, but I know you don't put out a high profile team unless you also have a black ops unit in the background. I suggest we use them and both teams get the chance to sharpen their tusks implementing strategy and stealth to outmaneuver the other team."

McCormack was stunned at the logic Daniel had displayed and it was obvious to Daniel that he had never considered the possibility that there might have been a second team performing operations that are more clandestine in nature. McCormack seemed disturbed by the notion and he leaned against his desk letting out a sigh.

"I think we're done, for now," concluded McCormack after a long moment. "I'll have Leonard work with your field strategies."

Daniel studied McCormack for a long moment.

"Damn," thought Daniel *"I guess he never thought about it."*

It was clear McCormack was shaken by the thought, which was obviously just a hunch, and yet, it made too much sense to disregard. He walked around his desk, collapsed into his chair and stared out the window in silence. There was nothing more to say.

Finally, Daniel rose and left to seek out Stonebreaker.

Four hours later, Leonard, red in the face, waved furiously at Daniel.

"No!" shouted Leonard, "That's final! I don't want to hear you make that suggestion again!"

"Why not?" retorted Daniel, waving his hands back at him. "Grenades is a perfectly acceptable solution in dealing with either a joint assault or a hostage situation."

"I said no. There is no way I'm going to be put into a situation where grenades are the standard operating procedure in dealing with other Specials. I don't want you bringing it up. Now let's move on!"

"No! I will not take it off the table! We've run through this scenario a dozen times and we still don't have an answer for the likely possibility of a group of Specials either attacking us in suicide runs or falling back and taking up hostages when we corner and overwhelm them."

"That's what negotiation is for!"

"Negotiation is for local law enforcement!"

"Federal too!"

"Our job is to nullify Special threats in general population theatres. Do you think that if they are breaking the law and get caught they are likely to put their hands up and surrender like a game of capture the flag? They lose, they go to jail. They're going to fight, and if we die so they can get away, 'oh, well.' I don't want to go out like that, do you?"

"And killing Specials with shrapnel is a perfectly good solution to you?" accused Leonard.

"We don't have to use shrapnel grenades, if that's such a problem for you."

"Maybe phosphor then?" said Leonard sarcastically.

"We could use flash-bangs or tear gas, or any number of things. Wholesale slaughter is not the only option."

"Yes, but the problem is, for you, it's still an option!"

Leonard sat down and kicked his legs up as though this would end the debate. Daniel ignored this gesture and pressed on.

"Look, I'm not gifted with super strength or invulnerability or super speed or mental powers. I'm just a guy from Brooklyn. And I sure as hell have no interest in getting killed while I'm fighting to ensure the bad guys get taken down and my team doesn't get injured or killed.

Leonard's eyebrows raised as he looked up at Daniel as though seeing him clearly for the first time.

"So now, Specials are 'bad-guys.'"

Daniel rolled his eyes.

"Give me a break, Leo. I've seen you use grenades in combat before during the Sol War."

"That was the enemy!" retorted Leonard, kicking his feet to a standing position. "And I've never used a grenade to take a life. If you'd recall, the Quill set us up against drones!"

"That's bullshit and you know it. We fought a lot of species."

"Those were slaves and clones, and I never used a grenade against them!"

"Don't go getting self-righteous on me, Leonard, we didn't even know they were slaves until after the war! And as I recall, you didn't have a problem with calling down bombardment on the cloning facilities."

Leonard grit his teeth and shut his eyes as though straining for control.

"I'm trying real hard," said Leonard, "to not make the connection you're putting Specials in the same boat with an intergalactic empire that was trying to make our sun go red giant. I'd hate to think I vouched for someone who would throw in against my kind like this."

"Your kind? You're human, Leonard. Special or otherwise. But if you're going up against a regular human and they used a grenade to drop you before you got to them, I wouldn't be surprised. As far as I'm concerned, we need to employ it and figure out a way to neutralize the same threat being used against us in the field. I'm not looking at Specials, I'm looking at the guy on the other side of the divide between cops and criminals, and if he has an advantage in reaching us at a distance, I want the same assurances."

"No, drop it!" snapped Leonard emphatically. "It's not us and them, for us! It's us ensuring we all get a chance at having a normal life! All of us! That can't happen if we kill some of us!"

"And the guys we will be going up against will not be so utilitarian user-friendly as you. They will be looking at it from the other end. They will be thinking 'I'm oppressed.' 'I've got nothing to lose.' 'I'm going to make myself great any way I can,' or 'I'm going to make the normal humans feel my pain.' You can't reason with them, because most of them are retaliating against society just by using their abilities. And with men like that, hard works best."

Leonard eyed Daniel in silence for a long moment, mulling over Daniel's words.

"Look," began Leonard, "I know what we're going up against, and I understand your perspective. I also have it in the back of my mind. But if we're going to have any kind of success with this, we're going to have to show we can take care of the threat, rehabilitate the suspect, and return them to society as a symbol of what can happen when you work with the system."

Daniel blinked.

"I never knew what a dreamer you were, Leonard," said Daniel at last. "I agree with what you seek, but that has no bearing on what we're discussing."

"And what do you think we're discussing?"

"That the guys we're going up against don't want to go through rehabilitation any more than the morgue. They lose time in their life, be it incremental or the whole thing. They will not go quietly unless we convince them it is best if they do so. That cannot be accomplished without shock and awe."

"Shock and awe?"

"At least in the beginning. A few big shows for the press, and then we can go softer, with the occasional show of force."

"These are human beings we're talking about!"

"Let's get this straight, Leonard, I'd toss a grenade into a pack of normal human thugs. I have no problem with it. Stop making this about Specials. Human is human. And I'd take the same measures with a street gang or a bank robber or a predator or a mob or a Special. It doesn't matter to me."

"And I say," replied Leonard, "It's a shame that Specials hold such company in your eyes."

"Give me a break!" snapped Daniel. "And stop twisting everything I say into some other thing."

"I think we've accomplished just about enough of what we can on this issue," said Leonard at last. "I'm tired. Why don't you go back to your room and write it up any way you want to, and we can pick it apart tomorrow?"

"Fine," scoffed Daniel, and he slumped toward the door with a confounded annoyance.

But when Daniel put his hand on the doorknob and gripped it tightly, he merely toyed with the thought of turning the knob and throwing the door open. He was exhausted, both physically and emotionally and wanted nothing more than to lie down in his own bed. But the nagging thought that Leonard viewed this argument as a friendship ending line that was crossed swelled to the front of his fogging mind and shook him. Daniel could only play with the doorknob absently.

"Hey, Leo, are we okay?"

"What?"

"You know, discussing this and saying something that bothers you or brings you low, I mean, I don't want to hurt your feelings, or anything."

"Hurt my feelings?" chuckled Leonard, as though silently pointing out how feminine this string of words sounded being uttered between men.

Daniel shrugged, perceiving how his choice of words must have been interpreted.

"Well," chuckled Daniel. "You know."

"Look," replied Leonard, with a conciliatory smile. "You've got a good point. I just don't like it. You're the boss. I'm just getting my objections on record, but I hope you'll listen and take my opinion into consideration on these touchy subjects."

"Yeah."

"We're good, Dan. Just write it up without me, and we'll discuss it at the 0830 meeting."

"Right," sighed Daniel, appreciatively, "Just so we're good."

"Goodnight, sir."

"Right."

With that, Daniel finally turned the knob and disappeared into the dark of the hallway, letting the door close softly behind him, concerned that a hard slam might be misinterpreted as anger.

With a sigh, Daniel felt his way in the darkness until his eyes adjusted to the semi-darkness of the hallway and perceived an obstruction in his path; there in the darkest shadow stood Stephen, propped up against a wall.

"You guys through?" scoffed Stephen, bleary eyed.

"What?"

"The walls are kind of thin in this place."

"Sorry if I kept you awake, then."

"Oh, don't sweat it," replied Stephen, "This was nothing. Don and Lizzie used to go at it all night." and Stephen pushed with his fist for visual effect. "That was a hell of a lot worse than this."

"Oh, I didn't know."

"Know what?"

"About Donovan and Meng being an item. That explains why she left after him, though."

"Oh, they weren't seeing each other. They hated each other. Donovan kept thinking Liz was Korean, and Liz hated Donovan, period."

"I don't get it then. If they weren't dating, why would they-"

"Man, Liz just liked the fact that Donovan could grow."

Daniel pursed his lips at the image of Meng and Henry together and shook his head to get the image out.

"Good night, Stephen."

"By the way, I think you're right about that."

"About what?"

"Grenades," replied Stephen. "It's about time someone showed some balls and said what needed to be said if we're really planning on taking down Specials in the field without risking our lives to do it. Just wanted you to know, those of us who are put in the middle of it, we appreciate the fact that someone's actually concerned about writing checks that the cannon fodder have to cash in. I'm not saying I like you, I'm just saying I like where you're headed."

"Well, don't fall in love with me just yet. I've got plans for you."

"Like what?" scoffed Stephen.

"It seems to me you've been underutilized as a team member, and that's something I'd like to see corrected."

"What," retorted Stephen, as though he had Daniel summed up. "You want to put me on the front lines to get a better body count? Man, that's where I've been since the Sol War. You've got nothing new for me. Now the only thing I see is an asshole that wants me on the front line and then wants to throw grenades at my back."

"You really are hard of hearing, aren't you? I'm not talking about using you as a human grenade. That may have been your function up until now, but that's not how I want to use you. I'll come right out with it. We lost Meng. That's a loss of power. We're stuck with you, and your ability is a hell of a lot more powerful, but also limited in use. I want you to take up Elizabeth's old position and use your abilities in a more long range capacity."

"I explode. You want me to drop the bomb? I'm the guy. But I don't shoot."

"I think you can. I think you're being lazy."

"Man, don't even think you can talk down to me! You thought Mammoth was a handful,

just try me!"

"Oh, I'm going to try you. Report at 0530. Be up and ready. I'm going to have Boatman's men put you through the paces."

"Science Medical? Been there, done that."

"Yeah? Then you'll know your way around. You're going to be in a bomb shelter with a cinderblock target, and you're going to stay in there until you can force the target to fall. You flare up—you lose, and the cinderblock target will be set up again. Pack a lunch, 'cause you're there for the day, Giordano. You got a problem with that?"

"Fuck you."

"0530. Don't be late."

Daniel left Stephen alone in the hallway and slipped into the dismal room, sat at the desk, where he pulled out a notepad and a pen. After staring at the notepad for a long time, he flipped it open and began writing a continuation of what he had argued so forcefully with Leonard. While he wrote, his vision blurred, and he shook his head vigorously to shake himself awake. Again, Daniel returned to the topic of hostage situations and running firefights with retreating Specials, his mind dizzy and fogged as he fought exhaustion to keep his point in the forefront of his mind. Slowly but surely, darkness crept in from the corners of his vision until all was black.

CHAPTER 7

TRAINING

When Daniel awoke, the alarm clock read 12:48. Somewhere between dream and awareness he blinked at the clock as the numbers slowly wended their way into his consciousness until at last he remembered he had an appointment at 08:30. He had missed it. He bounced up in alarm and pulled off the sheets of the bed, throwing himself to his feet.

Perplexedly, he glanced around the room, trying to get his bearings. He was sure he fell asleep at the desk writing up his belief that grenades were a necessary implement in their arrest operations, but the desk was neat, and there was no sign of a notebook to be found.

Finally, Daniel scoffed, threw open the door and darted down the hallway to McCormack's office. At the door, he heard what sounded like rancorous argument as violent muffled cries spread out by intermittent and frequent obscenities echoed thinly through the glass door.

Daniel swallowed hard, expecting to find them all in a frenzy over his grenade strategy. And with a hard sigh, opened the door to McCormack's office to be met with the sound of uproarious laughter. Inside, Leonard, McCormack and Bradley sat convulsing in hysterics, slapping their thighs.

They noticed Daniel, and cheered, like welcoming a regular in a neighborhood bar.

"Well," called Leonard chidingly, "look who's here! Hello, sleeping beauty!"

"Yeah," scoffed Daniel, "look, I'm sorry I overslept. I thought I set the alarm clock."

"You did!" chuckled Leonard, "I turned it off."

Daniel looked at Leonard in shock. He should have felt relief that there was an explanation for his oversleeping, but all he felt was annoyance.

"You did what?"

"Well, I couldn't disturb you." pouted Leonard, at the point of giggling. "You looked so cute sleeping there all cuddled up to your pillow."

Daniel felt the room shift beneath his feet uncomfortably, as embarrassment set in.

"I was asleep at the desk," recounted Daniel trying to remember exactly what happened to him after he left Leonard's room.

"Yeah. I had to carry you to bed." laughed Leonard with McCormack and Bradley chuckling behind him. "Kind'a like a little baby." Leonard leaned forward and slapped his thigh. "You know, picking you up is like trying to carry a sleeping cat? You were all over the place! I nearly dropped you twice. To be honest, I was a little uncomfortable about it, what with me carrying you like we just got married and here I am bringing you across the threshold. It felt a little gay to me," adding in an aside, "No offense, Brad."

Bradley socked Leonard in the arm and they both laughed heartily. Daniel shook his head to keep up with them.

"Why didn't you wake me up?" demanded Daniel, his rage building to a boil.

"I couldn't disturb your slumber!" replied Leonard sarcastically. "You looked so cute! All cuddled up and all. So I turned off the alarm clock and left you there."

"You let me sleep in," began Daniel, his anger barely in check as he pinched his nose and shut his eyes, "knowing we had a meeting at 0830?"

"You've been burning the candle at both ends for a few days now, Dan." said McCormack, finally. "We figured you could use the extra shuteye. So we let you get a few extra winks in."

"Knowing that we had a meeting at 0830," repeated Daniel, fuming.

"Is there a problem, Daniel?" said McCormack, his eyes scrutinizing Daniel's.

"Yeah," spat Daniel, "The problem is you guys aren't taking this seriously. You guys are on cruise control and we should be running. We have a limited timescale to accomplish a lot to get us ready for the task of establishing a cohesive working unit and you guys are fucking around. My problem is that we're two men short! My problem is we're going to need people of color and women to give the team a universal look."

"As far as the timeline," replied McCormack, "we're actually ahead of schedule. Barely, mind you, but you're picking up the necessary disciplines at the quick step, so we can get back into training at your leisure, now."

"Now," chimed in Bradley, "the people-of-color issue is something we do need to address."

"Yeah, Daniel's right," added Leonard. "We're going to look like the Aryan Special team, and we might as well have two lightning bolts on our logo."

"The problem is," rebutted McCormack, "we only have the list of Specials who were in the war. They were tested and proven, and we know what we're dealing with."

Daniel studied McCormack, hanging onto every word as McCormack leaned forward and folded his hands on the desk.

"The problem is the abilities," concluded McCormack. "Most of the documented people of color don't have the abilities we need."

"Why's that?" demanded Daniel.

McCormack merely shrugged.

"Most of the people of color who had the abilities we require were killed in the war."

"We lost a lot of energy emitters in battle," nodded Bradley.

"Why?" demanded Daniel. McCormack rolled his eyes as though the answer was obvious.

"Being able to project energy assaults doesn't mean you're invulnerable, Daniel." replied McCormack. "You can be killed as easily as you kill."

"Yeah," added Leonard. "I hate to break it to you, but the difference between a Special's durability and a normal human infantry man is that you carried a rifle into battle. We had our abilities. But that's about it."

"The reason why there are more white energy emitters is just the luck of the draw, actually."

"What about Plasma?" asked Bradley.

"Jeff Rodriguez got deported to Mexico," replied McCormack.

"I thought he was from East LA," said Leonard.

"Immigration's looking into it," replied McCormack. "But I think they're happier having him on that side of the border."

"He can't even speak Spanish," exclaimed Bradley.

"I hear he's learning," replied McCormack.

"What about Dragon's Eye?" said Leonard.

"Sent back to China," replied McCormack. "Junko Oshina was also deported back to Japan."

"Damn," scoffed Leonard. "She was cute, too."

"They took her student visa away from her?" gasped Bradley.

"That's the way it goes," replied McCormack.

"Mitra?" ventured Bradley.

"Ashoka was sent back to India," replied McCormack. "Matteh Al is back in Israel working for Israeli Counterterrorism. Reverb has disappeared."

"Corona's a possibility," said Leonard. "Anything happen with Reggie?"

"Mr. Estrin is currently in prison," replied McCormack. "He flared up at a park."

"How about Clarion?" ventured Leonard.

"Darell is out of the country," replied McCormack.

"He's American!" scoffed Leonard. "How'd he get deported?"

"He didn't," replied McCormack. "The government leased him out to work in the European theatre."

"Doing what?" asked Leonard.

"I don't know," replied McCormack. "But he's got the highest clearance possible. All I could find out is that he's somewhere in the French Alps."

"That lucky bastard," scoffed Bradley.

"Relax, Brad," mollified Leonard. "He's working, not working on his tan. Besides, I don't think they have your kind of clubs outside of Paris."

Bradley laughed and gave a crude gesture to Leonard, who affectionately touched his own heart as though the gesture were a gift.

"So basically," interrupted Daniel, "we've got nothing?"

"Not entirely," rejoined McCormack. "What you're failing to understand is that even though a lot of the requirements we're going by have limited our options, there are still thousands of undocumented Specials out there. Finding them will be a problem, though. Even the Specials we do know about will be hard to track down. A lot of them are hiding out in their own communities trying to do their best impressions of a needle hiding among a stack of needles. As long as they don't use their abilities, they could just blend in with the wallpaper, so to speak. It's hardly a problem, though. We may not be starting out with all the colors of the rainbow, but eventually, once the recruitment drive starts up, you'll have your pick of the litter."

"And until then," concluded Daniel, "we've got a bunch of white guys? This sounds like a bad comic book."

"Relax," soothed McCormack. "We're assembling the best team we can. What we need is ability. Color and gender will fall into place later. Until then, you'll just have to be patient."

"Now," said Daniel, "back to the part about you guys not training on my account. We should have been training every day, if that was your regimen. As you've already stated, I can pick things up on the 'quick-step.' What are we doing to rectify this problem?"

"What seems to be affecting you now?" asked McCormack.

"We need to get back in there and get our training back on," replied Daniel with an edge to his voice.

"We can start back up at any time," replied McCormack, leaning back in his chair.

"How about now?" challenged Daniel.

McCormack grinned and turned away from Daniel, facing Leonard.

"Leonard, go have the men change into the new sweats we got from Quantico this morning and have them assemble in five."

"You got it."

"And you too," added McCormack to Leonard. "You're getting a little thick around the middle."

"Thick around the middle my ass," grumbled Leonard as he left the office.

"Brad," continued McCormack, "go get changed into your sweats."

"Right on!" replied Bradley with a grin.

Realizing that they were actually getting ready for training, Daniel turned to leave the office to get ready when McCormack rose from his desk.

"Daniel," beckoned McCormack, "you got a minute?"

"This going to be your version of a pep talk?" snapped Daniel. McCormack glared at him for a moment and then sighed.

"You're annoyed right now," concluded McCormack, "and to some degree with good reason, so I'll let this slide. What I want to talk to you about is what we're looking at."

Daniel plopped down into a chair and looked over at McCormack.

"Okay," he replied.

"Our training will consist of SWAT training. Your infantry training is on par with Special Forces, and you've trained extensively in sting and no-knock warrant procedures, so what you're going to have to take into consideration is your function in all this. Your role will be that of an Anchor."

"Okay, I read that on your and Maximus' jacket. What's the function of an Anchor?"

"Anchors are field commanders. They hang back and call shots from a safe position, with the capability of entering the engagement at any time depending on enemy troop movements. In other words, you're to hang back until we are being routed and overrun. Not until."

With that, Daniel scoffed, waving his hand dismissively.

"That's not how I roll."

"Well," replied McCormack, "it's going to have to be a discipline you take on. We don't need a liability. We need orders and we need them to keep on coming."

"I can do that just as easily in the fray."

"And there will be too many variables that you will be too close to, to give the proper orders for. We will be committed to close-quarters combat, with the hostile target most likely in the next room, bracing for an attack. They will have more time to aim and act, while we are still locating the threats. If you go down, there goes our chain of command."

"We can sort this out later. Right now, I want to see how my team moves. I can't do that unless I'm going through the door with them."

"That's not how an Anchor functions."

"I could care less. I'm going through the door with my men. If you don't like it, you can stay here in your little office."

With that, McCormack leaned forward, his irritation showing on his face.

"Let me explain something to you. This office is not my office. It's your office."

"My office?" blinked Daniel.

"I'm holding the position of temporary team leader until you get up to speed." replied McCormack. "The office is for your use."

"And when were you going to tell me this?

"When you were ready." replied McCormack, matter-of-factly. "Frankly, I didn't know if you were going to make it this far to break it all down for you.

"We were going easy on you to keep you from being overwhelmed by the office you were taking over. In retrospect, we were kind of patronizing you, and I'm sorry for that. When you're ready, this office will be yours."

"Clear your things out and set up office down the hall. I'm assuming command of the Post."

McCormack smirked with a small glimmer of pride and stepped to the side.

"Yes, sir."

Fifteen minutes later, Daniel watched the road race by as they drove northwest down Grant Circle and continuing on New Hampshire Ave, jumping onto the 495 and switched over to the 95 exiting on Powder Mill Road. Daniel watched a stone and mortar wall rise up and fly past for a few minutes until the SUV finally turned into a driveway with a security checkpoint at 9200 Powder Mill Road. There, a sign bore the words James J. Rowley Training Center (JJRTC) Beltsville, Maryland.

The guard took his time reading the identification, then finally nodded and pointed down the road on the far side of the barricade.

"The urban warfare training facility is down this road. Be prepared to show your credentials again when you get there."

With a wave of his hand, the barricade slid away, parting to yield to the SUV. The driver waved to the guard and drove over the speed bump on the far side of the barricade, driving past the parking lot and the security building and down an elm-lined road, passing offshoot roads leading to different facilities and parking lots. In the distance, a concrete pavilion filled with people stretched out ahead with a series of houses and apartment complexes filling the lot. The driver pulled off to the left and parked in a parking lot just adjacent to the pavilion and turned to Daniel.

"Here we are, sir." said the driver.

"Right," said Daniel.

Daniel climbed out into the cold rain and studied the pavilion. It looked like a shopping mall surrounded by houses and apartment buildings. As Daniel approached the pavilion he was disconcerted by the notion that none of the people in the pavilion appeared to be moving. As he neared, their shapes seemed to come together until he was staring at a sea of mannequins. Just then, a Secret Service agent appeared from around a building and approached Daniel.

"You must be Agent Rooke," said the agent.

"Daniel," said Daniel, extending his hand. The agent shook it.

"I'm Agent Padilla." replied the agent. "You might want to step away from the mannequins. We have snipers training."

Daniel looked to the rooftops, and indeed, saw the muzzles of rifles protruding from the ledge, pivoting ever so slightly, and Daniel knew they were hunting the crowd of mannequins for something.

"We put a gun on one of the mannequins. When the sniper finds the suspect, he'll call it in to get the go ahead to take the shot."

"How long does this usually take?"

"Well, the record's inside three minutes from positioning to confirmed kill."

Daniel didn't find this at all comforting. A lot could happen in three minutes. He stared off in the distance.

"These are all training structures?"

"Every one," replied Padilla. "We've got your site set up over there."

Padilla pointed into the distance to what looked like an ordinary apartment complex.

"You ever run through one of these?"

"Not a simulation before," admitted Daniel, "But, yeah, I've been through hundreds of these."

"I hear you," said Padilla, "We've got your specifications set up and a Special Forces team is waiting for you."

"For the first run?" blinked Daniel. Padilla caught the trepidation in his voice and turned to him.

"You want me to send them home?"

"No," replied Daniel. "I want to see how my team handles themselves."

"Good. I don't want to be the one to tell these guys they wasted their morning. I'll leave you with Agent Morgan. He runs the GhettoFab."

"The what?"

"Ghetto Fabrication," explained Padilla, "It's for urban warfare training. Washington's Metro PD runs it twice a month."

Daniel and the others followed Agent Padilla as he led them around the back of the pavilion, showing the bare broken concrete and exposed bricks on the back of the buildings. The ground was broken asphalt with weeds shooting up through the cracks, and it was slick from the rain. In the distance, a trainer stood with his back to them. He turned and glared down the road at them and walked over to meet them halfway. Morgan was a short and stocky bald man in his late forties, with a handlebar mustache. He walked with a wide stance, his muscular arms swinging in a military rhythm.

"You're the Specials team, I take it?" said Morgan. It was not really a question.

"Agent Daniel Rooke." said Daniel. "This is my team."

Morgan studied them with a critical glare, sizing them up.

"Alright." replied Morgan. "Let me show you the staging area."

Morgan turned and walked off with a slight twitch of a gesture, indicating he wished them to follow him. Daniel turned and shook Padilla's hand and followed Morgan, and the others followed behind.

Morgan came to a stop on the far side of the pavilion, facing the apartment complex and stepped under a tarp. Daniel and the others followed him and shook the rain out of their hair. Morgan and Leonard merely wiped their bald heads and flicked the rain off.

Finally, Morgan turned and faced them again. He inhaled, and his chest swelled as he eyed them and when he spoke, his voice was loud and clear, like a drill sergeants.

"Welcome to the James J Rowley Training Center's Urban Warfare Simulation Station, also known as the GhettoFab. Here you will be running through an obstacle course with live hostages, being held by live hostage takers. This is a non-live training exercise, so no use of live rounds or extra-human abilities. We have special equipment for you to use within the facility, and we expect you to use them."

Morgan gestured to the table to the left and pointed to the first item on his mental list.

"Here is the Gel-Grenade. It is called the Gel-Grenade because when it is armed, it throws out a sticky goop that is very difficult to get off. It acts the same way shrapnel would, so if you get a little bit on you, you are considered wounded. If you come out covered in slime, it means you are dead."

Pointing to the rifles on the table next to the Gel-Grenades, Morgan continued.

"These are modified paint guns, manufactured to work in the same fashion as a SOPMOD assault rifle. The magazine holds twenty rounds of non-live ammunition and the rifle fires the same way a regular would handle, so be aware of the recoil."

Morgan then pointed to the item next to the rifles.

"These here are the headgear you will be wearing in infil scenarios. It provides night vision, targeting, building schematics and winvid, which is to say if you look at a wall, you will see the enemy like you're looking through a window at them. Please don't wave," added Morgan unnecessarily, obviously a joke at their expense, "the enemy can't see you."

Morgan then turned to face them straight on, again, and folded his arms.

"You will employ your training in stealth, teamwork and marksmanship to make your way through the urban facility, neutralizing all threats and determining the difference between threat and hostage, and you will be timed. The urban facility record is five minutes. You will be expected to not exceed 15. And questions?"

Daniel and the men just stood there silently examining the equipment, nonplussed.

"You heard the man, gentlemen," concluded Daniel, eyeing them all with his best drill sergeant glare. "Load up on the dope."

Daniel began passing out rifles and clips. And each took the rifle gingerly. Leonard gripped his and it cracked down the grip.

"Plastic," scoffed Leonard.

Daniel slid a magazine into another rifle and handed it to Leonard, who took it gingerly. Chad slung his rifle over his shoulder and put the butt of the rifle into his shoulder like Special Forces would do.

Daniel gave him a rare grin. Chad grinned back.

Leonard tucked his rifle into his shoulder and took a headset, lowering the visor over his eyes. McCormack and Bradley locked and loaded their rifles and put on their headsets.

Daniel noticed that all of them refused the grenades. Nonplussed, Daniel took a bandolier of Gel-Grenades and slung it over his shoulder.

"Let's move out," called Daniel, and turned to walk toward the GhettoFab.

"Time will start when you reach the gate." called Morgan.

"Alright, Chad and Leonard are on point. Tobias and Brad, follow my lead."

"Yes, sir," chimed the Specials.

McCormack and Bradley traded disappointed looks at Daniel's choice to have the physical force lead and followed skeptically into the rain.

Outside the complex, Daniel took a knee and checked his rifle. Leonard tucked his rifle into his shoulder with the barrels pointing down to the earth. Chad noticed this and followed suit. McCormack and Bradley knelt with their rifles at the ready and they all waited.

Daniel studied them all, noted they were ready, and with a wave of his hand raced up to the gated entryway with the Specials close at his heels.

"Time has started!" bellowed Morgan from behind.

Daniel came to the main door and found it locked.

"It's locked."

"Let me take a crack at it," said Leonard.

"No," said Daniel, "Chad?"

Chad nodded and flipped over the gate into the complex, quickly opening the gated entryway and standing sideways to make room for the team to enter the complex. Daniel covered Chad and Leonard took point down into the dark hallway.

Through the dark narrow corridor, they proceeded at a quick crouched step, their weapons pointed, darting from one possible attack point to another. Daniel tapped Leonard, who raised his fist to call for a halt. Daniel tossed a Gel-Grenade at an open doorway just ahead and in the burst of sound, light and debris, Daniel slapped Leonard's back and shouted out:

"Go! Go! Go!"

At the doorway, Leonard kneeled and pointed his rifle barrel into the room, and shouted:

"Clear!"

Chad took the far point and entered the room quickly, while Leonard entered into the apartment behind Chad and gave a more commanding sweep of the room he was responsible for:

"Clear!"

Leonard then took a kneeling position at the edge of the room and signaled Daniel to move in. Daniel entered the apartment, behind Chad. Chad turned at the kitchen and entered through the smoke and haze.

Chad made his way to the edge of the wall of smoke and dust studying the movements through the cloud barked into the room:

"Specials Investigations! Drop your weapons, now!"

The figures raised their weapons and Chad fired two shots, knocking the two men back, who bounced off the wall, studied their blue paint marks and nodded, sitting on the ground. Daniel darted into the hallway, moving straight past Chad, putting his hand on Chad's shoulder, signaling he had support. Leonard then signaled McCormack to enter the apartment with Bradley in support. Daniel made his way into the second bedroom, kicking the door open:

"Specials Investigations!"

Inside were two men with signs over their chests that read "HOSTAGE" and Daniel swept the room coolly, seeing no sign of threat. He made no effort to free the hostages, merely checked their bonds to ensure they were securely tied:

"Clear!"

McCormack studied the hostages, and gave a nod to Daniel, and Bradley pointed his rifle back toward the door leading out into the hall. Chad sighed and lifted his headgear.

"Well, that wasn't all that bad."

Just then, in the living room another "terrorist" rappelled down from a hole in the ceiling and fired at Chad, who moved with surprising speed, avoiding the paint balls, and fired three at the "terrorist," hitting him squarely. The man studied his blue paint marks, nodded and sat down, looking past Chad, snickering.

Chad turned to see Leonard glaring back at Chad with annoyance and pointed out the three blue paint marks on his back. Chad blinked as Leonard grit his teeth and sat on the ground disgustedly.

Daniel glared at Chad.

"Call your shots, call the targets," said Daniel, "and warn your teammates."

Chad waved a nervous apology to Leonard.

"Let's move on," snapped Daniel, and Chad snapped to attention. "Beach, you're point. Let's see if you've learned your lesson."

"Yes, sir," said Chad.

"Move out," ordered Daniel.

"Daniel," said McCormack. "Have you seen what you wanted to see?"

"Almost," replied Daniel, "give him one more sweep, and then we'll do it your way."

"Alright," replied McCormack, with a look of relieved comprehension.

"Whenever you're ready, Chad," said Daniel.

"Right," said Chad.

Chad proceeded down the hallway toward a bottleneck where two hallways converged next to an exit and an apartment door and took a knee, raising his fist.

Daniel, McCormack and Overman instantly kneeled. Chad made a gesture with his finger toward the exit door, and Daniel instantly proceeded down the hall warily, his finger playing with the release action down the center of the trigger.

Just next to the exit door, Daniel looked down at the hallway convergence and peered into the shadow warily. Daniel then gestured to the others with his finger over the winvid switch on the headgear. Chad and the others nodded, and studied their surroundings, seeing six armed gunmen, three in the apartment, one behind the exit door and two in the hallway.

Daniel signaled Chad behind him, and with a hand gesture, told him to cover the apartment door and prepare to advance on the hallway, tossing him a Gel-Grenade. Chad studied it warily then nodded his complicity. Daniel then signaled McCormack and Bradley to brace for clearing the room.

Daniel then stood at the exit door, and with a commanding nod, kicked in the exit door, knocking over the gunman, and quickly disarmed him, firing two paintballs into the backs of the gunman's knees, and sending him down the steps, turning to cover the apartment door and the hallway bottleneck simultaneously. Chad then threw the Gel-Grenade into the hallway and charged around the bend:

"Specials Investigations! Drop your weapons, now!"

There were four shots and silence until finally Chad's voice echoed through the hallway:

"Clear!"

Daniel then signaled McCormack and Bradley to the apartment door. The winvid displays showed the three gunmen take positions toward the doorway. Daniel looked up at McCormack, who returned an expression of impatience. Daniel scoffed and with a grin, gestured McCormack and Bradley into the apartment.

The apartment door blew off its hinges, striking the first gunman, and McCormack grit his teeth, and the other two gunmen stood straight up with their arms tight to their bodies, and their rifles were stripped from them:

"Clear!" called McCormack.

Bradley then entered into the apartment and fired three rounds carelessly, before exiting the unit.

"Three confirmed kills, sir," said Bradley with a bored intonation.

"Alright," breathed Daniel, "Chad, hold up."

Chad stopped and crouched down in his position, his rifle pointing down the hallway. Daniel turned to McCormack and Bradley and grinned.

"Alright," said Daniel, "let's see some shock and awe from you two."

"Yes, sir," replied McCormack.

McCormack and Bradley strolled into the hallway, casually noting all the gunmen stationed throughout the complex with their winvid displays.

"I'll lead," said McCormack to Bradley. "You sweep up."

"You got it," replied Bradley.

McCormack then grit his teeth and all the apartment doors blew open at once:

"Specials Investigations! Come out with your hands on your heads!"

Several gunmen pointed their rifles out of the apartment doors and fired down the hallway at McCormack. The paintballs exploded ten yards in front of McCormack who strolled up the hallway casually stripping the men of their weapons and dragging them out of the units by unseen hands, their legs kicking.

"Brad?"

"About time."

Bradley flew down the hallway, stripping the guns out of the gunman's hands and throwing them into a corner. The gunmen fired on Bradley, their paintballs seemingly exploding on him, covering him with blue. Overman kept fighting. The gunmen glared at Bradley with disgust.

"Foul! Foul! Sit down and wait for the exercise to be terminated!"

Bradley looked back at Daniel awaiting his orders.

"Alright, I've seen enough. I'm calling the exercise over at 1353 hours. Let's wrap this up and we can discuss strategies."

Bradley nodded, and all the paint fell to the ground, leaving not a drop on him. The gunmen stared in disbelief.

"Did you see that?" said one of the Special Forces operatives.

"Not a drop!" gasped the other.

Outside the GhettoFab, Daniel approached Leonard who stood next to an incensed field instructor.

"What the hell was that about?" demanded Morgan, "Which one of you kept fighting after being hit?"

"No one was hit." placated Daniel, "Sorry, I had to see what I was working with."

"What do you mean no one was hit?" railed Morgan. "I have twenty men calling foul!"

"And I called the training exercise," replied Daniel shortly, "I've seen what I needed to see." Then added dismissively, "Thank you."

"And I'm saying etiquette has to be followed! Now who broke the rules?"

"I said thank you," replied Daniel, narrowing his eyes at Morgan.

Morgan blinked at Daniel and stormed off in a fume. McCormack sidestepped and let Morgan fume and stomp past him then turned to Daniel.

"Alright, boss," began McCormack. "What's the situation?"

"I wanted to see the physically augmented Specials perform on a standard sweep," concluded Daniel. "As I suspected, Leonard performed above expectations, Chad needs work. As far as ability, you two can perform adequately with your powers. I just wanted to see Giordano run the GhettoFab."

"That's for later," assured McCormack. "He's going to be busy in the Explosives/Demolition Box for the rest of the day."

"What's he doing there?" asked Daniel, curiously.

"Trying to detonate a cinderblock from across the room without detonating," replied McCormack.

"Do you know how he's faring with that?" asked Bradley at McCormack's shoulder.

Daniel looked out on the GhettoFab and breathed deeply. He had virtually put his career on the line to prove that Stephen could perform as an energy projector on par with what they had lost when Burn walked out on the team in protest to his appointment. A fact that Boatman was quick to remind him at every turn. Daniel looked over his shoulder at Bradley and McCormack.

"We'll find out tonight."

CHAPTER 8

REBUILDING THE TEAM

The team shuffled into the Post with the weight of the day resting on their backs. Some carried it better than others. Leonard was grim with annoyance and Chad was lifeless as he walked into the flat and collapsed on the couch, immediately flipping through channels on the television in the obvious hope that he could be passed by as nothing more than a part of the couch. McCormack and Bradley nodded to Boatman in passing.

"General," they murmured as they passed leaving him to the only man he could possibly be seeking an audience with—Daniel.

When Daniel came through the doorway into the flat he stopped dead in his tracks, not altogether surprised to see Boatman, but wary of some possible fault he may have committed to draw his presence in the Post so soon after their last, and what he hoped was their final, talk.

Daniel approached Boatman, standing at a comfortable distance from him and greeted him.

"How did it go at the GhettoFab?" inquired Boatman with a scrutinizing expression.

"I saw what I wanted to see," assured Daniel, hoping that would be the end of the discussion on the matter.

"I heard you breached protocols with the Special Forces team," pressed Boatman, showing his annoying tactic for asking questions he knew the answers to and waiting for people to fall into his traps. Daniel pursed his lips and studied Boatman for a moment before speaking.

"Well," said Daniel, "I had to see what my men could do. I figured the Special Forces team could handle it."

"So you used Bradley and McCormack to prove a point?" pressed Boatman.

"No," answered Daniel, flatly, "To see what they could do."

"And your findings?" pressed Boatman.

"They can pretty much take on a squad of hardnosed grunts," replied Daniel coolly, "and disprove the notion that *you can't smoke a rock*."

Boatman smiled despite himself.

"Don't place too much on Overman and McCormack's abilities," counseled Boatman, "They make mistakes like the rest of them."

"I know that," assured Daniel. "I'm not putting all my trust into one basket."

"That's good," replied Boatman. "I need a team leader who can work with a rotating roster and not get hooked on reusing the same players."

"It's fine," assured Daniel. "Bradley and Tobias are good. I just needed to see them perform with my own eyes to see how they could be used. I'm pleased with what I saw."

"What are you not pleased with?" inquired Boatman.

Daniel felt a surge of annoyance at the feeling he was being tested and took a deep breath.

"One, I didn't get the chance to see Stephen in action," said Daniel, then added, "I would have liked to have him running the GhettoFab with the rest of the team."

"And two?" pressed Boatman.

"Chad needs to work with a team better," answered Daniel. Chad visibly cringed on the couch, lowering himself as to disappear entirely into the couch and flipped through the channels faster. Daniel ignored this, saying, "He made a typical green mistake and Leonard was taken out of the game as a result."

"You realize," said Boatman, "in real life Leonard is bulletproof?"

"You realize," snapped Daniel, "chances are we won't be encountering bullets on the missions?"

Boatman studied Daniel's flare-up with curiosity, and a trace of amusement.

"Just as long as you're aware," concluded Boatman.

"Oh, I'm fully aware," answered Daniel, "Any word on Stephen? How are things going at the Detonation Chamber?"

"It's about Stephen I wanted to talk to you about," replied Boatman as though they had finished with the pre-liminaries and were now ready to discuss the reason for his presence in the Post. "Or at least, I have an answer to the gap left in the team with the absence of an energy projector who can function on the team as I deem they should."

"Go on," invited Daniel.

Boatman led Daniel down the hallway to the kitchen. There, he stepped to the side and gestured to the door. Sitting at the table was a slender Asian man wearing jeans and a t-shirt, with long hair down to his shoulders.

"I'd like you to meet your newest team member," said Boatman with a keen smile, "Joshua Sung. Callsign Aura. He will be our new energy projector. I thought you'd like some color on the team."

Daniel studied Sung for a moment, turned to pick up a coffee cup, fill it with coffee and then turned away to face Boatman.

"What can he do?" inquired Daniel.

Sung sat there nervously, gesturing with his hand to get their attention.

"I'm right here, guys." said Sung, annoyed.

Daniel turned sideways and took a step back so he could look from Boatman to Sung with ease.

"Sorry," replied Daniel, though he did not particularly care how annoyed or frustrated Sung was. Boatman seemed to sense this and stepped closer to Daniel, enforcing his presence onto him, impressing upon him the necessity of smoothing things out between him and the Specials as part of his job. Daniel looked right back at him, defiantly.

"Mr. Sung," began Boatman, harshly, "has the ability to use his aura to create beams of energy."

"What's his level?" demanded Daniel.

"He's a Gamma level energy projector," said Boatman as though this should be enough.

"I've got a Beta, now," replied Daniel, taking a sip of his coffee.

"And as I've told you repeatedly," snapped Boatman, "Giordano cannot use his ability in the way that the team requires."

"And I think he can," answered Daniel.

"I will not have this discussion with you again," snapped Boatman. "As it is, Giordano is being trained to focus his ability. Until he produces, I don't want to hear another word on the matter."

"Fine," answered Daniel, irritably, then turned to the young Asian man with the long hair and studied his brooding eyes. "Sung, is it?"

"Josh," answered Sung in a murmur.

"Can I have a demonstration of your ability?" said Daniel.

"Is this a test?" stammered Josh, exasperated. "I thought I already had the job."

"Humor me," said Daniel, and he leaned against the counter and took a sip of his coffee.

Josh pursed his lips and eyed them, visibly annoyed. He then turned his attention to Daniel's coffee mug. Materializing out of thin air, a beam struck the mug, which exploded to marvelous effect. Daniel jumped as he wiped the hot coffee off his face and hand and shot a look at Josh. Josh merely smirked.

"Do I pass the test?" asked Josh, his eyes amused as Daniel shook the hot coffee off his hands and turned to throw cold water on his face and hands. He then pulled a wet towel and wiped his hands and face dry.

"Can you explain how you manipulate your ability?" pressed Daniel.

Josh blinked as though he were being asked to define something second nature and therefore never put into conscious thought before.

"You want me to explain it now?" repeated Josh, irritably.

"No," replied Daniel. "I think I'd like you to work with Giordano and see if you could help him with his own abilities."

"Wherever you need me, man," replied Josh. "I'm here for the paycheck. Anything's better than working at Costco."

"Oh, Sung," added Daniel, Josh stopped in his tracks and studied Daniel warily. "Welcome to the SITF."

"Cool," replied Josh with a grin.

Josh took a quick glance around the kitchen—as though he were evaluating a new home and found it to his liking—and then walked out of it.

Boatman could barely contain his irritation as he leaned in close enough that a whisper would do, though he spoke plainly his voice only quavering a little.

"I thought I told you to let it go," growled Boatman.

Daniel seemed to like seeing how much he could irritate Boatman. The time when he was nervous of the mood swings of Lawrence Boatman were quickly diminishing in intensity, replaced with amusement. He now understood he was too far in to be removed without a replacement being found, and that replacement would have to start from scratch gaining the team's trust and finding ways to implement them in a combat scenario. Daniel knew that Boatman's hands were tied in his gamble to produce a superhuman team at a rapid pace, and for better or worse, was for the moment stuck with him. Daniel smiled.

"You told me to stop talking about it," replied Daniel. "And I have. But if I can get Giordano a mentor, so to speak, maybe he could figure out a different way to project."

"I want Sung employed on the front lines," growled Boatman. "Not teaching."

"My team, Lawrence," replied Daniel, simply. Seeing Boatman flush of color, Daniel waved his hand in a mollifying fashion. "He'll get his training. This is above and beyond."

"Don't mess about, boy," growled Boatman. "You know how I am about results."

"You'll have them," replied Daniel. "But for now, the only people ready for collars are Leonard, Tobias and Bradley."

"Do you plan on making arrests with them?" demanded Boatman.

"As soon as possible," concluded Daniel.

"So I can consider the task force ready to begin?" pressed Boatman.

"Well," said Daniel cautiously, "we're near enough to begin."

"I'll send down the dossier of your first assignment, then," concluded Boatman.

This caught Daniel off guard and he blinked in surprise.

"You already have one?" inquired Daniel.

"One that's been operating with impunity for months," replied Boatman, scratching at his white moustache.

"So you've just been sitting on these?" said Daniel, incredulously.

"I have," answered Boatman.

"I'm surprised none of the other agencies wanted a crack at them," said Daniel, in a state of disbelief.

"You could say they're investigating them," replied Boatman. "For one reason or another they are having little results. Not enough to attain a warrant, at least."

"In this climate, I'm surprised."

"There are still laws in place that protect the average citizen from needless harassment. Those same laws protect the Specials community as well, last time I checked."

"I'll be sure to let the team know."

"Expecting a mutiny, are we?"

"Come on, Lawrence. I know you've got the flat bugged. You heard what McCormack said."

"Tobias is not about to abandon his responsibilities on a whim. You have him for a little while longer."

"That's good to know." scoffed Daniel at the timetable implications of having McCormack for only a while, depending on how things went and how he perceived the climate toward Specials to be on any given day.

"So I can assume the team active from now on?"

"Some of them." answered Daniel. "I'll take Bradley and Tobias with me to start out. Leonard can train Chad, Stephen and Sung until they get up to speed."

"It's your call." answered Boatman. "But I want my results."

"You'll have them."

"Then I think we're done here."

"A pleasure as always, Lawrence."

Boatman fixed Daniel with a laser stare and silently reminded him who ran things and who was in charge. Daniel understood his role was to run. Still, he couldn't resist smirking at Boatman's irritation. With nothing more to say, Boatman walked past Daniel and out of the Post.

Damn, thought Daniel. *You'd better be right, now.* Daniel scoffed and rubbed his forehead with a slight trepidation building at the thought that he would finally be beginning his job as official leader of a team investigating in the field. The butterflies began to whirl in his stomach and he felt his palms sweat.

Jitters, he thought to himself. *That's all it is. Snap out of it.*

He turned and walked to his office at the end of the hall when his notebook chimed. He pulled it out and saw the file Boatman had warned was coming had arrived. He ran his fingers across the notebook and the file opened. Daniel studied the name at the header of the file: Terry Lyons. His first Special. Daniel scrolled through the file with a brush of his finger reading it with a growing scrutiny at the bizarre case he was watching unravel page by page.

Damn, thought Daniel, *this looks more like fraud than Special activity. Boatman, what are you playing at?*

CHAPTER 9

PRINCETON PARK PLACE KINGS

Daniel could sense the mood of his team. Their brooding moodiness hung in the air like a foul specter. Everywhere he looked another face as dour as the next and the way they stalked about the flat, pensive and fatigued it was as if they anticipated some moment of surprise—as though some drill-sergeant would burst in disturbing their rest with more military exercises.

Daniel was aware enough to see the writing on the wall. These endless training exercises were wearing on the men. His need to get them battle ready was creating a divide between him and the men. He would need to correct that, soon. Enough was enough.

With a heavy sigh, he made his way out to the kitchen to find Leonard sitting with Bradley and McCormack. Bradley and McCormack were the only ones who appeared fresh. Daniel knocked on the doorframe unnecessarily.

"Leonard," said Daniel, "I think it's time we had a break from the training. Have the team assemble in the flat."

"We're two men short, Dan." replied Leonard.

"That's fine," concluded Daniel. "Giordano and Sung are making progress. That's important. We'll do this without them, this time. But I'll be sure to include them in the future."

"Right," replied Leonard.

Leonard rose heavily and stalked out of the kitchen to gather what men there were still in the flat leaving Daniel alone with Bradley and McCormack.

"Not even winded, you two." said Daniel, unsurprised.

"Daniel," chided McCormack. "the training exercise hasn't been invented that we haven't already aced. You forget. We're Anchors."

"Right," said Daniel, nonplussed. "You should file out too."

"Right away, sir." said Bradley as he rose easily and walked past him.

McCormack patted Daniel affectionately on the shoulder as he passed and walked out into the hallway.

Daniel watched as they sauntered down the hall to the open space filled with computer terminals and an entertainment center. Daniel followed behind them out into the flat and found the team assembled and ornery. Their eyes were wary, untrusting. Daniel saw the same wariness in each set of eyes, from Leonard to Chad, to the bored expressions of Bradley and McCormack.

Daniel stood before them a moment to fully appreciate their trials before he spoke, measuring his words carefully.

Finally he took a step forward and folded his arms across his chest.

"I've put you through the paces the last few days." announced Daniel to the men. "You've all done admirably. You really have. So I decided that I'd take you guys out for a meal."

Chad blinked and traded a glance with Leonard and Bradley. McCormack looked over at Daniel skeptically.

"Where is this meal going to take place?" inquired McCormack.

"Down the block." replied Daniel. "Get into your street clothes, guys. We're going for a walk."

Chad looked uncomfortable.

"You mean we're going out there?" said Chad, a note of discomfort in his voice.

"It's not so bad," replied Daniel, a trace of irritation in his voice for Chad's uneasiness.

Chad Beach was a man who could fight through a front line and inflict heavy casualties to the first wave of an assault making them think twice about advancing, yet he was nervous about walking down the street in a black neighborhood.

"I don't know," said Chad, thoughtfully. "Some of those guys look pretty tough."

"You're a Special," scoffed Daniel, as though intimidation was beyond the realm of possibility.

"I can still get intimidated by a look." wavered Chad. "I know I can win, but I still have to deal with that. Besides, I don't like conflict."

"Just stick close by me." replied Daniel, "You'll be fine."

"I'll stick close to Bradley," replied Chad.

"However you want it," scoffed Daniel irritably. "We'll meet down in the lobby in five minutes. Bundle up. It'll be cold."

Five minutes later, the team was standing in front of Daniel with heavy coats, jeans and boots.

"We ready?" asked Daniel, unnecessarily. The others nodded and grunted. "Alright, let's go!"

With that, Daniel turned and threw the lobby door open and stepped out into the ice-cold wind, turning left and marching down Georgia Avenue, the others following behind him.

Instantly, they drew attention. With Daniel in the lead, he nodded and greeted the storeowners as he passed, while the normally cordial business owners now turned cold and studied the new faces. Chad recoiled from the faces, and huddled closer to Bradley, until he caught sight of Bradley's apprehension to the cold faces and quickly hurried up to keep step with Daniel and Leonard.

McCormack walked like a priest next to Bradley, seemingly carrying on a silent conversation. From Bradley's eyes, it was clear whatever they were saying to each other was full of worry over the possibility of conflict.

As they pressed deeper into the neighborhood, the faces grew more pronounced with apprehension and outright malice.

Daniel ignored the occasional question: "You lost, white boy?" and pressed on until finally he stood in front of the corner restaurant with the marquee reading "Charlie's."

"What is this place?" asked Chad warily.

"Charlie's," replied Daniel, as though the answer was obvious. "The best soul food this side of New Orleans." Then added, "Or so Charlie tells me. I discovered this place my first week here."

"So this is where you disappear to?" said Leonard with a grin.

"It's better than the fast food we get shipped out to us," replied Daniel, as he pushed open the door and stepped in out of the cold. Leonard and the others followed him into the warmth of the restaurant and they all rubbed their hands together and stomped the slush from their feet on the welcome mat before daring step into the restaurant proper. Out of the darkest corner, a figure loomed in the shadow, and a Cheshire grin stretched his face as he stepped out into the warm light of the restaurant.

"Daniel," called Charlie, affectionately, "I didn't think I'd see your ass back here, again."

"What, and miss out on the ox tails and collard greens?" said Daniel, grinning. "Or maybe catfish on wonder bread?"

"You know," chuckled Charlie, "one of these days you're going to have to tell me how a white boy got so down."

"You can't live in Bed-Stuy without being intimate with Soul Food, Charlie. I thought you knew."

"Right, right," chuckled Charlie. "So you brought your friends, I see?"

"Yeah," chuckled Daniel. "Hey Charlie, can we have a quiet spot to sit?"

"Funny," grinned Charlie, "I have just the spot."

Charlie led Daniel and the others to a table at the far end of the room. There, sequestered in the semidarkness of the blinds drawn over the windows, Daniel and the others took their seats at a long table like a mafia family meeting for business with their backs to the wall and a commanding view of the restaurant. Leonard surveyed the room and nodded with pursed lips.

"This is a nice place," said Leonard, approvingly.

"Wait until you try the food," replied Daniel.

"That good?" replied McCormack.

"You're just going to have to trust me," replied Daniel.

"Fair enough," said McCormack.

McCormack and Bradley sat there curiously examining the restaurant, while Chad and Leonard pored over the menu. Charlie came over and pulled up an extra chair.

With a keen eye, he studied their faces until his eyes fell on Chad's innocent expression.

"You must be one of Daniel's friends," inquired Charlie with a grin.

Chad stammered for an instant unsure how to answer, until finally he said "Yes, sir."

"Well," replied Charlie, and he extended his hand across the table to Chad. "Any friend of Daniel's a friend of mine. I'm Charlie."

"Chad Beach," answered Chad at once.

"Well," teased Charlie, "that's a white boy's name if I ever heard one." And a flame in his cornea began dancing. "So, what do you do?"

"I'm on a federally funded task force that polices-"

Daniel jumped and slapped the side of Chad Beach's head.

"Chad," interrupted Daniel.

"Sir?" replied Chad, jerking to attention in his seat.

"You can shut up now," answered Daniel.

Chad blushed and his eyes fell to his menu.

"Yes, sir," said Chad.

Charlie chuckled, and scanned the table, looking over at Leonard, now. McCormack leaned forward and smiled, though his eyes were critical.

"You seem like someone who likes to talk," said McCormack, cagily.

Charlie rallied and focused on McCormack.

"Oh, I'm the guy to talk to about many things."

"Ol' Charlie here," said Daniel, "he's a celebrity in the neighborhood."

"I'll bet he is," whispered McCormack, not breaking eye contact with Charlie. "Tell me, Charlie, have you ever served in the military?"

"Me? Back in my day I was one of *the few and the proud*. But tell me, what about you?"

"Me? I'm a veteran of the Sol War. But that shouldn't mean anything to you, I guess."

Charlie appeared nonplussed and studied the faces at the table.

"I take it all of you are Sol War veterans?"

"What makes you think that?" replied McCormack, leaning forward, his eyes wide open.

"No reason, no reason," backpedaled Charlie, rubbing his chin, "But everybody's got a history."

"That's true," replied McCormack, his eyes boring into Charlie's, "Everyone does."

McCormack's eyes grew cold and his jaw set.

At that moment, Charlie swayed in his seat looking dizzy and touched his ear. He held his finger up to his eyes and examined a drop of blood on his fingertip, then looked up in shock at McCormack. McCormack tapped his temple and shook his head.

"Your friend, Ol' Charlie," said McCormack. "It turns out he's a Special."

Everyone looked up from McCormack to Charlie.

"Telepath," concluded McCormack, "Low-level from the looks of it."

Charlie rallied quickly, with a chuckle.

"Okay, you got me. I'm a Special. Just like everyone at this table."

"I don't know what you're talking about, Charlie." replied Daniel with a wry grin.

"How did you avoid the draft?" demanded McCormack.

"I didn't advertise my gift," replied Charlie. "I kept it as a sort of private joke. Besides, I'm a little too old to be drafted and my gift ain't that much use on the battlefield. Unless you want to find out what the enemy had for breakfast."

Charlie's eyes grew excited, and he turned in an effort to catch Chad's eyes, though Chad pretended to be engrossed by the menu, trying his best to avoid eye contact. Charlie then turned and saw Leonard was glaring dead at him. He turned and smiled at Leonard.

"So you're all Specials?" rallied Charlie. "What are your gifts?"

Then his eyes became focused and the light danced in the cornea. McCormack turned to Bradley.

"That'll be enough of that," concluded Bradley, his voice echoing in their minds.

Charlie's head jerked back and his hands flew up to his temples as though he was trying to keep his brain from exploding. A moment later he shot a malevolent glance at Bradley who leaned back in his chair. McCormack patted Bradley on the back, as if to say *"down boy."*

"It's polite to wait for someone to decide to tell you a secret," said McCormack.

"My bad," muttered Charlie, rubbing his temples. Charlie was put off by McCormack and sulked for a moment until he noticed the moods of the Specials at the table were growing pensive. Charlie quickly rallied with a winning smile, and the room spun back into his favor. "So who wants collard greens and ox tails?"

Daniel raised his hand.

"Oh," exclaimed Daniel, "you know I'll have that."

"Let me go get the order in," concluded Charlie.

With that, Charlie rose from the table on shaky legs for a moment, then straightened and walked back toward the kitchen as the door opened and a group of five rough looking men entered the establishment. The man leading them would have been handsome if he had not worn a hateful stare and a perpetual snarl. He led the men into the restaurant and approached Tamika, who stood with her back to the door.

"Hey, sweet thing," said the man with the malevolent eyes. Tamika ignored him, pressing her focus down on the pad she wrote down orders on. "Hey girl!" Tamika ignored them, seemingly praying they would give up and leave.

Finally the lead man seized Tamika by the arm and yanked her to him. "Hey, I'm talkin' to you!"

"Oh no you didn't!" shouted Charlie, storming out of the kitchen. "I won't have this foolishness in my restaurant! Get out!"

The lead man held onto Tamika's arm and grinned at Charlie, as though he were a prize. With a gesture of his hands, the others surrounded Charlie. The lead man stared down Charlie and stepped within inches of him.

"So, I hear you've been talking shit, old man." The men gathered closer around Charlie.

"Leave my grandpa alone, Chris," screamed Tamika, and tried to push the lead man away from Charlie. Chris reacted instantly, seizing Tamika by the hair and pulling her head to an awkward angle, shaking it violently.

"Oh, now you know me?" demanded Chris. "A second ago you didn't have time for me until I put my hands on you, but now you know me?"

Charlie grabbed Chris by the shirt and raised his fist.

"Leave my granddaughter alone and get out!" bellowed Charlie who was instantly seized by the others and restrained, slapped by several men. Charlie's eyes were wild as a froth built in his mouth. Chad looked over at Leonard, who waved him down. Chad turned to watching in horror as Chris's men manhandled Charlie and Tamika.

"What the fuck are you going to do about it, old man?" demanded Chris. "You can't do shit. Now get me some catfish and collard greens and all the money in the register. You old timers still deal in cash so I know you got money. And come to think of it, Tamika here is too fine to be working in a restaurant, so I'm going to do you a solid and take her off your hands. I can make money with that ass."

Finally, Daniel could take no more. He turned to the others and eyed them critically.

"No one does anything," commanded Daniel.

McCormack pursed his lips and then acquiesced with a nod, and the others nodded begrudgingly.

Daniel rose and walked up behind the tallest man, and tapped him on the shoulder, hard. The man jumped to see Daniel and instantly rounded on him. Daniel put him in an arm bar and applied pressure. The man winced and crumpled under the twisting of joints and Chris pushed through his own men to get to Daniel.

"Oh," exclaimed Chris. "I know this white boy's done lost his mind!"

Daniel twisted the man's arm harder.

"No, we're just talking." Daniel leaned down to the tall man's ear. "Isn't that right?"

Chris stood there nonplussed, taking in Daniel as a possible threat, and grew calmer.

"Talking, huh?" scoffed Chris. "Do you know who the fuck I am?"

Daniel pushed the tall man away and wheeled around on Chris.

"No," rounded Daniel, "tell me. Who the fuck are you?"

"Chris, don't!" begged Tamika.

In the back of Daniel's mind, a memory of Charlie explaining the tragic story of the neighborhood's history, and the source of his frustration being embodied by the elusive Chris.

"Oh, you're the Chris I've been hearing so much about?"

"PPK, baby," sang Chris with a malevolent grin, "Princeton Park Kings. You don't know who you're fucking with."

"No," challenged Daniel, "tell me, who am I fucking with?"

"You don't want none of me, white boy." threatened Chris, "I'm too much for you. I suggest you get the fuck out of my neighborhood. Why don't you take your ass back to Capitol Hill. Take some pictures and mind your own fucking business. I got business with this old assed man right here."

"Charlie's a friend." replied Daniel. "You got beef with him, take it up with me."

"Oh, I'll take up more than beef with you, boo." replied Chris, coolly. "I'll have that white ass turning tricks in a minute."

"You want to sample me before you pass my ass around?" challenged Daniel, "I'm right here."

Chris waved his hand and raised his voice.

"You got nothin'!" replied Chris, a decibel louder. "You breathe because I let you, bitch."

"And you eat solid foods because I let you," rounded Daniel.

Chris made an intricate gesture with his hands and the others nodded and began circling Daniel.

"No, wait!" called out Charlie with fear for Daniel in his eyes. "Why don't you tell me what you want, Chris?"

"I want this white boy's ass beat," replied Chris.

"Come get some," challenged Daniel.

"What?" scoffed Chris, in disbelief.

"See, you need your boys for me," replied Daniel. "I can see it clear as day. One on one, you don't stand a chance. Which is why you told your boys to attack me from behind. Bad mistake."

"What, you going to get all Jackie Chan with us? Is that it? You think you can roll?"

"I think I can drop you easy." concluded Daniel, then added "And I will, if you don't leave Charlie and his business, his customers, his family, his friends alone."

"What you got?" snarled Chris as he opened his jacket and showed the handle of his handgun to Daniel, "Nothing! Man, show this white boy what happens when a fool steps to Kings."

One of the men swung behind Daniel who heard the wind whip by the powerful swing. Daniel sidestepped, ducked and kicked wildly out behind him, taking the man off his feet to huddle on the ground. His next movement was into the man next to him, punching him in the abdomen while his left leg snapped against the other man's shin. Just then, Chris came up the middle and punched Daniel square in the jaw. Daniel hit Chris back, and Chris fell to the ground.

"I told you," taunted Daniel. "You can't take me without help."

Chris rose and pulled out the gun. Just then, the table next to him turned over and all of SITF was standing, eyeing Chris.

Chris looked over and recognized them as a threat, quickly pointing the gun at them.

"Oh," snarled Chris, "you want some of this too? I got something for all y'all!"

Just then, the gun exploded and the gunpowder and flecks of metal peppered Chris' hands and face as the bullets spilled out onto the floor. Chris hobbled against the wall in agony as Leonard stepped forward with a grin.

"That's okay," said Leonard. "We've got something for you. Chad?"

Chad rushed forward, grabbed two of the men, and threw them with such force they broke the drywall on the far wall. Bradley punched one and the sound of his jaw breaking seemed to echo through the room. McCormack swept his hand and it was as if a wind blew the remaining gang members into the wall where they crashed to the floor. Chris clutched his injured hand and rose, shouting at Daniel.

"Oh, you think you're bad?" railed Chris indignantly, his voice several decibels higher. "Don't you know who runs these streets? It's me! I run this motherfucker! You ain't shit next to me!"

Daniel grabbed Chris by the ear and yanked hard, slapping Chris hard across the face as he sent him spinning through the door onto the sidewalk outside. Leonard and Chad began throwing the rest of his crew out the door as though they were taking out the trash and left them in a pile outside the door. Daniel walked outside and knelt next to Chris.

"Remember what I said," said Daniel, mere inches from Chris' face. "This place and its people are protected. Anything happens to this place or anyone connected to it, when I hear about it, I promise you...I'll be running these streets by nightfall. You've never met anyone like me."

"Man, you're a cop!" spat Chris, knowingly. "I've seen you fools before. They either get bent or get dealt!"

"Well I ain't a cop." replied Daniel. "I'm the guy who does what he says and means what he says. And I'm telling you, I will dismantle your operation if anything happens to this place, these people or customers. I don't care if they buy a cup of coffee and walk out. They're protected. Got it?"

"Fuck you!" spat Chris.

Daniel backhanded Chris hard across the mouth.

"Watch your mouth when you talk to me."

Chris jumped to his feet, still favoring his right hand.

"You don't know what you done!" railed Chris, even louder than before, a froth building in his mouth. "You dead, man! I'm looking at a dead man!"

Daniel rose and went nose to nose with Chris, eyeing him coldly.

"I've been dying for years!" bellowed Daniel, "You think you can speed my clock? Come on up and try. But you'll be needing way more boys than the ones you brought. And I'm not some old man you can push around. I push back."

"You ain't shit!" railed Chris, walking backwards away from Daniel, his voice raising even louder the farther he stepped, "I'll be seeing you, white boy!"

"I'll be waiting, Chris." murmured Daniel.

Chris walked backwards down the sidewalk with his men shouting and flashing the gang signs P-P-K with his good hand until he cleared the corner. Leonard walked up to Daniel.

"Where do you think he's going?" asked Leonard ominously.

"The hospital, probably," replied McCormack. "That's a bad burn he's got."

Daniel turned to see Charlie standing in the doorway with a doomed expression.

"You okay, Charlie?" said Daniel, concerned.

"Boy," began Charlie forebodingly, "you shouldn't have done that."

"Come on, Charlie." said Daniel. "You looked like you needed the help. Tamika certainly needed it."

"You don't understand," said Charlie dismissively. "The Kings control the neighborhood. It's more than drugs and skin. They control trash take out. They control the delivery trucks. They control protection. Everybody pays. And everybody obeys. He doesn't have to touch me. He can just stop the delivery trucks and tell the grocery stores to not sell to me. If I'm lucky, he'll just raise the protection fee."

Daniel studied Charlie's defeated expression and instantly felt low.

"I'll make this right," said Daniel, apologetically.

"How?" scoffed Charlie. "You ain't a cop. And you roll with Specials. No cop is going to touch you."

"I still have some connections," replied Daniel.

"They'll just turn the neighborhood upside down again," replied Charlie knowingly, "We just recovered from that. We don't need it again."

"So what can I do?" asked Daniel, uncomfortably.

"Come back in and eat your food," said Charlie, somberly. "Get in out of the cold."

When they entered the restaurant, they were taken aback seeing the damage they caused. Broken drywall and burn marks on the wall and turned over tables. It looked like someone tossed a grenade in the room. Daniel felt a surge of guilt that welled up in his throat and threatened to close it off. He couldn't possibly think about eating, now.

"Look, Charlie." began Daniel, "We can pay for the damages, at least."

"No," said Charlie, emphatically as if his pride was hurt by the mere suggestion, and then cracked a smile to mask his dread filled expression. "I've been looking for an excuse to remodel anyway. Go on. Sit. Eat. It's the least I can do for you protecting my granddaughter."

Daniel and the others took their seats and sat there uncomfortably.

Tamika came out with the plates of food. Her hands shook as she set the plates down and she refused to make eye contact with any of them.

Dinner was a somber experience and they ate with their heads low over their plates. No one spoke. All that was heard was the sound of forks scraping plates and the occasional sighs of discomfort.

When they had finished, each of them pulled out whatever money they could spare and left a pile on the table as an apology. As Daniel and the others exited Charlie's, Charlie stepped out behind them and pulled Daniel aside.

"Watch your back. 'Cause you just painted a big ol' target on it."

"We'll be fine. No one's going to come calling for a while anyway. Besides, we're too busy with our work."

McCormack stopped and turned to Charlie.

"We may come calling on you, before long."

Charlie swallowed hard. A cold wind rose up and sent a chill down his spine. Charlie hugged his chest and watched

McCormack walk down the street slowly behind Daniel and the others.

"Damn…" scoffed Charlie, as a lump rose in his throat.

He was not a man accustomed to fear, but the stare of Tobias McCormack unsettled him.

CHAPTER 10

CHARIOT

B ack at the Post, Daniel and the others shuffled in like the walking wounded. It had been a successful day, for the most part, at the GhettoFab, and Daniel was looking forward to giving the good news to Boatman. He had just sat at his desk when the phone rang. Daniel knew out of hand it was Boatman, and he picked up the phone ready to give him the good news.

"Daniel," said Boatman, not waiting for him to even say 'Hello'. "I'll need you to be ready with the team in five minutes."

"Where we going?" said Daniel, cautiously.

"Joint Base Andrews Naval Air Facility."

"What's at Andrews Air Base?"

"Let's just say some new appropriations have come in and I have diverted a portion toward your transportation issue." replied Boatman cagily. His tone noted some annoyance. "It appears that the US Marshals don't want to transport your prisoners to the North Brother Island facility. You'll need to transport them yourselves. Given that, I have a gift for you. One I think you'll personally like."

"You've gotten us a transport?" blurted Daniel in disbelief.

"Yes." said Boatman simply. "Are you interested in seeing it?"

"We'll be outside in five." responded Daniel, already rising and preparing to hang up the phone.

"Good." replied Boatman, and the line disconnected.

With that, Daniel launched out of his office and down the hall catching Leonard in the kitchen.

"Leonard, I'll need the team up and ready in five minutes, down in the lobby. Boatman's got us a transport."

Leonard looked up from his hoagie and a rare smile played on his lips.

"Well, it's about time!"

Leonard rose to fetch the team.

Fifteen minutes later, the SUV raced through Maryland, to Prince George's County, eight miles east of Washington D.C. to the Joint Base Andrews Naval Air Facility. The Air Base was a 4,320-acre land, comprised of an airstrip, control tower, dozens of hangars and a large housing community for its 20,000 active duty military personnel, civilian employees and family members.

Driving through the streets, Daniel watched the children playing football in the street, running to the sidewalk to watch the caravan of SUV's pass, before running back out and reclaiming the street as their own. Farther down the street, children stood in somber silence around a broken window with a baseball size hole in it—the boy with the bat looked frightened and studied his friend's faces as if to gauge how much trouble he was in by the widening of their eyes. Daniel smiled. Seeing this bit of Americana in dire contrast to the tension of the neighborhood surrounding the Post was a welcome sight.

Finally, the SUV passed the housing community, leaving it behind as they pressed into the industrial section of Andrews. Cold postmodern buildings no larger than five stories dotted the landscape like well placed board pieces with large parking lots joining them together. And beyond that, hangars stood in a row next to the road leading to the airstrip. Security was tight, here. Everywhere Daniel looked, military police presence was found. Daniel knew their job function only too well: Protect the secret projects being worked on in the buildings and hangars. Daniel turned to the driver.

"How long until we get there?" demanded Daniel, anxiously.

"We're just up here, sir." replied the driver.

"Good." replied Daniel to no one in particular, "I need to stretch my legs."

The SUV pulled in front of a hangar with a sign over it. It read: ANDREWS WIZARDS.

Daniel studied the sign for a moment and smirked.

"What is Boatman up to?" he thought.

Daniel stepped out of the SUV and took a few steps toward the hangar, admiring the magical implications of the declaration the sign made and wondered what this new turn had in store. McCormack and Bradley walked up to Daniel and gestured toward the hangar doors.

"Shall we get on with it?" said McCormack.

"Let's," replied Daniel, and walked through the hangar bay doors.

Inside, the working space yawned open to reveal a long concrete floor with a sheet metal ceiling. Throughout the hangar, workers busied themselves with large pieces of equipment that looked like science projects. Engineering feats were being accomplished here. It was clean and polished, and the engineers worked like car mechanics, unafraid to pick up a wrench and climb into their projects. Out from behind one of the projects stepped a tall, well built man with a thin notebook in his hands.

"You there!" he shouted.

Daniel stopped where he was and waited for the man to jog over to him.

"Where's your ID?"

Daniel reached into his pocket and produced his government identification. The man studied it for a second and then blinked.

"Oh, you're here early." said the well built man, "Malcolm Reynolds. I'll be with you to make sure you don't see anything you shouldn't."

Daniel looked around casually, before gesturing to Reynolds.

"Lead the way," replied Daniel.

With that, Reynolds turned and led them down the aisle between the projects down to the back of the hangar. Daniel and the others could not help but look back and forth from one project to another, out of overwhelming curiosity. They were met with the cold protective eyes of the engineers and workers. A few of the workers stepped out and blocked the path of their sight from the key components they worked on, offering challenging gestures and glares back at them as they moved on. Daniel scoffed.

"You'll have to forgive them," said Reynolds with a grin, "They take their jobs seriously. The words 'Top Secret' are big around here."

"I understand." replied Daniel, casually. "I'm just ready to see the project pertaining to us."

"Well, it's right here," replied Reynolds. "Just beyond these curtains."

Reynolds held apart the draping tarps and stepped aside to make way for Daniel and the others. Inside, the space was clean and functional. Steel platforms surrounded them like walls, and in the space, scrapped star fighters sat depressingly stripped of their innards. Reynolds looked straight ahead with a marveling gaze and gestured toward the chaos of the room.

"What do you think?" inquired Reynolds, proudly.

Daniel looked around the room and saw the stripped spacecraft and felt like an elephant next to a collection of elephant bones—somber, reflective. Finally, he looked at Reynolds.

"Is this where star fighters go to die?" scoffed Daniel.

"Funny," replied Reynolds, without mirth. "This is where they go to be reborn. I'd like to introduce you to the Phoenix Project."

Reynolds gestured to a ship in the center of the room, obscured by the metal frame erected around it like a protective cube. Daniel stood shocked by what he saw, his mouth agape.

"Is that what I think it is?" said Daniel, at last.

"Yes sir," chimed Reynolds, with a nostalgic reverence in his tone, "third generation Roman deep space fighter craft, modified to fly in atmospheric conditions."

The ship was both bulky and streamlined, all at once. The mad scientist mechanics had stripped the deep space fighter craft of all components that were deemed impractical for the Task Force's intents and purposes, and managed to reshape the oddly shaped craft into something almost animalistic. Daniel walked up to stare up at the craft from underneath.

"Where did you find it?" gasped Daniel.

"Don't rightly know that, sir," Reynolds responded, "We requested parts for the AFR-33's and we got half the order, plus this monster, and four other craft; a Reever, a Black Arrow, a Sioux, and a Harrier, if you can believe it."

Daniel blinked and turned his head so fast he felt a crick in his neck. He ignored it out of excitement.

"You've got a Black Arrow in the hangar?" said Daniel, like a child at an air show.

"We've got some of the parts in there, sir." replied Reynolds. "Along with the console systems from an AB-4 for atmospheric flight."

"You put an AB con in the helm?" blinked Daniel, eyeing the craft with disgust.

Reynolds chuckled and rubbed his chin.

"Yeah, it seemed sacrilegious to us, too." replied Reynolds sympathetically. "But the General's orders were very explicit. Make a craft that would do the job and do it well. A Roman would fall out of the sky like a stone in the atmosphere."

"Yeah, I know," scoffed Daniel, still reeling in his amazement over what Reynolds' team had accomplished. "How'd you get it to fly?"

"That's where the Black Arrow and Reever parts came into play.

Daniel's eyes pored over the craft, seeing the outline of a dragonfly intermixed with the look of a jungle cat in sphinx-like repose. It was as if the beast was cut down the middle to make room for the massive dragonfly, clearly a Sioux frame, to be laid down the center, occupying the role of the spine. As Daniel stepped around the craft, the segments became quite practical—where the hind legs was dedicated to engines and fuel, the forelegs were dedicated to weapons. The dragonfly spine was the power relays, connecting the four parts to the brain located at the helm.

Reynolds watched Daniel's eyes grow wide and a smile stretched his face. He *was* a kid at an air show. Reynolds leaned over to Daniel as though offering a little treat.

"You want to see inside, sir?" said Reynolds.

"Can I?" blinked Daniels, excitedly.

Reynolds pulled out his thin notebook and tapped his thumb on the glass screen face, which instantly illuminated. The side panel of the beast slid away, revealing the hull of the craft, and Daniel jumped at the sudden movement.

"You like it?" mused Reynolds knowingly, "I took the idea from the Iroquois and Blackhawk design. You could say we had fun trying to bring about the features in our girl, here."

Without a backward glance, Daniel climbed through the slide away door into the belly of the beast and was awe-struck by the lengths the mechanics had gone to, marveling at the ugly beauty of the craft. Beneath the helm were panels, clearly marked with stick-em notes, to mark which conduit connected to which relay; the blue to life support, the red to weapons, the gold to the battery and green to engines. A seasoned pilot familiar with the systems could, in effect, repair the ship in mid-flight. And a seasoned fighter pilot could reroute power at will to affect the outcome of a battle, limited to either success or death solely by their ability to outthink the ace pitting against them. As Daniel entered the cockpit, he was beside himself with the wonder and horror of seeing a state of the art fighter craft fit to more practical purposes—and at the same time being used so cruelly. The AB helm clearly did not belong in the craft, and seemed almost comical at how it jutted out as if it were a bus' bright yellow tire rim bolted to the marble floor of a luxurious palace for use as a coffee table.

For a moment, Daniel doubted Reynolds and his look told all. Reynolds merely smiled.

"Not to worry, sir." said Reynolds reassuringly, "We just installed the helm this morning. By the morning, it'll look right at home."

From behind them, a familiar voice echoed into the cockpit, bringing Daniel back to the realization he was not alone.

"What a piece of shit," said Stephen.

"She's beautiful," said Daniel to Reynolds, seeing the look of contempt on his face.

"Seriously," said Bradley. "This craft is far below the standards for our job description. If we're going to use a transport, could we at least get an AFR-16?"

"Now, that's a beautiful transport," replied Chad.

"No," replied Daniels, more to himself than to the men. "This is our baby."

Daniel ignored their protests, massaging the walls of the craft, with the affection of an aficionado praising the craftsmanship of a finely tuned hot rod, feeling every curve, gingerly, and he whispered to the walls, as though soothing a wild mustang.

"Don't listen to the bad men," cooed Daniel, "They just don't understand you. It's okay, girl."

"Since you and the inanimate object are now so close," chided McCormack, "have you decided what you're going to name it?"

"Oh," grinned Daniel, "she won't be inanimate for long. Besides, she's already got a name."

Daniel walked past his dissenting team and out of the hold onto the concrete floor of the hangar, where he turned and stepped to the front of the craft, approaching the section where the grease had smeared—obscuring the vibrant orange and yellow symbol and the warm red words outlined in black—marred by carbon scarring due to plasma and electromagnetic pulse blasts and flack. Daniel took his hand and wiped across the grease and grime to reveal the design and words underneath. The words were only hardly clear with the hand streak clearing most of the grease out of the way. Only one word was marginally unhindered by the burns and damage.

Chario.........t.......s

Chad stared at the writing, letting his eyes go out of focus to see if he could pick out what Daniel was seeing. His reward was a migraine, and he quickly pinched his nose and shut his eyes.

"I got nothing," said Chad, rubbing his eyes.

"Reynolds?" said Daniel.

"Sir," replied Reynolds.

"Clean this up as best you can and make sure 'Chariot' reads clearly."

"Right away, sir." replied Reynolds with a grin.

"And by the way," added Daniel, "She's beautiful."

"Thank you, sir," chimed Reynolds with pride and shot a disgusted look at the Specials for daring to impugn both the craft and his skill as a master engineer. He turned to Daniel and nodded knowingly. "She'll fly true. Rest assured."

"No doubt in my mind," replied Daniel.

With that small bit of praise, Reynolds walked off at a quick step and flagged down some men to fetch paint and prepare a laser writer to be brought down from Polishing to put the finishing touches on what would be the "Chariot."

Outside the hangar, Chad and Stephen rounded on Daniel.

"You can't be serious!" started Chad.

"Did you even see that piece of shit?" demanded Stephen.

"That's enough," snapped Daniel. "She's our transport. Get used to it."

"I've never seen a transport that ugly," blurted Josh. "We're seriously going to be flying in it? It'll fall apart on us! I didn't sign up on this team to die in flight."

"Then go back to Costco," replied Daniel. "I'm sure they'll have work for you."

Daniel turned and walked back to the SUV leaving Joshua standing there stunned. Finally Josh scoffed and followed Daniel to the SUV.

"I'm not going back to Costco," concluded Josh, at last.

Chad, Stephen and Josh followed behind Bradley, McCormack, and Daniel across the spans from the SUVs to the Lobby doors of the Post. Daniel had this natural ability to part the onlooking crowd with a gesture and a wave of his hand that would have made Moses proud.

Josh was still fuming from the Costco comment and his ears were burning, though he admitted silently that could just be from the cold D.C. winter.

Inside the lobby, Daniel made a sharp turn away from the elevator and manned the stairs taking the steps two at a time. The others followed in silence as they climbed the steps to the third floor flat.

One of these days, thought Daniel, *I'm going to drown that elevator in Lemon Pledge and bleach until the smell goes away.*

"I'm way ahead of you," scoffed Bradley.

"What, you reading my mind?"

"You're projecting your thoughts." answered McCormack. "It's not hard. It just gives me a little headache."

"Well," replied Daniel. "One of these days you two are going to have to teach me how to block out my thoughts."

"Well, it's easier when you let your mind go blank." replied McCormack.

"So when I have my own personal dialogue, I'm open to be probed?"

"Not really." answered Bradley. "Like I don't know your exact words you say in your head. I just feel your contempt for the smell in the elevator."

"This whole building needs a bath." spat Daniel scathingly.

"That's why I don't bring my dates back to the Post," replied Bradley.

"Oh," chided Leonard. "Is that the only reason?"

"Well come on," pressed Bradley, "if I have a room and it's my room, why can't I entertain guests?"

"Define 'guests,'" said Leonard pointedly.

Bradley looked over his shoulder and rolled his eyes at Leonard.

"Knock it off you two," said McCormack, warningly.

"Look," said Daniel, flatly, "your rooms are your rooms. If you meet a pretty girl and she's down, by all means, use the flat. As long as you separate the business from the personal, you can use your rooms as you see fit. This isn't boot camp."

"So you mean," said Josh, tentatively, "we could bring dates up to the Post?"

"Hell, I don't care," replied Daniel, "As long as it doesn't interfere with our job and training, I say go for it!"

"That's all well and good, Daniel," replied McCormack. "But I think you should be clearing that with Boatman."

"I'm not looking for warrior monks," said Daniel dismissively, "I can deal with a team that leads their lives off duty."

McCormack shook his head in disappointment. Bradley nodded his appreciation, but his chin nudged just a little bit of a *"no"* warning Daniel to let the matter drop out of hand. Leonard grit his teeth with frustration and Josh and Stephen high fived each other, with full expectancy to test Daniel's words at the first possible chance. Chad put his head down, his eyes heavy.

The thought of girls was something Chad had not had time to think about, and the thought only depressed him. He knew he would have to remedy that—with or without the consent of his team leader—as soon as possible. The thought frustrated him, leaving him isolated between his job and his heart. Both were important to define himself, but he suspected between the two, one would have to give. McCormack seemed to look right at him. And soon, Bradley looked warily after him.

Daniel was oblivious to all this as he entered the Post, and left his men in the flat as he headed down the hallway, into his office and sat down at his desk. His computer terminal flashed when he put his hand on it, scanning his fingerprints and then blinking to life.

//Good evening, Daniel\\

Daniel read through the emails scanning through them like so much clutter until he found one from JJRTC. Curiously he clicked on the email and the contents caused his heart to leap in his chest.

SPECIAL AGENT IN CHARGE DANIEL HENRY ROOKE, SPECIALS INVESTIGATIONS TASK FORCE... THIS EMAIL IS TO INFORM YOU A SLOT HAS BEEN FILED FOR USE OF THE GHETTOFAB TRAINING CENTER BY LAWRENCE BOATMAN BETWEEN SITF AND SPECIAL INVESTIGATIONS EMERGENCY SERVICES UNIT AT 10:30AM....SINCERELY, AGENT HENDRICK MORROW, US SECRET SERVICE, JAMES J. ROWLEY TRAINING CENTER

Daniel leaned back from the email startled. Boatman was finally pitting his team against a viable threat for assessment of battle readiness. This could either be the greatest favor he paid or the greatest chance for public embarrassment he had been presented with. Either way, he could not refuse this boon. There was too much he could learn from this exercise. He couldn't give that experience up, and would not be deterred by the butterflies churning and warring in his stomach. He would own this. With a barely contained glee, he rose from his desk and left his office to tell his team the "good news."

CHAPTER 11

SCRIMMAGE WITH BLACK OPS

JJRTC-GHETTOFAB

Daniel stepped out of the SUV and smelled the air fresh from the rain. The sun was high in the sky, breaking free from the clouds and worked feverishly to evaporate the water that clung to the tarmac and GhettoFab structure. He strolled through the pavilion toward the GhettoFab, anxious to find what was in store for the day's scrimmage. In the distance, Lawrence Boatman stood huddled with a team that would take control of the GhettoFab for the scrimmage.

Boatman turned at the sound of the SUV's brakes, grimaced as he recognized Daniel in the distance and left the team standing there in their lazy huddle. He walked grimly, yet Daniel sensed an anticipation in the old man's eyes. At last, Boatman reached Daniel and grimaced.

"Rooke," Boatman began, "I hope you know how difficult it was to put this little scrimmage together."

"I can appreciate the difficulties in uniting a visible team with a Black Ops team, of course."

"Not Black Ops," corrected Boatman, sternly. "My Specials Emergency Service team is not some group of black bagger thugs."

"Whatever."

"You're trying my patience Rooke," growled Boatman. "It took a great deal of assurance to persuade my colleagues to allow these two teams to so much as breathe the same air."

"Look," answered Daniel, "you're just as curious about what happens as we are. And don't tell me you aren't going to record the scrimmage, either."

Boatman's eyes flashed cunningly.

"Of course I'm going to record it."

"And I'd like to see the results of the video feed." said Daniel.

"No video."

"Then how do you plan to record this?"

Boatman beckoned Daniel to follow him and turned, making his way toward the tarp that hung over the fold out tables. A Secret Service agent stood inside, apparently waiting for Boatman's commands. Boatman turned with a grin and waved his hand over a case of metallic balls sitting in neat rows. Boatman held one out for Daniel to observe up close.

"Rooke, I'd like to introduce you to the Joint Unmanned Combat Operating system. You might have been familiar with it during the war?"

Daniel studied the softball sized metal object with a sense of awe and skepticism.

"I knew you had JUNCO's standing guard around the battleships during the war. But that's a hell of a lot smaller than any JUNCO I'm familiar with."

"It's a new technology," replied Boatman, "reverse engineered from Quill machinery. It was in use by the middle of the war as assistance for the Specials teams fighting on the front."

"That looks like a drone, to me."

"A drone implies someone with a remote control would be operating it. As I said, this is unmanned—as in *man has nothing to do with it*. It is a marvelous piece of technology that allows for a 'freethinking' machine to dedicate itself to the purpose of protecting its 'master' through a proximity attack/defense protocol." Boatman reached into the case and pulled out a harness. "During the war, Specials wore these bandoliers with four or five JUNCOs on them. The bandoliers acted as a master marker. The JUNCOs would float close by, analyze enemy movement and fire on their positions as they appeared. If the enemy got too close, the JUNCOs would act as grenades and detonate. The bandoliers hindered their wanderings, keeping them close to the master marker. Say, five feet. *These* JUNCOs will have a wider net than that."

"And it also records?"

"Precisely."

"So these things will be flying around recording the movement of both teams?"

"Yes."

"I want bandoliers for my team." said Daniel. "I want the recordings up close and personal. I need to see how they perform in this scenario."

"I believe we're thinking along the same lines."

Boatman looked over at a Secret Service agent and gave him a nod. The agent nodded and turned, exiting the tarp out into the sun and disappeared around the side of the GhettoFab.

"So I wouldn't have gotten this if I hadn't asked for it?"

"You're responsible for your own team. I have to look after my own."

"So that team is yours?"

"Your team is not my sole responsibility, Rooke," answered Boatman, rather coarsely. "It will rise or fall depending solely on your ability to evaluate and command."

"Right," scoffed Daniel.

"Don't pout." reprimanded Boatman. "Your wish may not be my every command, but I will provide. Have I failed in any respect to supply in answer to your requests?"

Just then, the Secret Service agent appeared around the side of the GhettoFab carrying a heavy looking suitcase. He seemed to lean into the case as he walked with a painful looking arch of the spine. Within moments, he was beneath the tarp again, and placed the suitcase on the foldout table with a clatter and a heavy sigh. Daniel quickly walked up and threw open the case which folded open to reveal several bandoliers and a series of JUNCOs resting in soft divots at the bottom of the case. He studied the units closely, noticing eight lenses surrounding the devices with what looked like the multifaceted eyes of bees. In between the "eyes" were ports, which Daniel surmised were the weapons systems. He held one of the JUNCOs in his hand and tested the weight of it in his palm, feeling the almost circular shape with his fingers like a blind man.

"And these things float?" said Daniel, skeptically.

"They generate EM fields that allow them to float and move about," answered Boatman. "Yes."

"How fast are these things?"

"They can travel as fast as the master in most cases. The JUNKOs don't work well with speedsters, however. And there's a catch. If they float outside the proximity of the master, they arm and detonate."

"So what's to keep these from detonating?"

"I've set up master towers around the GhettoFab to keep them from getting confused," said Boatman. "However, just in case, I've had the weapons systems deactivated on the JUNCOs. This is going to be a test of wills between two teams, not a pitting of technologies against each other."

"Good to know."

"Yes, it is," answered Boatman, grimly. "You should know how pivotal the introduction of JUNCOs into the battlefield really was. Being a Special did not make them invulnerable, but the army with the bandoliers becomes unstoppable. It's an edge sought by many."

"I want it," said Daniel, quickly.

"I thought you might," said Boatman, his eyes scrutinizing. "For now, you'll have to settle for them acting as an impartial observer."

"As long as I get them," answered Daniel.

Just then, two SUVs pulled up and came to a halt at the edge of the pavilion. The car doors opened and out stepped Stephen Giordano, Joshua Sung, Leonard Stonebreaker, Chad Beach, Bradley Overman and Tobias McCormack. Boatman patted Daniel on the shoulder.

"I'll leave you to speak with your team, then."

Boatman walked away with a grim sense of purpose and his team of Specials turned to face him as he approached. Daniel turned away and walked up the pavilion and met his SITF team halfway.

"Good morning, men," said Daniel, grinning with anticipation.

"Good morning, Agent Rooke," replied McCormack. "Is that the team we're going up against?"

"That's a fact," replied Daniel. "You recognize any of them?"

"You could say that," replied Leonard.

"From the looks on your faces," concluded Daniel, "I can see this won't be a walk in the park."

"No," answered Leonard.

Daniel looked up and saw the clouds swallow the sun, and a light mist of rain fell.

"Let's get some cover," said Daniel.

Daniel led them to the tarp and ducked his head underneath it walking directly to the suitcase filled with bandoliers and JUNCOs. Leonard took one look and grimaced.

"I haven't seen those in a while," said Leonard, apprehensively.

"Yeah, well I just got introduced to them just now. Since you know all about them, I won't go through the trouble of telling you about them, just that you are to wear these during the scrimmage and that they will be recording your every move inside the GhettoFab. Got it?"

"Yes, sir." answered the team. McCormack merely nodded.

A chime alerted Daniel his notepad had just been updated and he pulled it out and began running his finger down the page.

"Alright," began Daniel, as he tapped on his notepad. "Our mission is to enter the premises and arrest and detain seven Specials. Assume they won't go lightly, and prepare for close quarters combat. Dossiers are being uploaded to your notepads as we speak."

Within an instant, the chiming of several notepads alerted the team and they pored over the dossiers on their notebooks with looks of consternation.

"John Simpson-call sign Death—Can create radiation and release it from his pores." said Leonard, in a monotone.

"Laurence Kelson-call sign Warhead—Has the ability to explode."

"So does Kip Harris-call sign Ground Zero." added Bradley. "His explosions generate fire. Then there's Paul Hirano-call sign Ground Shaker. We'll have to take him and Simpson out fast. These others are fighters. Randal Simms, Francis Tibbs and Gregory Meyer. They shouldn't be too much of a problem."

Daniel looked down at his notebook and read through their dossiers his frown becoming more pronounced with each page he scrolled through. Not one of the men was under 6'4." Randall Simms, callsign Scrape was a borderline Abnormal Special—his massive strength and speed comparable to a bull's. Francis Tibbs, callsign Primal. His picture showed broad-chested man with severe red eyes and a grin that showed his filed needlepoint teeth. And Gregory Meyer, callsign Uproar, whose massive frame can swell into even more powerful musculature. These were to goons on the "Specials Emergency Services" team. Daniel could have cared less what they were called, the whole team reeked of Black Ops.

"Take nothing for granted," concluded Daniel, "Your job is to arrest. Their job is to evade you or wipe you out. Also, take into consideration they've had all morning to study the GhettoFab. Assume they know it like the back of their hand, and they're going to use it to their advantage. Now here's what I want. I want Leonard to lead a standard breach by sneaking along the wall to the entry gate. Use Josh and Stephen as back up—and I want Chad in the rear covering everyone. I want Tobias and Bradley taking the roof. They'll have snipers set up, it's what I'd do. I want to deprive them of their high ground superiority. Any questions?" The team stared back at him, visibly gearing up for combat with deep breaths and stern eyes, alerting Daniel that there were no questions, and even more, they were ready. "Everyone step forward and take one bandolier and one JUNCO each."

The team gathered around the case and began strapping on the bandoliers, palming the JUNCOs and fitting them on their harnesses.

Across the quad, Boatman stood with the Black Ops team speaking to them in huddled whispers.

"What do you think, sir?" asked Paul Hirano.

"They're trained," concluded Boatman, "but they don't work well as a team, yet. Exploit that."

"Yes, sir!" replied Hirano.

"Don't let them near the building," said Boatman, "This is your territory. Protect it."

"Yes, General," replied the men.

"Take your positions," commanded Boatman. "And give them hell."

"Yes General!" replied the men.

Boatman walked away from them and they turned and filed into the GhettoFab. Daniel studied Boatman suspiciously.

"What was that all about?" inquired Daniel.

"Never you mind." answered Boatman. "Worry about your own team."

"I thought they were both your teams." replied Daniel cagily, adding "You showing favoritism?"

"As I said," grinned Boatman, "Worry about your own team."

Daniel looked over at the paramedics leaning against their truck and looked back at the GhettoFab suspiciously. Boatman climbed into the trailer next to the tarp and beckoned Daniel to follow him. Daniel climbed up the steps into the trailer and found Boatman seating himself before a wall dedicated to perspectives—each perspective moving into a different area and stationing at key points. And

Daniel understood. The black ops team had taken their positions.

Daniel donned his headpiece and spoke into the com. "Activate JUNCOs."

Each of them depressed their thumbs into the touch screen on their bandoliers, and the JUNCOs illuminated and rose off their harnesses hovering close by, moving like insects in the air. In the trailer Daniel watched the screen dance and multiply in perspectives until every SITF team-member was accountable on the wall.

"Alright Leonard. Lead your men around to the north-east corner now."

Outside, Leonard nodded and with a wave of his hand, jogged across the asphalt to the northeast corner of the GhettoFab, the JUNCOs bobbing along behind them like little balloons tethered to their masters by invisible string.

Just then, the earth shook with a tremendous jolt and the asphalt and topsoil broke between Leonard's feet, and the team fell into a trench. A second wave crashed down around them, rattling their bones and sending spider-lined cracks up the wall of the GhettoFab.

Leonard rallied quickly, pulling everyone out of the newly formed trench, and pinning them against the wall. Above them, rifle fire cracked and the dirt around them exploded in fine puffs of powder.

"We're pinned down, here," said Leonard. "A little help would be nice."

Inside the trailer, Daniel ignored Boatman's comical expression and focused on the task at hand.

"Tobias, Bradley," said Daniel, lazily, "Anytime you're ready. Come out of the sun."

Outside, McCormack and Bradley launched into the air with blinding speed, soaring higher until they were in position above the GhettoFab. Down below on the rooftops, Two Specials stood there with rifles and Gel-Grenades.

McCormack and Bradley came down hard and fast, swooping down to the rooftop and engaged the two Specials. Bradley landed on Paul Hirano, who rolled and sent a shockwave at Bradley, blasting him off the roof. McCormack squared off with Laurence Kelson. Kelson tightened his hands into fists and an explosion emanated from his fists, pummeling McCormack's telekinetic shield. McCormack stood on the other side of the shield, unfazed. Kelson then directed the blast at McCormack's feet, and the roof collapsed. McCormack fell into the hole—to the third floor and the JUNCO followed him through the floor—down and out of sight.

"I'm okay," called McCormack over the radio, "but we've lost control of the roof. Leonard, move your men, now!"

Leonard turned and looked at his men.

"Alright," concluded Leonard. "If we can't make it to the main gate, we'll have to make a new one."

Leonard stepped away from the wall and turned to face it. With a powerful punch, his fist broke through the wall sending plaster and drywall everywhere. Leonard kicked the wall hard and the rest of the wall caved in with an impressive shower of shattered cinderblocks, making room for the team to enter the complex. Kelson and Paul Hirano watched as the SITF team entered the GhettoFab and ran back toward the fire escape, bolting down to the third level calling into their radios: "Reposition to beta posts!"

Hirano ran up to a support pillar and put his hands on it, sending a shockwave through the pillar down to the basement level and jumped back just in time as the pillar shattered, sending the northeast corner of the building collapsing inward on the SITF team on the first floor. Leonard and Chad dove through the debris, seeking stable ground, while Stephen and Joshua blasted the falling debris with their abilities, sending sawdust and drywall powder everywhere.

"Move!" bellowed Leonard.

Leonard and Chad jumped though a crumbling archway into a hallway and quickly scanned the area through their winvid visors seeing no movement. A cloud of dust and powder flooded through the archway and filled the corridor as a chalky colored Stephen and Joshua raced out in search of fresh air, finding only the cloud they had just escaped from and coughed and choked on the toxic powder. Leonard and Chad were also incapacitated by the cloud of drywall chalk and dust particles, and wiped at their winvid visors to clear their vision. Their JUNCOs spun like tops until their optics were cleared of dust and recorded chalky haze as it thinned in density to reveal the still dark corridor.

"Hallway clear." declared Leonard, "Chad, take point. Stephen, you support. Josh, you're with me. Move!"

With that, Chad charged down the corridor with Stephen hot on his heels, down to the joining hallways from the two wings of the complex. There Chad halted, and scanned the area with his winvid. He saw nothing. Then he caught the shadow of a JUNKO bobbing in front of him and quickly judged the angle from which it was coming. Quickly Chad surmised the assault party was somehow blocked from the winvid technology and that they were stationed down the left corridor. Chad signaled with his hand and pointed down the left corridor and Leonard nodded, coming up on the left with Sung in tow. Leonard signaled with his fingers, counting down from three, two, one and pointed with his index finger. Chad nodded and charged to the corner aiming his rifle around the corner.

"SITF, Freeze!" he shouted.

Chad blinked and noticed that a bandolier lay on the ground and the lost JUNCO floated there in place, faithful to the bodiless master. Chad then turned to scan the hallway to see an open window with a rifle pointed out at him. With a quick jump, Chad threw himself into the stairwell where he gripped the stairs above him and flung himself high to the second level where Lionel Johnson stood with a rifle pointed down the stairwell. Lionel jumped to see Chad seemingly materialize out of nowhere and fired wildly. Chad knelt down and fired two shots directly at Lionel's head, hitting him once in the face, the other shot clipping his ear. Lionel pursed his lips and sat down.

Down on the first level, Leonard crouched by the corner studying the bobbing shadow of the JUNCO.

"Leonard, there's a sniper in the apartment left of the JUNKO," called Chad over the radio.

"Got it," answered Leonard.

Leonard crept around the corner to see the hint of the muzzle of a rifle protruding from the window. Leonard crept without a sound, reached into the apartment window and yanked the rifle free. He then pointed his own rifle into the window and bellowed:

"SITF! GET DOWN ON THE FLOOR NOW!"

Inside, Gregory Meyer lunged through the window above Leonard's line of fire and gripped Leonard's face, clawing the winvid glasses from his face. Leonard, propelled himself backward to a lying position and fired upward toward the ceiling, pelting Meyer seven times in the chest and abdomen. Leonard rolled back to a kneeling position, his rifle trained on an infuriated Meyer, who examined his own riddled torso and scoffed, kicking at the floor before collapsing into a sitting position with disgust. Leonard took his finger off the trigger and put his winvid visor back on with a grin.

"Next time you play sniper, Greg," chided Leonard, "make sure the muzzle is inside the room."

"I'll keep that in mind" spat Meyer, "next time I see you, Stonebreaker."

Leonard chuckled to himself before calling: "Hallway clear!"

"Come up to the second level," said Chad over the radio, "I've got activity."

Leonard turned to Stephen and Joshua and waved them on to the stairwell. With a quick motion, Leonard picked up the discarded bandolier, claiming the free-floating JUNCO as his own.

Boatman watched as the perspective window for Gregory Meyer began moving again, leaving Meyer behind and entering the stairwell.

"What is he playing at?" rattled Boatman.

"I guess that's the thing about JUNCOs," chuckled Daniel. "They must respond to the one with the bandolier. Anyone can get one off a fallen man."

Boatman considered this as he watched Gregory Meyers' perspective move up the stairwell.

Up on the second level, Chad knelt in the doorway leading out onto the second floor hallway, his rifle in his shoulder as he peered out. Leonard put his hand on Chad's shoulder and pulled him back in. He then tossed the free bandolier into the hallway and the JUNCO floated at head height into the corridor, instantly painted blue. Leonard pursed his lips.

"They've got the second floor corridor covered." he said. "Any ideas?"

"I've got a Gel-Grenade." said Chad.

"Any other ideas?" scoffed Leonard.

"Leonard," called Daniel, over the radio, "I'm ordering the use of Grenades. Throw them into the hall."

"Yes, sir." called Leonard over the radio, not hiding his distaste for using them.

Chad braced with the Gel-Grenades at the doorway, waiting for Leonard to give the order.

"On three."

Leonard used his fingers to count down, and upon reaching one, leaned out into the hallway and fired down the corridor, the shots painting the wall at the far end while Chad jumped out and threw the Gel-Grenades with all his might at the far end of the hall where the corridor teed out. The Gel-Grenades collided with the wall explosively, filling it with blue from floor to ceiling, painting the walls with a thick coat. Leonard then led the team down the hallway to the joining hallway that crossed to yet another wing. At the corner, Leonard used his winvid to see a figure standing tensed five feet back from the corner.

"SITF!" bellowed Leonard. "Down on your belly and don't move!"

"Let's see how you like return fire!" shouted Kip Harris.

The ensuing explosion bent and contorted to the shape of the hallway and funneled out, billowing into the corridor around the corner. Leonard leapt back away from the curling flames and the others shielded themselves from the shockwave by pressing themselves to the wall. Leonard looked over at Josh.

"Sung," said Leonard, "You're up!"

"No," said Stephen, puffing up his chest, his aura crackling and burning. "I got this!"

Stephen stormed down the hallway and jumped around the corner to square off with Harris. Harris grinned.

"You think you got the stones to step to me?"

Stephen balled his hands into fists and his aura began to crackle and flare, like a building chain reaction. With a powerful thrust of his arms, a shockwave launched down at Harris, who launched another burst of flames down the hallway. The explosions met in the middle with disastrous results, melting the paint off the walls, scorching the carpet and blowing the doors off their hinges.

When the debris settled, Harris lay on his back, smoking. His ears bleeding.

"Yep," replied Stephen, staring down at Harris.

A cocky grin spread across Stephen's lips and he glared down at Harris' unconscious form. Stephen wasted no time in flipping Harris over and cuffing him.

"Kip Harris is out." announced Stephen.

"So are you," said a voice behind him.

Stephen looked up to see Randall Simms with a rifle pointed at his head. He fired once, before Stephen could react, and sent him onto his back. Leonard cleared the corner and fired once, striking Simms in the face.

"Scrape is down," said Leonard.

Simms looked up with disgust at Leonard and charged him, punching him in the face, sending them both tumbling through the hallway. Leonard quickly had Simms pinned to the wall by the throat and Simms clawed at Leonard, kicking and punching him.

Back in the trailer, Daniel grit his teeth at the exhibition playing out on six perspectives.

"Foul!" shouted Daniel, "Lawrence, control your man!"

"That will be enough of that, Randall," said Boatman, casually.

Up on the second level, Leonard had Simms pinned, some blood trickled from his mouth. He instantly went slack and grinned cockily at Leonard.

"Whatever you say, General." said Simms arrogantly, and grew limp smiling into Leonard's face. Leonard held Simms there, pinned to the wall. "You heard the General," chided Simms.

Leonard released Simms' throat.

"Move on." said Daniel from the control room. "I want this wing swept and cleared in fifty seconds."

"Sir!" answered Chad.

Chad led Josh down the hallway and Leonard turned away from Simms with disgust leaving him cackling in his wake.

Chad crept down the hallway, activating his winvid and peered through the walls to see a figure crouched down next to a fire escape around the corner. Chad held his hand up and Josh came to a halt behind him, sucking in his breath as he did so. Down the hall Franklin Wang crouched down, edging out into the hall with his rifle clearing the edge and taking aim. Chad grabbed Josh and threw him down as the gel pellets whizzed by.

"Thanks." said Josh.

"Don't mention it." answered Chad.

"You coming, or what?" taunted Wang.

Chad rose to a kneeling position and fired several rounds at the corner. All that was heard was the cackling laughter of Wang.

"Oh look, you're painting the walls," crooned Wang. "And I didn't even have to pick you up from Home Depot, either."

Leonard caught up with Chad and Josh, tapping Chad on the shoulder. Chad pointed down the hallway and Leonard activated his winvid—there Wang stood crouched against the wall, his rifle pointed around the corner.

"If this was a live ammo scrimmage we could just shoot through the walls," griped Leonard.

Leonard flipped a switch on his rifle setting it to fully automatic fire and riddled the wall and corner. Through his winvid, he saw Wang retreating to the fire escape and disappear behind the shielding of the stairwell.

"I want Chad on point," ordered Daniel over the radio. "Let's see how he leads."

"You heard the man," said Leonard. "Up and at 'em."

Chad swallowed hard and set his jaw, crouched down and proceeded down to the corner which he quickly swept and cleared. He then turned to the fire escape and kicked the door open. A thin wire snapped free holding a pin on end. Chad quickly jumped back from the wire and pin screaming "Grenade!" and fell backwards, away from the ensuing explosion of blue paint. Leonard came around the corner and stared down at Chad, quickly pursing his lips.

"Agent Rooke, Chad's down." said Leonard. "Proceeding on."

Chad looked down at his legs and took in the sight of his legs covered in blue paint. With a heavily exasperated sigh, Chad leaned his head back and shut his eyes fighting the wave of embarrassment. From the stairwell, Wang cackled maniacally.

Leonard looked up and grunted at the stairwell.

"Grenade..." Leonard demanded.

Josh walked over to Chad and took a Gel-Grenade off his belt, then turned leaving him lying stupidly on the floor and handed the Gel-Grenade to Leonard. Leonard set the Gel-Grenade for three seconds and then pulled the pin, counting as he stepped into the stairwell and threw the Gel-Grenade up to the third level. Overhead, the sound of a gasp and hurried footsteps marked Wang's recognition of the threat and his speed at retreating from the stairwell out onto the third floor hallway as the Gel-Grenade detonated. Blue paint rained down on the second floor landing and Leonard grit his teeth through the blue mist knowing his target evaded the worst of the explosion.

"Damn." scoffed Leonard. "Alright team, follow me. We will avenge Beach's 'death', alright?"

"Yes, sir." said Josh.

Chad watched in a sitting position as Leonard charged up the stairwell with Josh following in support capacity until they were all out of sight.

Up on the third landing, Leonard took possession of the top step and peered out into the hallway. Wang has paint covering his left arm. He smiled.

"I'm not dead yet!"

Wang fired at the doorway and Leonard threw out another Gel-Grenade. Wang's footsteps could be heard retreating from the Gel-Grenade. Leonard pointed his rifle out of the doorway and trailed after Wang, leading his movement in his rifle sights just a little bit and fired. The shot exploded directly in front of Wang who stopped, spun and fired back, as Leonard took cover in a doorway. Wang then turned and sprinted down the hallway disappearing around the corner.

"Come and get me, Stonebreaker!" bellowed Wang across the open hallway.

Leonard held up his arm and Josh came to a halt next to him.

"We're out of range here. He's drawing us into something. Sung double back the other way, take the bridge on the far end of the complex and wait for instructions."

Josh nodded and turned on his heels, racing down the corridor. All that was heard was his footsteps racing down the hall.

"Fury's coming your way, Josh. Heads up!"

On the far end of the complex, where the roof gave way to the walkway adjoining two complexes, Josh received the warning over the radio. "Roger that. I have the bridge."

Josh walked warily across the bridge staring down toward the darkness of the hallway on the far end. Above him, Francis Tibbs fired down on their location pock marking the bridge with blue paint. Josh turned and projected his energy blasts back up at the roof—blasting a section of rainwater gutter away—Tibbs quickly retreated.

"Sung, report!" ordered Daniel over the radio.

"I'm okay."

"What's your situation?" demanded Leonard over the radio. "How many unfriendlies?"

"Bloodcry."

"That's all?"

"That's all I saw."

"Damn it!" spat Leonard, "They have the high ground! Get into the cover of the hallway."

Josh nodded to himself and pressed across the bridge into corridor ahead and into darkness.

"They took out the lights." said Josh into the radio. "This feels like an ambush waiting to happen."

Josh braced himself and his aura began to hum and grow luminescent when the thought occurred to him that his aura could be used to track him. With a cooling sigh, his aura diminished in intensity to a low glow. He activated his winvid and scanned the hallway. Down the hall he saw a figure lurking around the corner.

"I've got Fury cornered." said Josh.

"Roger that," said Leonard. "Hold position and wait for orders."

"Roger that."

"Try to take Franklin Wang in for questioning." ordered Daniel over the radio. "We need intel to press further. I want to know why they're not using their heavy hitters."

"Yes sir," replied Leonard over the radio. The next instant, Josh heard Leonard Stonebreaker bellow clear as a bell down in the darkness of the corridor.

"Fury," shouted Leonard. "You're trapped. Throw down your weapon and lie flat down."

"Fuck you!" shouted Wang.

Wang fired down the hallway at Leonard. Leonard charged down the hallway and tackled Wang. Wang dropped his rifle and began fighting Leonard in hand-to-hand combat. Josh saw the scene unfold through his winvid visor and raced down the hall to intervene. The two quickly escalated into a full-fledged brawl. Wang threw Leonard against a wall and Josh blasted Wang so hard he bounced off the wall and lay on the ground unconscious.

"Fury's down," chimed Leonard dryly over the radio.

"Good." replied Daniel over the radio. "Find out where the rest of the Black Ops team is."

"Fury's not going to be able to help us. He's not conscious."

"Well slap him around! I want intel."

"Josh hit him a little hard. He's out cold."

"Alright, cuff him and move on. I need eyes on the roof. Paladin?"

"I'm busy right now." said McCormack dryly over the radio. His JUNCO monitor was obscured by dust and debris.

"Busy with what?" demanded Daniel.

Just then a shockwave shook the entire complex, throwing everyone around sending a cloud of debris wisping through the corridor.

"I'm engaging Paul Hirano." answered McCormack.

"Brad," called Daniel, "can I get some eyes on the roof?"

Everyone waited in silence for Bradley's reply, only to be shaken when a dark drawling voice clicked on the radio.

"Maximus can't hear you, Agent Rooke," said the voice. "He's not doing so well."

"Who is this?"

"This is John Simpson and Maximus is currently experiencing a wave of nausea. It's hard to focus your telekinetic shield when you're suffering from radiation exposure."

Leonard and Josh looked at each other as a sense of dread crept up their spines, making the hairs on the backs of their necks stand on end as the cruel voice mocked them over the radio.

"Seriously," said Simpson, his jovial voice mocking them, "if this is the best you can throw against me, you might as well call it in now. I can keep this up all day."

"Simpson, this is Leonard Stonebreaker. If Maximus is down, he'll follow the protocols."

"That's nice, Lenny. But I'm just having too much fun watching his hair fall out. But you're welcome to come up here and try and stop me."

Simpson clicked off the radio and Leonard grit his teeth at the silence, staring at Josh's wide eyes.

"Alright, kids," growled Leonard. "This just turned personal. Chad, Stephen… get up here."

"I'm on my way." chirped Stephen.

"Coming!" called Chad.

"Paladin?" said Leonard.

"I hear you." answered McCormack. "I'll be there in a minute."

"Roger that." acknowledged Leonard.

Down in the trailer, Daniel stood shocked watching the perspective belonging to Simpson stare down at a writhing Bradley, vomiting on the rooftop and collapsing in the puddle. Daniel cupped his microphone and glared at Boatman.

"Tell your man to stand down, Lawrence," demanded Daniel.

"If your team can't handle a Special threat in a training exercise," replied Boatman, coldly, "how do you expect them to deal with it in the field?"

Daniel stared at Boatman in shock, as though seeing him for the first time and not liking the view. With a scoff, he stripped off the headset and threw it at the viewscreen, making Boatman jump.

"I say-" began Boatman as Daniel pulled out his sidearm and racked a round in the chamber before reholstering it and turning to walk out of the trailer. "Where are you going?"

"My team needs me," replied Daniel over his shoulder.

Boatman followed Daniel out of the trailer.

"May I remind you your job is to give commands at a safe distance?"

"You can shove that directive." spat Daniel with a scowl.

"This is not a professional decision, Rooke." criticized Boatman, though an approving grin seemed to haunt the corner of his mouth making his mustache twitch.

"Neither is letting your man kill my man." spat Daniel.

Daniel sprinted across the wet field and into the GhettoFab, hurtling debris and vanished in the cloud of dust rising into the air.

On the third floor, Leonard broke out into the light of the bridge connecting the two complexes together and pointed his rifle skyward at the edge of the rooftop. Chad raced up and caught sight of Leonard.

"What's going on?" called Chad, looking nervous.

"We're going up there!" replied Leonard.

"What about the snipers?" said Chad.

"This scrimmage is over," replied Leonard. "Now it's a fight!"

"So it doesn't matter if we got shot?"

"I could care less."

Chad instantly flipped himself onto the rooftop like a bird, and Leonard led Stephen and Joshua to the ledge. Leonard flung himself to the lip of the rooftop and swung himself over to join Chad above. Stephen and Joshua had more trouble with scaling onto the roof than Chad or Leonard and Chad had to turn and help them up—once up on the rooftop they saw Leonard surveying the rooftop with his rifle sights. The rooftop was barren.

"Clear!" called Leonard.

Leonard raced off toward the ledge of the rooftop pointed to the higher rooftop in the distance, which claimed the highest ground. Leonard and Chad raced off while Stephen and Joshua trailed after them. Within fifty yards of the higher ground blue paint rained down around them. Chad was pelted on the leg by a blotch of blue paint.

"Someone thinks this is still a training exercise," scoffed Chad.

Francis Tibbs crouched down firing on their position, pelting Leonard and Chad in the chest laughing maniacally. Leonard and Chad ignored this and launched themselves into the air onto the rooftop in front of Tibbs.

"Foul!" called Tibbs with a look of disgust. He glanced at Chad and grimaced. "Hey, you're covered in paint!"

"This isn't a game anymore." replied Leonard. "Get out of the way."

"Not if you're going after my team," replied Tibbs, and he threw his rifle aside as he rose and cracked his knuckles threateningly.

"Fine by me," concluded Leonard, and without turning his head, "Chad?"

Chad launched himself at Tibbs and the two began rolling on the ground fighting each other—kicking, punching and wrestling each other like wild cats.

Leonard led Stephen and Josh further through the obstacle course of rising loft spaces and air conditioning units until they came across a figure standing over a fallen man—Simpson stood casually over Bradley, his open hand caressing Bradley's face with a giggle. Leonard fired one shot at Simpson's head in the hopes that it would end the game—the paintball melted before it touched him. Simpson raised his finger and wagged it at them as though reprimanding a child.

"Come on, Leonard," crooned Simpson. "You'll have to do better than that."

At his feet, Bradley vomited and pulled out a clump of hair. Simpson looked back at Leonard and grinned.

"He doesn't have much time…"

Simpson laughed to himself, as the wave of radiation emanated out toward Leonard, who realized he was sweating and feeling queasy. Leonard stood stock still and watched in horror—knowing the only way to end this would be to surrender—lowering his rifle, he took his finger off the trigger and raised his right palm up in submission.

"Say it," crooned Simpson, a Cheshire smile warping his face into a look of gloating madness.

A loud crack sounded in the air—Simpson spun and rolled across the rooftop propelled by some unseen inertial force, his body coming to a halt against an air-venting pipe protruding from the roof's surface. Every Special on the rooftop turned to face this new threat, following the sound of the crack to see Daniel Rooke standing at the ledge, his sidearm pointed at Simpson's collapsed form. Chad rose from Tibbs—who spat blood on the ground—his mouth agape. Daniel surveyed the faces of shock surrounding him and pursed his lips.

"What?" demanded Daniel.

Simpson rolled onto his back slowly, breathing shallow as he stared at the sky and assessed his injuries. Finally, he looked over at his left shoulder and saw blood trickling out of a small hole just above his collarbone. He looked up and saw Daniel standing there braced—his gun pointing at his heart. A fury welled within Simpson as he sat up and braced himself to clamber to his knees.

"You shot me!" spat Simpson as the ripple of radiation colored the air around him.

"Power down, son." said Daniel.

"You son of a bitch!"

Simpson rolled to his feet and braced, as the ripple of radiation poured into the air and ignited with a loud crack like a live wire—his skeleton glowed through his skin as his clothes burned away. The radioactive fire burned and billowed forth seemingly responding to the cues made by its conductor.

Leonard grabbed Chad and pulled him back toward the edge of the rooftop, while Josh dragged Bradley to their side. Stephen stepped forward and cracked his knuckles. The sight of his bravado brought a dark chuckle to rumble like fire in Simpson's throat. Stephen's aura crackled and hummed and he rocked his legs into a ninety-degree stance as he braced his arms and balled his fists.

Simpson raised his hands like a maestro commanding the flames and they swelled and threatened to rush out only to hold and contort into a perfect sphere. Simpson studied the shape his flames were making and a puzzled expression took his face—on the edge of the rooftop stood McCormack, carrying Paul Hirano's limp frame over his shoulder while his free hand balled into a fist.

"That's enough of that, John," said McCormack, a finality ringing clear in his voice.

"Stay out of this, Paladin," spat Simpson.

"This is my team," said McCormack, setting Hirano's limp body onto the graveled rooftop. "I'm in this. You can end this now."

"Or what?"

"Or I'll end it."

"Get real," snapped Simpson with a dry laugh. "You're just a telekinetic."

"No," answered McCormack. "I'm more than that."

Simpson braced his legs and summoned the flames like roiling waves and sent it out as an explosion—the flames rushed out toward the telekinetic shield and stopped dead against the perfect sphere, growing brighter within the rippling envelope McCormack had created around him.

McCormack tightened his fist and the sphere shrank— Simpson screamed within the confines of the sphere as his fires rushed back over him. Finally, the flames died down to reveal Simpson kneeling on the rooftop nursing his gunshot wound—the flames evaporated into nothing.

McCormack walked over to Simpson and stared down at him. Simpson glowered back up at him.

"You know this would have gone differently if I wasn't shot," spat Simpson.

"Still," replied McCormack. "I'll take it."

"Fine," spat Simpson.

"Let's get you down to the emergency medical technicians and get that bullet wound checked out."

McCormack lifted Simpson easily into the air and his feet left the ground.

"I won't forget this," spat Simpson, eyeing Daniel.

"Neither will Maximus," replied McCormack.

Simpson seemed to consider this as McCormack lifted him off the rooftop and disappeared from view descending down to the medical teams standing by at the edge of the GhettoFab's perimeter.

Daniel turned to his team.

"Are you guys okay?" asked Daniel.

"Present and accounted for," answered Leonard, briskly.

With that, all eyes fell to Bradley who was struggling to rise.

"I'm starting to feel a little better," answered Bradley.

"Can you use your telekinetic ability?" said Daniel.

"Not right now," answered Bradley.

"I got it," said McCormack, as he touched back down on the roof. "I need to pick up Hirano, anyway."

Bradley gave a wan smile and rose to his feet dizzily as he staggered over to McCormack and collapsed in his arms. McCormack took the extra weight and adjusted his stance to keep himself from falling over.

"Woah there," startled McCormack. "I got you."

"Thanks," sighed Bradley.

McCormack waved his hand and both Bradley and Hirano floated over to his side. With that, he turned and hopped off the rooftop taking his burden with him.

Daniel walked to the roof's ledge and stared down after McCormack who touched down lazily next to the medical crew, and gingerly passed Bradley and Hirano over to the waiting gurneys. Daniel grinned.

"I'll never get over that," said Daniel.

"Did you get what you wanted?" inquired Leonard, coolly.

"Yeah," answered Daniel, noticing the cold edge in Leonard's tone and returning it with interest.

"Good," concluded Leonard, "Because this won't be happening again."

"Actually, it will." snapped Daniel.

"What?" demanded Leonard, the edge in his voice marking Daniel's response was unacceptable.

"You don't seem to comprehend what happened here," continued Daniel, hotly. "We got our asses handed to us."

"No," Leonard snapped back, "What happened is you put us up against that psychopath John Simpson. There's a reason his call sign is 'Death.'"

"Hey, I didn't get a choice in who you'd be going up against. Don't bring this down on me."

Leonard eyed Daniel for a moment, mulling over his words as the veins in his forehead throbbed less and less fiercely until finally he seemed amicable.

"Look," said Leonard flatly, "I'm sorry. I'm just in a foul mood because of the way things played out."

"Hey," replied Daniel, "I just had to shoot a man. I'm not proud either."

"No, I understand. And thank you for the backup. It was good of you to intervene."

"What was I going to do?" scoffed Daniel.

"Yeah," nodded Leonard, his eyes burning into the gravel of the rooftop.

Chad helped Tibbs to his feet, staring blankly at Daniel and Leonard.

"So where to now?" inquired Chad, his blue hands at his side. Tibbs wiped his mouth and walked away toward the fire escape at the far end of the complex, shooting malevolent glances at them as he walked away unhindered.

"Now we go to check on Brad," replied Daniel.

"Right," said Leonard. "You heard the man, back the way we came. We'll pick up Frank on the way."—Noting Wang was probably still unconscious in the hallway on the third floor.

Daniel turned to Leonard and gestured him to lead the way and with a commanding wave of his hand, Stephen, Chad and Joshua turned and followed them to the ledge to the third floor walkway and with a quick hop, they were down the corridor to collect Wang. Down in the darkness, a figure struggled to his feet, and pulled his legs through the handcuffs until his hands were in front of him. Daniel entered into the darkest part of the hall and called out to Wang.

"The exercise is over!" shouted Daniel. "You want those cuffs off?"

Wang put up his hands and Daniel uncuffed him. Wang looked past him to Leonard.

"Who won?" said Wang.

"Boatman'll probably declare victory," scoffed Daniel, "but we subdued everyone."

"What's that supposed to mean?" snapped Wang.

"Agent Rooke shot John Simpson for trying to kill Maximus," replied Leonard.

"With a real gun?" gaped Wang.

"Sue me," snapped Daniel, "I didn't have a paint gun."

"That's fucked up," said Wang, half-caring. "Where's John now?"

"He's being checked out by the medics," replied Leonard. "He'll be fine."

"How do you know?" snapped Wang.

"I didn't shoot him anyplace vital," replied Daniel.

"Any place vital?" parroted Wang, at a loss for words.

"He shot him in his left trapezius," replied Leonard. "It's non-lethal, but it'll hurt like hell."

Wang winced at the thought and rubbed his wrists, feeling where the cuffs had dug in and chafed his skin.

"So what happens now?" said Wang.

"Now," said Daniel as he led them down the corridor back to the stairwell at the far end of the complex, "you go back to your team and plan how best to take and hold territory for next time."

"You just shot one of my team members," replied Wang, "and you want to set up another scrimmage with us?"

"Well maybe next time," replied Daniel, "Mr. Simpson will let my teammates tap out instead of trying to kill them. He had it coming. Now he knows not to pull that with my men."

"You're talking a lot of shit for a norm hume."

Daniel stopped at the stairwell and turned to stare down Wang—who stared right back at him, anticipating a fight—Leonard and Chad closed ranks on Wang.

"I roll just as hard as I talk," said Daniel, defiantly. "Remember that about me."

"Alright," said Wang, and noticing how close Leonard and Chad were to him, edged away and walked past Daniel down the stairs to the first level.

"So," said Leonard as Wang's footsteps faded in the distance. "You're really thinking about pitting us against them again, after all this?"

"Who else do you have in mind?" replied Daniel, walking into the stairwell and down the stairs. Leonard and the others followed.

"I don't like it," said Leonard, his frustrations clearly underlining his words.

"Neither do I," said Daniel, "But what choice do we have? We need the practice and so do they. We might as well exploit it for training purposes."

"They're a bunch of animals," spat Leonard, his gravelly voice almost a growl.

"They're a bunch of animals who managed to slow down the entire team," corrected Daniel, "whittling at its numbers with booby traps and ambushes, all the while dividing the team into individual assaults throughout the complex. Besides, before I called the exercise we were already behind schedule. We need to be faster, better and prepared. I won't lose to these guys twice."

"What do you expect us to do?" said Leonard, exasperated.

Daniel stopped short at the first level hallway and turned to face Leonard. His eyes were clear and his tone was comforting.

"I'm not coming down on you, Leonard," said Daniel, "Don't think that. You did a great job leading the team, and you tested their strengths in there. That was good of you. But I think I need to be going through the door with you guys, next time. I'm not built for this sideline bullshit."

"So the next time you're taking part in the scrimmage?"

"That's how I see it needs to be." replied Daniel. "You all have been gaining proficiency as a cohesive unit. This is something I'm not gaining from our partnership. It's time that changed."

"So you're giving up being an Anchor."

"I can be an Anchor in the field. These aren't all going to be arrests. This can be done in a suit and tie. I just need us to be ready for the firefight, because I'm sure we'll be going up against some hard fights in the future. We need the Black Ops team, at the moment. And they need us. Without a sparring partner there's no way to know if you're really ready."

"Whatever you say."

"I'm sorry, Leonard. I know how this must be for you."

"Hey, you're the boss, right?"

"Come on. Let's load up."

Daniel led the team through the wreckage of the first level. Plaster and rubble covered the ground and clouds of chalk darkened the air—all this destruction in just a training exercise.

"Can you believe the amount of destruction two teams of Specials could cause?" scoffed Daniel. "The GhettoFab was built to last."

"Right," replied Leonard, not entirely sure how Daniel meant what he was saying.

"Something tells me we're going to get a bill from the JJRTC."

"I wouldn't be surprised."

Daniel held his breath and clambered over the rubble to the main gate. Leonard and the others followed, walking easily through the debris, seemingly unaffected by the dust cloud that hung in the air.

When Daniel broke through into the light of day again, he took a long draw of fresh air and walked on, knowing Leonard and the others would follow him around the shambles of the GhettoFab to the medical teams around the corner. As he neared the medic station, Boatman appeared out of the trailer and walked briskly toward him.

"Go on, guys. I'll meet up with you in a minute."

Leonard didn't say a word. He merely nodded and led Stephen and Joshua to the medic station.

"So, Rooke," began Boatman, "did you get what you wanted? I know I did."

"No, I didn't," replied Daniel. "I don't think the team's ready yet."

Boatman did not appear surprised. His tone was matter of fact.

"Why not?"

"Two arrests out of eight targets?" said Daniel, "The rest are dead. I don't think that's a very good ratio for success."

"One arrest," reminded Boatman, "Tibbs was attacked and restrained by a 'dead' man, as I recall."

"Whatever," replied Daniel. "The point is the team needs to work as a unit and have the wherewithal to foresee the dangers inherent in the mission at hand, if I'm not mistaken. I'm not satisfied my team is up to snuff yet."

"What do you suppose you should do about it?"

"We've been out of action and wearing ourselves thin on the GhettoFab. I think the team should be divided. Beach, Giordano and Sung should have more time running the GhettoFab while McCormack and Overman take part in small arrests until the team is ready to act as a team. Leonard can run them through the hoops until they perform up to standard."

"Is that your executive decision?"

"That's my executive decision."

"Very well, I'll have your first arrest file sent to you this afternoon. You can proceed tomorrow."

"So it's not a priority?"

"Possible Fraud."

"That sounds like FBI work."

"The bureau won't touch it. She's one of ours."

"Fine," concluded Daniel. "Now if you'll excuse me, I need to check on my team."

"By all means," replied Boatman. "I'll have your note-books updated."

Daniel gave Boatman a curt nod and walked away, resentful at the treatment of his team.

What's Boatman playing at? thought Daniel as he walked to the medic station.

When Daniel arrived at the medic station, he found both teams of Specials hovering around the medical technicians as they patched up Simpson's wound and treated Bradley for radiation exposure. The Black Ops team listened to Wang's retelling of everything that transpired since Daniel removed his handcuffs and they all turned and glowered down at Daniel as though he were an unwanted commodity. In fact, the mood was so hostile, Leonard signaled Chad, Stephen and Joshua to stand at the ready, and they edged just so subtly closer to the Black Ops team in anticipation for the fight that seemed almost surely to come. Daniel waved them down casually, and walked up to Simpson.

"You okay?" asked Daniel.

"Get away from me," spat Simpson. "Norm hume."

"I'll take that as a yes." scoffed Daniel.

"Fuck you!" bellowed Simpson indignantly, his aura flaring for an instant.

"Next time," goaded Daniel.

"There won't be a next time," said Hirano.

"Actually," replied Daniel, "there will be. You need this just as much as we do. You may not like the school, but you're learning just as much as we are."

"What am I learning?" spat Simpson defiantly, "Other than how to be shot!"

"To not be so cocky, for one." replied Daniel. "You controlled that rooftop. But you were careless."

"You shot me." railed Simpson.

"You tried to kill my team member." answered Daniel, calmly. "Now, Brad, he's a forgiving type. I'm not. You come up against me, you better be prepared. Because I will be."

"Oh, I'll be prepared." scoffed Simpson.

"Good," smiled Daniel, "because once the GhettoFab is repaired, we're going to have another scrimmage."

"Are you going to be there?" demanded Simpson, liking nothing more than a chance at Daniel.

"Yes." answered Daniel.

All the Black Ops team stared up in shock. A normal human fighting against Specials? Insane.

Daniel proceeded as though they were not even there, and turned his attentions solely to Bradley.

"How you feeling?"

"Better. They just gave me a shot of something."

"Vitamin X-32," chimed in the medic working on Bradley. "It counteracts most forms of radiation poisoning by speeding up healing in the body through nanites and steroids, increasing the durability of the individual. He'll be fine in a few hours."

"I feel great," said Bradley, and began to rise. The medic put his hands on Bradley's shoulders.

"Don't get up so quick. Let it do its job."

"Hey, how's my hair?" asked Bradley self-consciously. "Do I have any bald spots?"

"Not really," said Daniel, "I can't see anything, but then again, you've got a lot of hair. It hides it well. You're fine."

"You're a long way from having my condition, Brad," chimed in Leonard, jovially, though his eyes still showed concern.

"That's good," sighed Brad, "All I remember is pulling out a clump of hair and I freaked out."

Simpson said nothing. He stared at the medic with annoyance when he handed him a sling for his left arm.

"Give it a rest, for a while and let the wound heal on its own."

"What about that Vitamin-X32?" scoffed Simpson. "Or do you only give that to high ranking Specials?"

"I gave you VX-32. But you still need time for the wound to knit. I've patched the wound with second skin, so it will heal rapidly. Still, you're looking at a few days with your arm in a sling."

Simpson gave a murderous glare to Daniel who shrugged it off.

It's not my fault you decided to be an ass and got it handed right back to you. thought Daniel.

Finally, Simpson snatched the sling out of the medic's hand and stalked off. Kelson, Harris, Simms, Meyer, Hirano, Wang and Tibbs followed.

"Well," said Leonard sarcastically, "that went well."

"No kidding," scoffed Stephen.

"So what now?" asked Chad nervously.

"Now we go home so you can get some rest," answered Daniel, exhausted.

"But I feel great," begged Bradley. "Besides, I've got a date tonight."

"A date, huh?" said Leonard, his eyes wide.

"Yeah," replied Bradley, as though it was perfectly normal.

"Oh, okay," said Leonard, "I'm just saying…from the neighborhood?"

"Yeah." answered Bradley.

"I didn't know you swung that way." said Leonard.

Daniel eyed Leonard with surprise.

Is he really bent out of shape about Bradley dating a black girl?

"Leonard," said Daniel, "*I* swing that way."

A wry knowing smile stretched Leonard's face.

"You *might* want to rethink that statement."

Daniel ignored Leonard and turned his attention back to the medic working on Bradley.

"Is he good to go?" asked Daniel.

"I'd say as long as he doesn't overexert himself," surmised the medic, "he'll be fine."

"You hear that, Bradley?" said Daniel. "Let *her* steer."

Leonard laughed to himself, but said nothing. Just then, McCormack appeared around the side of the trailer.

"I just had a talk with Boatman." said McCormack. "Apparently we're a go to start making arrests in low profile cases."

"Yeah," said Daniel, answering the surprised expressions of his teammates.

After the moment of shock wore off, Leonard grinned and patted Bradley on the shoulder as he rose to his feet anxiously.

"Good to know," said Leonard.

"Not for you, Leonard." said Daniel. "You're responsible for training Chad, Stephen and Josh in making arrests in an urban environment."

"What?" scoffed Leonard.

"That's the word from the mountaintop." answered McCormack. "They need you guys humming when you move through the GhettoFab. Since the GhettoFab is in need of some repair, you'll be running the exercises at the urban warfare center for Metro Police. Understood?"

"Right," growled Leonard.

"This is good practice," continued McCormack. "You need a new environment to train in. You guys know the GhettoFab like the back of your hands. I need you guys in new locations running at top speeds."

McCormack gave Daniel a knowing nod and Daniel nodded his thanks. He was not looking forward to having to explain his executive decision to Leonard. McCormack saved him the trouble of doing so, and made it seem as though unseen parties had made the decision for the entire team. Daniel was grateful.

"Alright, let's get Bradley home in time for his date."

Bradley rose to his feet and stretched like a cat. Leonard watched Bradley with a mixture of protectiveness and discomfort, as though the thought of him dating was in some way distasteful.

Daniel noticed this and shrugged. He never noticed Leonard to have any discriminatory feelings before. This was enlightening to him. On the drive back to the Post, Daniel busied himself with his notebook, which had already downloaded their first case to investigate. A Special with dozens of aliases using the same social security number and bank account. All follow ups found that someone was working and filing taxes on time, but the entirety of the money withdrawals were taken out from an account in Boston.

We're going to Boston. thought Daniel. *There's a lot of collateral damage in a big city case. A lot that can go wrong.*

Daniel began to second-guess himself. Maybe he should have the entire team brought in…

CHAPTER 12

JOSEPH LITTLE BIRD

APACHE COUNTY, ARIZONA

Teec Nos Pos was a small working class community in the northeast corner of Arizona located in the Navajo reservation near Four Corners. With a total population of 800 people, half of them single mothers, there was a large gossip mill rolling around ranging in topics from cheating spouses to what actor was dating whom. Mostly, the community avoided certain topics of conversation, deeming them too uncomfortable. At the top of the list of subjects whispered nervously was Joseph Little Bird.

Joseph was an oddity to the people of his community. There he stood, a proud 230 lb. Navajo, standing at 6'3" with a body that seemed to have been carved from wood to perfection. He lived in a beat up trailer parked out far from the community, nestled near the foot of the Carrizo Mountains. On hot days, people could just make out his powerful elbow jutting from his pick up truck's window amid the dust cloud kicked up by his tires. On cool days, he walked. In the early morning, before the nighttime snow could melt, he could be found hiking in the Carrizo Mountains, or scaling the walls of rocks that rose precariously at the base of the mountains.

People would ask him why was he always going somewhere. Or where did he think he was getting to? Or why would he only rest when his legs gave out?

Joseph would always reply, "Because I can get places on my own."

Joseph was an odd man. But that had become expected from men who had seen war.

"Leave him alone," the elders would say. "He's got a road to walk. If he's got someplace to be, let him get there. Most who have come back from war would have drunk themselves to death or put a gun in their mouths long ago. If going places gets him to a place of peace, let him work to get there."

His neighbors gave him a wide berth, and Joseph did not seem to mind. He acknowledged most people he encountered with a nod, and a handful of words that quickly grew repetitive, which seemed to annoy him. So before long, he stopped that altogether.

Occasionally you could find him sitting outside his trailer home on a bucket driver's seat he had converted into a lawn chair and had placed on a carpet of Astroturf. There he would sit with a cold beer and a cigarette, looking out past the desolation and the trailer houses with a foreboding stare, as though something malignant merely loomed beyond the horizon, slowly making progress on its march toward him and he was just waiting for it to reach him.

It was a chilly day, and most of the neighbors anticipated Joseph's usual walk through the neighborhood, or into the badlands. But on that day, he decided to drive off the reservation into town for a beer. His coarse, grey streaked hair was pulled into a ponytail to keep his hair out of his eyes; and he wore faded form fitting Wrangler jeans, tan suede boots, a military sweater, and over it, a long multicolored Navajo print coat with wool lapels. He pulled his silver and turquoise dressed tan suede leather gambler hat low over his eyes.

People watched him pass by in his beat up Ford F-150—a hand-me-down truck from his grandfather that seemed defiant against breaking down—with his powerful elbow jutting out the window and wondered where he was going now.

Maybe he's leaving us, some of his neighbors whispered.

There was little emotion in the thought. Joseph was an odd man.

Just across the highway, Joseph studied the invisible line dividing the reservation from the world of the white people. The highway had been a source of annoyance for the reservation since the land was divided between Indian and white—the whites occupying the highway strip malls that dotted the asphalt road—and as a child he would sit on reservation land watching the cars roll by drinking a beer. Sheriffs would signal for the kids to approach them, and if they did, they were immediately arrested for being drunk on a state highway. The smart ones just sat where they were and continued drinking, to the annoyance of the Sheriffs. Joseph chuckled at the memory of running from the Sheriffs and marveled how long ago it had been.

On the other side of the highway, a strip mall stretched out and Joseph crossed the invisible line, pulling in to the parking lot. It was not often he visited Billy's Bar, but they were nearby and the patrons usually left him alone, and he liked it that way. He climbed out of his F-150 and it shuddered as the engine cut like a hot-tempered horse, sighing as Joseph's feet made purchase on the gravel parking lot.

His feet crunched as he made his way for the door to Billy's Bar and entered like a lone gunman, standing tall in the doorway and surveying the room. It was not long before every eye was on him, nervously watching his progress to a stool at the bar. The bartender, Billy, watched Joseph— slide onto the stool and open his coat—with some trepidation. After all, it was not every day an Indian came off the reservation for a beer. Not when the reservation provided its own little world for them.

But then again, Teec Nos Pos was a small community. Reservations typically had their own bars and community centers—in fact, this one had its own Navajo University on it—and had everything it needed to exist separately from society-at-large. Only the unwanted came off the reservation to venture into town. This was a well-known fact. And the unwanted were unwanted universally.

"Heineken and a shot of Jack," said Joseph, in his low commanding voice. He meant to sound friendly, but that was the best he could ever muster. Something was missing.

Billy gave a curt nod and tried his best to appear amiable to the tall Indian. Not that Joseph cared. He was quite used to being excluded. Behind him, a few patrons paid their bill and hurried out of the bar as though anticipating trouble. Joseph watched them leave with a shrug and turned to Billy.

Billy put the bottle of beer next to a shot glass and poured the whiskey into the glass expertly. Only a drop or two betrayed his nervousness.

Joseph threw the shot back and let the warm liquid burn his throat and warm his stomach, then chased it down with a sip of beer. He would nurse the beer in silence, as he always did when he ventured into town. He was not particularly concerned with his environment. People usually feared him and gave him a very wide berth.

As it happened, that day was not one of those days.

As is often the case with bars so close to the reservation, the occasional "problem child" will make a mess of things and the community had grown keenly aware of it—which was why it was no surprise to Joseph when Deputy Owens appeared in the doorway. Owens was two inches shy of Joseph, and was not built for power. His presence was commanding, standing with his feet wide apart giving him a sense of gravity, and his right hand rested on his side arm grip like a cowboy gunslinger.

Joseph gave him an appraising glance and returned to his drink. Owens walked into the bar with a wry grin, as though dispatch had given him a treat. He walked over to where Joseph sat and leaned against the bar next to him.

"What are you doing so far from the reservation, friend?" asked Owens, coolly.

"Friend?" scoffed Joseph, and eyed Deputy Owens as though he knew everything there was to know about the redneck and bit back a chuckle. *It's amazing how many of you call people 'friend' with such disgust,* thought Joseph. *I'm curious how they say momma.*

Owens glared at Joseph with a quickly rising rage toward the "uppity Indian" who did not even attempt to kowtow or turn his eyes downward.

"You going to be a problem, boy?" demanded Owens, looming menacingly next to Joseph.

Joseph tightened and glared back at Owens, who reached for his pistol grip, eying Joseph as though his face was close enough to "brandishing a firearm," as he needed. Joseph tensed, ready for the fight when Billy lurched forward nervously.

"Now, we don't want no trouble from you people," warned Billy, timidly, putting down the check for the drink and chaser. "We treat you good and nice when you boys want a drink, and Sally Two Trees is a nice, sweet Indian— all the boys keep telling me. So we don't need no situation, okay?"

Joseph glanced over at Billy with a sudden boiling fume that made his eyes water. Sally Two Trees had gone missing from the reservation weeks ago. Her mother called the reservation police to search his trailer for her twice.

"Why don't you be on your way, then?" soothed Billy, "You can always come back tonight when the bikers are here to keep you in line."

"I wouldn't even bother, friend," chuckled Owens. "Unless you come up here with some of your women. A man's got to pay to get into a bar. Understand?"

"I understand perfectly," said Joseph, his eyes boring into Owens.'

Joseph shook it off and rose to leave, only to find Owens' hand attempting to force his weight back down into his seat. The attempt was unsuccessful, but Joseph sat back down to avoid being charged with assaulting an officer.

"Now pay the man," gloated Owens.

Joseph turned on Billy.

"You're throwing me out of your bar and you expect me to pay?"

"Now, now," soothed Billy, as though he were talking to an unruly horse. "We don't want no trouble. You had your drink, now you can go. But this is a business."

Joseph stood up and faced Billy, picked up his beer, took a long deep swig, set the bottle back down on the counter and pulled out his credit card, which he swiped over the reader, debiting the money directly from his bank account.

Owens patted him hard on the back and squeezed his shoulder, attempting to inflict pain. Joseph's shoulder seemed made of wood, and Owens, taken aback, squeezed harder in his attempt to intimidate him.

"See?" crooned Owens. "That wasn't so hard now was it?"

Joseph glared down at the hand on his shoulder with disgust and his eyes found Owens daring him to act on the impulse.

Joseph turned and tried to walk away, but Owens was right there blocking his path.

"You know," said Owens, eyeing Joseph with disgust. "You'd be good to remember they have bars on the reservation, and don't be mixing with no white people. We don't need your money. Though we appreciate your contribution. Get along, now."

Joseph walked toward the door.

"And you might want to rethink driving back to the reservation, friend." grinned Owens. "You've just been drinking." Then Owens added with a chuckle, "I'd hate to have to arrest you."

Joseph walked out of the bar to find the Sheriff's cruiser parked directly behind his Ford F-150, blocking him in.

"Now don't you worry about a thing," mocked Owens, the laughter barely concealed in his voice. "Your truck will be nice and safe here until all that alcohol gets out of your system. You know how you Indians are when you drink. Go on, now."

Owens gave a hard slap to the back of Joseph like sending a horse running away, and Joseph grew rigid and turned to face Owens.

"You know," began Joseph, hardly bothering to conceal his disgust for Owens. "I've been nice. I've paid my way and I let you see yourself as an authority figure-"

"Oh," spat Owens, "you've let me?"

"Yeah," laughed Joseph sharp and cool, "I have. But on the one, I'm not drunk. On the two, you're parked illegally."

"Oh is that a fact?"

"And on the three, I ain't leaving my truck with some white trash hicks."

Joseph turned from Owens, climbed into his truck and slammed the door shut leaving Owens shifting stupidly on the walkway. He stepped down to the gravel and approached Joseph in the truck.

"You don't know who you're fooling with, boy," warned Owens.

"No, you got that backwards," said Joseph, "And I'm telling you, I'm not your problem. I'm the rez police's problem, when the Sheriff calls to complain about what I did to one of his squad cars."

Joseph started the engine and the F-150 roared to life. Owens grabbed the handle of his side arm threateningly, Joseph, with a grin, ignored it as he reversed full force into the patrol car— the cruiser rocked onto two wheels — while Joseph spun out, and the tail of his pickup truck spun around in a wild fishtail motion. Owens jumped free and landed in an oil stain on the graveled parking lot. Joseph gunned it and the truck launched for open parking lot and swung out on the highway, across the road, and onto the reservation. Home free. Owens rose from the asphalt and eyed his oil stained uniform.

"I'm gonna get that red nigger," seethed Owens.

Joseph fumed as he drove up the dirt road and gunned the engine hard as he dared, knowing children would be playing in the street ahead.

That wasn't smart, thought Joseph. *That's asking for trouble, there.* Joseph replayed the events leading up to the reckless adventure he plunged into and sighed. *Fuck 'em,* thought Joseph. *He had it coming...*

Joseph caught himself and lifted his right foot off the gas and the F-150 slowed down to a crawl.

"Looks like I won't be going into town for a while." sighed Joseph to himself.

He returned to his trailer and set in on the porch, waiting for the reservation police to come around and talk to him. He would probably have to pay for the damages and promise to stay out of town for a while. It had happened before, when the locals informed him he was an unwelcome commodity.

The sun had set and no one came calling. Joseph waited next to his propane heater a while longer, and then gave up, going inside to make himself something to eat.

Later that evening, Owens drove slowly onto the reservation with his headlights cut, creeping past the houses of Indians, looking for the beat up red F-150. In the backseat, off-duty deputies Burns and Fox picked through the plastic rings of a six-pack of beer and downed their cans, tossing them out of the window. Their logic being: it was not territory where they had to uphold laws, so littering was a problem for the residents of the reservation. Burns leaned forward and belched into the front seat, blowing the foul stench of beer into the enclosed space, looking glass eyed at Owens.

"You're not going to find him, Earl." said Burns.

"That Indian's halfway to Mexico, right now," laughed Fox. "He'll be in a mariachi band by sun up."

"No, he's still here. I can feel it." replied Owens, angrily. "That sumbitch is gonna pay for what he did."

The houses pulled away, and Owens drove down a dark road with the wilderness closing on either side as coyotes' eyes reflected through the trees and rocks in the night.

"Did he really mess up your car?" said Fox, a giggle in the back of his throat as loud as he dared around Owens.

"Shut up," warned Owens.

"Come on," said Fox, "It's just an Indian."

"I believe they want to be called Native Americans," corrected Burns with a laugh.

"Shit, it's a Navajo," replied Fox. "You don't get no closer to rodents than that."

"True," answered Burns and then peered out at the dark road blindly. "What are we looking for, anyway?"

"There it is." answered Owens as the beat up F-150 came into sight next to a trailer nestled close to the foot of the mountains.

They took in the sight collectively—a beat up bachelor's trailer with the door tilted on its hinges. Before it, Astroturf carpet rolled out over the dusty earth with a propane heater propped next to a bucket car seat that had been haphazardly propped against the door, balancing on cinderblocks and stabilized by rocks—the look of absolute squalor in the eyes of the off duty deputies.

"What a dump," gaped Burns.

"What do you expect from an Indian?" replied Fox.

"Well," replied Burns, "we passed some nice houses coming all the way out here."

"Probably casino money." replied Fox.

"Shut up," spat Owens, and opened his car door and climbed out. "Let's go."

Owens led Fox and Burns to the trunk and flung it open revealing a shotgun, a crowbar and a sledgehammer. Owens took the shotgun and Fox and Burns were left to fight over the remnants—Fox won the scuffle over the crowbar and Burns reluctantly took the sledgehammer.

"Why don't we use our guns?" asked Burns, not at all pleased to have a sledgehammer in his hands.

"And get them traced back to us?" pointed out Owens

"Right," said Burns with the realization Owens was right.

"So what's the shotgun for?" asked Fox.

"I got this off a dead meth dealer," replied Owens, "down in Cow Springs." Then added in a whisper, "Follow me." And he took off toward the trailer.

At the trailer door, Owens kicked it in and pointed his shotgun into the room to find it empty.

"He's not here!" spat Owens.

"Come on," said Burns to Fox as he turned to head back to the car. "Let's go home."

"Yeah," sighed Fox, and he shivered from the cold before shuffling off after Burns.

Just then, Joseph came around the corner of the trailer with a mangy coyote dogging his heels like a loyal pet. In that instant, Joseph eyed the three men noting the crowbar, the sledgehammer and the shotgun, and his eyes raised to meet Owens' eyes.

"What the fuck?" said Joseph as his eyes pored over Owens. The coyote growled at Owens who turned and pointed the shotgun at Joseph's broad chest and barked like a drill sergeant.

"GET DOWN ON THE GROUND!" railed Owens. "GET DOWN ON THE GROUND, NOW!"

The sound spooked the coyote and it warily circled around Fox and Burns and trotted into the night. Joseph grit his teeth and put his hands up as he knelt down on the ground. Owens ran at Joseph and hit him with the butt of the shotgun across the jaw and Joseph glared at him, spitting blood out of his mouth.

"I said get down on the ground!" spat Owens, pressing the muzzle of the shotgun into Joseph's temple. Joseph glared back at Owens defiantly. His tone, however, was pragmatic.

"You don't want to be doing this, boy."

"No," grinned Owens, "I really do."

"I'm telling you," said Joseph, "this road I've been down, and there's nothing but pain at the other end. You don't want to do this. It'll fuck up your entire life."

"You're just some stupid Navajo," rationalized Owens, seemingly talking himself up to something. "No one's going to miss you. I bet not even the Navajos will miss you."

"I'm tellin' you right now, son," warned Joseph, "you don't want none of this. I'm tryin' to reason with you. There's things you only think you know-"

Owens laughed loud and pressed the barrel of the shotgun deeper against Joseph's temple.

"This red nigger's been to college," scoffed Owens, leaned in close to Joseph, clenched a clump of his grey streaked hair and yanked his head back, peeling Joseph back until he bent backward over his heels. "Alright, I'm darin' you, Joe, what do you think I don't know?"

"A lot of things, white man. And I'm tellin' you, you don't want me doin' to you, what I know I can. An' I don't want to do it, neither."

A flame swirled in the back of Owens' eyes, and the veins in his neck and scalp pulsed as his face went red.

"No, I think I want you to show me how you're smarter than me," whispered Owens and he convulsed as he released Joseph's hair and backhanded him across the mouth. "You hear me you drunk assed Indian? Show me!"

Owens slapped, punched, and kicked until Joseph's right eye was shut; he brought his boot heel down on Joseph until his teeth were cracked and Owens' legs were sore from the exertion. Fox and Burns tried to pull Owens off Joseph, but Owens broke free of them, charged at Joseph and grabbing at the back of his scalp yanked Joseph's head back so hard there was an audible pop in the back of his neck. Owens darted his face at Joseph threateningly, holding the shotgun awkwardly against his skull.

"Show me!" railed Owens.

Joseph merely smiled through the slit his vision had been reduced and looked back up at Owens—his vision had been reduced to a red blur and seeing Owens in red seemed so comical to Joseph, he chuckled.

"Your skin's redder than any Indian I ever saw. At first I just saw it on the back of your neck, but now; I guess the only thing I don't know is: 'who raped whose ancestors, yours or mine?'"

Owens stared down at Joseph absently released the clump of Joseph's hair let him drop to the dusty ground and stood there for a long moment, trying to process what Joseph had said to him. He looked back at Burns and Fox for some bearing as the earth shifted beneath his feet. All he saw were shocked expressions, turning to resigned sighs of complicity as though Joseph had just signed his own death warrant, and the last reason not to kill him had been stripped away.

Joseph lay on his back smiling with a queer expression back up at them; not one of resignation, but defiance and something else they could not place. It was as if Joseph held a doorknob with a terrible beast behind the door, and merely waited for them to come just a little closer.

"You boys going to help me with this or what?" demanded Owens, darkly.

"I'm not digging no hole this time," muttered Burns. "Sally Two Trees was enough."

"What are you complaining about?" scoffed Fox "Sally was some nice piece of cunny."

"Yeah," replied Burns "Was a shame, though."

"Yeah," agreed Fox with a dark chuckle.

"We doing this or what?" demanded Owens.

"Sorry, Earl," said Burns as he made his way over to where Joseph was lying.

"Hold his arms," said Owens. "And get him up on his knees."

Burns and Fox scooped up Joseph while Owens emptied the cartridges from the shotgun and let it fall to the ground; walked methodically around behind and applied a chokehold to Joseph to keep him compliant—then produced a switchblade.

"You know," whispered Owens in Joseph's ear, "I should really get this knife engraved. And you know what it should say? It should be called the Indian killer, or some-thing. This here knife carved up Sally, Bill Garcia and Joe Pony Rider, and I'm going to put this into you. You heard me? First I'm gonna cut off your pecker, since you men-tioned a dirty Indian raping my grandmother or someone. Then I'm gonna scalp you, 'cause you Indians like that so much. What'che got to say about that?"

Owens laid his hand on Joseph's shoulder and moved the switchblade lower toward the inseam of his pants. Joseph just smiled up at him, and spat in Owens' face.

"Buckle up, kids," sang Joseph, as if he were a carnie adjusting seatbelts on a rollercoaster. "We're going for a ride."

Owens stared down at Joseph perplexedly and near-ly stabbed Joseph in the eye when a crack rang out and a stiff wind hurled toward them. For the briefest of instants, Joseph, Owens and the deputies grew long, and seemed to swirl like a twisting of ribbons toward a central point, their heads touching, as they grew together into seemingly one mass screaming in agony. Their bodies grew long and spa-ghettified as they swirled around a central point as if they were being forced to fit through the eye of a needle. The next instant, Owens, the deputies and Joseph vanished and the sound of rushing wind collapsing in on a free space with a terrible crack was all the evidence of that there was ever someone there.

All that was heard was the rushing of wind violently trying to process the sudden void in space, and the jostling of air and dust to fill it back again. The wind then slowed and the dust dropped back toward the earth like a fine mist, sparkling in the moonlight like flakes of gold and silver until the air was once again still, with only the slightest breeze.

Silence crept back into the night and the loss of four men was seemingly inconsequential to the life of the

barrens of the reservation when a point appeared, seemingly out of the horizon. Out from it poured four streams of
substance, where whirling particles rushed back into place
rapidly—like a film of statues that had been rendered into
dust being run in reverse. Owens, Burns and Fox seemed
to reform into their full shapes, as their skin reformed onto
their bone and muscle frames, and Owens' potbelly took the
longest to form. They fell away from the point in the horizon and Joseph appeared, gritting his teeth, caught between
unbearable agony and hysterical laughter as tears streamed
down his face and he shook in the chill winter night. Joseph
glanced about him and saw Owens and the deputies convulsing, weeping and railing on the ground.

"Oh," groaned Joseph, beating his own head as he tried
to escape from the wailing men, stumbling and stagger-
ing away from them in a crippled form of flight. "I hate
that part."

Joseph tripped over his own feet, pawing at the ground
in a fright and did not stop until he found the security of a
large boulder jutting from the Arizona earth at a safe distance from the off duty Deputies. He made his way behind
the stone and leaned on the far side against the slab, trying
to catch his breath. He pulled out a thin bottle of Southern
Comfort from his back pocket of his jeans and took a swig
from it, then shakily lit a cigarette.

Behind him, the Sheriffs continued to scream as though
devils sat on their chests, ripping bits of flesh off them while
Joseph shook and twitched, as beads of sweat dotted his
face and hands and he fought the urge to vomit.

Look at the moon. thought Joseph in shallow breaths
growing deeper as he could dare. *Look at the stars. You're
in the world now. You're not there. You're here!*

A moments later, the visions were dancing behind his
shut eyes, and the screams of the Deputies brought the
visions back to him again until Joseph couldn't bear it any

longer, and, realizing his eyes were closed, opened them again and stared up at the white gibbous moon.

"Hey, shut it!" railed Joseph over his shoulder to the Deputies, who continued to scream despite the cruelty in his voice. "It goes away in a few minutes!"

Whatever they suffered, it was infinitely worse than anything Joseph could offer by way of cruelty in his voice. So potent were the cries of agony, Joseph's mind washed with the suffering he had been victim to only three minutes earlier, and almost without his deciding to do so, pushed off the rock and began walking away from the twisting and writhing bodies; seeking a refuge where their cries could not penetrate.

Behind him, and fading to a mingled wail in the distance as the wind rose, the Deputies shoveled the earth into their mouths, gasped, and railed even louder, with mouthfuls of dust pouring back from their mouths in long streams of saliva to the dust again.

"Christ almighty," grumbled Joseph. "It's not that bad. I used to go there five times a day on a slow day."

In the distance, a loud cracking sound echoed across the night, and a rock next to Joseph launched into the sky and flipped back to the ground alerting Joseph instantly to the fact one of the men fired his gun at him.

"What in hellfire?" Joseph exclaimed as he dropped his thin bottle in a start. He then listened to their screams with immeasurably less pity that mounted to almost a desire to go back and give the men a second ride when he realized his Southern Comfort was now a muddy pool at his feet.

"Serves 'em right," concluded Joseph, at long last as he threw the empty bottle at the mountain before walking back to his trailer. "Fucking assholes."

WASHINGTON D.C. –POST

Daniel woke up feeling excited knowing that within a few hours, he would be making his first collar. And he had something to prove. He threw off the covers, grabbed his travel kit and made his way down to the bathroom for a quick shower and shave. In the shower he went over the case he had virtually memorized. Terry Lyons, black female, standing 5'11" weighing 132 lbs. Telekinetic. Mastering in something called the psi ball. Somehow this telekinetic had managed to have aliases across three states holding down steady jobs by somehow convincing corporations she was on the payroll. Possible telepathy?

This troubled Daniel, imagining himself approaching a woman who could just as easily "convince" him to forget about her and he would be helpless to stop her.

No, he thought, *Bradley and McCormack will be there with me. Two telepaths against one. No sweat.*

Daniel took his time shaving, going against the grain, running his fingers across the path of the blade, searching for missed stubble. His razor was new and sharp. He managed it with very few cuts. With a slap of aftershave Daniel rubbed the burning liquid into his smoothed face and let the pain wash over him and subside. He threw water on his face and cleaned off the excess shaving cream with his towel and loaded his travel kit back up, walking down the hallway to his room where he found a note pinned to his door. It was from Leonard.

> Daniel,
> Took Chad to the Metro urban warfare center. Joshua's with Stephen working on his control at the Explosives Detonation Chamber at JJRTC. Good luck in Boston.
>
> Leonard.

Daniel took the note off the door, set it down on the desk in his room, and quickly changed into a black suit.

He looked himself over in the mirror and frowned. He had always hated the way Feds looked, and here he was—a carbon copy.

With a self-deprecating scoff, he turned from his reflection, and as an afterthought, picked up his duffel bag and stalked out of the room and into the flat.

He found Bradley and McCormack sitting watching the local D.C. news. The newscaster was glorying his own ability to predict snow in the wintertime and McCormack chuckled at the way he patted himself on the back. With state of the art Doppler technology enhanced by Quill technology the ability to predict weather patterns forming had become eerily omniscient in feel, and the weatherman never let you forget it, praising the new technology as he predicted icy conditions on the highways.

Bradley looked up and paused surveying Daniel in a suit. He seemed torn between something, but his eyes were bright as he quickly looked down to Daniel's duffel bag.

"What's in the duffel bag?" said Bradley.

"Don't worry about it." deflected Daniel. "Let me talk to you two about our agenda for the day. Have you checked your notebooks, yet?"

"We're going to detain Terry Lyons for questioning," answered McCormack, mechanically.

"Right," said Daniel.

"I don't like it," said Bradley, looking disgruntled. "Terry wouldn't be part of any fraud. It's not in her character."

"With the treatment of Specials by the government," answered Daniel solemnly, "we can't put anything to chance."

"So you think we could be walking into a hostile scenario?" said McCormack, with a critical stare. "Is that what the duffel bag is for?"

"I'm not taking anything to chance," answered Daniel, unconsciously swinging the duffel bag out of sight behind the couch. "We go in prepared. Then we talk. Are you with me on this?"

"I'm not against you," replied McCormack.

"That's good enough for now." concluded Daniel and he checked his watch. "Get dressed. We'll go in professionally. If we can reason with her there'll be no cause for violence."

"But you're ready for it," said Bradley, knowingly.

"Yes." answered Daniel. "Meet me in five minutes ready to go."

McCormack rose to leave. Bradley sat there studying Daniel.

"You heard the man, Brad." called McCormack. "Five minutes."

Finally, Bradley rose and left the flat for his bedroom.

Daniel turned and walked down the hallway to his office and loaded his notebook into the duffel bag. As he was zipping up the bag the phone rang. Daniel looked at the phone and sighed.

"This can't be good."

Daniel walked into the flat to find Bradley and McCormack dressed in similar suits, Bradley's suit was more stylish, with a black leather smoking jacket in lieu of a sports coat. The look on his face was crystal clear: this was the closest Bradley would be getting to the federal mold. Daniel sighed and dragged his hand through his hair with frustration.

"What's up?" said McCormack.

"Boatman just got a call from the FBI field office in Arizona." said Daniel. "We've got a rogue Special down there who attacked three cops and are now being treated at a local hospital. He's hiding out on a Navajo reservation and causing a big stir with the locals. The feds were called in but the reservation police force isn't being very cooperative."

"So what's the plan?" said Bradley.

"The plan is to go get him," answered Daniel. "The Lyons case is on hold for now."

"Lucky her," muttered McCormack.

"What about the rest of the team?" said Bradley.

"I don't want to interrupt their training," replied Daniel.

"And you don't know what you'll be walking into," concluded McCormack. "So you decided to bring along some Alphas."

"Can you blame me?" answered Daniel with a grin.

"How are we getting there?" said Bradley, already knowing the answer and dreading it.

"We'll take the Chariot," answered Daniel. "I just got the call that it's ready for use, and we now have a pilot we got on loan from the Bureau."

"What's the travel time?" inquired McCormack, more for curiosity on the airworthiness of the Chariot than any expectancy of when they would actually arrive in Arizona. As far as McCormack was concerned, the chances were likely that the Chariot would lose power and fall out of the sky like a brick.

"Forty minutes," replied Daniel. "I don't want to break any records with her."

"Not bad," breathed Bradley, nervously.

"How do you want us?" said McCormack, looking down at his suit and judging it to be out of place for a hostile engagement.

"We'll go as is," answered Daniel.

"Who's the target?" said McCormack.

"Joseph Little Bird," answered Daniel. "You know him?"

"Heavy Gear?" gasped Bradley.

"We're familiar with him," replied McCormack. "He was on our team. Hang on, I'll pull up the file."

McCormack pulled his notebook out of his breast pocket. His fingers raced across the notepad and data scrolled across the viewscreen.

Joseph Little Bird – call sign: Heavy Gear aka Crazy Joe [Rank: E/IGFOEEV-Gamma Status BLACK ANCHOR]

"Crazy Joe?" picked up Daniel, critically.

"His ability leaves a lot to be desired," answered McCormack.

"Will he be a problem?" asked Daniel.

"That depends…" answered Bradley.

"…On what?" demanded Daniel.

"On how hard a time he's had since the end of the war," concluded McCormack.

Daniel studied Bradley and McCormack critically in silence. No one broke the electric stillness between them, and they seemed to verge on a purely psychic dialogue as Daniel's mind raced over the possibility that a "crazy" Special was waiting for them at the end of the road to their first collar. Finally, Daniel's notebook chimed. Daniel pulled it from his duffel bag and studied it, reading the urgent message before putting it in his left breast pocket.

"Let's get going," said Daniel, picking up his duffel bag. "Our ride is here."

Daniel, Bradley and McCormack walked in silence down the three flights of steps to the lobby and walked out onto Georgia Avenue. The SUV was parked and idling in the red zone directly in front of the lobby doors. Daniel walked straight for the front passenger seat and Bradley and McCormack piled into the back.

"Andrews Air Base." said Daniel. "Go!"

The SUV lurched forward, cutting off a passing car and pulled out onto the avenue amid a stream of blaring horns. The next second, the SUV was peeling around the corner and was gone.

The SUV pulled up to the tarmac outside Andrews Wizards Hangar. There, the hulking Chariot sat hissing fume as the slow whine of the power conductors raised in pitch. Daniel climbed out of the SUV, took out his duffel bag and stood next to the Chariot. McCormack and Bradley walked up and studied Daniel. His suit was thin and office efficient.

"It'll be cold there," said Bradley, eyeing his wardrobe critically.

"I'm not worried about the weather," replied Daniel cautiously.

McCormack nodded knowingly and put his hand on Daniel's shoulder.

"Relax," said McCormack. "It's a simple arrest. You've done this a thousand times before."

"Feels like my first time," admitted Daniel with a self-deprecating scoff as a slim built man in a flight officer's uniform walked past them and stepped into the Chariot's cabin. He turned around and glanced at them with a cocky smile.

"Everyone on board," called the pilot, and he vanished from view into the belly of the beast.

Daniel gave a nod to McCormack and followed him into the Chariot. Bradley eyed the craft untrusting but boarded despite his better judgment. Inside the cabin were rows of seats with harnesses along the walls, and a viewscreen for data updates and news reports that might shed light on the situation they were en route to, whatever that may be.

The pop of the intercom alerted them that the pilot had finished with his preflight checklist and all three of them sat up straight and craned their ears to hear the message from the new face who held their lives in his hands.

"Ladies and gentlemen," chimed the pilot as though he were addressing commercial flight passengers. "we will be travelling at an altitude of fifty-two thousand feet, reaching supercruise speeds that will bring us to our destination in just under forty minutes. Please feel free to light 'em if you got 'em. I'm turning off the no smoking light."

"Funny guy," scoffed Bradley, looking miserable.

The Chariot lifted off the ground and quickly gained altitude with little jerks and tremors.

"Hopefully we make it to your first time alive," chided McCormack, grimly.

"Relax," said Daniel, "Chariot's a good ship."

There was another tremor and a jolt of speed that quickly slowed, sending them jerking in fits. Daniel, Bradley and McCormack eyed the cockpit. Bradley turned to Daniel nervously.

"Has this guy ever flown this thing before?" inquired Bradley nervously.

"The guy's AB-4 certified," replied Daniel. "He should be able to fly it."

Just then, another jolt of speed sent the cabin shuddering and the unmistakable sound of metal whining as it bent sent chills down their spines. Daniel glanced back at McCormack and Bradley and noticed their jaws were set. With a sigh, Daniel undid his harness and kicked his duffel bag firmly under his seat.

"I think I'll have a talk with the pilot," announced Daniel.

"You do that," replied McCormack with a critical glance.

Daniel walked up to the cockpit, leaving McCormack and Bradley alone staring at Daniel's duffel bag.

"Any ideas what's in it?" said Bradley curiously.

"Knowing Daniel?" said McCormack. "I'd say body armor, a high powered rifle and grenades."

Neither Bradley nor McCormack made a gesture toward the duffel bag. They didn't want to know. All they knew was Daniel was shouting at the pilot who continued to stress the hull with sudden on pours of speed and the subsequent slowing that sent the cabin rattling.

"Thank God we can fly," said McCormack.

"For real, though." sighed Bradley.

The forty-minute flight felt much, much longer, and with a sigh of relief, they felt the Chariot making its descent, slowing down all the while.

Daniel's argument with the pilot seemed to have some effect on his piloting skills as the ride was far less bumpy for the remainder of the flight. Bradley and McCormack could not hear exactly what Daniel said to the pilot, but whatever it was left him shaken, as he kept glancing over his shoulder, peering down to the cabin and gave a nervous "thumbs up" as if asking if Daniel approved of his piloting skills. Daniel would curtly nod back and with a sigh of relief, the pilot would turn to face the console and return to his duties. Daniel shook his head.

This asshole's going to ruin my transport, thought Daniel.

Finally, the ship took a static position and slowly low-ered to the highway 504 at the Teec Nos Pos Trading Post. The Chariot touched down on the desert floor, kicking up dust as the engines whined and dulled to a low roar that reduced to a purr.

"Thank you for your patience," called the pilot over the intercom to the annoyance of Daniel, who shot him a death-ly look. The pilot shivered slightly and continued talking, as though his braving the icy looks of the three passengers would make their collective grievances with him go away. "It is currently 9:30 am, and the temperature outside is 49 degrees. Good hunting."

With that, the pilot released the cabin doors, which slid open to a gust of chilly wind blowing through the cabin. Daniel shivered for an instant and then shrugged it off, stepping out of the Chariot onto the dusty ground and surveyed the surrounding area dotted with desert foliage and dry twisted trees. It was an inhospitable environment.

Just a little ways away, beat up SUVs squared off against late model SUVs, lights flashing on both sides, like a law enforcement standoff.

Daniel could just make out the boundary dividing the reservation from federal jurisdiction just by staring at the SUV's. Standing between the cars, a group of men huddled together, staring at the Chariot warily. Finally, one of the men from the non-reservation side of the territorial dispute walked over toward Daniel, with his hand over his eyes, shielding himself from the swirling dust.

"I'm Special Agent Flannery," said the man, flashing his FBI credentials. "I'm assuming you're my Specials liaison?"

"Agent Rooke," replied Daniel, shaking his hand. "Specials Investigations Task Force. These are agents McCormack and Overman. We'll be handling the manhunt."

"Not much of a manhunt, Agent Rooke." replied Flannery, rubbing his chin. "Little Bird's got himself holed up at his trailer just on the other side of the reservation border. About a ten minutes drive from here."

"And you haven't taken him into custody?" blinked Daniel.

"We're having problems with tribal authority right now," replied Flannery as though this was nothing new to him—merely the business of the day. "It's a minor problem that is usually rectified by showing respect, but then again, there's the problem. Too many hicks with badges, out in these parts."

Daniel looked over at the men squaring off with each other and noted how many times the Sheriffs spat dip on the ground at the Reservation police's feet. The reservation police glared back at the Deputies with disgust.

"Got it," said Daniel. "Well, why don't you give us a quick briefing then, and catch us up."

"Not much to it," said Flannery, rubbing his chin perplexedly. "Joseph Little Bird is a Navajo standing at six feet three inches, weighing two hundred thirty pounds. Last seen wearing blue jeans, cowboy boots, a matching hat and a tribal print coat. He's big, he's ornery, and he's a Special." Flannery leaned in conspiratorially, "We can't get a handle on his ability, but from the stink he's made we figure he's a telepath."

Daniel did not want to know how or why Flannery came to that conclusion but his curiosity was piqued.

"What's the story with the victims?" demanded Daniel.

"Well, that's the thing," said agent Flannery, rubbing his chin speculatively, "we don't know. They're perfectly healthy, they're just insane. Whatever he did to them, it's having a lasting effect on them."

"Okay," concluded Daniel, "and his house is just over those hills?"

"Yeah, it'll be the one at the foot of the mountains."

"Got it. Put me in touch with the tribal police. "

"I'll get him. Good luck calming him down."

Flannery walked away warily and Daniel turned to look at Bradley and McCormack.

"What do you think?" said Daniel to McCormack.

"Well," replied McCormack, "first off, Joseph isn't a telepath. He's a long distance teleporter."

"He was responsible for teleporting supplies to the front during the Sol War. His designation was Heavy Gear. But by the end of the war we just called him Crazy Joe. His teleportation leaves a lot to be desired if you follow."

"What are the side effects of his teleports if he's taking other people with him?"

"Intense agony and insanity. You feel like your skin's being ripped off and your blood boils. You also lose your equilibrium and you lose track of everything. Up, Down, Sideways, beginning and end. You feel like you're dying. On the other side, you feel it all over again as your body reconstructs."

"Reconstructs?" repeated Daniel.

"Joseph opens up wormholes," said Bradley.

"Wormholes," repeated Daniel.

"Don't get all bent out of shape," said McCormack, anticipating Daniel's subsequent head exploding, "The wormholes aren't that big. In fact, they're pretty minute. That's the problem with them. Stable wormholes require a lot of energy depending on the size of them. So his are like microscopic tears in space/time. Pulls whatever it can into them and makes them fit by ripping them apart and then reconstructing them on the other side. Wherever that's going to be."

"Usually it's just him," said Bradley, "and he doesn't handle the effects all that well either."

"Okay," said Daniel, grimly. "Take no chances, then. If he looks like he's going to Jump or take one of us with him, take him down hard."

"Done," answered Bradley.

"You read my mind," concluded McCormack.

Just then, the tribal police chief stepped up to Daniel. He was a sturdy man with hard eyes lined with frustration but his jaw was set defiantly. Whatever grief the Deputies were giving him was beginning to show in cracks on his face.

"So," said the police chief, "I hear you're the ones who are supposed to get me to play ball?"

"Actually," said Daniel, thoughtfully. "I'm here to ask your permission to cross onto your jurisdiction and make an arrest of one Joseph Little Bird."

"And why should I be agreeable to you?"

"Because I'm asking nicely," replied Daniel, a faint edge in his voice. "I can ask nicely in other ways, but you wouldn't appreciate that. Look, I'm not here to ruffle feathers."

"Ruffle feathers," repeated the reservation police chief, "That wouldn't be a crack, would it?"

"Look, I have a job to do and I need to do it quickly and quietly. Can you help me with that?"

The police chief studied Daniel for a long moment staring blankly for a moment and then his face flooded with an amicable smile.

"What do you need?"

"An escort and a perimeter set up," replied Daniel with a friendly smile. "And then I need you to let me handle my job."

"Yeah, I can help with that."

"I appreciate it," said Daniel, shaking the man's hand. "I'll be along shortly and then we'll head on up."

"No problem."

The tribal police chief stepped away. Daniel glanced at McCormack. McCormack smiled.

"Just keeping things moving forward." said McCormack.

Daniel grinned.

"I've got no problems with that."

In the distance, the tribal police chief signaled Daniel to follow and then climbed into his beat up SUV. Daniel signaled Flannery and he flung himself behind the wheel of his SUV with purpose as Daniel, Bradley and McCormack piled in. Within seconds, they were across the highway and on Indian Route 5028 heading southeast.

"We've got company," said Bradley.

Behind them, five Sheriff cruisers followed them onto the reservation, like a legalized lynch mob, waiting for their chance at their suspect.

"This could turn ugly real quick." said Daniel. "Can you keep an eye on them and tell me if they decide to play cowboys and Indians?"

"That's already on their minds," answered Bradley looking like he was battling with a bad flavor being inside their heads, "but I'll tell you if they're gearing up to a mob mentality."

"Good to know," replied Daniel.

With that, Daniel turned and looked out the window at the dusty view. The scenery was barren and desolate, and yet there was a beauty to the place that Daniel could not put his finger on. He would not want to live there, but to come and commune with nature in silent contemplation for a few hours—that could last him years, spiritually.

"It's coming up on the left," said Flannery, pointing the direction the SUVs veered toward the foot of the mountains. Finally they came to a stop some fifty yards from a beat up trailer. The Deputies stopped short about twenty yards behind them and climbed out of their cruisers with shotguns, gripping them tightly but otherwise not moving or speaking. Daniel climbed out of the SUV for a better look at the residence of Joseph Little Bird.

Before him, the beat up trailer hitch sat propped on stones to keep the trailer level.

"This is it?" demanded Daniel to the Indian police chief.

"Yeah." said the police chief. "Joseph's an interesting guy. He lives like a spirit walker out here on his own. It's the way he likes it."

Daniel looked back at the trailer and the surrounding area with some sense of what bordered on pity. Here was a war hero, returning home to hard times. Living in a trailer no bigger than a prison cell, his bare comforts being a television, he surmised, from the dish on the roof of the trailer, a beat up pickup truck and a makeshift "lawn."

Honestly, thought Daniel, *he could pick up and move anywhere. And he lives out in the cold alone like this.*

"Wait here." said Daniel. "I'll go in alone."

"You sure?" said McCormack, eyeing him doubtfully.

"Yeah," sighed Daniel, not at all sure.

Daniel stepped forward toward the beat up trailer and studied the surrounding debris critically. Out in front was a driver's seat that had been converted into a lawn chair and had placed on a carpet of Astroturf.

Daniel stood at the doorway and knocked. It seemed a stupid thing to do. The bite of the gravel muffled by the Astroturf was enough to alert the trailer's lone inhabitant.

"That was a nice touch," said the grizzly man in the trailer.

Daniel peered into the trailer and let his eyes adjust to the semidarkness highlighted by streams of dust filled light that trickled in through the window and reflected off the grime covered television screen. Daniel stared at the reflection through the screen blinking back at him and was instantly aware of the presence of the man as he turned to face him. Joseph Little Bird was a man who seemed to have been carved from stone to perfection yet warm as wood. Even in sitting, he was formidable.

"Joseph Little Bird?" said Daniel.

Joseph peered up at him. He wore a raw steak over his right eye, obviously to bring down a swelling.

"You the guy who thinks he's got my number?" challenged Joseph with a wry smile.

"That depends," replied Daniel, "did you mean to attack those men?"

"Didn't attack," corrected Joseph. "Returned fire."

"You left those hicks in a bad way, Mr. Little Bird."

Joseph swiveled around in his chair and let the steak drop from his eye revealing the black and blue swelling.

"Served 'em right," spat Joseph, and with a dismissive wave of his hand. "They'll be fine in a few days. And maybe they won't be stupid enough to come onto the rez lookin' for a fight."

"Or maybe they'll be more inclined to shoot you from a distance," mused Daniel.

Joseph considered this for a moment and then grit his cracked teeth.

"They can try."

"My point is," pressed Daniel, "you're not thinking things through here."

Joseph studied Daniel for a moment, amazed he was having a rational conversation after what had transpired the night before.

"Who are you?" demanded Joseph.

"Agent Daniel Rooke," replied Daniel. "with the Specials Investigations Task Force."

"Never heard of you," replied Joseph with a shrug.

"We get that a lot," grinned Daniel.

"So," began Joseph, musing over Daniel, "a super se-cret government organization checking up on Specials who use their abilities without being asked to use them by the government, even under the threat of death. Have I got your number right?"

"About," admitted Daniel.

"And you're here to arrest me for defending myself," continued Joseph, with an air of clarifying the situation. "Still with you?"

"Still on the same page," said Daniel.

Joseph studied Daniel critically.

"I don't know you from the war," said Joseph, carefully. "So you can't be a Special. At least not a Special worth a damn." Joseph threw the steak on the floor and a mangy coyote trotted over from the corner and began devouring it. "You can't be here on your own. Who'd you bring with you?"

His eyes were curious, almost begging. Daniel smiled.

"Agents Bradley Overman and Tobias McCormack."

"Maximus and Paladin?" replied Joseph, his eyes wide, and then a grin broke on his face. "Two Alphas just for me? I'm flattered."

"I would appreciate it if you'd be inclined to settle this situation amicably."

Joseph seemed to consider Daniel for a moment, and then clicked his tongue as he rose and fetched his shirt and coat, donning his suede gamblers hat.

"Just for the sake of seeing old friends," said Joseph, and then added with a wide grin, "why the hell not?"

Joseph cozied past Daniel and walked out to face off with Bradley and McCormack. He seemed to study them mutinously for a moment and then cracked the wide grin again.

"Hellfire," grinned Joseph. "You boys look like right lawyers in those outfits."

"Hey Joseph," said Bradley with a grin.

"So, what's the pitch?" said Joseph, wild with anticipation. "Your boy didn't mention one." "Well," began McCormack. "We've got a resort with dorm rooms picked out for you on North Brother Island in New York."

"Sounds like a nice little prison," scoffed Joseph.

"Well, considering we're Specials," replied McCormack, "and most of us are hard to cage, they made it nice for us."

"Are the guards there good in a fight?" inquired Joseph with a queer grin.

"The guards will be in the water," replied McCormack.

"Lot of good it'd do 'em." chuckled Joseph.

"Well, with your ability," replied McCormack, "I think they just expect you to be back by lights out."

"Three squares and a cot and I'm on the honor system?"

"Knowing you," chided Bradley, "it'd be the ornery system."

"Brad," crowed Joseph, "you wound me."

"So, is it true?" inquired Bradley.

Joseph paused for a moment and studied Bradley as though admitting to an unseemly indiscretion.

"Yeah, it's true."

"Did they have it coming?" said McCormack, looming in his presence.

Joseph pursed his lips and studied the ground, his eyes reddening.

"Probably even more than I know from what they were saying while they were working me over. Like I told your boy over there. They had it coming."

McCormack's eyes bored into Joseph's for a long lingering moment. Joseph looked right back. To Bradley and Daniel's surprise, Joseph did not flinch under the X-raying eyes of the telepath.

"So," said McCormack, finally. "You want to ride in the front seat?"

Joseph grinned and looked over his shoulder at the perimeter of reservation police and the Deputies in the distance.

"No account going to the extra lengths with me," said Joseph with a wry grin. "I'll go the hard way for the news cameras."

"No news," answered Daniel, emphatically.

"An Indian beats down white Deputies on the Rez? There's bound to be press."

"Not yet," answered McCormack. "No."

"Still off the books?"

"For now," answered McCormack.

"Gotcha."

Joseph pulled on his coat and adjusted his gambler hat. "So, where's the transport?"

"On the other side of the reservation," answered Daniel.

"So we're going for a walk, then?"

"Unless you'd rather *jump*'there." replied McCormack.

"Walking's nice," replied Joseph, coolly.

Bradley chuckled and escorted Joseph across the Astroturf carpet and onto the dusty road. The coyote watched their progress pensively, and Joseph stopped in his tracks. He knelt down and the mangy dog trotted up and licked Joseph's palm, as he scratched behind the coyote's ears.

"Good boy," cooed Joseph. "Be seeing you." With that, Joseph stood up and eyed the crowd of lookeyloos who had gathered to witness his arrest. "Feed my dog while I'm away. I come back and find out one of you shot my dog, I'm coming round for a talk."

The lookeyloos looked down at the wild coyote, then back up at Joseph's stern glare, and backed away up the path to their homes.

"Damn, Joe," scoffed McCormack. "Only you would take in a feral coyote."

"He's a good dog," answered Joseph. "Aren't you, boy?"

The coyote woofed and trotted away into the barren wilderness.

"They don't like him because he knocks over their trash cans for the food, but we hunt and kill his game, so he's gotta eat something."

"Right," said Bradley, without thinking.

"I'd take him with me, if I could," continued Joseph. "But I don't think the ride would sit well with him. Besides, he's meant to be in the wild."

"What about you?" inquired McCormack, fishing—for what Bradley had no idea—Daniel studied him carefully.

"Well," replied Joseph, "that's something me and that dog have in common. We don't do well in society."

"You want to give it a go?" said McCormack

"What do you mean?" said Joseph

"I mean we don't have to go to North Brother Island," said McCormack, coming to the point.

"Where else could we go?"

"Washington," answered McCormack.

"State?"

"District of Columbia." corrected Daniel, now seeing where McCormack was leading. A teleporter for the team might give an advantage on the next scrimmage against the Black Ops team. Joseph studied the ground and kicked at the earth, mulling it over.

"That's a wilderness of another sort," breathed Joseph.

"I need someone who can do a decent sweep of a room," said Daniel. "And knows how to take some initiative."

"What sort of initiative?" asked Joseph warily.

"Like taking some courses on criminal investigation" said McCormack. "And being able to step up to the plate on a team."

"You're offering me a job?" said Joseph with a slight trepidation in his demeanor. "A job in law enforcement?"

"You look capable," said Daniel. "And you can obviously take a punch."

"What do I have to do?"

"I'll settle for a suit and a haircut," said Daniel.

"I'll settle for a suit and a ponytail," countered Joseph.

"This is a high profile team," pressed Daniel. "We'll be out in the public. I want a professional look for the team."

"And I got scars I'd rather not show," answered Joseph plainly.

Daniel looked at him as an oddity. He looked fine. Was Joseph being literal or metaphorical? Did he have some issue with people not from a reservation? And how important was it to weigh his words at that moment? Daniel was not used to the whole negotiating process as a whole and found it distasteful.

"I'm not asking you to strip and play Indian," snapped Daniel.

"I recognize that," replied Joseph. "But I have my vanity."

"Fine," answered Daniel.

"We have a deal?" said McCormack.

"For now," answered Daniel.

"Well then," said McCormack. "Let's get out of here."

Bradley sighed.

"What about them?" he asked, eyeing the Deputies who gripped their shotguns so tightly their knuckles were white.

"What *about* them?" scoffed Daniel, and he pulled out an earpiece, placed it in his ear and tapped it. "Pilot," said Daniel in a clear voice. "Pick us up at these coordinates."

"Do I have authorization to fly onto reservation land?"

"You're already on reservation land."

"Right," replied the pilot. "I'll be there in a few minutes. Let me clear the yokels out of the cabin."

"What?!" bellowed Daniel.

"They've never seen a bird like this before and they were getting pretty riled that I wouldn't let them take a look."

Daniel waved and signaled Flannery.

"Get the car ready." ordered Daniel. "We're coming fast."

Flannery turned on his heels and climbed into his SUV.

"Let's go." called Flannery from the driver's seat.

The Deputies stepped forward squeezing their shotguns so tight they chafed the skin on their hands.

"He's not going anywhere with you," shouted a belligerent Deputy.

Daniel looked over his shoulder toward Bradley.

"Brad…"

Bradley stepped forward and squared off with the Deputies.

"You want to go home, now." said Bradley. "Thank you for your assistance."

The Deputies stood there slack-jawed for a moment and then slowly turned and shuffled toward their cruisers, climbed in and pulled away. Bradley stood there looking back at Daniel with a leisurely smile. McCormack patted him on the back, and Joseph grinned.

"Thanks for that," said Joseph. "Those Deputies had me a mite nervous."

"After you, Joe," said Bradley, and Joseph stepped toward the SUV with a nod to Agent Flannery and climbed into the back of the truck. Bradley followed and clambered in after him. Daniel made his way to the front passenger seat to be blocked my McCormack.

"We're walking into a delicate situation, Daniel." said McCormack.

"I know," scoffed Daniel.

"How you handle it," he pressed, "is going to reflect on us."

"I know," answered Daniel.

"How are you going to handle it?"

"I'll be discrete," said Daniel.

McCormack studied him for a moment and then stepped back, making way for Daniel to enter the SUV. McCormack climbed in next to Bradley and Joseph.

The drive back to the Teek Nos Pos Trading Post was quicker than the ride in. It seemed Agent Flannery was in a hurry to be off reservation land and be shot of his cargo. Daniel could not bring himself to blame him. Currying Specials around most assuredly was not on the list at the beginning of the day. Still, he was amicable and did not fidget much. Daniel would remember his professionalism at the end of this.

Back at the trading post, a mob surrounded the Chariot, lifting hatches and peering in, or walking around the cabin while the pilot waved helplessly to get them out of the craft to no avail.

When Flannery pulled up it was to a mob of people glaring at him for pulling up too hard and sending a wave of dust and small stones at them like shrapnel. Daniel flew out of the car seat and jumped onto the ground, marching like a drill sergeant.

"Can I have your attention please!"

No one responded.

"Hey!" bellowed Daniel, and a small group turned to face him. "Get away from the federal transport, now!"

The small group who held his attention moved sheepishly out of the way, while the remainder ignored him.

Daniel caught one man walking away with his duffel bag.

"Hey!"

He snatched the bag out of his hands.

"Give me that!" barked Daniel, his jacket coming open to reveal his side arm. "And get the hell out of here!"

The man backed away nervously.

"Pilot!" bellowed Daniel. "Get on the com and make the following announcement: 'This craft is preparing for takeoff. Please proceed to a safe distance.'"

The pilot stood there jerkily, his mouth agape, but he quickly rallied and ran into the cabin, sending people out as he ran.

Daniel took to swatting people with his duffel bag as they ran and ordered people away from the craft. He pulled at his tie, undid the top button, and shouted for attention.

"Ladies and gentlemen," echoed the pilot's voice over the intercom. "This craft is preparing for takeoff. Please proceed to a safe distance! I repeat, please proceed to a safe distance."

More of the mob poured away from the craft, however there were a few stragglers who would not be distracted from their investigation of the craft, and they shot dirty looks at Daniel as he approached. One of them, a ferret looking man, had a camcorder and videoed his approach.

"Get the hell out of there! What the hell are you doing?!"

Just then, he spotted the ferret man videoing the entire scene and he snatched the camcorder out of his hand.

"I'm confiscating this."

The ferret man glared at him with disgust and made to snatch the camcorder back. Daniel pulled his side arm and he now had the mob's full attention. Just then, their eyes seemed to glaze over and they turned and walked away calmly to a safe distance where they turned and faced him resigned looks on their faces.

Daniel perplexed over this and looked around for something to explain the odd behavior of the mob. Just then, McCormack patted him on the shoulder.

"Subtle." chided McCormack.

"Shut up," sighed Daniel. "Let's get on the bird before anything else happens."

"My thoughts exactly," said Bradley.

Joseph said nothing. He smiled ear to ear, apparently pleased by the mayhem around him. Joseph stepped onto the transport and took a seat, adjusting his hat as he sat down. Bradley and McCormack climbed in after him and took their seats around him, instantly falling into banter about the old days during the war.

Daniel traded a glance with McCormack, who sat silently staring at him. In Daniel's mind, the sentence was pushed with a seeming ease: *"Well, you've got some color for the team. Happy?"*

Daniel grinned at McCormack and climbed into the cabin, sealing the sliding door and climbed into the cockpit.

"We ready to go?" said the pilot nervously.

"At your leisure." replied Daniel, a stern glare in his eye for the pilot.

"Yes, sir." said the pilot with a sigh of relief that the debacle was now over.

The pilot's fingers rode the console and the Chariot roared to life, rising into the air and angling Easterly toward the horizon, climbing in altitude higher and higher. With a short on pour of speed, the Chariot hummed and cracked as it broke the sound barrier and, within a moment, was gone.

CHAPTER 13

TERRY LYONS

CAMBRIDGE, MASSACHUSETTS

Terry Lyons walked into the lobby of her apartment complex on Binney Street and 5th with a shiver. She was an elegantly dressed black woman with a regal stride and a youthful face and body that belied her true age of 47. Her hair was pulled back and bound into an elegant bun with her scarf pulled tight across her mouth and nose, leaving only her brown almond eyes showing—her eyelashes tinted with snow.

Once inside the lobby, she tugged at her scarf, which yielded to her delicate fingertips as she walked to the stairs. The elevator had been out for two days, and with the snow, it was unlikely the elevator repairman would be making the journey to Cambridge this evening. With a sigh, she climbed the steps to her apartment on the third floor.

On the third floor landing, Terry caught sight of Rebecca Goldberg, an elderly woman in a weathered frock raincoat, pulling her grocery cart up the steps one by one, laboring with the two wheeled contraption as she neared her destination.

"Hi Rebecca," sang Terry, "Here, let me help you with that."

Terry quickly took up the cart and pulled it onto the landing.

"You are so sweet," sang Rebecca, "Always helping out. I'm always telling Sol that."

"Oh," replied Terry with a wave of her hand, "it's nothing at all."

"Sol," called Rebecca toward the open door at the edge of the landing, "Get down to the car and help bring up the groceries. We can't infringe upon Terry's generosity any more than necessary."

"Alright, alright," answered Sol, "I'm coming."

Soon, an elderly man, bent by the weight of age appeared in the doorway.

"Hello, Terry." smiled Sol and his eyes took in her business attire. "I see you're dressed in your winter's best."

Terry smiled at her thin dress pants and dress boots underneath her coat wet from the snow and clinging to her calves.

"I try," said Terry, in a dry singsong. "As best as work allows."

Sol rubbed his face as though checking for whiskers.

"It must be tough weathering the elements in something so thin."

"Oh," sang Terry, "I get by."

"I bet you do at that," smoothed Sol, like a younger man at a nightclub.

Rebecca rolled her eyes.

"Well, Sol," reprimanded Rebecca, "are you going to stand here chatting it up with every pretty girl in the building or are you going to get down to the car?"

"Alright, alright," answered Sol, his subterfuge dashed to pieces. "I'm going."

"Night Sol," sang Terry as Sol made his way down the stairs tightening his coat around his waist.

"Good night, Terry," replied Sol with a youthful smile for the young exotic woman with the deep brown eyes.

Rebecca rolled her eyes again.

"Honestly," scoffed Rebecca, "That man. He's too old to be acting like such a playboy."

"Oh," sang Terry, "I don't see anything wrong with being young at heart. Do you?"

"Well when you put it that way," replied Rebecca, in a communal whisper. "It is nice when he gets frisky like this."

"There, you see? He's definitely in the mood tonight. Light some candles for dinner and see what happens."

Then, Rebecca blushed uncontrollably, and slapped her hands to her cheeks to cover the telltale rosing of her cheeks.

"Oh Terry," sighed Rebecca, for her teasing. "You're terrible."

"What?" protested Terry, "You deserve it. You're a beautiful woman. There's no reason why you can't let yourself be desirable."

Rebecca studied her for a second, a thought on the tip of her tongue.

"You really think-" said Rebecca, stopping short and second guessing herself. "I'm too old for such things…"

"You're never too old to be young," replied Terry, knowingly.

Down below, the lobby door banged open with a clatter, and Sol could be heard cursing under his breath, intruding on their moment. Rebecca grew flustered and began to physically steer Terry toward the hallway.

"You'd better hurry along, dear," said Rebecca, "Before the letch comes back and monopolizes more of your time."

"Just as long as you monopolize his tonight," replied Terry, over her shoulder, playfully struggling against Rebecca's thrusts.

"Well," said Rebecca, at last, "we'll just have to see what happens, dear."

"Good night, Rebecca."

"Good night, dear."

Terry walked down the hallway toward her apartment and Rebecca watched after her, as though she were something precious. Sol cursed on the stairwell and Rebecca glanced down expectantly, comforted by the sound of Terry's keys jingling. Rebecca turned to grab a second glance at Terry, but she had vanished.

Obviously inside her comfortable apartment, thought Rebecca, *bless her.*

Sol puffed as he made it to the third landing laden with grocery bags.

"One more trip ought to do it, Rebecca."

"That will be fine, dear. Hurry and I'll begin making dinner."

"Fine, fine."

Sol passed the bags on to Rebecca, who took them with surprising strength and he turned to head back down the stairs, and into the snow. On the second floor landing, he nearly collided with a rushing Terry Lyons. She was dressed in a red sweater and jeans with thick socks protruding from her tennis shoes and her hair was down.

"Oh, sorry Sol." said Terry, recognizing the shock in his face. "Are you alright?"

"I'm fine," replied Sol, "I'm fine. My heart's strong as a horse."

"Well, that's good to know."

"Did you forget something?"

"No," said Terry, curious. "Why?"

"I-" began Sol, then thought better of it. "Nothing. Forget it. I'd better get the rest of the groceries out of the car before someone steals it. You know how Rebecca gets."

"Oh," said Terry, her eyes alight. "Tell Rebecca I said hello. I do enjoy talking to her."

Sol looked at Terry for a long moment, and finally stammered—

"I will," said Sol at last.

"Thanks Sol," sang Terry, kissing him on the cheek. "You're a dear."

With that, Terry hurried up the stairs and disappeared at the third landing. Sol looked after her, half expecting her to reappear. When she did not, he turned and walked down the steps, a little worried for Terry.

That was odd, thought Sol. *And wasn't she wearing a different coat and pants?*

Sol shook it off as a lapse of old age setting in, as confusion transformed into the reality that he was not a young man anymore. With a heavy sigh, Sol made his way down to the car to fetch the rest of the groceries. Trudging out in the snow, he tightened his coat's belt around him and found the trunk of the car still open. He buried his head in the trunk and grasped at the bags, hefting them up and struggled with his elbow to close the trunk. It was a juggling act he was losing when a familiar gloved hand grasped the trunk and closed it. Sol blinked in the falling snow to see the beautiful features of Terry Lyons dressed in warm winter clothes and snow boots. The colorful clothing was matted with snow as if she had been walking for hours.

"I hope you don't mind," said Terry looking thoughtful. "It looked like you could use a hand."

"You won't hear me complaining, pretty lady."

"You're such a flirt," reprimanded Terry playfully. "But don't let Rebecca hear you talking like that. She's such a sweet woman."

"I'm smart enough to keep such things to myself, thank you very much."

"Rebecca's right about you. You are a playboy."

"She said that?"

"All the time."

"Do you need help with these bags?"

"I think I got it, thank you, dear."

Just then, one of the bags tore and the milk fell out of the plastic bag onto the snow-covered asphalt. Terry quickly retrieved it and smiled.

"Just a little help, then?"

"Oh," contemplated Sol for a moment, and then resigned himself to the company. "Alright."

Terry smiled warmly and took a bag from Sol and led him toward the building.

"So, how are you?"

"Oh," said Sol, patting his chest, "strong as an ox."

"I have no doubt." replied Terry playfully.

"So, I see you decided to enjoy the weather with some warm clothes like I told you."

"I always wear this when I walk to work."

"I thought you took the train."

"Sol, I work down at Costco."

Sol blinked, slightly confused.

"In management?"

"God, I wish. I fold clothes and do boxing in the evenings."

Sol looked pitiably on Terry, never realizing the hardship she lingered in.

"I didn't know."

"Well, we all do what we can."

"How can you afford your apartment on a Costco salary?"

"Oh," sang Terry with a warm smile, as though it was not really a problem, "I get by."

"You'd think you'd live somewhere more in your means."

"Sol," pouted Terry, "I could take it to mean you don't want my company."

"Walking alone with a beautiful woman, if you'll excuse me saying, I don't have a problem with you at all."

"That's sweet," said Terry, and she kissed Sol on the cheek.

Inside she pulled off her knit cap to reveal cornrows pulled back into a ponytail. Sol was amazed.

"Isn't that a tricky hairstyle to have?"

"I don't follow you."

"Doesn't something like that take a while to do?"

"Oh, the cornrows? Yeah, it takes a full evening to put together, but it keeps my hair out of my eyes, and I think it looks pretty. What do you think?"

"I find you breathtaking however you wear your hair."

"Sol, you keep talking like that, you're going to get into trouble."

"I wouldn't see it as trouble," winked Sol.

When they reached the third landing, Terry passed the milk and bag back to Sol.

"You have it from here, I take it?"

"I do." replied Sol, politely. "And thank you for your help back there."

"It's no problem," replied Terry, "Oh, and do say hi to Rebecca, will you?"

"…I will," stammered Sol, utterly perplexed by the notion of her repeating herself as though each meeting was the first.

Terry waved and turned to walk down the hallway. Sol watched her make her way to her doorstep and pull out her keys but was distracted by the sound of his wife banging pots in the kitchen, a "silent" sign she was impatient for his return. He dared a second glance down the hallway to see if Terry had inserted the key yet only to find she had vanished. Apparently already in her cozy apartment.

Sol was just about to enter his apartment when the clatter of stiletto heels on the steps alerted him to someone's presence close behind him. He turned in time to see Terry Lyons grunting up the steps. Her long coat had come open revealing black stockings, thigh high black leather boots, a black miniskirt with a top that allowed her cleavage to show prominently and her hair teased and permed. Sol's jaw dropped at the sight of her, as he turned between her apartment and the vision on the landing, with a double take expression.

Terry stopped dead and glared at Sol with disgust.

"What the fuck are you looking at?" challenged Terry. Sol was astonished at her harsh voice and saw nothing but coldness in her eyes, like she had seen and done everything before. "Pervert." she spat.

Sol stood aghast as Terry walked past him, a swish of her hips as her backside butted him out of the way and he watched her proceed down the hall to her apartment. Sol turned to look for Rebecca, and when he turned back, Terry had vanished. A cold sweat broke out all over his body, and he went lightheaded. Sol quickly turned and entered his apartment, not daring to watch Terry make her way the rest of the way to her apartment. He closed the door as softly as he could for fear he would annoy her and she would come back, perhaps looking completely different and sent him calling 911 for the men in white coats to take him away.

"Rebecca," said Sol, as he set the milk and bags down on the counter. "I'm not feeling well. I'm going to lie down."

Rebecca looked up at his frightened eyes and was filled with dread at the sight of him.

"Are you alright?" she said, nervously.

"I'm fine, I'm fine." assured Sol. "I just need a good rest. That's all."

"I'll call Doctor Lieberman," said Rebecca, and she quickly picked up the phone.

"No," answered Sol, "no doctors. I just need to shut my eyes for a little while. I'm fine dear."

"But Sol," begged Rebecca, "if you tell me what's the matter-"

"I said I'm fine, woman." snapped Sol, instantly regretting it as his tone took a kinder tenor. "I just need to lie down. I don't want to alarm you. Everything's fine."

"If you're sure," replied Rebecca, hesitantly, clearly unsure in Sol's self-assessment.

"I'm sure." reassured Sol.

"Alright, then," said Rebecca, "I'll make some matzo soup. How does that sound?"

"It sounds good, dear."

"Alright, you lie down, and I'll make dinner for you in bed."

Sol turned to head to the bedroom when he stopped nervously and faced Rebecca.

"Rebecca," said Sol, lingering at the kitchen archway, "I don't know what I'd do without you."

And Sol took her hand gingerly, looking deep into her eyes with gratitude. Rebecca's eyes welled up and she smiled, patting the back of his cold sweaty hand.

"Lie down, dear," assured Rebecca, "I'm here."

"I'll just be a minute," said Sol.

Sol clambered into the bedroom and laid down on the firm mattress and shut his eyes. Hoping that he was not going mad, and at the same time hoping that the visions of Terry were just a hallucination—he couldn't bear to think of his neighbor being that troubled. But more he hoped he was not suffering a heart attack. He laid in bed, his eyes shut, the cold sweat continuing to drench his shirt and it clung to his body. He tried to remember being a young man, dealing with stress with deep long breaths. Little by little, his heart slowed and his breathing grew regular, and he sighed as he drifted off to sleep.

WASHINGTON D.C., THE POST

Daniel sat at his desk poring over his notebook reading the dossier on Terry Lyons anticipating his lack of understanding and striving to correct any problems digesting the text to greater facilitate his formulation of a strategy. Daniel was running in circles.

McCormack knocked on the door and stood in the open doorway.

"Maybe we can help," offered McCormack.

Daniel looked over McCormack's broad shoulders to see Bradley standing easily behind him. With a gesture toward the seats in front of his desk, McCormack and Bradley filed in and took their seats, gesturing for him to speak.

"Where are the others?" inquired Daniel. It was McCormack who answered.

"Leonard took Chad and Joseph out for a jog through the neighborhood and the SUV already picked up Stephen and Josh for their training session in the Detonation Chamber."

"Alright," said Daniel, satisfied he did not need to worry about the rest of the team in his absence. "Here we go again. We are looking into one Terry Lyons, callsign Avatar. [Rank: Special Operations Covert Operations-Beta Status BLUE ANCHOR]. The bureau has calculated over twenty-seven aliases, all of them using the same social security number and bank account. All of the checks are deposited into the bank account, and-"

Daniel glanced down at his notebook and scrolled through a few pages, his brow furrowed. Bradley and McCormack sat in silence in wait for Daniel to continue. When the acceptable amount of silence lapsed, McCormack leaned forward.

"And?"

"And," continued Daniel, "that's where things get weird. There are no withdrawals from any of the cities in any of the states save from the Cambridge Massachusetts branch."

Bradley and McCormack traded a knowing glance and grimly stirred in their chairs. This did not go unnoticed by Daniel.

"Is there anything you can tell me about her?" pressed Daniel.

McCormack leaned closer to the desk, pulling his chair closer. Daniel set down his notebook and leaned into the confidence being offered.

"What you have to understand," said McCormack, "is Terry was a gifted telekinetic."

"Not a bad telepath, either," added Bradley.

"But she got pulled off the front line," continued McCormack, "for a black box project and never returned to the front. Her record reads like a ghost. That's a telling thing. Whatever she was doing, she was buried deep. Frankly, I don't see how the government let her go."

"Perhaps they didn't," mused Bradley, "Perhaps she escaped."

"If she did," replied McCormack, "she's been doing a piss poor job of hiding herself." McCormack shook his head and leaned back, staring at the dust motes travelling through the air in the beam of sunlight that broke through the clouds. The intensity of his stare was so total, it was with a dark tone that he continued. "No, something else is going on."

"This could just be a dead end," said Daniel in frustration, "where she's a victim of identity theft. That's what the bureau seems to be thinking, anyway."

"But you don't think so," concluded McCormack.

"No," replied Daniel, "I think she's probably tapped a little deeper into her abilities. Maybe brainwashing people into thinking she's working for them when she's not. Drawing paychecks by using her telepathy illegally."

"Seems like you've already made your mind up about her," said McCormack, critically.

Daniel met his eyes and shifted in his seat as a wave of shame swept over him.

"Sorry," said Daniel with a self-deprecating scoff, "it's a bad habit I've picked up as a detective. I'm trying to see things without jumping to conclusions, but this case just doesn't make any sense."

"Do we have any background on her?" said Bradley.

"She's divorced," replied Daniel, scrolling through his notebook. "Husband took the kid and disappeared. No one's seen him since. Wherever he is, he's hid himself well. Ms. Lyons made several attempts to search for her child through the courts, claiming her daughter was kidnapped. The courts haven't been very accommodating."

"Of course," said McCormack, darkly.

"So we've got a woman who's a Special," mused Daniel, "she's got a grudge. She's not going after anybody. All she's doing is making a truckload of money by somehow being at near thirty places at once, and as far as I can tell, having residence in only the Cambridge area."

"So we're going to Massachusetts, then?" said Bradley.

"SUV's waiting outside," said Daniel, "We leave in five minutes."

"You'll be bringing your duffel bag, I take it?" said McCormack snidely.

"You have a problem with my wanting to be prepared?" challenged Daniel.

"Not at all," replied McCormack. "Just wondering what it is you're bringing along with you on these collars."

Daniel eyed McCormack for a moment and then pulled out his duffel bag and opened it, revealing a flak jacket, two side arms with laser sightings, two tazer guns, winvid sunglasses with targeting systems, an earpiece communications device and a first aid kit.

"Happy?" said Daniel, sarcastically.

"You planning on invading the apartment?" said McCormack.

"If I have to," replied Daniel, darkly.

"Let's just try knocking first," offered McCormack.

"I think I can handle this, Tobias." snapped Daniel.

"Fine," replied McCormack, coolly, "I'm just going on record, here."

"Duly noted," replied Daniel.

McCormack turned and headed down the hall to his room to change. Five minutes later, Bradley and McCormack appeared as different as two men in suits could be. McCormack wore a classic black suit with a thin black tie, while Bradley went for the more stylish suit with a black on black fashion statement complemented by a red tie. Daniel clicked his teeth with irritation at Bradley's choice of apparel.

"We ready to walk down the runway, Brad?"

"I'm ready," replied Bradley, coolly.

"Good," said Daniel, shooting his cuffs out. "Let's go."

JOINT BASE ANDREWS NAVAL AIR FACILITY, ANDREWS WIZARDS HANGAR

The SUV pulled up alongside the Chariot and the doors flew open. Daniel slung his duffel bag over his shoulder and led McCormack and Bradley toward the Chariot with

TERRY LYONS

determined strides, as though he were already marching on Lyons' front door. McCormack and Bradley traded uncomfortable glances as they followed in silence. With a hop, Daniel was inside the cabin of the Chariot and he quickly made his way to the cockpit, where the same pilot as last time sat nervously at the helm, expecting Daniel's disappointment.

"You again?" snapped Daniel.

"Sorry, sir," said the pilot. "I've been assigned to pilot this craft. I'm not happy about it either."

"Can you fly like a sane person this time?"

The words stung the pilot, and he reddened, tucking his head down and nodding. Daniel did not care if the pilot was angry or ashamed.

"I'll do my best," muttered the pilot.

"Good," sang Daniel with a clap of his hands. "I'll be in the cabin if you decide to fly stupid again."

"I got a feel for her now," spoke up the pilot, the red in his cheeks spreading across his forehead. "There won't be any more problems with the flight."

"Good. Then I'll leave you to it."

"Yes sir."

Daniel threw down his duffel bag and sat down next to Bradley and McCormack with a disgusted look on his face.

"Same pilot?" surmised McCormack.

"Same pilot," replied Daniel, nonplussed.

"I expected as much," said McCormack. "We're a Specials team. No one wants to work with us." With a shrug he added, "What can you do?"

Daniel kicked the seat across from him for all the good it did, then sat back and locked his harness. He then pulled his notebook out from his breast pocket and began scrolling through the pages, quickly becoming engrossed in the files he had read a dozen times, and had all but committed to memory. He grunted through his nose as he stared at the notebook with disgust.

"You seem troubled," said Bradley.

"I'm just looking over my notes," replied Daniel, "It's really unclear how she is committing fraud because all the jobs report her as hardworking and reliable. Never late. There are overlapping work schedules, which would make it impossible to be in two places at once, but her records show she is in two places at once. Or rather, twenty-seven places at once. At first I was thinking she was hacking human resources databases and inputting her own personal data, then using her telepathy to convince key people she was working there, but I don't know..."

"Well have you found a trend in employment?" said McCormack.

"The jobs are all different," replied Daniel, "Bank manager, waitress, DMV clerk, postal employee, escort, personal assistant to a CEO, personal assistant to a congressman, etc. Each with a winning letter from the employer."

McCormack nodded in thoughtful silence while Daniel pored through the file looking helplessly for an explanation that was satisfactory. Finally, he reached over and put his hand on Daniel's shoulder.

"There is a possible way she could be in two places at once," said McCormack, at last. "I'd hate to think of the ramifications to her psyche in dividing it to micromanage each one but it is possible, for her."

Daniel blinked.

"Go on," he urged.

Bradley knew where McCormack was going with his reasoning and quickly chimed in.

"Back in basic," said Bradley, "we were put through a battery of tests to push our abilities further than we had previously conceived. One test was the psi-ball."

"A what?" stammered Daniel.

"A psi-ball is a construct of pure psionic energy," McCormack explained. "It can be measured, weighed and tested. During basic, we used to try to bring one out into being. It was hard, frustrating work. But Terry was a natural. While the rest of us could only make a glob, or a sphere, she could make geometric shapes... likenesses of statues... she made the statue of David once, perfectly. There was talk that she could make them take on even greater dimension than what I've just described to you. Depth of shape, consistency in form. Color. It's possible she can create psi-balls that perfectly mimic people. Her ability would be very useful, if she's developed it to such a degree. Seemingly independent entities."

"A psi-ball," said Daniel, in disbelief. "But that implies just a ball."

"A ball is all the test subjects could ever muster. But Terry, she was different." McCormack paused and shook his head darkly. "Like I said, if she's micromanaging twenty plus psi-balls and sending them out into the workforce, I'd be wary about her state of mind in meeting her."

Daniel met his gaze and with understanding nudged his duffel bag with his foot.

"That's why I bring the duffel bag," said Daniel.

"We might need it," said McCormack, grimly.

"Why do you say that?" said Daniel, sensing a threat in the air.

Bradley watched them with a growing sense of severity.

"As a telekinetic," said McCormack, "she is very powerful. If she's mastered the psi-ball and is able to keep the shape and form coherent enough to pass by unnoticed in the workforce, with all the eyes watching for any subtle defect, and finding it flawless... She would have exceeded her potential that you have listed in her dossier. We would be walking into a situation unlike anything any of us have witnessed. I hope I'm wrong, on a few levels. But I have to admit, I'm curious to see her progress with the psi-ball."

"Curious," parroted Daniel, staring at McCormack.

"To see a perfect human construct," continued McCormack, his eyes showing a glint of wonder. "walking around, talking, breathing, thinking... Like cloning."

"Cloning?" parroted Daniel.

"If she thinks she's cornered," warned McCormack, "she can just dissolve the psi-ball, and it would be impossible to cover twenty-seven locations in the hopes that you had the right one. My suggestion, we take her when she gets home from work. Her psi-balls will be predictable. They will all go home or fade out of existence."

"You're sure of this?" asked Daniel, disbelievingly.

"You don't know the strain of making something like a psi-ball," replied McCormack. "The less effort in making one, the better off your psyche. If you are going to make more than one, then you would be wise to keep their constructs simple. The more you make, the less potent they become...unless you push yourself. We are talking about a psi-ball on an entirely different playing field, though. Mastering one psi-ball is tricky. Twenty plus is a mental breakdown waiting to happen."

Daniel sat back in his seat and let his notebook rest in his lap as his mind processed this frightening phenomena... To be able to summon a human being out of nothing and send it out to do the master's bidding. This Terry Lyons could be the single greatest threat Daniel had ever come across. Daniel's mind filled with assassins evaporating into thin air after the commission of their contracts. A chill travelled down his spine, and he shuddered at the thought of someone who was truly a one-man army.

LOGAN INTERNATIONAL AIRPORT

The Chariot landed on the tarmac with a slight bounce, before leveling out and touching down in a secluded section of the airport, far removed from the terminals. Daniel grit his teeth at the bounce and shot a severe look toward the cockpit only to find the pilot waving back weakly. Daniel traded glances with McCormack and Bradley and with a shake of his head at the inadequacy of their pilot, picked up his duffel bag and hit the panel that released the slideaway cabin door which pealed back to reveal three SUVs waiting for them. McCormack stood looking at the cars and frowned.

"You think they were expecting the whole team?" asked McCormack.

"No, it's as I ordered," said Daniel. "I wanted a perimeter and surveillance set up on Lyons' residence. Real low key. Just a tap on the phones and cameras on her apartment window."

"So you've thought ahead," said McCormack, with a nod.

"This has been in place since yesterday," replied Daniel.

Daniel stepped off the Chariot and strode across the tarmac, up to an aging agent from the bureau.

"Agent Rooke?" said the agent.

Daniel extended his hand but the agent was not forthcoming.

"Agent Rollins," announced the aging man, his jaw set. "I'm not happy about being here. I got pulled off a joint task force with ICE to be here. Tell me you're not going to get me into a long drawn out ordeal so I can get back to my job."

"This should be fairly straightforward," replied Daniel, assuredly, then added, "Your men will be standing by in an assist capacity should things go awry."

"By 'things go awry' you mean what, exactly?" pressed Rollins.

"I mean the suspect manages to kill me and my men and attempt to make good her escape."

"Is that likely?"

"You never know, dealing with Specials."

"Specials?" snarled Rollins. His lips turned down and his eyes hardened. "Tell me you're not actually going to use my men to track down freaks."

"I'll use your men as I see fit," snapped Daniel. "And get used to it. You're mine until I make the arrest or clear the suspect. Understood?"

"And I'm pointing out that I'm a little old for this dance," spat Rollins with a wave of his hand as though the thought of dealing with Specials were beneath him. Daniel eyed Rollins with contempt.

"But not too old to deal with smugglers and skin traffickers," challenged Daniel.

"That's a thinking game," replied Rollins. "You're talking about a game a little more physical than my team is trained to handle."

"That's why you're on perimeter and surveillance. You're not going through the door with me. This is a Specials situation. My team is trained for it."

"Two men?" scoffed Rollins, his eyes wide as though McCormack and Bradley were a joke, his eyes trailed over Bradley's choice of wardrobe and turned up his nose to him for dressing unprofessionally. Daniel sensed the problem and stepped forward until he was swimming in Rollins' vision.

"They have Special training," said Daniel, coolly. "More advanced than your Bureau leisure course. They're certified for the job at hand. You're not."

"You won't hear any complaints from me there."

Daniel gestured toward the SUV and Rollins turned, walking around to the driver's side and climbed into the lead SUV. Daniel led McCormack and Bradley to the SUV and climbed in.

"So," said Rollins, "what is this special training you were talking about that you guys receive that makes you such bad asses you can take on Specials?"

"We train against Specials in an urban warfare center."

"So you guys get paid to fight Specials, huh?" mused Rollins. "Are these Specials you're fighting against inmates?"

"That's classified," concluded Daniel, hoping Rollins would drop the matter and stop indirectly offending his teammates.

"Sure, sure," said Rollins. "But you must come up against some real nasty pieces of work. What do they look like, anyway? All deformed and beastlike, I'll bet."

"You've never met a Special before have you?" said McCormack, a wry smile on his face.

"Why would I be consorting with the likes of them?" scoffed Rollins, though he eased up a little as he looked into the rearview mirror at the professional cut of McCormack's manner. "My job is to track down and arrest criminals, not hang out with them."

"I should advise you," said Daniel, warningly, "that you have two Specials sitting right behind you."

Rollins went rigid and cold, as his eyes slowly climbed to the rearview mirror and scowled at Bradley and McCormack, who scowled right back at him.

"We should be there inside fifteen minutes," said Rollins, an edge in his voice, and he pressed his foot down on the accelerator as hard as the icy conditions would allow.

It was a quiet fifteen minutes. Rollins ground his teeth in annoyance at being a chauffeur for Specials, and he let them know it with glares into the rearview mirror, as though he expected to be attacked my McCormack and Bradley at any moment. Rollins took Interstate 90 to Exit 18, and took Storrow Drive to Monsignor O'Brien Highway and took it across the Charles River to Cambridge. All in all, a quick drive, though the silence lingered and made the drive seem much, much longer. Rollins turned onto Binney Street and stopped at 5th Street at a dog park, parking behind four SUVs and two black vans.

"Here we are, Agent Rooke," said Rollins, a cool edge in his voice that clearly screamed *get out of the car!* Daniel chuckled, and grabbed his duffel bag.

Daniel stepped out of the SUV and surveyed the dog park and the street. Elm trees lined the sidewalks of Binney Street and the snow had taken the consistency of slush in the warming sunlight breaking free from the clouds. Daniel looked at the conditions favorably and turned serious as he rounded on Rollins, sitting comfortably in the heated SUV.

"Have your men hold the perimeter," commanded Daniel. "Each point of escape I want covered."

"What if we got a Special breaking free," mused Rollins, a playful smile starting to twist into a leer, "what then?"

"Hold your fire until I give the kill order," replied Daniel. Rollins clicked his tongue and gnawed on his cheek, displeased with his instructions. "That's all," concluded Daniel, and he closed the door on Rollins.

Realizing he was dismissed, Rollins exited the SUV and walked over to the black vans signaling the men to meet with him. They gathered in a huddle at a distance from Daniel and traded moody looks which quickly turned to expressions of shock and trepidation. McCormack walked up to Daniel, and stood next to him grimly.

"You ready for this?" inquired McCormack, steeling himself as much as Daniel.

Daniel pulled his duffel bag off, set it on the slush covered ground and opened it—he dug in, pulling out a taser gun and a Sig 9mm. Bradley watched in horror as Daniel slid a magazine into the Sig and locked and loaded the weapon. Daniel caught the look of anxiety on Bradley's face and stowed the Sig into his holster, closing his jacket as he heaved the duffel bag back into the SUV's passenger seat.

"Let's go," said Daniel.

"Yes, sir," muttered Bradley.

McCormack and Bradley followed Daniel across the street and into the main lobby for the complex, shaking the cold off them as they penetrated deeper into the lobby. An elevator repairman stood in the elevator. He smiled and waved.

"You gentlemen going up?" said the repairman cheerily.

"Yes," said Daniel.

"Step right on," said the repairman with a smile. "I just got her working again. What floor you headed to?"

"Three, please," said Daniel.

The repairman hit the three button warily and looked up at the ceiling of the cab as though he could see through it all the way to the third floor.

"I hear there's a lot of weird happenings on third floor."

"Really?" said Daniel, suddenly alert. "Like what?"

"Like tremors. Voices and the like."

"You've heard voices?" pressed McCormack.

The repairman looked uncomfortably at Daniel and McCormack. Bradley stood with his back pressed to the wall of the elevator cab looking forlorn.

"No," replied the repairman, as though he wanted to divorce himself from the gossip as much as possible. "I take the people in the building at their word."

The elevator doors opened to the brass three dimly shining in the florescent lighting. The repairman poked his head out and scanned the floor as though straining to hear a voice. He turned and smiled at Daniel and the others.

"I'm just saying, you might want to be careful. Something's not right on that floor."

"Thank you," said Daniel with a smile.

"It's probably just ghost stories," offered the repairman, "but you never know."

"True," said Daniel kindly. "Thanks again."

The elevator repairman tapped the lobby button repeatedly, as though he could coax some speed out of the door and the elevator to get as far away from the third floor as possible, just in case. Finally the doors closed and Daniel heard the repairman audibly sigh through the doors. He turned around to face McCormack and Bradley.

"You may be right about her abilities increasing," said Daniel, darkly.

McCormack said nothing, he stood like granite. Bradley seemed to be listening to something. Finally he said: "She's close."

"Is she in her apartment?" demanded Daniel, his hand slipping unconsciously to the catch on his holster.

"Yes," replied Bradley. "She seems divided. Part of her is aware we're here, but the dominant part of her consciousness is distracted by something."

"What?" demanded Daniel. "What is distracting her?"

Bradley focused on the static in the air and seemed to grow distant, removed from them. Finally a tear fell and Bradley wiped his eyes.

"Oh, Terry," stammered Bradley.

"What is it?" demanded Daniel.

"It's what we feared," said Bradley. "She's divided her consciousness into compartmentalized independent units. Each with a distinct function."

"How is Terry?" demanded McCormack.

"She's not good," said Bradley, his voice trailing off eerily as he stared off into nothingness. "She doesn't know how bad she is. I don't know how we can solve this. She's too unstable. Anything could set her off."

"Daniel," said McCormack, "I'd like to go on record and suggest we come back with the rest of the team."

Daniel shook his head.

"We go," concluded Daniel. "If it seems like she won't go quietly, I think we can contain it between the three of us. If things go south, that's what the guns are for."

Neither Bradley or McCormack were pleased to hear his thoughts and studied him with grit teeth. Daniel ignored it as he led them down the hallway, fighting the creeping sensation of unease that seemed to infect him with every step. The closer he got to Lyons' apartment door, the stronger the sense grew as though she were willing people to leave her alone. Daniel suppressed the shiver travelling down his spine and unbuttoned his jacket, an action that did not go unnoticed by Bradley, who rushed forward and stopped Daniel.

"What are you doing?" demanded Bradley.

"Stand down, Overman," commanded Daniel.

"That's it?" scoffed Bradley. "You're going to go in there gun blazing? Is that how you intend to lead us?"

"Brad," soothed McCormack, "read him."

"You know I can't read him," spat Bradley. "You put the block on him yourself."

"You're a much more talented telepath than me," coaxed McCormack. "Go in there and take a look."

"Guys," said Daniel, uncomfortably. "I'm right here."

Bradley looked deep into Daniel's eyes for a long hard moment—his eyes scrutinized Daniel and the veins in his temples pulsed. Finally Bradley exhaled and pulled back away from Daniel.

"Fine." said Bradley, "Sorry, Daniel. I just don't like guns."

"My gun is my way of evening the playing field."

Bradley studied him another moment and then pursed his lips.

"Fine."

"Now if we're done here," said Daniel. "I believe Terry's door is right over there."

Daniel, McCormack and Bradley stood staring at the door near the turn in the hallway. They stared at the room number and Daniel checked it with his notebook, seeing clearly the apartment was indeed 317.

"Here we go," said Daniel, taking a trepid step toward the door.

"Daniel," offered McCormack, "Perhaps if she saw a friendly face?"

Daniel studied McCormack and Bradley for a moment, and then stepped back.

"Go on, then."

McCormack knocked on the door and stood there in the silence of the hallway listening to the activity on the other side of the door. The door to 317 embodied everything unknown to an arresting officer. To Daniel, it was a series of fortifications and barricaded doors. To McCormack it was a room filled with psi-balls. To Bradley, the door embodied a mere construct barring a world from seeing pain unendurable.

No one was prepared for what was on the other side. When the door latch clicked and the door opened, three chins dropped, their mouths agape at the activity in the apartment. Terry Lyons stood there in the doorway, an apron tied around her waist looking at McCormack and Bradley with a pleasantly surprised smile.

"Tobias? Brad?" she let out a squeal of excitement as she launched herself forward and hugged them. "How are you? How did you find me? What are you doing here?"

"Hello, Terry," said Bradley, with sad eyes.

Terry turned and noticed Daniel standing there, waiting patiently.

"I'm so sorry," said Terry, "You must be on the outside looking in with me hogging Toby and Brad like this. I'm Terry."

"Daniel Rooke."

"Any friend of these guys is a friend of mine," said Terry with an unmistakable comrade in arms edge in her voice, "Come in, come in. You must think me so rude keeping you out in the hallway."

McCormack and Bradley entered the apartment and Daniel followed politely into the world of discrete luxury. There was a minimalist quality to the room decorated with Persian rugs and African fertility idols and African warrior statues carved of dark wood. The leather couch and chairs were inviting and elegant and with a quick gesture, they made their way toward the couch. Inside the spacious and elegant apartment, a tall and muscular black man sat on the couch watching ESPN Highlights while a little girl around three years old drew on papers set on the floor with crayons—her face screwed up in concentration as she tried to stay in the lines of her coloring book. The black man rose looking caught off guard, not knowing whether to smile or fight. He merely stood there and waited for Terry to speak.

"Everyone," sang Terry, "this is my daughter Nailah, and over there is my beautiful black husband Dion."

Daniel shook Dion's hand, finding it a firm handshake with calloused hands. McCormack and Bradley stood back looking grim, saying nothing to Dion. Dion did not seem to have an opinion on the matter of respect and any potential for tension was broken by Terry.

"He's a construction worker," said Terry. There was a note of pride in her voice as if announcing her husband was a successful architect.

"Stop saying it like it's something glamorous," said Dion, embarrassed, a note of annoyance in his voice. "I wear a hard hat for a living, and I work in the cold."

"You have an important job," soothed Terry. "You help bring buildings up. I can be proud of you."

Dion grimaced and rubbed the back of his neck as if it was the only thing he could do to keep the loving words from annoying him.

"I'm going to go wash up," said Dion. "Nice meeting you."

And with a pleasant smile, Dion turned and walked out of the room. Terry turned to Bradley and McCormack and gave an irritated stare.

"You remember Dion, right?" asked Terry, wonderingly. "From the Message From Home feeds?"

"I remember Dion," muttered Bradley sadly.

"Well you could have fooled me," scoffed Terry.

"Sorry," replied McCormack. "It's just odd seeing him here."

"I know what you mean," sighed Terry, "All those years seeing him on a monitor screen, and now we're together again. It's like a miracle."

"A miracle..." parroted Bradley with a subdued tragic tone in his voice.

"Honey," called Dion, "is dinner ready?"

"Yes dear," called Terry, "You wash up and I'll set the table."

"We're sorry to catch you a dinner," said McCormack, shifting nervously as he surveyed the room.

"No, it's alright," said Terry, "I've got plenty of time for old friends...and new ones." Giving a friendly smile to Daniel.

Nailah walked up and tugged on Terry's apron.

"Mommy?" asked Nailah tentatively, "Can I watch TV?"

"We're about to sit down for dinner, dear," warned Terry, staring dotingly on her little girl. "Are you finished with your ABC's and numbers?"

"I can count to ten!" sang Nailah.

"Well let's hear it then."

"One, three, two, four, five, seven, nine, ten."

Terry laughed and hugged Nailah, burying her face in her stomach and squeezed lovingly.

"Oh," sang Terry, "you're becoming such a big girl. We can work on your numbers later. Now how about your ABC's?"

Nailah began singing the ABC song with a soft angelic voice, and she dazzled Terry as she stumbled through the alphabet in a singsong. When Nailah finally stumbled her way to Z, Terry hugged her again, the proud mother, and Nailah struggled to reach her arms around her tall frame before finally giving up, and being satisfied with hugging her arms. Terry kissed Nailah on the forehead, and then attacked her cheeks with a flurry of kisses that sent her into mad giggles. Finally Terry released her and Nailah ran off past Daniel, plopped down and returned to her drawings.

"They grow up so fast," sighed Terry to Daniel.

"Yeah," replied Daniel, "they do."

"Do you have any children of your own, Mr. Rooke?"

"No ma'am," replied Daniel, "I'm still a bachelor at heart."

"I envy men," sighed Terry, "They can wait forever and start a family in their fifties. Women, they pass thirty-five, chances are they've missed their chance to have a child. I'm blessed."

McCormack and Bradley appeared concerned and saddened.

"Miss Lyons," began Daniel, "if I could ask you a few questions?"

"Mrs. Greene." corrected Terry. "Lyons is my maiden name."

"Of course," said Daniel, trading cautious glances with Bradley and McCormack who met his gaze with sadness. "Mrs. Greene, I've come here calling because of a discrepancy file held by the Department of Justice saying you are currently holding over twenty-seven jobs in three different states consecutively."

"I beg your pardon?" replied Terry, surprised, and then chuckled. "I'm a housewife and a fulltime mom. I wouldn't know anything about twenty-something jobs."

"I see," said Daniel, watching her movements carefully. Terry wiped her hands on the apron walking along the couch where she stopped and wheeled around to face him.

"Do you suppose someone's stolen my social security number?"

"That's always possible," replied Daniel, as though considering it when he was really just leading her to the next question. "Sure. Someone must have your information." Daniel looked around the living room, taking in every detail and decoration, lingering on the large lithograph of *The Kiss* by Gustav Klimt. "Tell me," continued Daniel, "how does a construction worker and a stay at home mom begin to afford a place like this? You'll forgive me, but it is impossible to live in a building like this without pulling six figures."

Terry's smile left her face for the briefest of instants, only to return with a chill.

"My husband provides," answered coolly, as she sat on a comfortable leather chair. "That's all you need to know."

"Tell me," pressed Daniel, "how does he 'provide'?"

Terry glared at Daniel for a moment, and then looked to McCormack and Bradley for aid. When she saw none was coming, she quickly returned her attention to Daniel, her eyes scrutinizing.

"Are you a cop?" demanded Terry.

"I work for the government," answered Daniel, somewhat cryptically.

Terry nodded, calculating her words.

"Am I under arrest?" she asked, finally.

"Not at this time," replied Daniel, assuredly.

Terry crossed her legs and leaned back in her chair.

"Then I think it's time you left."

Out of the bedroom, Dion came and loomed close to Daniel. He spoke to Terry, but never took his eyes off Daniel.

"Is there a problem, honey?" said Dion, coolly.

"No problem, Dion," replied Terry, "Mr. Rooke was just leaving." Terry then turned and shot a disgusted look at Bradley. "And Bradley's about a step away from leaving as well. Boy, don't go poking around my head."

Bradley gave a worried glance to McCormack.

"Forgive us, Terry," offered McCormack. "We're just concerned about you."

"What's to be concerned about?" scoffed Terry, "I'm perfectly fine. I've got a beautiful baby, a husband who provides, all I have to do is keep the house tidy. What's wrong with me being happy?"

"Nothing," replied McCormack, "But Terry…all this? And what about your husband and daughter."

"What about them?" retorted Terry. When McCormack hesitated Terry rose and stood before them confrontationally. "No, I want to know what you're trying to say!"

"Terry," said Bradley, tentatively, "your husband and daughter are-"

"What?!" demanded Terry, "What you got to say? Spit it out, already!"

"Terry, you must understand this from our perspective," said McCormack, "A highly talented Special with the ability to-"

"Oh, okay," cut in Terry with a dark chuckle, "I see. You think I'm using my telepathy to con people out of money, is that it?"

"It's a popular notion," replied Daniel, "One I've exercised some thought over. Sure."

"Well I don't use it often," admitted Terry with a shrug, "Sure I used it to get past the credit check to get the condo, but I'm not using it willy-nilly." Terry then crossed her arms and glowered at them. "And I'm no thief."

"I never said you were," replied Daniel.

"Well tell me what you think I am, Mr. Rooke," spat Terry.

"Terry," begged McCormack, "we're getting off on the wrong foot here."

A long uncomfortable silence stretched out between them and Terry swallowed hard and lowered her head in apparent shame.

"Maybe you're right," replied Terry softly, "Maybe I'm just reading into things. Why don't you speak plainly? What do you think is happening?"

"Well," began Daniel, "to discuss that, I'd like to ask you a specific question about your time in the Sol War."

"I have no secrets," replied Terry, "Though I'm sure the government wishes I did. Ask away."

"What is your proficiency with the psi-ball?"

Terry blinked, astonished.

"What did you say?"

"What is your aptitude in generating a three dimensional independent construct," said Daniel, "out of pure thought?"

"I don't know what you're talking about," answered Terry, nervously.

"Really?" pressed Daniel, the interrogator inside him taking over. "I have witnesses who tell me you're quite advanced. I'd like you to demonstrate your most sophisticated psi-ball for me, if you please."

Terry wheeled around on McCormack and Bradley.

"Is that what you've been telling him?"

"Terry, please," begged Bradley.

"Miss Lyons," began Daniel.

"Mrs. Greene," snapped Terry.

"Miss Lyons," pressed Daniel, fully aware he was pushing her buttons.

"Stop calling me that!" demanded Terry.

A chair slid across the room and several idols fell from their positions on the shelves. A wind seemed to blow from nowhere, sending Nailah's papers and crayons blowing about the room. Nailah watched with a curious expression on her face—like a cat hunting. McCormack leaned toward Terry and raised his hands.

"Terry, please!" demanded McCormack.

Terry turned and stared at McCormack in shock; the papers and crayons fell and rested where they landed. Nailah continued to stare as though ready to pounce.

"You too?" said Terry of McCormack.

"We're gravely concerned for your state of health, Terry," said McCormack. "Please, let us help you."

"But I'm perfectly fine," answered Terry, a note of worry in her voice.

"No," answered Bradley, "you're not."

Terry eyed Bradley as an unwelcome voice.

"What do you think is wrong with me?" demanded Terry.

McCormack pointed to Dion and Nailah.

"That is what's wrong!" said McCormack, his words harsh, as though he were describing a great sacrilege. Terry followed his finger and found Dion and Nailah staring back at her.

"My family?" asked Terry, slowly.

"Your husband," said Bradley as delicately as he could, "kidnapped your daughter and abandoned you over ten years ago."

Terry's eyes welled up with tears for the briefest of instants before clearing and staring at Bradley with disbelief.

"Well that's just ridiculous," replied Terry, "They're obviously right there."

"Your husband," said McCormack, "ran off with Nailah because you were a Special. It happened during the War.

You could do nothing about it. You were on deployment. You don't remember his last transmission?"

Terry stared at McCormack and Bradley as though she had never truly seen them before, and was horrified by what she saw. For bearing, she turned to Daniel and saw only grave understanding there. She shook her head and turned to McCormack.

"Why are you saying these things to me?"

"You never heard from them again," answered McCormack.

Terry points to her husband and child.

"What do you call that?" demanded Terry, "Some figment of my imagination? You see them too. The checks my husband brings home are real enough!"

"They're not real, Miss Lyons," answered Daniel.

Terry welled up with fury in her eyes and the papers began to pick up off the ground and dance around the room again. McCormack put his hand on Daniel's shoulder.

"Daniel, please," insisted McCormack. "You're not helping."

"My job right now is to get to the truth of the matter," replied Daniel, shaking out of McCormack's grip.

"The truth?" snapped Terry, "You look more interested in making an arrest, Mr. Rooke. Or is it Special Agent Rooke?"

"Agent Rooke is fine."

"Well, *Agent Rooke*," answered Terry with a cold smile, "you should know I don't go down easy."

"What's that supposed to mean?" asked Daniel.

"You really think you can stand up next to me?" laughed Terry darkly, "You've sat here for the past ten minutes looking down your nose on me and my family. You think I'm about to stand for that?"

"Terry," said McCormack, "please."

"So you're with him?" challenged Terry.

"Terry," replied McCormack, "I'm for peace. But I've got a job to do."

"Tobias," began Terry, methodically, "if you and I fought we would level this building and rain bricks in the street. You ready for that?"

"No," answered McCormack.

"A wife and mother would do a lot to protect her family," warned Terry, "Don't push me."

"We won't." replied McCormack. "But our concern for you is real. You're in a dangerous place, right now."

"I'm with my family," rebutted Terry, "What danger is there? Unless you brought it with you."

"Terry," begged McCormack.

"Terry nothing!" snapped Terry. "I think you've said about enough, Tobias."

"I've had enough," said Dion, his muscles coiled under his long sleeve shirt. "I think it's time the three of you left. I won't be having you gang up on my wife in front of my daughter."

"Are you seeing this, Terry?" pressed McCormack, "Answer me this, if this is really Dion, don't you think it's strange he looks exactly the way he did ten years ago? What about your daughter? Isn't it interesting she hasn't aged since the last time you saw her?"

"If you don't leave now," warned Dion, "I'll make you leave. Believe me, I can do it."

"Miss Lyons," said Daniel, and he produced from his pocket a cell phone, "if this is your final answer-"

Dion threw himself across the coffee table and tackled Daniel, propelling him out of and over the chair, and on his back to roll on the ground. The cell phone flew out of his hand and Daniel quickly turned and grappled with Dion, wrestling himself behind him and put him in a strangle hold—only to have Dion's muscles swell, and with ease, threw him off.

McCormack stepped toward Terry, who reacted teleki-
netically, sending McCormack bouncing off the wall. The
walls trembled and the figurines tumbled from their shelves
and littered the floor while Terry, wild eyed, jumped to her
feet.

"Get out of my house!" shouted Terry.

Nailah crouched like a cat ready to pounce and hissed
at them.

"Terry," begged Bradley, "you're not well. Come with
us. We can get you help."

"I don't need any help!" screamed Terry, "My family's
not gone, they're right here!"

Nailah began to cry. Terry picked her up and held her
and she nuzzled into Terry's breast.

"See what you did!" railed Terry, "This is my life! My
family! My daughter! Don't you tell me they're not real! I
don't know what kind of game you're playing but it's time
for you to leave, now!"

Bradley stepped forward.

"I'm sorry, Terry."

Bradley put his hands against his temples and focused
on Terry. Their minds linked and Terry was awash with
Bradley's memories of Terry telling him all about how her
husband kidnapped her daughter. *How could he do this to
me? My daughter! It's like he cut a piece out of me! A
piece so big nothing can fill it.* Terry reeled from the power
of the memory and relived the moment in her own mind
again and again until she dropped to the ground clutching
her ears, screaming long and hard. Dion jumped off of
Daniel, leaving him on the ground, and rushed to Terry's
aid. He knocked Bradley to the side and supported Terry's
heaving shoulders.

"It's okay, baby, I'm here!" said Dion soothingly, then
turned on Bradley. "What did you do to her?!"

"I'm sorry, Terry," said Bradley, undeterred. "But your daughter is not a baby anymore. She'd be fourteen, now, wherever she is."

Daniel rose from the floor and joined McCormack and Bradley in watch over Terry. Terry shook and her eyes grew clear and filled with tears. She looked up at Dion.

"Dion, that's enough."

Dion knelt back and sat down next to Terry obediently, not saying a word. Finally, Terry looked up at Dion and gave a wan smile.

"Do you have any idea how much I love you? How much you hurt me?"

Dion sat there crying.

"I forgive you," said Terry, and she kissed Dion on the cheek.

Terry then turned to Nailah, who rushed into her arms. Terry held her tightly, kissing her forehead, as though each last kiss could hardly be enough for her. Nailah squeezed her back and Terry rocked her like an infant, as though she could stay there forever rocking her in her arms. Finally she kissed her eyelids and bent down to Nailah's ear.

"Goodbye," whispered Terry, sweetly as though she were wishing her a good night's sleep in a crib.

Slowly, light crept in through the window, as the setting sun broke free of the clouds, bathing the room in warm red hues. Dion and Nailah slowly grew transparent. Terry seemed to fight the transparency for an instant, resiliently holding onto Nailah, fearing her leaving again. Finally, with a heavy sigh, Terry looked down and watched as Nailah faded away and the room grew still. Terry collapsed on the floor weeping.

Daniel, sensing a new calmer personality had risen to the surface, knelt down beside Terry.

"The other psi-balls?" asked Daniel.

"Gone," replied Terry darkly.

"Are you okay?" asked Bradley, helplessly.

"No," replied Terry, "I'm not. I lost my family all over again."

"Well," said McCormack, "you have something you didn't have before, Terry."

"What's that?"

"You got the chance to say good-bye."

"Yeah," scoffed Terry, "to a figment of my imagination."

"Sometimes," said McCormack, "that's all we have."

"I miss them, you know." said Terry.

"I know," sighed Bradley, hardly able to contain his grief.

Terry fixed him with a patronized stare.

"No, you don't." snapped Terry.

"Terry," replied Bradley, "I was inside your mind. Believe me, I know."

Terry looked at Bradley and her eyes welled up. Normally she would have resented the invasion of her privacy, but after watching her husband and daughter disappear into thin air, all she felt was hollow.

"It's funny," said Terry, "All the things I wanted to say to them, and all the things I wanted to do…"

"You took your daughter to the fair." soothed Bradley, "You took your husband to the opera. You took your daughter to the museum. You did everything a mother could do. That was real. What you felt was real."

"Yeah…" sighed Terry.

"Come on." said Daniel at last. "Let's get you out of here."

He reached down and took Terry's hand, pulling her to her feet. She moved like an automaton, rigid and jittery. Terry did not fight the tears. She didn't know if she even knew how.

Daniel opened the door and Bradley escorted Terry into the hallway filled with onlookers. For a moment their eyes locked. Terry and her fellow tenants. Her first impulse was to turn and go back inside, seeking the safety of her apartment. Bradley held her firm.

"It's okay," said Bradley, "I'm here."

Terry looked into his eyes and found only empathy. She nodded and took solace in his arms as he led her through the crowd of lookeyloos and onto the elevator. McCormack turned to Daniel.

"I don't think I care for this run," said McCormack.

"No," replied Daniel, "Neither do I."

Outside in the dog park, the agents were on high alert, scattered across the park with shotguns and assault rifles. Terry only half acknowledged them as she stumbled toward the SUV Daniel directed her to. When Daniel opened the door the hot air from the heater blasted out of the SUV and mingled with the frigid air outside. Terry clambered up into her seat and Daniel helped her with the seatbelt.

"You're going to be okay," said Daniel.

"Anything's better than this," replied Terry, on the verge of tears again.

The door on the far side opened and an agent climbed in with a shotgun, which he held at the ready, eyeing Terry as though she were something dangerous. Terry cringed away from the cold eyes of the agent.

"Easy," said Daniel to the agent. "She's not under arrest."

The agent nodded, but did not relax or ease his grip on the shotgun. Instead, he signaled the others to climb into the van.

"Clear!" said the agent to the others. "I got her."

Terry wheeled around in her seat and peered into Daniel's eyes.

"What's going on?" demanded Terry, her eyes wide with fright.

"Relax," said Daniel. "They're just scared. It'll be okay once we get you to the transport."

"That's not exactly so, Agent Rooke," called the voice behind him, belonging to Agent Rollins. A cold leer on his upturned face.

"What's that supposed to mean?" demanded Daniel, coldly.

"Well," said Rollins, "I didn't like how our last conversation went, so I made some calls."

An agent walked up to Terry and stabbed her with a syringe in the arm causing Terry to yelp with pain and alarm. Daniel lunged forward grabbing the agent.

"What the hell are you doing?!" bellowed Daniel.

At this, several other agents found their way around the SUV and pointed their shotguns and rifles at Daniel. Bradley clenched his hands into two fists and eyed the men threateningly. McCormack put his hand on Bradley's arm, telling him silently to stand down. Bradley looked helplessly at Terry who slipped out of consciousness, her head rolling back onto the headrest. Rollins smiled a hideous grin.

"Apparently this Special's got a warrant on her, so it's a federal matter." said Rollins, then added coldly, "She's mine. But thanks for doing the footwork for us. All that Special training sure came in handy."

"You haven't heard the last of me," said Daniel coolly.

"That's fine," replied Rollins with the broken toothed smile. "I'm retiring soon anyway. Let's see what you got."

Rollins slammed the door shut on Terry and slapped the door twice, indicating it was secure. The SUV peeled out and raced away down Binney Street, turned the corner and vanished. Daniel turned back to see Rollins climbing into an SUV.

"If you'll excuse me," said Rollins with a chuckle, "I need to get my collar back to headquarters." Rollins reached down and tossed Daniel's duffel bag out the window at him—which Daniel caught. "Don't worry. I've left you a van to drive you back to your transport. Have a safe flight home."

With that, the SUV pulled off, the sound of laughter echoing in the cold. Behind them, a van loaded with scanning equipment and cables was all that was left.

"Come on," said McCormack. "Win some, lose some."

"I ever tell you how I hate losing?" said Daniel as he climbed into the passenger's seat.

"I'll make a note of it," said McCormack.

Bradley climbed into the back of the van and shut the doors, taking a seat on a pile of cables. He looked like a terrible bird perched on a branch, so foul was his mood. McCormack took a seat next to him at the terminal.

"It'll be alright, Brad," said McCormack, soothingly.

"No," fumed Bradley, "It's not."

CHAPTER 14

BROWNSVILLE

BROOKLYN, NEW YORK

Raheim Washington darted through the Tilden House building lobby, and burst out into the night air in a daze. He had run down the stairs hurtling flights at a time to outrun her. He didn't know how she was doing it, but he knew his friends were being murdered, listening to the distant screams emanating from the elevator shaft. He told them not to use the elevator. It was unreliable and slow, sometimes opening on the same floor after a minute's wait. But he was sure of one thing. He was the sole survivor. As long as he kept moving.

Thoughts raced through his head so fast he hardly had time to filter them. *How was she doing this? What was that thing she was carrying?* The answers were not forthcoming.

She was a force of nature. Unstoppable. She entered the apartment with cold authority, glaring at everyone with a fury that sat oddly on such a beautiful young face. She had been fun the night they found her and invited her back to their apartment, and she was beautiful, even when they forced her down and beat her unconscious. Raheim remembered how the lights in the apartment blew out with a shower of sparks when the final blow fell. And how they laughed that ghosts were trying to protect her from their carnal urges. It did not matter. She was claimed by them again and again in the dark. No impulse of compassion or ethics interfered with their plans to climax inside her, or their plans to turn her out and put her to work.

Christine was going through the process called *Breaking the Bitch*—where pimps beat and raped her for hours to teach her she cannot stand against them, and the only safe place to be was firmly under them, working for them, bringing the money home at the end of her tricks.

This was the Christine he met a month ago; the one who disappeared in a car and vanished into the night leaving them furious that their money ticket had vanished on them. But the anger didn't last long. They would catch up to her eventually. And there were other younger girls to train. Such was the world of pimping. So why did they laugh at her when she appeared at their door that night carrying that heavy metal rod? What was so funny about it?

Raheim did not think it was funny. He was angry with Christine for escaping them. But he was not the first to his feet to discipline her. The others pounced on her. Eight able bodied men charging this petite little girl of sixteen—a frightening spectacle to behold as they clenched their fists and prepared to rain blows down upon her. But Raheim was glad he had not charged her—because as they neared her, she lifted the rod, pointed it at them and smiled. There was a flash of light—no, lightning—and Marshawn and Darrell fell to the ground and did not stir.

She wheeled the rod above her head and again the lightning flashed in the apartment, and the lights went out. There in the blackness, his friends screamed. "She's got a gat!" and then there was the running, bowling her over and escaping out into the hallway, racing toward the elevator.

Raheim called to them to take the stairs, but they piled into the elevator, and Raheim heard them pounding the lobby button repeatedly, as fast as his heartbeat as he raced down the steps, tripping, falling, rolling to his feet, racing again, faster. Their screams in the elevator shaft echoed in the lobby, and Raheim was grateful that the icy winter wind in his ears cut out their cries. Raheim darted toward Stone Avenue like a deer, and headed north in the direction of Brownsville Baptist Church. After all, if you had just seen the devil, where would you go?

Tears stung Raheim's eyes and he ran with a wild determination to stay alive—spurring him on, faster and faster. He never looked back to see if she was following him. Of course she was following him—like in those horror movies where the killer walked determinedly behind their victim— it was only a matter of time before she caught up to him, and he would see the lightning again. He eventually reached his objective, and stormed the steps of the church, grasping for the door handle only to find it was locked.

Raheim pulled on the door harder and harder with all his might trying to force the door open. Finally he gave up and began pounding on the doors, screaming.

When the dark shadow of the archway illuminated he screamed even louder, wheeling around expecting to see the girl with the lightning, and he fell to his knees prepared to grovel on the steps of the church for mercy.

The police in the cruiser held the spotlight on him as they stepped out into the cold staring at the oddity of a young black male dressed in jeans and a tank-top shirt sweating in the cold. Automatically they assumed Raheim was under the influence of some heavy drug and called for backup and a paramedic bus to fetch the young man up as they ordered him to walk toward them slowly.

Raheim was so elated he ran to the police officers with his hands in the air and put his hands on the hood of their patrol car.

"Arrest me!" he begged. "Please! Don't leave me out here!"

The police officers traded incredulous looks and called for more backup.

The Chariot blazed across the nighttime sky leaving a white trail of vapor in its wake that spiraled back for miles behind them like a comet's tail. Inside the cabin the mood was grim. Daniel sat in his seat gloomily, his harness locking him safely in place. McCormack finally broke the silence offering a question that he already knew the answer to, but merely wanted to get Daniel out of his silent funk.

"You doing okay, there?" asked McCormack, feelingly.

"I just got outmaneuvered by a flatfoot Fed." scoffed Daniel. "No, I'm not happy."

"Take it easy." soothed McCormack. "Terry will be fine. Once Boatman hears about the interference we received tonight, he'll have the Deputy Director of the Bureau breaking out in a rash."

"Besides," said Bradley supportively, "they can't hold her. They don't have the means to hold a Special. We do."

"They could just keep her drugged indefinitely." replied Daniel, bluntly.

McCormack and Bradley grew quiet and nodded. It was certainly an option for agents who were terrified about what they were dealing with.

Daniel dwelled on the problem with the Bureau and felt the weight of office pressing down on his shoulders. Just then, the intercom cracked open and the pilot's voice rang in the hold.

"Agent Rooke," chimed the pilot, trying to be brave in light of the verbal reaming he had received earlier from Daniel. "I've got a call for you from Director Boatman."

Daniel undid his harness and walked over to the terminal built into the hold.

"Put him through." said Daniel and waited a moment until he heard the steady breathing on the other end of the line and Boatman's face flooded into view on the screen. Daniel's grim expression set as he opened communications to Boatman: "You've heard about what happened in Boston, I assume?"

"That can wait." answered Boatman as though trying to clean his palate of a bad taste. "There's a situation brewing in New York. I'll need you to reroute and handle it. It's local jurisdiction, so I think you'll have an easier time than against a special agent."

"What's the situation?"

"Apparently there are two Specials tearing through Brooklyn." replied Boatman. "There is a body count. Four survivors have stated that a young black woman is electrocuting people at random. I don't buy it, but that's the word from the Brownsville police."

"Brownsville?" repeated Daniel, surprised.

Boatman shot him a knowing smile.

"Do you feel like going home?" said Boatman, wryly.

"We'll reroute now," responded Daniel, "Send us what you've got on our notebooks."

"Already sent."

Just then, Daniel's notebook pinged and illuminated as he pulled it from his breast pocket.

73rd Precinct report: //SPECIALS ALERT\\ Two possible Specials have been sighted chasing down

men and attacking them with phenomenon described as "lightning". Victims are known gang members of "Jonas Pimps" – IN CUSTODY: Raheim "Finesse" Washington, 22, CRITICAL CONDITION: Darrell "Breaker" Jones, 24, STABLE CONDITION: Marshawn "Popcorn" Goodings, 19. DECEASED: Mike "Bone" Owens, 37, DECEASED: David "King David" King, 33, DECEASED: Lorenzo "Enzo" Thomas 39, DECEASED: Jaleel "Godzilla" Walker, 28. Attack occurred on the 8th floor of Tilden House I at Stoner Avenue and Dumont Avenue beginning in apartment 832 at approximately 8:18pm. Raheim Washington was taken into custody at Brownsville Baptist Church on Stoner Avenue.

At 8:23 pm, Officer Cruise and Bolton found Raheim "Finesse" Washington at Brownsville Baptist Church attempting to gain entry. Upon questioning, Washington confessed to multiple counts of rape, solicitation and human trafficking in order to facilitate being arrested for protection against a possible rape victim with the ability to fire bolts of "lightning." Please Advise: Due to the fact that this is most likely a SPECIALS matter, does local PD have the ability to investigate and make arrest?

Be Advised: This is a suspect in 73rd Precinct jurisdiction. Continue investigation. Suspect description as follows: Black female approximately 16 years of age, 5'5", 115 lbs. Dressed in black pants and a black hoodie carrying a metal rod or rifle. Possibly SYNKR-22.

No other report at this time.

Daniel finished reading the report and looked up at the viewscreen. Boatman sat there with his hands folded waiting patiently.

"Lawrence," said Daniel, "get in contact with the 73rd Precinct Senior Officer and explain to him Federal assistance in en route."

"Already done," replied Boatman, "Don't waste time landing at La Guardia and driving in. Just land at the Tilden Houses projects."

"Understood."

"I'm uploading coordinates now."

"Incoming Coordinates," said the pilot, "40°39'48"North 73°54'26"West. Strap yourselves in, we land in five minutes."

Just then the hull shook and nearly unseated Daniel.

"Just watch those bumps," scolded Daniel.

"Yes, sir," muttered the pilot.

Tilden Houses was a federally subsidized public housing project. It stood as a series of eight sixteen-story buildings on a superblock of land with open space between the buildings dotted with trees, like an urban forest equipped with concrete walkways cutting and zigzagging through the trees and grass covered expanses. The area was well lit with security light towers illuminating the shadowed underbellies of the trees and with the exception of the areas where the lights were shot out, seemed relatively safe to walk without fear of being mugged in the dark. Unfortunately, the victims would be—mugged in the light, and therefore—worked over much harder to make it impossible to make a positive identification to police.

The Tilden Houses lost none of its dangers over the years. It remained the last ditch between shelter and home-lessness, and the home of gangsters and dealers. Still, many families dwelled here, and they stared out their windows to watch the patrol cars drive onto the grounds, casting their lights to the trees and the buildings, waking the sparrows in the trees that confusedly began to chirp as though it were daylight as the police converged on Building I. Outside the lobby to Building I, a crowd had converged, filled with lookeyloos and those suspicious of police activity in their neighborhood. Their eyes were wary and cold as the police pushed their way through into the building.

The Chariot veered hard in a circle above the tree line like a predatory raptor and hung in the air imposingly before descending to the playground outside Building I. Inside the cockpit, the pilot cringed, expecting to be chastised for his aggressive flying. Daniel said nothing. Too tired to complain. Instead, he looked back at McCormack and Bradley and shrugged.

"You ready for this?" said Daniel.

"Backing up New York's finest?" said Bradley, dryly. "Should be a hoot."

"Funny," scoffed Daniel.

Daniel hit the airlock button and the door slid away revealing the playground outside of Tilden House I. He hopped down and his shoes bit into the gravel of the playground. Bradley and McCormack followed at his flanks like enforcers as they approached the police that cut a swath through the residents to gain purchase in the lobby drawing many stares at their entrance. Daniel pulled out his credentials and raised the SITF badge high over his head like a torch lighting the way. Police and lookeyloos alike craned their heads to read the credentials high in the air to see what new intrusion had entered their homes and jurisdiction. Daniel marched past them without a second glance and hopped onto the elevator with Bradley and McCormack, squeezing in with the other investigators until it was tight. The investigator closest to the buttons stood claustrophobically.

"What floor?" offered the investigator.

"Same as you," replied Daniel, and said nothing else.

The investigator nodded uncomfortably while Daniel and the others turned to face the elevator doors. The elevator was relatively swift, considering the age of the building and the condition of the elevator, which apparently had not been updated with the building since, at least, the 1990's. It allowed time to realize how they were probably over the weight limit for the lift, and every cough was an uncomfortable breeze that the others tried not to breathe in. When the elevator doors parted again, it was to the relief of everyone inside, breathing the stale air of the 8th floor as though it were pumped in from the mountain tops, fresh and clear.

Daniel followed the investigators to apartment 832 and found the place buzzing with activity. Forensic detectives scanned the burn marks on the walls, ceiling and floor with their notebooks, took samples of burnt carpet and drywall and dusted down every surface. Several forensic detectives stopped working to look at Daniel, Bradley and McCormack and waited nervously to discern whether they were authorized to be on their crime scene. Daniel stepped forward and produced his credentials.

"Agent Daniel Rooke with Specials Investigations," said Daniel. "Who's in charge here?"

"I am," said a middle-aged man in a long coat. He approached Daniel, his eyes trailing over the credentials methodically before looking up again. "Inspector Lockhart."

"Inspector Lockhart," repeated Daniel, committing the name to memory. "I've come to offer my assistance in arresting and detaining the suspects, if they are indeed Specials."

"Well, we've got three eye witnesses that claim Special activity, but I don't have a clear picture yet. It could just be a girl with a gun. Burn marks suggest fire. It doesn't smell like gunpowder, but we'll run it anyway."

"The report said lightning."

"Yeah," replied Lockhart, scratching his chin. "Weird case. We've got several shots fired here, and down the hall on the elevator. We just finished our investigation and cleared the bodies out of there and now we're turning to the apartment with a fine toothed comb."

"What about the weapon?" demanded Daniel. "What it a Shiotani-22?"

"No, that was left behind in the elevator." replied Lockhart. "We've got prints off the metal rod, but there's nothing in the database. And judging from the size of the prints, this is obviously a first offender."

"Or someone young enough to evade the draft," offered Bradley.

"How old is the suspect?" said Daniel.

"We can't get a specific age off the fingerprints," said Lockhart, "As I said, they're not in our system. But whoever it is, they're very petite."

Behind them, a young investigator jumped up.

"Sir!" called the young investigator.

"What have you got?" said Lockhart.

"We've got fingerprints," said the investigator.

"Let's see them," commanded Lockhart calmly.

The forensic detective ran the notebook over the fingerprints and lasers cascaded over the surface of the door. The notebook blinked and an identification scrolled onto the viewscreen with the word SPECIAL blaring across it like a threat: ROLLEY TYLER-[SODEM-Chi STATUS]. Bradley blinked.

"Roller?" gasped Bradley.

Inspector Lockhart looked up at Bradley critically.

"You know this man?" inquired Lockhart.

"Rolley Tyler, special operations and demolition," said McCormack. "He was in the war with us."

"We have a Rolley Tyler who pokes around the precinct from time to time," replied Lockhart. "The dicks all hate him. They say he has a real bad habit of appearing on their crime scenes. This is the first I've heard that he was a Special. What's his ability? If you don't mind my asking."

"Olympian strength," said McCormack. "Low level invulnerability, and senses like an animal's. Good tracker. Last I heard he was a private investigator."

"So he could be working for us?" ventured Lockhart.

"Or he could be assisting the suspect," countered McCormack. "These types are right up Tyler's alley. He's got a bit of a hero complex."

"Do you know the places these Jonas Pimps congregate?" demanded Daniel.

"They've got another place over at the Van Dyke Houses," said Lockhart. "Rumor is that's where they break the girls in. We haven't been able to get a warrant on the residence yet."

Daniel smiled and took out his cell phone.

"You don't have my lawyers," said Daniel.

The Van Dyke I Houses is comprised of 22 buildings on 22 acres of land. The buildings vary from three to fourteen stories high with over 1,600 apartments housing some 4,300 residents. The buildings, dating back to 1955, showed the utilitarian function of low-income housing in cold steel, concrete and glass warmed by the trees and grass the way Tilden Houses were comforting. But here, there were no lights, save the stars overhead and the full moon blanketing the dark trees in ethereal luminosity giving the project an eerie glow.

The cruisers—multiplied by the addition of officers from the 65th Precinct—entered the property off Livonia Avenue with an unbelievable show of force, ducking under the trees and rolling over the grass. Behind them a three Emergency Service Unit armored trucks followed them onto the property completing their caravan as they glided toward a three story building in the distance, seemingly swallowed by the larger properties surrounding it. Like the Ark of the Covenant being carried into battle, the ESU armored trucks gave comfort to the officers in the cruisers as they crossed an invisible line into what had become to be known as the literal *heart of darkness.*

Coming around the edge of a fourteen-story building, the cruiser came to a halt facing a three-story building. Daniel stepped out of the cruiser and stared off to the buildings. Bradley and McCormack stepped out and surveyed the area, prepared for anything. As the other officers stepped out of their patrol cars they studied Bradley and McCormack, who stood silently studying their surroundings as though listening to something they could not hear. Many of the officers shrugged it off and unsnapped their holsters, checking their side arms to make sure a round was in the chamber.

"Do we know where we're going?" said Daniel, unsure what the next move was.

"We're heading to that three-story building right over there," said Lockhart. "Top floor."

"How much of it is controlled by the gang?" inquired Daniel.

"All of it," replied Lockhart as though the question was surprising to him coming from Daniel. "They'll be running the girls out as we run in."

Daniel looked over at Lockhart and grinned.

"Why don't we kill two birds with one stone?" said Daniel and Lockhart turned and looked back at the armored trucks.

Emergency Service Unit personnel exited the back and sides of the armored trucks in riot gear—with special operations modified rifles—donning their helmets and lowering the visors over their masked faces. Out of the trucks, trained attack dogs hopped down and barked with anticipation of the chase, seemingly giddy to be a part of the operation. Their masters held onto the leashes, pulling the dogs back into focus for the job at hand.

"That's why I brought ESU," said Lockhart with a grin.

"Let's go get 'em," said Daniel.

"ESU teams," said Lockhart over the radio, "move out."

The ESU teams moved across the lawn converging on the three-story apartment building—their assault rifles pointed ahead of them as they quickstepped in a crouched position. Inside the building, a window flew open and a man appeared waving to the ESU officers.

"Hurry up!" he called frantically, "He's here!"

The ESU came to a halt at once and the radio cracked to life.

"Lockhart," said the ESU commander over the radio, "we've got a situation, here."

"I see it," replied Lockhart.

Just then, a helicopter flew overhead and illuminated the building with spotlights that dazzled the project as though the noonday sun had made its appearance in the night, casting shadows at odd angles across the lawns. The man in the window was dazed and hid his eyes in the glare of the helicopter's spotlight.

"Go ahead," said Lockhart, "Proceed with caution."

The ESU unit converged at the exits, pressed in on all four emergency exits at once, and disappeared into the building. Daniel watched as window by window, the flashlights attached to ESU team's rifles illuminated window after window to the screams of the inhabitants.

"We call this *shaking the hornet's nest*," said Lockhart with a wry smile.

"Been there," replied Daniel, "done that."

Lockhart looked away from his binoculars and stared sideways at Daniel.

"How do you get into your line of work," inquired Lockhart, the curiosity about Daniel seeming too much for him to take any longer, "If you don't mind my asking?"

"Honestly?" said Daniel, weighing his words in order to best encapsulate how he got there. "You get tapped on the shoulder by the boogey man and you don't flinch."

Lockhart gave him an appraising look and turned back to the building, looking through his binoculars.

"We've got something," cracked the radio.

"Freeze!" cracked the radio, as though it were necessary as they could plainly hear the commands echoing across the lawn. "Get down! Get down! Don't fucking move!"

"What have you got?" demanded Lockhart into the radio.

"Hold for verification," clicked the radio. "We have one of the suspects. Rolley Tyler."

"And the girl?" demanded Lockhart.

"There are plenty of girls in the building who fit the description. Young black girls, all of them. We'll run them all through the database and see what falls out."

"Understood." said Lockhart. "Bring out Tyler." Then added to Daniel, "Now maybe we'll get some answers."

Rolley Tyler was led out of the building in handcuffs. He was a tall muscular man, standing at six feet four inches, and weighing easily two hundred seventy pounds of muscle. His arms were so massive, his hands had to be cuffed in front of him. Three ESU team members followed Tyler with their weapons trained on his head. Despite this, Tyler appeared to be untroubled by his predicament and strolled along toward Daniel, verging ever closer to where he stood.

"You must be the man to talk to," said Tyler. "Where's Paladin and Maximus? I can smell them on you."

Bradley and McCormack stepped out of the shadows, Bradley walking up to Daniel's side, while McCormack lingered at the edge of the darkness, watching.

"Hello, Roller," said Bradley.

"Long time no see," replied Tyler with a grin.

"What are you doing here?" demanded McCormack.

"Personal business," replied Tyler, dryly.

"Does your business involve a girl who shoots bolts of lightning?" inquired Daniel.

"Maybe," replied Tyler, coolly.

"I want her," said Daniel, coolly.

"There's a line around the block for that," replied Tyler. "Mostly comprised of Jonas Pimps and their associates in the project. I gotta say," he added with a grin, "the line's been getting shorter."

"What do you know about the deaths at the Tilden Houses?" demanded Daniel.

"Only that if I'd gotten there first, they'd have suffered a lot more on the way out."

"What do you know about the lightning girl?" demanded Daniel.

"Lightning Girl?" scoffed Tyler. "You make her sound like a superhero."

"Cut the crap, Rolley," warned McCormack.

Tyler shot a glare at McCormack of warning. McCormack did not flinch. Daniel quickly stepped in and stepped toward Tyler.

"I just got one question for you," said Daniel. "Are we dealing with a Special?"

"Oh, she's a Special, alright," replied Tyler. "She came to me for some guidance. I grilled her for information about what gang branded her and the locations of their associates. Then I told her I'd handle it and left her at my office."

"You got a name?" pressed Daniel.

Tyler studied Daniel critically.

"What do you want with her?" asked Tyler evasively.

"She's murdered people," spat Lockhart.

"They killed her first," snapped Tyler.

"What's that supposed to mean?" demanded Daniel.

"What do I mean?" spat Tyler and he glowered at Daniel for being so ill informed. "Gang rape. Branding.

Turning the girl out onto the street. She's now HIV positive. That's what I'm talking about. They killed that poor
girl a month ago. Anything that happens tonight is divine
justice. What are you all concerned for? You're getting the
projects cleared of an entire gang of pimps and drug dealers.
The community will sleep a lot better tonight, believe me."

"So this is about revenge?" concluded Daniel.

"This is more than revenge," said Tyler ominously.
"This is payback."

"What's your involvement in all this, Rolley?" said
McCormack, suddenly becoming the principle interrogator.

Tyler considered him for a moment, and then shrugged.

"I was hunting down Jonas Pimps," he replied simply.
"They've been running too hard, and jumping too many
girls. Drive down Rockaway or Stoner and you see ten
new youngsters every week. These punks need to be dealt
with."

"So you're running around playing superhero," concluded McCormack. "What about the girl?"

"I'm looking for her too," replied Tyler, "I keep catching the aftermath."

"What's your body count like, tonight, Rolley?" pressed
McCormack.

"I may have roughed up a few," answered Tyler, slyly.
"Hung the occasional punk over the balcony…"

"You let anyone drop?" pressed McCormack.

"Occasionally," grinned Tyler.

"Do you know where we can find her before she gets
the needle?" asked Daniel, reasserting his position as
interrogator.

Tyler looked back at Daniel and studied him.

"You going to help her," clarified Tyler, "or arrest her?"

"Both," answered Daniel.

"Trust us, Rolley," added McCormack. "We're all
you've got."

Tyler looked up at McCormack for a moment, and then looked over to Bradley for confirmation. Bradley nodded his agreement with McCormack and his eyes fell to Daniel with a scoff.

"Man," exclaimed Tyler. "I've got a community out there. They take care of me. My meals are all comped everywhere I go in Brownsville, my rent is always free, and then there are the jobs that pay real well. I make off like a minister 'round here. I'm like the straight one man A-Team. Lock me up. I'll make bail in an hour."

"That's not technically how it works," warned Daniel.

"Oh, really?" spat Tyler, sensing Daniel was both threatening him and offering him a line.

"Not for Specials, no," continued Daniel, "You've been cushioned from the reality of being a Special in the rest of the country, so let me fill you in. You're looking at no bail, an indeterminate amount of time before you ever see the inside of a courthouse and with your actions, today, and no constitutional protection. Words like 'aggravated assault,' 'attempted murder,' 'terrorism' and 'kidnapping' will haunt you when you finally see a judge."

Tyler sensed Daniel was telling the truth and shifted in his stance.

"What do you want?" said Tyler at last.

"I want her name," answered Daniel.

"Christine," said Tyler at last. "Christine Turf."

Lockhart wrote the name down on his notebook and ran through juvenile school records.

"Got her." said Lockhart, a note of victory in his voice that faded quickly as he read the file. "Christine Turf. Went missing three months ago. Turned 16 this Sunday. Posted missing by her grandmother. Father's dead. Mother's is currently in the House of Detention for drug abuse."

Daniel turned back to Tyler, and his eyes narrowed and bored into him.

"I want to know where she's headed," pressed Daniel.

Tyler put his head down and nodded to himself in thought before finally answering.

"There's nowhere left to go," said Tyler at last. "She's headed to the street."

"What?" said Daniel as the thought of young Christine going public flashed through his mind. Special killer executing civilians in cold blood, would run the headline on the eleven o'clock news.

"Dumont." clarified Tyler. "That's all that's left of Jonas Pimps. The enforcers. She's going after the thugs who kept her working and made sure she didn't run off. The ones who beat her and strip searched her for money. The ones who kept her working when she was in too much pain to keep going. The ones who choked her into unconsciousness."

"Inspector Lockhart," said Daniel, over his shoulder. "Get me a bird over Powell Street and Dumont Avenue. And move your cruisers into the street."

"My men won't engage a known Special, Agent Rooke," warned Lockhart. "These are family men and women. They won't risk their lives against a superhuman."

McCormack stepped forward and put his hand on Daniel's shoulder.

"Daniel," said McCormack, "Put us in, coach. We'll bring her home."

"Yeah," said Bradley, stepping forward.

Lockhart turned to consider alternatives, and then snapped to attention.

"I can have ESU set up snipers at a quiet distance, though."

Bradley, McCormack and Tyler looked at Lockhart stymied.

"Do it," replied Daniel, "But give me the frequencies. I want to be in contact with them. No one fires without my say so."

"On it," answered Lockhart, and he turned and walked over to the ESU Detective standing by the armored truck.

Daniel turned away from Lockhart and wheeled on Tyler.

"Tyler," said Daniel, "You want things to go easier for you in court?"

"What do you want?" asked Tyler, his reality crashing down around him.

"You will be placed under the temporary federal standing as an acting law enforcement agent working in tandem with my offices."

Tyler blinked as the words sunk in and then a wry grin stretched across his face.

"So you're assembling a posse?" clarified Tyler.

"You are the posse," answered Daniel.

"Cool," grinned Tyler.

"You don't have cart blanch, here," clarified Daniel, "You will move in to diffuse this situation while Law Enforcement personnel move in to make arrests of the pimps on the street level. You will walk her back to me and I will take her into custody."

"Wait, you expect me to hand her over after what she's gone through?" scoffed Tyler. "What she's doing is justified."

"What she's doing is illegal," clarified Daniel, "She will be arrested. But I can spare the needle. That's within my power."

"How?" demanded Tyler, eyeing Daniel critically.

Daniel reached into his breast pocket and produced his cellular phone.

"See this?" Daniel held up the phone before Tyler's critical eyes. "This is my magic wand. I press send and I can pull wondrous things out of my hat. On that, you can bank."

"Really?" scoffed Tyler in disbelief.

"He can," said Bradley, supportively.

Tyler glanced at Bradley as if his words were of more weight and credibility than Daniel's was and mulled it over for a long moment, glancing back between him and Daniel.

"Alright," haggled Tyler, "My and the girl's freedom for my time and assistance."

"*Your* freedom," concluded Daniel, "The girl has to be processed."

"What happens to her?" demanded Tyler.

"She'll be tried and sentenced within a week," replied Daniel, "Then she'll slip through the cracks and disappear into my hands. From there, we'll place her somewhere where words like extradition are ridiculed."

"By waving your magic phone..." scoffed Tyler.

"That's right," grinned Daniel.

Tyler looked over Daniel's shoulder at McCormack.

"He really got it like that?" challenged Tyler.

"He does," replied McCormack.

Tyler studied Daniel with a hard-eyed look of approval.

"Looks like you guys are backing the right horse," concluded Tyler.

"You have no idea," replied Bradley.

"Better to do the devil's bidding," said McCormack, "than be in his path."

Tyler blinked in surprise and glanced at McCormack, taking in his words and weighing them carefully.

"I'll remember that," replied Tyler.

"Do we have an accord?" pressed Daniel.

"Yeah, we do." replied Tyler. "You're not expecting me to sign anything in blood, are you?"

"Just bring her to me," answered Daniel and gestured to Tyler to step forward. "Here, let me take those cuffs off you."

Tyler gave a sly smile and twisted his wrists, coiling the chain on the cuffs together. With a powerful wrench, the chains shattered and Tyler had free movement.

"Don't worry about it," said Tyler with a grin. "I got this."

He reached into his pocket and produced a handcuff key and unlocked the bracelets, letting them fall to the ground. McCormack and Bradley gave him disparaging glances as though the display of strength was wasteful and unnecessary. Daniel pursed his lips at the destruction of a perfectly good pair of handcuffs and was impressed by the thought that if a Special did not want to be detained, there was very little that could be done but fight. Tyler grinned cockily as though he had made his point with the theatrics and rubbed his palms together with anticipation.

"What next?" inquired Tyler.

Daniel turned away to Lockhart who stood in heated conversation with the ESU team commander.

"Lockhart," called Daniel. "We'll need to acquire undercover surveillance trucks."

"They're on their way." replied Lockhart.

Daniel turned to face Tyler.

"Now we hit the street," said Daniel.

DUMONT AVENUE

A beat up van parked across the street from the Van Dyke Houses, with a clear view of the foot traffic parading down the avenue. The girls were young. Far younger than Daniel felt comfortable with and he grit his teeth that he was not a cop and could do nothing for them. He was a federal agent working strictly on Specials assignment. He told himself over and over again his job was Christine Turf. That these under aged girls being pimped were collateral damage. Still, it ate at him as he looked into the viewscreen at the scene outside. And more girls came out from the Van Dyke housing project to join them on the avenue, walking down the cold icy street in their high heels and tight form fitting miniskirts with makeup smeared on their faces like real painted ladies.

His real resentment was for the pimps who congregated together around the tree line, just off the sidewalk dressed for the cold weather while the girls wore barely anything at all. The pimps stood there talking and laughing. Once in a while one of the pimps would break off from the group, approach a girl and slap her to get moving and get in a car, or choke a girl for not giving him the money fast enough, or glancing at another pimp. Daniel watched all this with a building rage for the pimps, and it took everything inside him not to throw the back door open, run across the street and beat down the pimps where they stood.

You have a job to do. You have a job to do. thought Daniel. *Your job is the girl. Let local PD handle these girls and those men...*

"Tyler," said Daniel into the radio, "you in position?"

Across the street, Tyler put his finger to his ear.

"I'm here," cracked the radio. "I don't see her."

"Stay cool," replied Daniel into the radio, "You're doing fine."

"Detective Cummings, here," cracked the radio on ESU's frequency. "We've set up birds eye post at Stone Avenue Branch Library. Got a clean run of the street. If she's coming out, we'll see her."

"No one shoots without my authorization," clarified Daniel. "Confirm?"

"Confirmed." cracked the radio. "Waiting on your authorization."

"Outpost two," cracked the radio, "set up on the rooftop of Temple Beth-El Church on Powell Street. There's a lot of traffic down here."

"The girls are out," replied Daniel, needlessly. "Keep a lookout for a petite girl dressed in black with a hoodie carrying a metal rod."

"Roger that."

Most of the girls on the street were dressed in bright tight clothing with short jackets that did little to block out the cold. The cars were welcome respites for the freezing girls, and they literally jumped into the cars that stopped in front of them. It would have been almost comical if the police detectives weren't already keenly aware of their ages. It was the worst form of heartbreak to watch the cars roll away unmolested by police, for fear of ruining the sting arranged to capture a rogue Special.

The detectives grit their teeth and searched harder through the streets for the suspect, to make a quick arrest and then to move on to getting the girls off the streets as quickly as possible. But as the minutes stretched into an hour, and the streets quieted down as the last of the girls was taken, the detectives sat helplessly watching the cars come back to drop off the teenaged girls and raced off into the night. The pimps routinely stepped away from each other, collected money, disciplined their girls and sent them back out into the street. Finally, the local PD had a breaking point.

"Request permission to photograph license plates and drivers for future investigations?" cracked the radio.

"Go for it," sighed Daniel.

"Thank you," groaned the radio.

"Just keep your eyes peeled," said Daniel.

"Roger that," chirped the radio.

Just then, out of the tree line, a shadowed figure stepped out into the street carrying a steel rod. She was small and petite by even the girl's standards, and looked almost foolish as she half supported/half dragged the metal rod as she crossed the street toward the enforcers. She pointed the rod at the pimp choking the girl and with a flash of light and a loud crack, the pimp flew backward smashing through the glass of a bus stop.

The street came alive as cars peeled out at the sound of the crack and raced away down Dumont and Powell, squealing around the corner and out of sight, while the girls in the street began screaming and scattered like rats when the lights were thrown on. The pimps turned to recognize the new threat instinctively, reaching for their guns—only to be scattered by the second bolt that struck a parked car's tire, bursting the tire at once.

An able-bodied pimp made eye contact with the shadowed figure and his chin dropped as the figure stepped toward him. He raised his gun and fired aimlessly as he turned and ran—as though the bullets would find her heart by his will alone—the bullets smashed windows, ricocheted off the asphalt and struck random girls as they raced across the street in a mad rush to get out of the line of fire.

The figure, undaunted by the bullets flying past her, raced off in the direction of the able-bodied pimp, throwing the rod aside and tearing up Powell Street in hot pursuit of the man.

"That's her, move in!" shouted Daniel, "Tyler, where are you?!"

"I'm on her!" cracked the radio.

Daniel saw Tyler burst into the street and tore down the block after the girl.

The able-bodied pimp ducked down an alley leading off of Powell under the watchful eyes of the snipers hidden on the rooftop of Temple Beth-El Church and Christine followed running full tilt in running shoes, while the pimp stumbled in his flat bottomed high tops—vanity slowing his strides as he slipped on the icy street—trying not to get them dirty as he ran. He turned and fired again at Christine, who kept running toward him in a madness.

"Outpost two! We got her," cracked the radio. "What are your orders?"

"Hold your fire!" shouted Daniel into the radio. "I have an agent in pursuit!"

"Roger that, we got him." chirped the radio. "Black male, roughly six foot five, two hundred fifty pounds."

"Confirmed," replied Daniel. "That's my guy."

"That's Rolley Tyler," chirped the radio in a tone of disbelief, "Didn't he get arrested earlier tonight?"

"Right now he's working with the Specials Task Force," replied Daniel into the radio, "Cover him."

"Roger that," chirped the radio, "Covering."

Daniel wheeled around to face Bradley and McCormack.

"Bradley, Tobias, I'll need you down there." said Daniel. "No theatrics. We got eyes on us on this one."

"Understood," said McCormack.

Bradley nodded and followed McCormack out of the van.

Bradley and McCormack raced across Dumont and up Powell, following Tyler around the corner into the parking lot of Temple Beth-El Church.

Up ahead, the pimp splashed through a puddle of water as he raced for a chain link fence separating the parking lot from an adjacent property leading out to Junius Street. In hot pursuit, Christine pulled her hoodie off and scowled at the able-bodied pimp, out of breath.

She put her hands on her knees to breathe against the stitch in her chest when she noticed the pool of water that stretched out down the parking lot to the chain link fence that her quarry was now scaling. He landed on the other side winded, and supported himself on the chain link fence, laughing at her, thrilled to be alive.

A smile stretched her face and she took her shoe off and stepped into the puddle. The cold water lit up and lightning travelled the length of the parking lot to the chain link fence—which found her target—his muscles froze and convulsed as his hands clenched the chain link fence, his feet in the puddle on the far side. He seemed to bend backward against his will, threatening to break his own spine in the exertion of muscles not regularly used until finally Christine took her foot out of the puddle and the pimp collapsed in a heap of steam and a shower of sparks.

Tyler raced up to Christine who turned prepared for the fight, though not exactly sure what she could do without her metal rod.

"Damn, girl," said Tyler, "You're a regular live wire!"

"What are you doing here?" said Christine.

"You were supposed to wait in my office," reprimanded Tyler.

"Yeah, well, I had things to do," scoffed Christine. "I'm not going to rely on any man. I'm going to get mine."

"Yeah, well, you got yours," scoffed Tyler. "Look, the cops have this place surrounded. You killed that man under surveillance. I can't do anything for you."

Just then, McCormack and Bradley ran up and Christine's eyes burned white with static.

"It's cool!" said Tyler. "They're with me."

"You set me up?" scoffed Christine, not altogether surprised.

"They're here to help you," replied Tyler. "But you got to go in. They can't help you unless you're in the books."

"Yeah, right." scoffed Christine, disbelievingly.

"Miss Turf," said McCormack, "We can help you. But you've got to come with us."

"Men," spat Christine. "You think you can push me around because I'm a girl." Turf's eyes grew white with static and sparks played in her hair—the puddle she stood in bubbled—as she glared at McCormack, adding: "But I got skills."

"I know you do," said McCormack. "I've been seeing your handiwork all night."

"Then you know what I can do," answered Christine defiantly, "if you don't let me walk out of here."

"Your ability doesn't work that way and you know it," snapped McCormack. "Bluffing won't help you."

"Bluffing?" countered Christine. "I just killed an entire gang."

"Yes," answered McCormack, "but you need to channel your ability. You can't fire lightning. You need conductivity. Wires. Metal rods. Water. Without that conductivity, you're powerless. Which is why you ended up getting put out on the street."

Christine's jaw locked and she glared at McCormack.

"You don't know nothing about me," spat Christine.

"I know you need a lifeline," answered Bradley, "You need one badly. You're drowning."

Christine studied them nervously, her eyes welling up as she wavered between defiance and breaking down.

"Why should I trust you?" asked Christine, her voice quavering.

"Because we're the best option you've got," answered Bradley.

"I just wanna go home," whined Christine, and her age came through. She was not the hardened killer. She was not the personification of vengeance. She was a child.

"We can talk about that, eventually." said McCormack. "For now, you're coming with us."

"Am I under arrest?" asked Christine.

"You have two snipers trained on you," answered McCormack. "Local law enforcement is a death sentence for you. They're afraid of you. Killing you is just easier for them. But if you come with us, we can protect you. You'll be tried, convicted and sentenced. Then you'll come to us."

Christine stood there shaking like a leaf, her eyes dazed.

"I can't go home again, can I?"

"Not now, dear." answered McCormack.

Christine's eyes welled up with tears and she collapsed onto the asphalt.

"I want my grandma," said Christine, "I want my momma."

"Trust us, Christine." said Bradley, his own tears welling to the surface as he bent down and placed his hands on her shoulders. For some strange reason, the feminist inside her did not object to the touch of this man, and she held her arms and swayed as she wept.

McCormack bent down and offered his hand to her.

"Come on." said McCormack. "It'll all be over soon."

Slowly Christine rose from the ground supported by McCormack's hand, Bradley's hands on her shoulders, squeezing them in support. Tyler watched as they walked away down the parking lot toward the street. A van pulled up hard and the doors burst open as police officers flooded out, guns drawn, shouting commands. Christine studied them in shock and saw the fear in their eyes. Christine pulled against McCormack's hand and retreated back into the safety of Bradley's arms.

"Don't make me go with them," she whispered like a child.

"It'll be fine," replied Bradley, kindly. "We're going with you."

A second van pulled up hard behind the first van and the back doors flew open as Daniel hopped out.

"That'll be enough of that, men." said Daniel to the jittery police officers. "Stand down."

The officers turned and glared at Daniel who approached Christine. Daniel's smile was sincere.

"My name is Daniel Henry Rooke," said Daniel. "You'll be coming with me."

CHAPTER 15

SE RECRUITING

ANDREWS AIR BASE

When Daniel stepped out of the Chariot, it was with a wry grin that he pulled out a long carrying case along with his duffel bag. The trip to Brownsville had been productive, and far overshadowed the disastrous Cambridge affair, providing him with a new candidate for the team and the chance to stop by his brownstone in Cobble Hill.

Bradley and McCormack offered to stay behind with Christine Turf, to help smooth things out with the judge, to ensure she was delivered swiftly into their custody.

A small matter. he thought. *It should be taken care of in about a week.*

The judge would see things their way. As much as he hated using that aspect of his abilities, Bradley Overman would see to it. McCormack was just there to hold Christine's hand and talk to the judge. Bradley would do all the heavy lifting on this expedition.

Daniel walked across the tarmac and into the waiting SUV with a hop, pulling his gear in and throwing it into the back seat.

"Home, James." said Daniel with a grin.

The ride home was fairly quick, the SUV blaring its lights all the way as it weaved in and out of traffic like a real emergency was pressing and the overall trip was completed in roughly twelve minutes. Once the SUV took to traffic streets, the ride was slower. Pedestrians in the neighborhood had the unpleasant and annoying habit of waiting for the light to turn red and then walk into the street, defiantly and provokingly glaring at cars as they made their way across the street.

The flashing lights on the SUV and the blaring of the horn only made them walk more slowly, or stop entirely to stare down the driver. Once or twice Daniel fought the impulse to jump out of the car and pummel the pedestrian who stood there threateningly. There was nothing to do. Pedestrians still had some rights—even when jaywalking.

When the SUV finally pulled up to the Post, it was nearly one in the afternoon. Daniel hopped out and pulled his bags out of the back, turned and walked through the usual crowd of onlookers as if they weren't even there. He had grown accustomed to the neighborhood. So similar to Bedford-Stuyvesant, it was hard not to read the foot traffic and recognize their hard looks as an aftereffect of hard lives. The need to check every new face and gauge their strengths and weaknesses was just an unconscious twitch that everyone in the harder neighborhoods suffered from.

Daniel made his way into the lobby where no one would follow, held his breath and entered the elevator. The ride was slow and jerky, and he had to suffer a few inhalations of the acrid urine scent but finally the elevator doors parted and he stepped out onto the third floor landing. He walked into the flat to find Leonard at the table with Joshua and Stephen, looking mutinous. Joseph sat there alone with a grin on his face. Leonard folded his arms and glared at Daniel, not at all happy.

"Did you get what you were looking for?" said Leonard.

"And then some," replied Daniel with a grin.

"I heard we lost Terry," said Leonard.

Daniel paused. He knew he would eventually have to discuss the Cambridge affair, but he was in good spirits up until now, and did not want to discuss it yet. It still sent a wave of bile into his mouth.

"Yeah," said Daniel, "we were outmaneuvered in Boston."

"Outmaneuvered." scoffed Leonard. "That's one way of putting it."

"How would you like it entered into the record as?" snapped Daniel.

"I'm not talking about a goddamn record," snapped Leonard, "I'm talking about Terry Lyons in some Bureau experiment."

"There's nothing that can be done about it now," said Daniel, somberly. "I have Boatman on it, but that's as far as my hand can reach without losing a few fingers."

"I can see that," replied Leonard, forgivingly. "and I'm not blaming you."

Daniel scoffed and gestured to the table full of Specials as if it said something far different to him.

"Then why the huddle?" demanded Daniel.

"We're feeling a little left out," replied Joshua.

"Three arrests," added Stephen, "and we're sitting here on our asses."

"By the way," added Joseph, "thanks for the job."

"Don't mention it," said Daniel.

"Yeah, Joseph," growled Leonard, "Stop mentioning it."

Joseph leaned back and chuckled at the way he annoyed Leonard.

"Sure, sure." sang Joseph.

"So that's it?" pressed Leonard with a wave of his hand, bringing the point back to Lyons.

"Terry's beyond our reach, right now," concluded Daniel. "She'll be back with us as soon as possible."

"I don't like it," replied Leonard, folding his arms and flexing his biceps unconsciously.

"Your discontent is noted," said Daniel, "Is that all?"

"What's in the case?" inquired Stephen.

"Just a little something I intend to implement in future arrests."

Leonard leaned back with a surly expression.

"Why do I get the feeling I won't approve of what's in the case?"

"You might not approve," replied Daniel, "I could care less. I need an edge. And since we all know how you feel about grenades…"

Leonard studied Daniel critically but said nothing. Then his eyes took in the length of the case in Daniel's grip and his eyes went wide.

"That's not-"

"Is that all, gentlemen?" interrupted Daniel.

No one said anything.

With that, Daniel turned and walked down the corridor to his dorm room and closed the door. With a half-caring toss, his duffel bag landed on the bed. He set the long case down on the floor and made to open it when there was a knock at his door. Daniel slid the case under his bed, making sure it was out of sight. Not an instant after, Stephen opened the door and peered at the case being slid under the bed. Daniel pulled the sheets down and the case disappeared under the curtain of the comforter.

"What is it?" demanded Daniel.

"Phone," said Stephen.

Daniel hurried down the hallway to his office and found the door ajar, the phone off the hook. Daniel pursed his lips. He would have to speak to his people about answering his line.

"Agent Rooke," said Daniel.

"This is Agent Morrow of the Secret Service," chimed the voice on the other end of the line. "JJRTC GhettoFab reconstruction is complete and ready for use by your agency."

"That's excellent news," replied Daniel, pleased to hear something good for a change.

"You also have a bill of eighty-thousand, nine-hundred fifty-three dollars for repair and redesign of the GhettoFab," continued Agent Morrow in the same friendly voice as though the money was of no real consequence to Daniel. Then added, "To whom should I contact about payment?"

"What?!" exclaimed Daniel, clutching the phone tightly.

"The GhettoFab was partially destroyed with foundation damage occurring throughout the structures," continued Agent Morrow with a perfunctory politeness in his tone, "Very little of the original frame could be left standing and the foundation had to be ripped up and re-laid."

"We didn't do that to the structure," stammered Daniel.

"We have video footage of one of your operatives punching through a wall, and moments later three stories imploded due to structural damage to a support column."

"I'm telling you, you're billing the wrong team."

"You do not have one Leonard Stonebreaker on your team? He's clearly on the video footage transmitted by your own probes. Should we turn this over to collections?"

"The team you should be billing is the—I'll need to talk to my superior."

"Understood. I'll turn it over to collections and submit the bill in writing."

"Fine."

"Would you like to reserve your team for training at the GhettoFab?"

"Yes."

"I can schedule you in for tomorrow at oh-eight-thirty."

"That'll be fine."

"Have a nice day, Agent Rooke."

Daniel hung up the phone and looked over at the wall. Someone had painted an arrow pointing to a dot in the corner of the office. Daniel instantly recognized the dot as a surveillance microphone/transmitter. He walked over to the corner and craned his head up to the dot and said in a clear voice:

"Boatman, I'd like a call from you."

"Then it's a good thing I came by," said Boatman from the doorway. "I see your men found the bug."

"Yeah, I noticed."

"So, why don't we get down to business?"

"By all means," said Daniel, sitting down behind his desk, gesturing toward the seat in front of the desk. Boatman took the seat and sighed as he sat down facing Daniel. "You might want to start with Lyons."

Boatman's face was long and worn at the mention of Lyons.

"She has fallen through the cracks into the Bureau's experimental Specials Unit. A group of normal men and women, much like yourself, who deal with Specials solely."

"That sounds like our team."

"No." clarified Boatman. "There is a great difference between the two units. For one, you work with Specials. For them, all Specials are the enemy. And the greatest difference between your teams is that the Bureau's Specials Unit continues the studies held by Base Camp Gamma Science/Medical and the Science Medical Division 552nd. Brutal experiments used to coax out the abilities of the more latent Specials into the open, with often-disastrous results. They've been refining their practices on Specials. Their agenda with Lyons will be to push her abilities to their limits and see what happens, documenting everything. Pain means nothing to them. That is where Lyons is. That is where I am focusing my attention at the moment."

"How come Specials Unit didn't make the arrest? It was a Bureau file we got handed."

"The Specials Unit is not equipped to take down Specials. They let you do the dirty work with every intention of stealing the collar once she was properly subdued."

"So we got used," concluded Daniel.

"Yes." agreed Boatman. "And you're right. We need assurances this sort of thing won't happen again. That is even more important than getting to Lyons."

"What do we do?"

"Let me make a few calls. Loosen up a few doors. It will take some time, so the calls will have to be enough. As it is, I have a date with Congress. These other agencies making off with our collars has gone on long enough, don't you agree?"

"Yes."

"Is there anything else on your mind?"

"Yeah," replied Daniel. "We just got a call from the JJRTC. GhettoFab's up and running."

"Good news," said Boatman with a grin.

"Followed by bad news." replied Daniel. Daniel's smile was filled with his displeasure. "They're billing my team for the destruction and reconstruction of the urban warfare set. Since it was your team that caused the collapse, I don't want to see the money coming out of my team's funding."

"Ah," said Boatman, rising to his feet and stretching his back out. "Alright, I'll take care of it. Have the bill sent to me."

"Very good," said Daniel.

And with a smile, Boatman left.

Daniel sat back down in his chair and faced his computer terminal. He depressed his thumb on the security lock and the screen illuminated. Daniel pulled his keyboard to him and began typing.

"Open SITF file."

The screen blinked and a window blinked open.

"Open new file in this location. Name, Christine Turf."

The screen blinked and filled with data, before Daniel could input any: Christine Turf-Designated Callsign: Current [Non-Military Special-Epsilon Status] Female, 5'7", 135 lbs. African American. Ability to generate static electric charges which can be projected through contact with conductive material [proven examples of this are water and steel rods. PSYCH REPORT//Turf suffers from posttraumatic stress disorder as a result of gang rape and psychological conditioning to make her more pliable to handlers [pimps]. Turf's PTSD has brought about a severe break from the ability to follow social norms—evidence of this is underscored in attached file New York People vs. Christine Turf—and antisocial tendencies. All reports from New York City Psychological Evaluations points to deep resentment and distrust of authority figures. Long-term therapy recommended. PHYSICAL REPORT// Blood work run on Turf's DNA confirms she is an HIV carrier—further medical examination required to isolate strain and properly manage. Estimated time since infection is three months. Evidence also points to HPV infection, with precancerous cells in urine suggesting advanced strain attacking cervix. Due to cause of PTSD, Turf is unwilling to allow male OBGYN to examine her further than blood and urine testing. Requesting female OBGYN. If not treated within the next year, she will lose the ability to conceive.

"Poor girl," sighed Daniel.

WASHINGTON D.C., HOTEL MONACO

John Simpson stood in a business suit with his arm in a sling and Paul Hirano, similarly dressed, stood at the carriageway portal entrance on N 8th Street with their backs to the tree-lined street. The Hotel was located in the Penn Quarter of Washington D.C. located on a residential street with row houses, and apartments nestled in around it. It was a neoclassical design built of marble and was patterned after the Roman Temple of Jupiter blueprint. It was austere and beautiful with marble Corinthian columns rising proudly from the second floor to the roof. The richness of the area seemed to cling to the air and it reminded them they were far from home.

Simpson stepped forward nervously followed closely by Paul through an elegant courtyard and up a stone staircase. Inside, they stood frozen and took in the room with its sixteen-foot cast iron ceilings and skylights. The dining room was a lounge area filled with elite Washingtonians and hotel guests sipping wine and vodka at a modern bar and a dramatic dining area set in raised platforms with the highest tier giving a bird's eye view of the kitchen below. Both men swallowed hard, looking at the room. There was no way they could afford to even breathe in this room.

Slowly the two men approached a beautiful hostess who stood by a podium smiling at them as they approached. Simpson stepped forward and leaned his good hand on the podium.

"We're here to see Lesley Ayers," said Simpson, expecting to be told she had never heard of him. Instead, she smiled warmly.

"He is waiting for you." said the hostess. "Right this way."

The hostess turned and led Simpson and Hirano through the dining room and up a staircase. At the far corner of the empty platform, a single man sat sipping a cocktail casually staring out on the vacant courtyard, which was closed during the winter months. He rose with a smile and gestured to Simpson and Paul to come forward. Simpson recognized Lesley Ayers—callsign Fume— at once, and a nervous smile played on his face. Ayers stood, his warm smile infectious to the recipient.

"Good of you to come!" said Ayers, and gestured to the seats across from him. "Please, sit down."

Simpson and Paul took their seats across from Ayers, studying him cautiously. The hostess, oblivious to their standoffishness handed out their menus which Paul and Simpson took nervously.

"Nonsense. My friends will be having the Lunch Special." And then added, "And what would you like to drink?"

Simpson took a look around the room and knew he could not afford anything they had to offer by way of amenities.

"Thanks," scoffed Simpson, "but I didn't bring my wallet."

A pout played on Ayers' mouth as he looked out at Simpson and Paul.

"Do you honestly think I would allow my guests to pay?"

A silence yawned between them as Simpson studied Ayers coolly. Ayers was a calculating man, gifted with setting elaborate traps. One could get a headache trying to keep up with him. *What is he up to?* thought Simpson.

Paul Hirano broke the silence with a slap of his thigh.

"Well, in that case," said Hirano greedily, "I'd like a Johnnie Walker Blue Label."

"That's the spirit," exclaimed Ayers brightly.

"Water," said Simpson, coolly.

Ayers stood stiffly as though he had been doused with some himself but his smile quickly returned.

"A chaser, I'm sure." concluded Ayers, embarrassed. "Let's add some Johnnie Walker to that as well."

"Whatever you say, Mr. Ayers. I will inform your waiter."

Ayers slipped her a hundred dollar bill and folded his hands over hers.

"As always, my dear."

The hostess looked down at the hundred in her palm and blinked in astonishment, then quickly slipped it into her pocket and smiled at Ayers, leaving him with a slight shake of her hips. Ayers hardly paid any attention as he sat back down and crossed his legs casually. Simpson and Paul sat there for a moment and then Simpson, to appear respectful, leaned forward.

"Thank you for the invite," said Simpson, and looked around the posh restaurant. "It seems you're doing well."

"Company benefits," replied Ayers with a grin.

"What company you working for?" said Simpson, conversationally.

"A little startup LLC with big plans. SE Services. You might have heard of us."

SE Services was hardly a startup. It was the biggest security company in the United States with its own private army of ex-military looking for higher wages and a no-bid deal on contracts—that freezes out bidding by competitors—with the United States and Mexican, Saudi and Iraqi governments; along with whispers they could get contracts with Japan, South Korea, El Salvador and Switzerland.

"A little startup…" chuckled Hirano. "I like that."

"Well," said Simpson slyly, "why don't you hook a brother up?"

"Well," said Ayers, leaning forward, "that's what I called this little meeting for. You could call me something of a head hunter for this little firm I've fallen in with."

"A head hunter, huh?" replied Simpson, fishing, "Tell me, what are you looking for?"

"Specials, of course." replied Ayers, "Preferably Specials I've worked with before."

"I see." said Simpson, "So, someone like us?"

Ayers leaned forward conspiratorially.

"Let me pose you with a question," said Ayers, "Are you happy with your lot in life?"

Simpson shrugged and winced, quickly rubbing his ruined shoulder.

"It's a gig," said Simpson.

"A fair paying one, I'd wager." fished Ayers. "One with time off with pay? Medical and Dental?"

"Not particularly." said Simpson.

"No?" pressed Ayers.

"We get checked out at a college by interns," said Paul, disgustedly.

"And that sling you're wearing," pressed Ayers, "you've gotten the best care possible?"

"My arm is in a sling because I got shot a week ago." grumbled Simpson, bitterly. "It's stiff and it hurts. The interns tell me I'll always feel some pain and have lost some motor control."

"It's a bullet wound," scoffed Ayers with a chuckle. "We were patched up from far worse in the field."

"Tell me about it," replied Simpson, his bile rising in his mouth. "These arrogant interns think it's the best job in the world that they did because they did it to the best of their knowledge."

"True," replied Ayers. "The interns will learn a lot about dressing and cleaning wounds from experimenting on you."

"I have a staph infection," grumbled Simpson. "I gotta go back and get it cleaned again after this meeting." Simpson looked out the window at the view of the courtyard and found it ugly, as it came to personify the man who shot him. "That asshole…"

"How did you get shot, anyway?" inquired Ayers, pointedly. "In the course of your duties?"

"A training exercise," spat Simpson. "I was purposely shot during a training exercise."

Ayers leaned back in his chair, flexing his fingertips together.

"Such is to be expected when working for the government," said Ayers. "They don't trust us. They don't like us. They just want us to follow orders and take the meager pittance they offer us by means of salary. That is where you stand."

"We're not standing," said Paul through grit teeth. "We're kneeling."

"Truer words were never spoken," replied Ayers.

"And how would you remedy our situation?" said Simpson, bringing Ayers to the point.

"I'd offer you jobs," replied Ayers.

Simpson and Paul traded glances for a moment, gauging the other's surprise and finding only intrigue at the notion of working in the private sector.

"Doing what?" said Simpson.

"You would do a little of this, a little of that." said Ayers, with a grin. "More to the point, you would assist me in completing and keeping contracts, elevating the standard and status of my firm through appearance, conduct and overall professionalism."

"So you want us to represent your firm and just look impressive?" said Paul, not entirely trusting Ayers by first impression.

"I need people under me," clarified Ayers, "who will be able to add that military spit and polish touch to impress the clients, and that little extra ability to be the perfect protection to my firm's assets."

"You're being rather vague," scoffed Simpson with an irksome jerk of his head, his hand rubbing his shoulder.

"The job is fluid," corrected Ayers, "One assignment you will be security, another you'll be the tip of the sword. Think of it as multiple job distinctions which you would be paid handsomely for taking on."

"Handsomely?" said Simpson, keenly. "You got a price you want to fly by us?"

"The salary will put your current pay grade to shame," replied Ayers. "Some of the contracts are government, so you will have a pay grade higher than most agencies because you will be privy to their secrets and non-disclosure agreements are, as you well know, not worth a damn without incentive. And then there will be the private sector missions dealing far and wide in the way of purpose for presence and execution of contracts. You'll just have to take it from me that you will never be bored, and never have to worry about arrests as a result of your actions on duty. Does that ease your concerns? Or am I still being too vague?"

"For the right amount of money," replied Paul, "we'll be whatever you need."

"I thought that might be the case," smiled Ayers.

"So you're just looking for two Specials?" said Simpson.

"Good Lord, no." exclaimed Ayers, as though the thought was laughable. "I'm looking to recruit your entire team. But I am very keen to keep this as close to our original lineup as possible. However, some of the men on your current team can add the muscle we need to impress the clients who lack imagination for their needs."

"So, you need some thugs," concluded Simpson.

"A few would be nice," admitted Ayers, with no shame betraying his smile. "But as I said, you two are what I envision my team to be built around."

Just then, the waiter arrived with their drinks. A silence set over their discussion and they watched in stillness as the drinks were set down. Sensing he was interrupting, the waiter made a hasty exit down the stairs. Simpson then leaned forward toward Ayers.

"What would be required of us," said Simpson, "exactly?"

Ayers mulled over his words and spent a moment formulating his response, flexing his fingertips together calmly.

"The specificity of your requirements would be made clear in the fine print of each account you are assigned to, and it is uniformly different every time. I don't offer specifics because, to date, there are none. Just please the assets by performing your duty within the confines of the legal wording with exceptions to be made and clarified through our offices. In other words, they can't boss you around. *We* boss you around. But the pay is considerable, and I assure you, it will override any feeling of mortification or need for retaliation against the assets, that may arise. You are paid to put up with the eccentricities of the clients, and your ability to point out their need to read the fine print of the contract. Our contracts are very well written, and clearly state what your duties will be. Any problem with following the stipulations can be remedied with a call to the account manager who will quickly contact the asset and discuss modification of the contract with a raise of fee for you."

Hirano and Simpson traded a hungry look at the words "raise of fee" and silently communed for a long moment. Finally, Hirano turned to Ayers.

"What about medical?"

"It is within my means to give you a taste of our medical treatment for employees," said Ayers shrewdly. "I can arrange someone to look at that shoulder within the hour."

"Sounds good to me," said Simpson, rubbing his sore shoulder, absentmindedly.

"I thought that might," smiled Ayers.

Daniel sat in his office poring through emails filtered through Homeland Security fitting the broad speculation of *Special Involvement*. He stared at the screen so long flipping from one file to the next his eyes began to ache from the constant glare of the computer screen. *God,* he thought, realizing that flipping through emails and X-File documents could detail the majority of his job as task force agent in charge.

A knock at the door startled him, and blearily he looked up at the ragged expression on Lawrence Boatman's face.

"You got a minute, Rooke?"

"Just give me a second," he answered.

Daniel fished in his drawer for eye drops, leaned his head back and let the drops burn the skin of his eyes and bring him to watering. When he turned back to Boatman he was blinking bloodshot and his tear ducts went on overdrive producing lubrication for his strained eyes. "How can I help you, Lawrence?"

"I have a problem that is soon to become your problem, and I saw it only fitting to have a meeting with you to get a firm grip on the problem before it becomes…explosive."

Daniel cocked his head and stared at Boatman thinking *okay, not too ominous…*

"Well why don't you lay it out there so I can get a clear view of the battlefield."

"I've had a few…AWOLs… and I thought it best to bring it to your attention."

"AWOLs?" blinked Daniel. "I'm assuming you're talking about your personal team you've felt necessary to keep in the dark from me?"

"That would be the same."

"How many?"

"The entire team!" snapped Boatman, irritably. "Hirano, Simpson, Kelson, Harris, Simms, Townsend! All gone."

Daniel felt a lump rise into his throat. A Black Ops team under the heel of Boatman was a powerful tool. But free to do as they pleased with military training and a Special's dis-enfranchisement? Daniel knew if they stepped out of line it would fall to him to make the arrest. And judging how poorly they did in fighting a scrimmage against them, he would hate to see real blood in their eyes. The only thought that occurred to him was to find out how much training and augmentation they went through. How much they were holding back during the scrimmage?

"So how much was invested in them?"

"Considerably more than your team in training and team cohesiveness." answered Boatman shortly. "They were the best of the best."

"They were also missing a few screws."

"They acted within their roles."

"If you recall, Simpson tried to kill Bradley Overman."

"That was nothing that could not be remedied with a word from me, and would have been wholly unnecessary if Maximus was working on his telekinetic shields and not slacking."

"Slacking?" blinked Daniel in astonishment.

"*Yes, slacking.*" snapped Boatman. "Don't rely on your team being perfect, Daniel. They are all taking it easy, with the exception of Giordano, who I will admit, is becoming more effective in long distance attacks and suppressive firepower. He just might be able to replace what was lost when you let Meng walk out the door, with enough time and training."

"I didn't let anyone walk," snapped Daniel, indignantly.

"You didn't go out of your way to *keep* them on the team, either, did you?" replied Boatman with vinegar.

Daniel stood where he was for an instant and then nodded.

"No," admitted Daniel. "I didn't."

"This is not a reflection on your leadership since then." soothed Boatman, pinching the ridge of his nose as though putting pressure on an annoying headache. "You've made the correct decisions on how to implement change and have experimented with arrest methods in the field, learning lessons and seeing problems that would need to be addressed if we were going to continue with the unit beyond the experimental. But this team that I have invested in was a challenging fighting force with a military background. They have successfully been in training and combat for over ten years before I invested my time and funding in them." Boatman paused and took a breath before continuing. "As an asset they are a force to be reckoned with. As free agents, they can prove...problematic."

Daniel studied Boatman for a long moment drinking in every word and finding it not to his liking.

"Why are you telling me this?" asked Daniel.

"I'm afraid," said Boatman, "they will be on the board before we like it."

"You mean our most wanted list?" said Daniel.

"Your team will need to be prepared for this possibility," said Boatman smoothly. "You've trained against them, and you've lost."

"I didn't see it as a loss," replied Daniel, folding his arms indignantly.

"Then you weren't paying attention." snapped Boatman. "Beach taken out by grenades, Overman taken out by radiation exposure. And all the while, Paladin was absent. Get on your team and see that they perform. I want you running the GhettoFab in less than five minutes. None of this ten, twenty minute bullshit I'm seeing from you. If you can't run it in five you can't run it against Specials in the field."

Daniel swallowed hard and nodded his agreement.

"Right."

"I'm not playing around, Daniel." snapped Boatman. "These men are dangerous. I need you prepared for the eventuality you run up against them."

"I'll get the team on it first thing in the morning," promised Daniel.

"See that you do," said Boatman, and he stormed out of the office leaving Daniel there alone with new problems to occupy his mind. New nightmares to form in his consciousness. And a new threat to dominate his task force.

Daniel sat in his office calmly. Hours ago he had informed Leonard that the team would be running the GhettoFab in the morning, and they had now stopped their griping, accepting the inevitable jumping through hoops, kicking in doors, clearing rooms and floors, taking out targets using their powers or their weapons depending on who was an energy projector and who was just powerfully built. Joseph would be the real test in this exercise. He had never run the GhettoFab before. It would be a test for him to act with a team again, after so long. Each of the men had fallen short the first time through the GhettoFab—the closest thing to real urban warfare they would get before the real thing confronted them when the task force was up and running—and each of the men had learned the hard way that without teamwork, they were as good as dead.

Now he was listening to the flat grow silent as one by one his team went to bed early anticipating the early morning exercise. Five minutes for a cul-de-sac. They would be running, dizzy from turning left and right at neck-breaking paces. And they would be in full gear. Daniel did not envy the men. But this was something they had to do alone. He was forbidden to participate by mandate of what a team leader's function was...to bark orders and to keep those orders coming. To watch. To be helplessly underutilized. This was frustrating to Daniel. He was made to move. He was built to be in the action, not sidelined to a babysitter's duty. But that was exactly what he was expected to be. He sat back in his chair and reclined, shutting his eyes, when a knock interrupted his brooding.

Daniel turned to the door to see McCormack leaning against the doorframe. The sight of him standing so casually should not have surprised him in the least, but he was shaken just the same. He was sure it would take a week before he saw him again. His presence could only mean his work in New York was completed successfully and far ahead of schedule.

"You look like you're ready to explode," chuckled McCormack.

"Wish you could read my thoughts?" smiled Daniel.

"Not particularly," replied McCormack.

"When did you get back?"

"Just now." replied McCormack. "Brad's unpacking Turf into Meng's old room, giving her the rundown before she meets you." McCormack fixed his eyes on Daniel's and added, "You want to do this now or tomorrow?"

"I'll meet her now." said Daniel without a moment's hesitation.

"You sure?" measured McCormack, thoughtfully. "You don't look too well."

"Yeah well," scoffed Daniel, "Boatman just gave me a mouthful of his problems and left me feeling like it was my fault."

McCormack gave a knowing nod.

"Boatman must be on edge."

"The edge of a razor blade, from what I gathered."

"Don't worry about him," soothed McCormack. "There isn't a plot against him he hasn't managed to turn against his enemies. He's just good at it."

"Yeah," answered Daniel, "well this one might require us to get involved."

"Do tell," said McCormack, curiously.

"Boatman's Black Ops team went rogue today."

McCormack blinked in astonishment and stared at Daniel for a long moment.

"How many of them?"

"The whole team."

McCormack pinched his nose and closed his eyes at the headache that threatened to erupt at the thought of a rogue Black Ops team in their future.

"Not good at all."

"Nope."

McCormack released his nose and waved his hand in the air at the inevitable question that he already knew the answer to:

"We running the GhettoFab, I take it?"

"First thing in the morning."

"Maybe meeting Turf can wait," decided McCormack.

"No better time than the present," shrugged Daniel.

"I'll tell Brad." McCormack did not move, or even speak. He did not shout down the quiet hall or gesture. He just closed his eyes and exhaled. When he opened them again he smiled. "They're coming."

Bradley led Christine Turf into the room with a warm smile, encouraging her steps into the office to face Daniel for the second time. The first time she encountered him he was hard and cool, but he wrangled in the police officers who were keen on opening fire if she so much as moved wrong. Seeing him standing at his desk watching her intently made her nervous, and she clenched her fists and released them alternately as a coping mechanism with stressful moments. Daniel recognized how nervous she was and an encouraging smile played at his lips as he gestured to the chair in front of his desk. Christine did not sit. She stood there next to the chair studying Daniel carefully, as if every word would be measured and weighed. Realizing this was the closest to comfort Christine would allow herself to get in his presence; Daniel walked around his desk and sat on the edge of his desk, looking at her unblinking eyes.

"So," opened Daniel, unnecessarily for the sake of beginning. "I take it you've gone through quite an experience."

"Yeah." said Christine.

"Do you know why you're here?" questioned Daniel.

"Mr. Overman," began Christine, but corrected herself with a glance at Bradley, "Brad…told me it was for a job."

"Well, not yet." corrected Daniel. "You're too young for the kind of work we'll be doing. But I can train you and make sure you receive proper education so you can carry out the duties my team is mandated to perform. Does that sound interesting to you?"

"I guess," shrugged Christine, glancing nervously at Bradley. Bradley nodded back to her encouragingly. "I mean, it's not like I can go back home, right?"

"Not now, no."

"Well I guess I'd rather be here."

"This isn't a prison sentence, Christine."

"So I can go home?"

"If you want to go home, I can make that happen, but you'd be facing the same problems you were facing before. Plus, you've been outed as an active Special. It will follow you on your background check, and make it difficult to find work."

Christine wiped tears away, flicking them off her fingertips trying to maintain her composure.

"Can't you make it go away?"

"That's not in my power. But I can offer you something better. I can offer you community. A family. I can offer you job security, which may mean nothing to you now, but out there, you'd find it very difficult to find that."

"What do I have to do to get back to my family?"

"I'll tell you what, I don't want to come between you and your family. How about we enroll you in classes here in

D.C. and start you out right, and I can write it up where you take two weekends a month to be with your family."

"You can do that?"

"I'm not sure, but I can try."

"Thank you."

"This doesn't have to be a prison sentence. It can be a new start, if you'll let it."

"I know." "I just want my grandma."

"I'll make the necessary arrangements to get you enrolled in classes and get you clearance to visit your grandmother."

'Thank you."

"Well, you've had a long day. I won't keep you. Why don't you get some rest."

"Okay." Christine turned to Bradley who smiled and with a gesture, she followed him out of the office.

"That was nice."

"You being sarcastic?"

"Just a subtle manipulation with the mention of the background report, but overall you handled it fine."

"Sarcasm…"

"Relax. You got what you wanted. You got a black girl on the team to add some color to it."

"You don't have to put it like that."

"Isn't that exactly what you wanted?"

"A traumatized sixteen year old with posttraumatic stress and HIV?" scoffed Daniel and he shook his head. "Hardly."

"But it's a start," said McCormack, plainly.

"It's a start," agreed Daniel.

"It's late." said McCormack, lifting off the doorframe, "I should go."

"Yeah," sighed Daniel. "Let me finish up in here and I'll turn in too. We've got a busy day tomorrow at the GhettoFab."

"Then I will leave you to it." concluded McCormack. "See you in the morning, Agent Rooke."

Daniel listened to his footsteps on the wood floor down the hall and finally a door close softly. Sitting in silence he heard Christine talking in hushed voices with Bradley. Stephen and Joshua playing video games raucously. Leonard snoring. Only Chad and McCormack were silent.

Damn, thought Daniel, *Stephen was right. You* can *hear everything in this place...*

CHAPTER 16

BREAKING MANDATE

D aniel sat in his office glued to the computer, reading reports about suspected Special activity and pursed his lips as he read the article before him. A house had burned to the ground in the middle of the night plainly due to the fact that the owners, who had not paid their heating bill had been warming themselves with a barbecue they kept in the living room with wood and paper burning. The locals suspected Special involvement. What utter nonsense!

Okay, he thought. *I need a break.*

He rose and cracked his back with a long and thorough stretch, and with a twist for good measure, squeezed out an extra crack in his hips. With a long yawn, he turned away from the 150 unseen emails and made his way outside into the flat. There he was greeted by the welcome sight of Leonard in sweats, stretching. He was chipper this morning, in deference to his attitude yesterday. Daniel waved his hand like a white flag, just to be sure. Leonard turned and grinned at him and cocked his head back toward the remaining members of SITF, consisting of Chad Beach, Josh Sung, Stephen Giordano and Joseph Little Bird, all in sweats.

"We're going to run down to the reservoir," said Leonard. "You coming?"

"Actually," said Daniel, "I was thinking of going down to Charlie's for something to eat."

"Sounds good," said Leonard. "Maybe we'll swing by after we work up an appetite."

"Sounds good," replied Daniel.

With that, Leonard turned to face the sweats clad file behind him.

"Alright!" barked Leonard, "Come on you loafers, let's get out there!"

Leonard led them out of the flat and down the stairs—the sound of their heavy footsteps creaking on the wooden plank steps on the way down sounded like an army marching—Daniel stood there until the sound of their footsteps faded into the street and left him alone in silence.

With a hop over the barricade, Daniel followed them down the steps at a leisurely pace, taking his time down the steps and out into the street. The neighborhood hardly paid him a second glance. He had become just a side attraction, a passing curiosity; as though the population of Shepherd Park and Georgia Avenue were saying *You're still here?* He took it all in stride, and turned south, crossing Quebec Street and making his way past the barbershops and pool halls.

As Daniel turned the corner to see Charlie's Soul Food, he stopped dead in his tracks at the sight that greeted him. The front of the restaurant was graffitied with the words

Princeton Place Kings, *PPK*, and random other tags naming the taggers and people who claim the territory, including Chris' street name, "Jonas." A section of window was boarded up with plywood, easily telling that someone had thrown a rock or brick through the window, or something far more sinister. Daniel felt his blood run cold and then a wave of heat overtook him at the sheer arrogance of the gangsters who desecrated his favorite restaurant.

"Chris," he muttered.

Daniel pushed the door open and entered the dimly lit soul food restaurant feeling grim as soon as he looked around seeing it empty.

This is all my fault, thought Daniel.

"Daniel!" came the familiar welcoming voice of Charlie from the darkest corner of the restaurant. He appeared worn and beaten down though his resilient smile shone through and almost put Daniel at ease. Almost. The most he could offer Charlie was a wan smile.

"Hey, Charlie." moaned Daniel.

"Tamika," called Charlie to the kitchen, "Daniel's here! A cup of coffee, please!" Tamika poked her head out, rolled her eyes and disappeared into the kitchen again, returning with a mug of coffee, which she set down on the table in front of Daniel with an odd expression, as though she were torn between conflicting emotions. Charlie noticed her expression and leaned toward Daniel conspiratorially. "My granddaughter's a stubborn one. Won't give an inch even though she wants to."

"I don't follow."

"Well, considering how you two met she's got a bit of a grudge against you. Now on top of that, you saved her and her grandpappy over here… it would be reasonable for her to express gratitude, wouldn't you say?"

"No thanks are necessary, considering all the problems we must have caused by interfering."

"Oh, but thanks are necessary for your assistance. She's smart enough to know it. And let's not forget, you saved her from getting turned out, too. She owes you. Even though you'll never hear it from her. Like I said—stubborn."

"How are things?" said Daniel, anxious to change the subject from expressions of gratitude for causing more harm than good. Charlie instantly shifted in his seat, serious and wary, knowing his choosing of words could affect the mood of the conversation and wanting to choose carefully.

"I'm surviving."

"Hey, sorry about last time. I didn't think things would get out of hand like that."

With that, the youthful spark twinkled in Charlie's eyes.

"And it doesn't help that you got some black in you." Charlie grinned.

"I'm sorry?" stammered Daniel.

"Man," exclaimed Charlie to the heavens, "I never seen a white boy as down as you. You straight old school, too. Stepping to these young turks like you the real deal. And you deliver. You and your *'special'* friends. Man, I never would've known you had so much juice just by looking at you, but man, you deliver."

"Well, I'm sorry just the same for bringing it to your doorstep. How's business?"

"Slow. But we got cops coming in again. And for some reason the feds have been pouring in here like they already know the menu. I suppose I got you to thank for that."

"Just a little."

"Well, thanks. Some business is better than no business."

"It'd be a shame if you lost your roots in the neighborhood, though."

"Man," exclaimed Charlie, rolling his eyes and puffing up his chest. "The neighborhood ain't leaving me. I told you, they call me 'pops' for a reason. I'm the one the neighborhood turns to when they look for sage advice. I'm like a big bad voodoo daddy reading fortunes and cards. They can't get enough of me."

"That is until they find out how you do it," chided Daniel.

"Well," replied Charlie, smoothly, "let's just keep that between us, okay?"

"Hey," chuckled Daniel, "my lips are sealed."

"I appreciate that," said Charlie, closing the messy chapter of his ability before Daniel could make another sleight of hand comment. Charlie then looked around the room as though looking for eavesdroppers, even though the restaurant was empty, and leaned in conspiratorially toward Daniel. "So, I hear you got yourself a big Indian in your corner, now."

"Yeah," chuckled Daniel. "I'm not surprised you'd know about that."

"Shit," replied Charlie with a wave of his hand, "a big assed Indian jogging around the neighborhood with a skin-head and a little white boy? That tends to stand out a bit given our color over here."

"I hear you," laughed Daniel, "Actually, they should be stopping by for lunch. You should get to meet Joseph your-self when he comes in."

"Joseph, huh?" parroted Charlie, scrutinizingly. "Not Dog-Barks-At-Morning-Sky or something like that? But an actual name?"

"Let's not get racist, now."

"You're right. You're right. Joseph it is, then…" Charlie sat still nodding sagely for a moment, until he couldn't take it anymore. "He's not Mormon, is he? Tell me he's not Mormon."

"Why?"

"A man from the plains named Joseph? Nine times out of ten, he's a Mormon."

"Fair enough," conceded Daniel. "I don't think he has a religion. He's kind of to himself in a strange way."

"You need any help cracking him?" said Charlie with a wily glint in his eyes. "I'm always up for some practice."

"He's on my team," said Daniel flatly, "He's off limits. Besides, he's pretty direct. I don't think you'll need your talent with him. He'd probably tell you straight out and then tell you where you can stick it."

"Oh," chuckled Charlie, "a sweetheart."

"I'm just forewarning you."

"I can dig it."

Behind them, the entrance door swung open and in walked Chris flanked by two large thugs. Chris eyed the pair of them like a prize.

"So I heard there was a white bitch up in my restaurant," taunted Chris with a cocky grin in finding Charlie and Daniel—especially Daniel—alone.

"Get out of my restaurant," growled Charlie, balling his fists and rising from his chair. Daniel leaned back in his chair and looked over his shoulder back at Chris, expecting anything.

"Don't get it twisted, old man," mocked Chris, "This place is mine. You just work here, but the checks come to me. Starting today. You feel me?"

"No, I don't 'feel' you," snapped Charlie, standing firm and tall like a younger man. "Get out of my restaurant and crawl under your rock you little cockroach."

"Sit your ass down, old man!" retorted Chris, opening his winter coat to reveal the pistol tucked into the elastic of his underwear and pants. The two thugs laughed at the turn of events, eyeing Charlie cruelly. Daniel turned even more in his seat, studying Chris as critically as the ten steps between them, and the lengths to get to him before he could pull the gun from his pants and aim with surety. Chris then turned to meet Daniel's eyes, gloating over the sureness of his superiority to Daniel without his team in tow.

"What about you, white boy?" goaded Chris. "You got something to say?"

Daniel locked eyes with Chris and grit his teeth, disgusted with the man before him, yet unwilling to race the ten steps to take a life. He had known too many thugs to be rehabilitated by a prison stretch to want to end a life when all he saw before him was unused potential. Unused, not wasted. In the end, he merely played the game of words, offering Chris some of his own, letting him know how dangerous he was and how explosive this conflict could become with a simple push.

"You don't want to see how I roll, son." said Daniel.

Again, the enforcers laughed cruelly, and Chris looked from one to the other with mock surprise before leaning closer to Daniel.

"Now, see?" replied Chris, taking a step closer to Daniel. "That's where you're wrong. I want to see what you got without your boys backing you up."

"That's a hell of a thing to say," retorted Charlie, "when you don't go anywhere without your boys."

"Shut up, old man," snapped Chris, reaching for his pistol, "before I cut your buck-fifty ass in half to make change."

Charlie stopped dead in his tracks, and eyed Chris as though he estimated him as nothing more than a weak man with a gun to tip the odds in his favor and with his weapon, lord over those who would otherwise be superior to him.

"I got you," declared Chris, his hand clutching the pistol in his pants, "You got nothing! And no one's going to help you!"

Daniel was distracted by the sounds from the sidewalk, the scuffle of several feet, the shadows that warped and refracted through the window on the wall beside him, and the voices, out of breath and heavy. One voice commanding the others and Daniel chuckled.

"But that's the thing, see?" said Daniel with a grin, "I'm never alone."

Just then, the door opened and in the doorway appeared Leonard, Chad, Joseph, Stephen and Josh in sweats just in from a run down to McMillan Reservoir and back. Leonard looked down at Chris and the two thugs and grinned.

"We heard there was a party," said Leonard, eyeing Chris, "and decided to come in and check out the bitches."

"Who you calling a bitch," demanded Chris, wheeling around, "bitch?"

Leonard blew a kiss to Chris, and Chris' eyes went wide with rage as he reached for the pistol tucked into the elastic of his underwear. Daniel rushed up and kicked Chris with his right leg in the back of the knee, driving Chris to the floor in agony, and with his left foot, Daniel kicked the gun out of his belt and sent it spinning across the floor. Leonard walked into the room with cold authority and glowered down at the two enforcers who stood cowed under Leonard and Joseph's collective shadows.

"If I were you," said Leonard, "I'd be…"

"…Leaving?" offered one of the enforcers, nervously.

"See?" said Joseph. "And I thought these bitches were going to be dumb."

"Off you go," said Leonard, and the two enforcers sidled against the wall, and edged their way past the small army in the doorway until they reached Josh, Chad and Stephen—their size and wiry frames made them seem perfect targets—the thugs pushed their way forcefully into them. Chad kicked one in the face and put the other in a stranglehold, tightening his grip all the while.

"Bad move, pal." said Chad.

The enforcer patted Chad's arm as a universal sign for *"enough, you're choking me!"* and Chad relaxed his grip and let the man go. Stephen stepped forward and flicked his fingers at them; a loud pop sounded and the force knocked the two enforcers back to the ground in utter disbelief, patting the flames out as they struggled to get up and ran down the street, clearing the corner on Quincy Street and disappearing from view, Stephen laughing uproariously at their exit.

Inside, Chris knelt before Leonard and Joseph glowering up at them as Leonard slid Chris' gun into his own waistband. Daniel walked over and crouched down next to Chris.

"This could get real bad for you, Chris," said Daniel, methodically. "Or you can call it quits and forget about this place, the staff and customers. Because I've reached my limit with you. Next time we meet, you had better have more than a nine millimeter between you and me. Because I'll have at least a forty-five."

"You ain't got shit," spat Chris, defiantly.

Daniel opened his coat and revealed the forty-five in his shoulder holster.

"Bluffing is for boys without the means to even the odds for themselves," said Daniel, dispassionately. "As you can plainly see, I don't have that problem."

Chris eyed Daniel with contempt and watched cruelly while Daniel stepped away and returned to Leonard's side.

"Let him go," said Daniel, at last.

Leonard nearly choked on the words, and turned his wide eyes to Daniel.

"Are you sure about that, Daniel?" said Leonard, unsurely.

"I'm sure," replied Daniel.

"Sir," pressed Leonard, "I don't advise we do that."

"Let's just call the cops," said Joseph, as though the solution was obvious.

"And have the gang clamp down on the area in his absence for revenge?" replied Daniel firmly. He shook his head. "No. There's not enough to make this worth our while, anyways."

"Let the cops have this little bitch," pressed Joseph and smiled down at Chris expectantly. "I'd love to be a fly on the wall of the gen-pop shower tonight."

Chris glowered back at Joseph contemptuously as his fate was decided in pragmatic fashion.

"What are we going to get him for," replied Daniel, "brandishing? If I get this guy, it'll be for something good. Not a three-month stint with good behavior, then kicked back out to the street due to overpopulation. I want him a way for a long time."

Leonard and Joseph seemed to mull over Daniel's words as though they had a bad taste in their mouths—neither of them were happy with his bringing a cop's logic into their fantasies of having Chris arrested and the problem being solved. Daniel looked down at Chris as though disappointed.

"Get out of here," said Daniel, at last. "And don't come back."

Chris rose slowly, as though sensing some trick. His eyes trailed from Daniel, to Leonard, to Joseph and finally on the remainder of their retinue who glared back at him with disgust. When no one rushed him, he walked to the doorway, leaned against the door, and paused. As though he could not help himself, he turned to face Charlie and shot him a dangerous look.

"I'll catch up with you and your daughter later, Charlie."

"No you won't," interjected Daniel. "If you do, I'll finish what you started right here on this floor."

"And we'll watch," smiled Joseph.

"Whatever," scoffed Chris.

Chris walked out of the restaurant, and glowered at them through the sections of window unmarred by graffiti as he made his way down to Quincy Street and vanished around the corner. With that, Charlie sat down and sighed.

"You know he's never going to stop, Daniel," said Charlie, exhaustedly. "Right? He's going to keep coming back until someone puts two in him."

"Don't think I wasn't tempted," sighed Daniel.

"I know," said Charlie. "I know."

"So what, now?" said Joseph, impatiently.

"We let him think it over," replied Daniel. "Maybe he'll change his mind."

"More likely his tactics," concluded Leonard.

"Then we'll deal with him later," replied Daniel. "For now, I'll settle for getting surveillance on this location."

"Surveillance?" scoffed Leonard. "We don't have the resources."

"Installing cameras and linking it up to Metro and DOJ is no big problem," soothed Daniel. "Besides, they all eat here, now. They should be interested in keeping the place up and running for the next time they have a craving for catfish on Wonder Bread."

"So we document their activity on the block and at the restaurant," reasoned Leonard, "Then what? We sweep up after they roll through, and if we're lucky, someone smiles for the cameras so we can ID 'em?"

"This is a Metro problem," concluded Daniel. "We are not authorized to engage the general population. We have a mandate and we'll stick to it until we get authorization. Is that clear?"

"Yes, sir," snapped Leonard, grimly.

"Whatever you say, Agent Rooke," said Joseph.

"Hey look," offered Charlie. "I appreciate the help, again. But you don't know this cat. Chris won't stop. He'll just keep coming. He's hardheaded like that."

"I didn't say we wouldn't help," clarified Daniel. "I'm just saying that my team can't engage Princeton Park Kings. I said nothing about me."

"What are you going to do?" blinked Charlie.

"I don't want to get into it with too much detail," mused Daniel. "But I'm seriously considering burning a house down to make a point."

"You want to go on record with that?" warned Leonard, hinting the restaurant is in all likelihood bugged by the SITF Surveillance Tech Teams.

"I'll settle for having a house seized and put up for auction," clarified Daniel.

"Man," exclaimed Charlie, "Chris don't care about nothing."

"How about his momma's house?" answered Daniel cagily.

"You wouldn't," gasped Charlie.

"Bet me," replied Daniel.

"Damn," exclaimed Charlie, and gave Daniel an impressed look. "You are hard."

"Hard's got nothing to do with it," said Daniel.

Charlie stared at Daniel unconvinced, but acquiesced.

"Alright," concluded Charlie. "We'll play it your way."

"My way's your best bet," said Daniel.

"You stake my life on it?" clarified Charlie, "My daughter's?"

"I only stake my own life on it," answered Daniel.

"Our lives are together in this," answered Charlie. "Come hell or high water."

Tamika walked out of the kitchen where she had been hiding and approached Charlie, shaking.

"Grandpa," warned Tamika, "tell me you're not going up against Chris."

Charlie stood there in silence, mulling over his reply until finally he sighed and looked at Tamika.

"I remember when Chris was a sweet boy," said Charlie. "Loved his momma, always polite. This Jonas, I don't know him. Let's hit him where it hurts."

"Let me make a phone call," said Daniel, pulling out his cellular phone.

"While Daniel handles his business," said Charlie, "why don't we take orders?"

Chad, Joshua and Stephen entered the restaurant and sat down at the far table away from the cold blast of wind from the door. Leonard and Joseph followed and sat down, and Charlie pandered to them like a group of rambunctious kids.

Tamika took their orders while Daniel made a call to the District of Columbia Metropolitan police and got Chris Young's address. Then placed a call to the IRS and inquired into the state of their tax payments…suggesting it was due time for an audit. The voice on the other end of the line jumped to attention when Daniel identified himself with Homeland Security and made the proper emails, alerting the proper departments that Chris Young was now on the investigative list. When Daniel got off the phone, he sat down with a grin on his face.

"You know," said Daniel, "I could get used to this job."

"Everything went well, I take it?" inquired Leonard.

"I haven't even begun to squeeze that little shit," replied Daniel. "But all this falls under my not using the team to handle non-Specials matters so I think Boatman will allow it."

"That's good to hear," said Joseph. "But taxes? Honestly?"

"You've never seen the IRS raid a house before?" replied Daniel.

"No," replied Leonard, a little nervous at the thought.

"You wouldn't want to see it either," said Daniel grimly.

"Especially if it's my house," added Leonard.

"There are ways to crack a nut without ever getting a nutcracker out of the drawer," said Daniel. "It's all about the proper application of leverage. And I intend to apply every possible pressure until Chris cracks. Maybe he'll get so caught up in his troubles he'll leave Charlie alone."

"You really think that could happen?" said Charlie, disbelievingly.

"I'm giving Chris the benefit of the doubt, here," replied Daniel. "He doesn't want to see my dark side."

Joseph eyed Daniel quizzically and grinned.

"This isn't your dark side?" quipped Joseph.

"This is me toying with him," corrected Daniel. "This has nothing to do with what I could do to him and his gang. And hopefully, none of them, or me, will find out just how dark I can get."

"Cheers," saluted Joseph, and took a swig from his mug.

When Daniel and the others returned from Charlie's, the Post was dimming as the last rays of light dipped below the buildings across the street. Daniel flipped on the fluorescent lights in the flat and made his way down the hallway, flipping on lights as he went. As he passed McCormack's cramped office, he saw the lights were on, and poked his head in, rapping on the door.

"Daniel," said McCormack with a smile. "Come in."

Daniel settled down on a chair, pushing a box out of the way so his knee wouldn't bang into it. McCormack waited for him to get settled before speaking.

"I heard you had an interesting day."

Daniel eyed McCormack suspiciously for a moment and then sighed rolling his eyes.

"Boatman?" asked Daniel, unnecessarily.

"You know he's got feelers everywhere," replied McCormack.

"I wonder if he's got the restaurant bugged," murmured Daniel suspiciously.

"I wouldn't know," replied McCormack. "But even if it was, it couldn't be used in court anyway."

"Yeah," replied Daniel somberly. "It's a shame."

"I hear you're making that kid really feel it, too."

"I'm doing what little I can do, just passing information along to people who can do something about it."

"Just the same, I'm impressed you didn't use the team to handle the gang, by now."

"Not our fight, on paper."

"No. It's not."

"I'll stick to the letter of the mandate. Don't worry about that."

"Oh, I know," replied McCormack. "Still, it's a shame that your friend has to suffer before Christopher Young feels the squeeze."

"That's what Metro's for. They eat there too. I put them on alert."

"And Boatman gave in to your little request and had the surveillance team set up cameras there at the restaurant and down the street, with feeds to Metro and DHS."

"Really?" said Daniel with a note of surprise. "They must have just shown up. We didn't see them anywhere near the place."

"Well, Boatman's made it very clear the surveillance teams are to be unseen, unheard and unknown."

"And how do you know so much about it, then?"

"Boatman can't shield his mind to me or Bradley. So, he doesn't waste his time. He just out and says what he's planning."

"I see."

"Don't tell him I told you."

"Don't you think he already knows you told me?"

McCormack reached for a jar of water and shook it. There was the dull clinking sound of metal colliding with glass mixed in with the slosh of the water. McCormack smiled.

"All the bugs in my office and the hallway just outside. I prefer my privacy."

"How nice for you."

"I'm just finishing up my updates to the Turf file. It should be ready for you in about five minutes."

"Good deal."

With that, Daniel rapped his knuckles on the doorframe and left McCormack to his work, walking down the hall to his office. Once he opened the door, he flicked the light on and took his seat at the desk noticing the email notice was flashing. With a few clicks from the mouse, the email window appeared and Daniel clicked through them.

Most of the emails were benign chatter about possible Special sightings that had been filtered through local law enforcement agencies and had fallen through the rabbit hole to his Task Force to be scrutinized over. Specials sightings were akin to UFO sightings, and most turned out to be the ravings of lunatics. However, they would all have to be investigated in one way or another. A description of a muscular furry man with wings had a tag on it which read: **//POSSIBLE GRIFFIN SIGHTING. GRIFFIN A.K.A. BRIAN OARSMAN HAS BEEN AT LARGE FOR 21 MONTHS. //ABNORMAL-SPECIAL\\ APPROACH WITH CAUTION\\.** Another email described a man who could turn luminous with the tag: **//POSSIBLE PHOTON SIGHTING—PHOTON A.K.A. TERANCE COONTZ. [RANK: BOFO-DELTA/BETA STATUS]. APPROACH WITH EXTREME CAUTION.** Daniel opened another email with an attachment to a sighting of the devil. Daniel groaned and then out of curiosity followed the attachment: **POSSIBLE AZAZEL SIGHTING—AZAZEL A.K.A. ELROY MATHERS—BROKE OUT OF AB-SPEC FACILITY 33 MONTHS**

AGO. //ABNORMAL-SPECIAL\\ APPROACH WITH CAUTION.

"These emails are weird," scoffed Daniel.

"Welcome to our world," chided Leonard from the doorway. "We live on weird."

"Take for example," said Daniel, and scrolled down on the list of emails. "*'Blackout in Nashville, Tennessee. Possible Special involvement suspected.'* Are they serious? They're blaming everything on Specials."

"When you don't have an answer, see the scapegoat."

"Something tells me the biggest part of this job is going to be persuading the public no Specials were involved with the catastrophe-slash-accident-slash-incident."

"Now you're starting to see things our way," said Leonard with a chuckle. "A lot of these calls are going to be shadows chasing ghosts. Some of them will be legit. But we're going to be investigating them all. But you know this. That's why you've got us all training as a team and as individuals. We're all going to be going up against a case on our own at one point or another, calling in for backup or not as it pans out."

"True," answered Daniel. "But these aren't even filtered. It's just a laundry list of X-Files with attachments suggesting possibilities by outing Specials who might not even be involved."

Leonard walked around the desk, looked over Daniel's shoulder and studied the first email.

"Okay, a word of advice, if Brian Oarsman is involved, it'd be to defend someone else. He's one of those hero-types. And he's smart enough to go for the Brazilian wax job all over to blend in."

"What about the wings?"

"Ever heard of trench coats?"

"Okay, so we put one file away. What about the luminescent man?"

"If it's Photon, we'll be in trouble."

"Why?"

"When he's in his other form, he's not all there. Crazy's more to the point."

"Okay."

"He's also not luminescent. Rather, pure energy. You could get burned trying to tackle him, let alone you'd fall right through him."

"So how do we stop him?"

"That's what Ab-Spec detainment centers are working on. Haven't got anything for us yet, otherwise he'd be on our most wanted list, wouldn't he?"

"So we go for the easier ones."

"Now you're catching on." Just then, the phone rang. Daniel and Leonard both looked down at the phone and traded ominous looks. "That can't be good."

"Specials Investigations," said Daniel, "Agent Rooke speaking..."

Daniel's notebook hummed as new data uploaded onto the driver. Daniel flipped over the notebook and examined the viewscreen studiously.

"I understand."

Daniel hung up the phone and looked at Leonard, who grew agitated by Daniel's silence.

"Well?"

"Gather the team. We've got a mission."

"Where?"

"DHS Headquarters," replied Daniel. "SUVs will be outside in three minutes."

"We're driving?"

"No," answered Daniel. "I prefer shock and awe. We take the Chariot."

"It's just across town."

"And I prefer not flashing credentials at every roadblock set up to contain the area," answered Daniel. "Wheels up in ten minutes."

"I'll tell the men."

The Department of Homeland Security headquarters was a four million, five hundred thousand square-foot facility in southeast Washington, D.C. located on the 182-acre west campus of what was formerly St. Elizabeths. Sitting on the bluffs overlooking the Potomac and Anacostia Rivers, the postmodernist building stood proudly on the manicured lawn, surrounded by the forested area that hid it from view of the average onlooker travelling down Martin Luther King Jr. Avenue.

To the average citizen, the only evidence that the Department of Homeland Security had any presence there was in the form of the assault rifle armed security post at the driveway entrance. This entryway was in full use 24 hours a day, 365 days a year, as the upper echelons of the DHS joked: "The homeland never sleeps. Nor shall we." A laughable expression considering how many deputy directors were woken with the news that someone had broken into the very heart of the facility and was downloading terabytes of information as they spoke. What's more, they could not find the suspect, and no walls seemed able to hold them as the security routinely sealed blast doors in the corridors, only to find the doors mysteriously open and close again.

Whoever had broken in, they were very good at overriding their commands and even better at concealing their identity. And what was even more bizarre, the guards seemed to be breaking protocol themselves, opening and shutting blast doors with no warning and no explanation. This was the state of affairs when Daniel received his first call from Boatman over an hour ago. Daniel stood on the manicured lawn looking at the activity surrounding the facility. Fighting vehicles veered around and faced St. Elizabeths, while Army infantrymen and agents from over a dozen agencies stood behind their SUVs pointing their side arms at the main doors of their own office building. From a group of onlookers, a uniformed agent stepped away from the group and made his way across the lawn to where the Chariot had parked and after studying them for a moment, made a beeline for Daniel.

"Agent King," said the uniformed agent. "DHS."

"Agent Rooke," greeted Daniel. "SITF."

King blinked at the initials, uncomprehendingly.

"What's your function here?" inquired King, cagily.

"There was an account about a ghostly woman appearing to your guards."

At that King rolled his eyes.

"Yeah," scoffed King. "I sent them off to the clinic to check for drug or alcohol use...Of all the days to make a slip..."

"You usually monitor your guards for drug and alcohol use?"

"Every week."

"Have these guards tested positive?"

"Never. But there's always the first. We have a zero tolerance for drug use and alcohol consumption before or during shifts."

"I think it's safe to say they didn't break protocol now."

"What makes you say that?"

"The ghostly figure described by the men... It could be a Special. That's why I'm here."

"A Special?" blinked King, his eyes widening at the turn of events and the potential ramifications raced through his mind. "You really think so?"

King shook his head as though it were impossible and laughed. Daniel leaned in close.

"Someone is accessing your secrets. Someone is getting it all, and there's no sign of it on your security feeds. But several of your men have accounted on a mysterious woman, and you have video footage of a woman walking into restricted areas all night."

"How would you know that?"

"I was briefed before I got here."

King studied Daniel, and took a step backward, narrowing his eyes on him skeptically.

"What agency are you with again?"

"I'm lead agent of the Specials Investigations Task Force, and I believe you have at least one Special in your building stealing government information at its source. The question is what are you going to do about it?"

King's face went long and then took a pained expression.

"What do you suggest?"

"Let my team go in and hunt them down."

"Not without my men."

"This is not a negotiation. I've been ordered to go into that facility and restore order. I need your men not to shoot us in the back when we advance."

"And just what do you expect us to do, while you play cowboy, stand here with our thumbs up our asses?"

"I expect you to not let anyone out of the facility until I give the all clear."

"We have men and women in there."

"And you may have a Special with the ability to change into different people. Anyone who does come out is subject to detainment. Understood?"

King did not look happy about the prospect of a Special in the facility. He looked back at the agencies lined up outside the building as though he needed a lifeline, and all he met were questioning glances, waiting for orders. Sensing King's inner turmoil, Daniel's tone softened.

"Look, you've been put in an impossible position here. My men know what they're doing. Let us do our job."

King nodded and Daniel signaled the team with a wink. Instantly, Leonard passed out bulletproof vests and assault rifles and the others took them and put them on, all except McCormack and Bradley, who stood there looking at the vests as though they were ridiculous. Daniel walked over.

"Guys, put on the vests."

"Why?" scoffed Bradley; the thought of wearing the vest was a joke due to the fact he was virtually indestructible with his telekinetic shields up.

Daniel glared at him for a moment until Bradley looked back at him swallowing his defiance to hear him out.

"These guys are freaked out at the thought of a Special in their precious building," said Daniel. "Just imagine how they'd feel if they knew they were letting at team of Specials in as well."

McCormack turned to Bradley and nodded, and Bradley took the bulletproof vest and pulled it over his head, while McCormack followed suit.

Daniel pulled on his vest and snapped the pieces in place, and pulled out his side arm, more for effect, than an actual intent on using it. The others grinned at him—knowing he was playing for the sake of the other agencies—and followed suit, choking up on their assault rifles and pistols. With a wave of his hand, Leonard took point with Chad following behind with Daniel at his side and Joshua, Joseph, Stephen, Bradley and McCormack hunched over and filed into the rear, entering the building and disappearing from view.

Inside the massive structure, Daniel was awed by the utilitarian look of the lobby; the polished stone reflected the Department Seal high above, mirroring its proud eagle outstretched beyond the borders of the enclosing circle, announcing the breaking of outmoded policies and management.

"Okay guys. Activate your WinVids and proceed carefully. We have at least one suspect."

"And each interviewee described her differently," replied Leonard. "How many people are we looking for?"

"We'll start with a 'ghostly' woman description and work our way from there," concluded Daniel. "I'll take Giordano and Bradley with me. Leonard, you've got the assault team. Head for that terminal in the basement."

"You got it," said Leonard, and slid a round into the chamber of his assault rifle.

Leonard trotted down the hallway with the others hot on his heels. McCormack walked casually, studying his surroundings, as though listening for something.

Daniel turned away and walked to the elevator. The security center was on the fifth floor, and Daniel led Bradley and Stephen onto the elevator and they watched the doors close, reflecting their expressions back at them—Bradley looked puzzled with Daniel, Stephen just looked annoyed. Daniel caught Stephen's glare in the reflection of the door and turned to the mirror image.

"You've got a problem, Stephen?"

Stephen kicked at the floor as though kicking up dust.

"The strike team is headed toward the action. And I'm headed away from it. Sounds like you're really using my resources well, sir."

"Cool it, Steve." scolded Bradley.

"No, it's fine, Brad," said Daniel with a wave of his hand, hushing him, instantly. "I want to hear what Giordano has to say about my leadership."

"Fine," snapped Stephen. "I'll say it. I've been trained to be a weapon with long range capabilities at great expense to the government, and I'm being shelved in a possible Specials encounter to sit in a security booth. It seems to me that my abilities might achieve greater use if I was a part of the strike team."

The elevator stopped and the doors slid open. Daniel led Stephen and Bradley off the elevator and onto the fifth floor, then turned to face them.

"That is a very thoughtful argument you just made, Stephen," replied Daniel, not intending to sound condescending, "But you're failing to remember, that twenty security personnel remember encountering a woman ranging in description from ghostly, angelic, beautiful, hot and sexy. Each agent and security personnel she encountered gave a completely different description of her."

"Why do you think there's only one?" said Bradley.

"Because the building monitors only show one breach in security," replied Daniel. "She's in the building, she's a Special, and I believe she's in the one place that can control the blast doors."

"The Security Room," exclaimed Bradley.

"The Security Room," replied Daniel with a grin.

Stephen did not look pleased, in fact, it looked like he had been doused with cold water.

"Let's move."

Daniel crept toward the Security Room at the far end of the hall, consulting his notebook for directions, and then stowed it in his cargo pant pocket and slid a round into the chamber of his pistol. At the door to the Security Room, Daniel looked back at Bradley and Stephen to gauge whether or not they were ready. Bradley nodded encouragingly. Stephen had a *just get on with it* expression. Daniel rolled his eyes and opened the door to the room, letting his vision narrow to the sights of his pistol as he panned the room.

At the far end of the room, an unattractive bony woman sat at the helm of a security station typing on the console. Daniel led Bradley and Stephen into the room, and pointed his sidearm at the woman's heart.

"Freeze!" barked Daniel.

"You can't see me," said the mysterious woman at the console, without glancing up. "You need to leave."

Daniel felt the tugging at the corner of his brain that he had quickly begun to associate with psychic violation and grit his teeth with annoyance. Before he could react to the threat the woman posed, Stephen went slack jawed, looked around the room questioningly, and turned to leave. Daniel and Bradley watched Stephen's bizarre behavior with minor surprise and Bradley stopped him with an arm barring his progress.

"There's nobody here," scoffed Stephen, defending his decision to leave the Security Room. Bradley steered Stephen back into the room and directed him directly toward the mysterious woman at the far end of the room.

"Daniel," said Bradley, "if I may?"

"By all means." said Daniel.

Bradley entered the room and narrowed his vision on the woman who instantly cringed and gripped her temples as though her brain were trying to explode free from her skull.

"Hello, Athena." said Bradley.

"Maximus?" she said, with slight shock. "It's been a while."

"Yes," replied Bradley, "Yes it has."

"I always wondered how you see me?"

"Does it really matter?"

"We don't have to begin like this, Bradley."

"Your tricks don't work on us, Samantha."

"What tricks?" said Athena, innocently.

"If you push me, I'll make you hurt. You know I can. You've gotten strong, I can tell, but so have I."

"So what happens now?" said Athena musingly.

"We place you under arrest," said Daniel.

"Oh well," said Athena, completely unconcerned. "I'm done here, anyway. Take me in, if you can."

Daniel stepped forward and threw her a pair of cuffs. He then trained his pistol at her heart again.

"Put on the bracelets, honey."

Athena eyed Daniel mockingly.

"So chivalrous."

"Modern world. Would you rather I pistol whip you and cuff you myself?"

"You're a brave one, aren't you?" chuckled Athena.

"Just the guy to get things done." replied Daniel.

"Tell me, how do you see me?"

Daniel looked at her thin long face. Her over-pronounced nose and her rampant freckles warring with her acne obscured by her alopecia-thin red hair.

"Honey, I've seen better."

Athena's features contorted in rage and glowered at Daniel and he again, felt the invasion in his mind.

"How about now?"

Daniel raised his pistol to her face and grit his teeth.

"You have two seconds to stop that before I shoot" said Daniel. Then said "…2."

"Alright, alright, handsome." chided Athena. "No need to get so macho with me."

Athena put on the handcuffs, snapping them in place, but cuffed herself in the front, instead of the preferred be-behind-the-back. She smiled up at him as though she had won a small victory.

"Now, we can be nice," said Daniel, putting his sidearm back in its holster. "What did you do?"

"You'll have to figure that out on your own, honey." scoffed Athena.

"You realize this could go a lot easier for you if you come clean." said Daniel.

"Come clean?"

"It shows contrition."

"You want me to be contrite?" said Athena. "Fine. I have been opening and closing security doors all night."

"For who?"

"Are we still being contrite?"

"You're not going to tell me, are you?"

"No." smiled Athena.

Daniel tapped his earpiece.

"Strike team," called Daniel over his radio. "you in position?"

"Strike team, here," chimed Leonard over the radio. "Our overrides don't work on the security screens. I guess DHS doesn't trust us with the keys to the kingdom. We're set up at the elevators. Security's so tight over here there's no way down. He's got to take the elevator."

"Hold your position."

"Was that Leonard Stonebreaker's voice I was listening to?"

"They've got your partner cornered," said Daniel with finality. "It's all over. Now why don't you tell me about your partner before we catch him? What is he, bulletproof? Stealth?"

"All that and more, you pathetic norm-hume."

"Who is he?"

"Wouldn't you like to know?"

"Yeah, I would."

Just then, McCormack walked into the Security Room.

"Leonard's men have the elevator shaft under tight guard. Anyone steps out of that elevator's walking straight into a firefight. What have you got?"

Daniel turned to glare at McCormack, annoyed he was not covering the elevators with the strike team. His teleki-netic abilities would be better served down there. He point-ed toward the unattractive woman and began his reply, but it was clear as he began that McCormack already had all the facts he needed.

"Samantha Kalinowski-"

"Callsign: Athena," McCormack finished their update. "Well, that explains a lot."

"What does it explain?" said Daniel, uncomprehendingly.

"Yeah, Paladin," crooned Athena, "do tell."

"The tingling in the back of my head as I made my way to the Security Room," chuckled McCormack, and he shook his head as though he found Athena a pathetic individual. "Sam here has the ability to invade people's minds and make them do what she wants. She's also insecure about her appearance, so she makes each individual see her as their ideal woman. What you get is a lot of sex hungry men chasing her, while others fall to her feet in worship. Either way, she likes the attention. Poor girl. You're still not comfortable in your own skin?"

"That depends on how you see me, lover."

"So," said Daniel, "I get the need to get into the Security Office to control the cameras and the doors to gain access to the central mainframe, but how did you plan on getting the data since your entry caused the security breach and sent the place on lockdown? You must know that everyone leaving would be subject to detainment and search."

"Wouldn't you like to know?"

With that, Daniel narrowed his eyes and leaned in toward her.

"I could just have Bradley dig it out of you."

"Maximus isn't strong enough anymore," she scoffed. "He's been exercising his brain muscles to make him bullet-proof and super strong, not to invade people's minds. I've been invading minds for years."

"Yeah, but you never used it this way before," replied McCormack. "You just used it for the sake of vanity."

Athena shrugged.

"People grow. People change."

"True," replied Daniel. "You're not going to tell us, are you?"

"Nope," she said with a cunning smile like she could not get enough of the torture she was delivering to Daniel with mere words.

"Fine," concluded Daniel. "Take her away. Make her comfortable aboard the Chariot. She's not slipping through our fingers."

Bradley took Athena by the arm and led her from the security helm down across the room toward the elevators. McCormack followed as Stephen followed along in Athena's wake like a puppy dog. Daniel glanced at the security monitor on the strike team set up around the elevator. All looked quiet. Then took up the rear. At the elevator, Daniel joined them in the cable car and the doors closed mirroring their faces back at them. Athena stood there smiling triumphantly. It annoyed Daniel how confident she was. As though their arrival was almost fortuitous. Stephen hopped from one foot to the next, stealing pained sideways glances at Athena, as though he were going to explode—a cold feeling began to claw at him, at the thought that she could affect the less shielded members of his team so strongly.

"What are we going to do with her?" asked Stephen. His tone had a note of longing—a fear for Athena that could only be attributed to Kalinowski's ability to bend the minds of men to her will—still, the question obviously needed clarification. They had honestly never gotten this far into an arrest before. The Task Force actually processing and detaining a suspect had never come up before.

"I've got new protocols in place for detainment of criminals through the Andrews Specials Detention Facility being set up at the airbase."

"There's a detention facility at Andrews Air Base?"

"Just a temporary one. The other one being built will be in Alaska. Until then, we've got the Andrews Facility."

"Well," mocked Bradley, "at least it'll be a short flight, Sammy."

Athena scowled at Bradley.

"Don't call me that."

"Whatever," scoffed Bradley.

The elevator doors slid open and Daniel stepped off the elevator leading them into the main hall of the lobby under the outstretched eagle seal and clicked on his radio.

"Strike team, report." Daniel stood listening for a moment to static in his earpiece and then clicked the radio again. "Leonard report."

Just then, down the hall came the sounds of an explosion followed by the screams of the strike team, then nothing. All that could be seen down the hallway was a wisp of smoke billowing out and quickly thinning in the air.

"Leonard, come in?"

"Leonard here," chirped the radio. "We're fine, but the explosion came out of nowhere. If there was someone in the elevator, chances are they got past us."

"Come meet up with us in the main hall. Double-time."

"Roger that."

Daniel turned to McCormack.

"Something's happening."

"You bet your sweet ass, something's happening," grinned Athena.

The sound of her mocking tone infuriated Daniel and he wheeled around on her, pulling his sidearm out and leveling it at her skull.

"What do you know?"

Athena cringed away from Daniel but he held her fast so she couldn't more than squirm under the barrel of the sidearm.

"I don't know what you're talking about!" she whined in a fright.

Just then, McCormack stiffened as though he saw something.

"Olsen?"

Out of nowhere a grenade flew into their midst and detonated, sending a blinding flash through the room, the explosion propelling them against the walls, their ears ringing.

Daniel looked up in time to see Samantha rippling into a mirage state and vanishing before his eyes.

"What the?"

Instinctively, Daniel fired in the direction of the ripple effect, leading the target as he fired, predicting where she would be standing if she were running toward the door. The door opened and swung closed. McCormack put his hand over the back of Daniel's hands gripping the pistol.

"What are you shooting for? She's gone."

"Where did she go?"

"She stepped inside Mirage's sphere of influence."

"Mirage?"

"Olsen Cadiff" said McCormack. "Callsign: Mirage. He has the ability to disappear without leaving a trail to follow. Not footprints, not shadows, nothing. He was our Espionage, Black Ops Reconnaissance man."

"He was very good," said Leonard, appearing through the smoke.

"Apparently," snapped Daniel, infuriated they had lost yet again. "So he could just take another person with him for the ride, then?"

"So to speak," said McCormack. "Yes."

"Great," spat Daniel. "So we lost them."

"Yes," said McCormack, simply. His tone reassuring there was nothing more that could be done. Athena and her cohort had escaped with the terabytes of information they had sought. Whatever that was. Daniel grit his teeth, his skin burning in embarrassment and rage.

"Just perfect."

Leonard stood respectfully in the silence of Daniel's mood swing, giving him a few moments to vent. Then leaned forward.

"What now, boss?"

Daniel sighed.

"Get back to the Chariot. I've got to explain the egg on my face to Agent King."

Daniel turned from Leonard trying to hide his disgust, but the team felt it. It was obvious a part of him blamed his team for the escape of the two Specials. A telepath and a stealth operative. This should have been easy. Go in, corner them and make the arrest. Instead, Daniel found himself trotting down the lawn toward the waiting DHS teams, all with weapons trained on him. He knelt to the ground and placed his hands behind his head, and waited for the Anti-Terrorist Team to converge on him and secure him. They led him under guard to Agent King who looked at him with wild eyes.

"What's going on in there? We heard explosions and shots fired."

"My team was neutralized with grenades. They got away."

Daniel explained to a bewildered King how they had cornered one Special in the Security Room and identified her for the record, then explained how the second Special had scattered their forces and escaped with Kalinowski.

"You let them escape?"

"We didn't let them do anything. We were routed."

"You mean to tell me while we've been sitting on our collective asses letting your men do whatever you pleased inside, that two lone suspects managed to escape? How come we didn't see them?"

"Cadiff has the ability to be undetectable to camera, heat signature, scent, hearing or vision. He's a ghost. If he was in there, he could walk out the front doors and you wouldn't know it."

"We can still set up a road block. What are their descriptions?"

"Cadiff is a classified black op Special. I don't have access to his picture at this time." He was more helpful in describing Athena, explaining her ability to enter a person's mind and convince them of anything. "A regular road block wouldn't work."

"So we just let them go?"

"There's no way to track them," sighed Daniel, exasperated. "Unless they separate, you won't find them. And if you found only one, either way, they would elude you."

"You!" cried King, jabbing his finger at Daniel. "I'm holding you personally responsible for this breach! I want your superior's name."

There's something to be said about having a trump card on the tip of your tongue, because as soon as Daniel uttered the name Lawrence Boatman, a chill spread over the surrounding men and King himself shivered.

"You haven't heard the end of this."

"I'm sure." replied Daniel. "Now if you'll excuse me, I need to see to my men."

"This isn't over, Rooke. Not by a long shot!"

"Gentlemen," said Daniel, with a grim nod, and turned from them; walking away, feeling the collective eyes of the DHS teams boring into his back like laser targets flickering across his torso and head. Daniel shivered as he made his way back to the Chariot. Once onboard, he slammed the door shut and collapsed against the wall, eyeing his men. He opened his mouth to speak but Leonard beat him to it.

"There was nothing you could have done." reassured Leonard. "We were unprepared for what we were going up against. Simple as that."

"Simple as that..." concluded Daniel, his voice going hoarse. "We were beaten by two suspects. Soundly. I'm not at all happy."

"This is the real world, Daniel." said McCormack. "We learn as we go. What we've just been through? We'll need an edge."

"What kind of edge?" said Daniel.

"We should take a serious look at the JUNCOs," concluded McCormack. "I think that will even things up a bit."

"We can discuss this in greater detail back at the Post," concluded Daniel, who then turned and pressed the intercom icon on the touch screen next to him. "Pilot. Take us to Andrews Air Base."

"Yes, sir."

The Chariot lurched into the air, climbing faster than any in the cabin would have preferred, leaving their stomachs behind as it climbed to a higher altitude. Daniel muttered something about finding a replacement pilot as soon as possible, and collapsed in his seat. The estimated time for arrival to Andrews Air Base was three minutes at normal flying speeds. Daniel shut his eyes and counted toward ninety on their way back to Andrews Air Base.

"Sir!" chimed the pilot, unexpectedly.

There was something urgent in his tone, and Daniel hoped against hope that the night's adventure was still alive, and not over. He depressed the intercom icon on the touch screen.

"What is it?"

"I'm getting a call on all police bands calling all nearby agencies in for assistance."

Daniel perked up, hopeful that maybe his two suspects had appeared and were being cornered by Metro Police.

"Where is it located?"

"Fort Lincoln Cemetery," said the pilot. "Maryland."

A pit grew in Daniel's stomach and rose to his throat as the thought he would not be getting a second chance at redemption. He nearly gave the order to turn home and head for Andrews, when the live feed of the chaos on the ground rattled in his ears from the radio of the desperate calls on all law enforcement frequencies. At that moment, the cop in him switched on.

"Let me bring it up on the viewscreen."

The firefight was heading in a southeasterly direction through the woods toward New York Avenue Northeast. Daniel ran his fingers across the viewscreen pulling up satellite surveillance footage of the park and scrolled down to the latest image of the area—a barren section of road next to a tree line, which met the Paint Branch Stream to the east and New York Ave NE to the south. The police and bureau bands were chilling. Reports of fallen officers and agents broadcast along both bands independent of each other and overlapping each other through the broadband feed. An image of dead and dying officers and agents painted a picture confirmed by helicopter and satellite imagery on the scene and something snapped inside Daniel. *Not tonight,* he thought. *There's been enough of this tonight.* His fingers brought up the latitude and longitude of the woods and with a flick of his finger, transmitting the coordinates to the pilot.

"Pilot, reroute to the following coordinates."

"Yes, sir!"

Daniel then activated the communications window and began speaking into the microphone next to the viewscreen.

"This is Agent in Charge Daniel Rooke from SITF. Bureau agents—cover the 50. Local police advance with K-9 units into the woods to the river and flush the suspects south. Hold at the tree line and wait for support."

The chaotic voices from different agencies took a collective breath and then began chattering along their frequencies following the new plan set out by Daniel. McCormack looked over at Daniel with a wary expression.

"Are you sure you know what you're doing?"

"I'm saving a bad night."

"Our mandate…"

"People are dying down there." retorted Daniel.

"Are you ordering us into a firefight against armed normal human combatants?"

"Yes, I am."

McCormack studied Daniel carefully for another moment, and then nodded.

"Yes, sir."

McCormack traded a nod with Leonard, and Leonard quickly began re-strapping his armor over his cargo pants and t-shirt.

"Alright ladies," called Leonard down the cabin, "you heard the man. Gear up and get ready for contact."

The cabin moved with excitement as the Specials slapped their gear back into place and took up their weapons, checking the sights and loading rounds into the chamber again. Within the span of a minute, the Chariot slowed abruptly and became static.

"We're at the coordinates, sir." said the pilot over the communications link with the cockpit.

"Bring us in." commanded Daniel.

The Chariot touched down at Fort Lincoln Cemetery to a bustle of controlled activity. The scene was less chaotic than before on the video feeds and Daniel was grateful for that. He jumped off the foot railing, crunching into the snow and mud followed by the entire team. Before him, a burly Sheriff's Deputy studied Daniel, approaching him and his team, trying not to allow himself to be rattled by the strange aircraft that hovered and touched down light as a feather in the snow.

"Were you who spoke to us over the radio?"

"Agent Rooke," said Daniel, offering his hand. "You are?"

"Deputy O'Neil," answered the Deputy. "What do you need?"

"I need you to close the door behind us when we enter the woods. At the first sign of contact, get on the radio and give us the coordinates to meet you there. We're going to corral and close in."

"Right!" said O'Neil, and he clicked on his radio about to give orders. Daniel put his hand on his shoulder.

"Just watch our backs, okay?" Daniel turned to Bradley and McCormack, who were apprehensive about what was about to be said, as though they already knew Daniel's strategy. "Bradley, you and Tobias I need in the air."

"You sure about this?" said McCormack critically.

"I want some good press to come out of this," said Daniel. "Just a bit to keep Boatman off my back as hard as he'll be looking to be."

"And this is your plan?" chided McCormack.

"Hey, it just feels right."

"Alright," said McCormack. "I hope you know what you're doing."

And he and Bradley turned and marched off toward the tree line leaving Daniel where he stood.

"Me too." sighed Daniel.

Daniel turned to Leonard and with a nod, led the team into the tree line and walked to the tundra brush of the water's edge. Daniel looked up and saw Bradley and McCormack fly overhead. He couldn't shake the feeling that this would have spooked the Deputies and sent them into a tizzy, but he couldn't concentrate on that right now. Leonard brought him out of his thoughts.

"Now what?"

Daniel looked around to see they had entered a clearing.

"Fan out. Keep each other in sight."

"Right."

They fanned out across the forest line and walked due south toward the distant lights on the highway 50. As they neared the edge of the clearing, the glint of metal alerted them there was something in the shadows at the base of a withered tree. Daniel crouched down and trained his gun on the glint of metal and shouted at the darkness.

"Freeze! Don't move!"

Daniel signaled Leonard to flank the position with Chad, and Leonard covered him as Chad came up through the tree line behind the shadows. Finally Chad poked his head out and waved to them.

"Just two bodies." he said. "Apparently shot and bled out."

Daniel sighed.

"No time to check vitals. Mark the area for the medics."

Chad and Stephen broke and dropped glow sticks into the snow while Leonard and Daniel surveyed the looming shadows of the forest coolly. Josh looked nervous as he stared at the two bodies as though doused with cold water and waking up in a world where he can be killed at any moment. Joseph knelt and said a silent prayer before picking up and pressing on into the woods. Daniel watched him enter the canopy without orders and gestured for him to return to standing formation. Joseph paid no attention, and marched deeper into the shadows.

"Joseph," called Daniel.

Joseph didn't answer. Within a moment, the night had swallowed him up. Daniel gave Leonard a look of annoyance and Leonard returned it in silent agreement that they would be having a chat with Joseph after this jaunt was over and pressed on. With a flick of his arm, the Task Force fanned out again, standing ten feet away from each other as they ducked into the woods.

In the distance, the highway 50 glittered with the lights of Federal SUVs corralling the area. Joseph was nowhere to be found. Ahead, out by an outcrop of trees and rocks they saw movement, like shadows, dark as the night with the speed of deer making their way just out of reach of the lights of the SUVs across the river, and darting in and out of the naked pines, skillfully avoiding the searching helicopter's spotlight. Daniel rushed forward, his feet crunching in the muddy snow, as he maneuvered between the rocks for a better view of his target.

"Freeze!" bellowed Daniel and the shadow was still. "Get down!" he commanded. The shadow broke into a run and fired on his location. Daniel, Leonard and Chad fired back instantly.

The shadows ahead were dotted with light like firecrackers popping off as several shooters began firing on the shadow's positions, and vice versa. Chad crouched down next to a tree and took aim at the muzzle flashes of the gunmen and fired calm and easily. Leonard charged their positions, sweeping along the right and swinging east toward the stream. Suddenly Daniel sensed movement and looked up to see Joseph take position behind a tree, peering out to see into the distance where all the commotion was, his gun pointed down at the snow. Stephen appeared out of nowhere next to Daniel and charged toward the gunmen's position and flanked right, travelling westerly, to meet Leonard in the middle. Daniel came up behind Stephen and yanked him back.

"Are you nuts?" bellowed Daniel in Stephen's ear. "You're not bulletproof, you know."

With a quick jerk of the shoulder, Stephen pulled free of Daniel's hold and shot him a disgusted glare.

"Like you care!" snapped Stephen.

Just then a shadow broke free of a tree and raised his arm outstretched at Daniel and Stephen. As the figure stepped out into the light of the moonlit night, the figure froze and eyed Daniel.

"You!" snarled a familiar voice.

Daniel froze too recognizing the dark face lit up by moonlight reflecting harshly off the muddy snow as Chris "Jonas" Young.

Chris fired at Daniel and Stephen. Instinctively, Daniel pushed Stephen down and out of the way, then experienced a familiar sense of violation and inertia as the bullet penetrated his armor and sent him backwards, where he crashed down, hitting his head against a rock.

Daniel fought the blurry haze, shaking his head to clear his vision. Out of the corner of his eye, he saw Joseph lunge forward and disappear with a loud *crack*.

Next thing Daniel knew, he was in a long black tunnel, with two pinholes of light marking the edge of his vision. He fought against the surrounding blackness and he felt his heart rate accelerate with urgency as he told himself he would not black out. When the pinholes of light zoomed back up, dispelling the darkness out of the corners of his vision he saw the starlit sky overhead and the probing light of the helicopter sweeping the tips of the trees searching for, in all likelihood, another escaped suspect. Daniel was so disgusted he sat up hard and he instantly felt nauseous. Hands pushed him back, but he continued to fight them in an effort to rise. They were speaking to him, but it sounded far away. Muffled. His vision and hearing came back to him only to find EMTs placing a brace on his neck and attempting to strap him to a board. Daniel sat up and shooed the medics away.

"I'm fine," growled Daniel. "You can stop now."

The medics protested. "You've been shot. Are you aware of that?"

"Yeah, I'm aware. I'm even aware I'm using a rock as a pillow. Tell me something I don't know."

"Well, your cognitive reasoning seems to be returning. How about this: Let us check your head for signs of trauma and let my partner work on that nasty bullet wound. How about that?"

He unzipped a carrying case he had strapped over his shoulder and laid it on the ground, opening it to reveal a touch-screen which illuminated with the logo for Emergency Medic/Triage Systems, followed by the letters MTS-4 [Medical Triage System Series 4: a battlefront kit for the soldier in the field providing all the technology of an Emergency Room and Intensive Care Unit]. The paramedic fastened devices to Daniel's chest and head, then produced a thin device like a pen.

"What's that?"

"That's a wand." said the EMT, almost boastfully. "It analyzes patients and gives us the results right in the field. All the information gets transmitted directly to your medical file so when you get to the hospital, they just check your name and boom...they got all your information right there. It saves them the time of doing it because, frankly, a lot of people who go to the hospital die while waiting to get diagnosed. Thanks to this, we skip all the headache with admitting and get right to the problem."

"What does that say?" asked Daniel, mildly curious.

The paramedic glanced down at his MTS-4 and flicked his finger along the touch screen. It instantly illuminated and an outline of a human form came into view with red blips appearing on the screen over the form's head, neck and abdomen.

"It say's you're pretty lucky. The bullet passed between the intestines, not compromising them. So, no colostomy bag for you. The neck and head appear to be up there with high school football injuries. You've got a concussion.

You're also in shock, so I need to take you to the hospital for a doctor's approval that you're free to leave."

"So I'm going into a hospital?"

"Afraid so."

"Negative. I've got a medical team that can treat me at Andrews Air Base."

"Hang on, lay back. We're still dealing with that GSW."

One of the medics pulled out a hypodermic syringe filled with a nearly phosphorescent green solution. Daniel blinked at the needle and raised his hand to the medic in protest.

"What's that?"

"Vitamin X-32," said the medic. "A little saline solution, some multivitamin, a little pain killer, nanite workers to help stitch the wound and fight off staph infection, it's got everything a growing boy needs."

Daniel lowered his arm and allowed the medic to tie a rubber strip around his bicep to find a vein to inject the concoction into. He had had VX-32 a few times before, during the war.

"I thought that was still just for military use."

"Well, it's still for use by the government to treat police in the field. You'll be fine."

The second EMT put a cold compress on the back of Daniel's neck, and slapped his hand over it. The cool sensation shook Daniel, and he drifted on the feeling of the coolness against his flesh and almost passed out. He shook himself awake.

"Is Giordano okay?"

"Right here, boss."

Stephen looked down at Daniel oddly, as though he were suffering some great inner turmoil—somewhere between mistrust and appreciating for the fact Daniel saved his life.

"What happened to the suspects?" demanded Daniel.

A powerfully built man stepped into Daniel's frame of vision. Leonard looked down on Daniel with worry lines on his brow, but a soothing smile the way men look when they are concerned, but do not want to make others worry.

"We got them," answered Leonard. "Three were dead from loss of blood, but we collected seven others. Including, and you're not going to believe this, but-"

"Chris."

"I thought you might remember him."

"So we just took down the head of Princeton Park Kings?"

"That we did."

"Who got him?"

"That would be Joseph." said Leonard and nodded to Joseph Little Bird who sat a little ways away looking grim and worn as he always did after wormhole travel.

"He jumped right behind him and took him for one of his rides, then disarmed him. Chris isn't doing well." Leonard glanced over to his right and there was Chris being strapped to a gurney and carted off over the rough snowy landscape toward a waiting helicopter. "The helicopter was originally meant for you. You feel up to taking a ride?"

"I can walk."

"I thought you might feel that way." grinned Leonard.

"Where is McCormack and Bradley?"

"They're explaining to the local police how they never saw two men jump into the air and fly. Unless you feel like letting the cat out of the bag and revealing to the world our little team."

"No, memory modification is fine with me."

The two medics gave sideways glances to each other as though they weren't sure they were hearing them right. Daniel looked at them and waved it off. The medics paused for another second and then continued with their work treating Daniel who continually tried to rise, but the EMT kept pushing him back down.

"Hang on, there." ordered the EMT. "Give the nanites time to knit your wound together."

"I feel fine."

"Not yet, you're not."

"Hurry up. I'm cold, here."

The EMT unfolded a warm blanket and wrapped it around Daniel.

"How's that?"

"Fine," admitted Daniel, reluctantly. "Can I sit up?"

After a moment's deliberation, the EMT assisted Daniel in leaning his back against the rock he had cracked his skull on, propping him into a seated position. Daniel pulled the blanket tighter across his midsection and shivered as he realized he was wet all over from the snow. Then he realized he was actually feeling feverish. His skin was hot.

"Hey, I'm feeling a little hot, here. Is that normal?"

The EMT pulled out his wand, and pulled a cable out with a plastic needle at the end of it. He inserted the needle into the artery on Daniel's right arm and waited for the screen to blink. The data rushed across the touch screen of the MTS-4 until windows opened and gave up-to-date reports on Daniel's body condition.

"It sounds like hypothermia, but your systems show you're fine. I'd say this is a side effect of being shot and the nanites working. Just the same, I'd like to take you along to the hospital for a checkup."

"We've got doctors on standby at Andrews Airbase." said Leonard, dismissively.

"How do you plan on getting there?" snapped the EMT.

Daniel touched his earpiece, which illuminated at the touch.

"Chariot, come in."

"Chariot," chirped the radio, "standing by."

"Lock onto my GPS and come in for a pick up."

"Roger that. ETA is two minutes. Out."

Daniel pursed his lips together. *Two minutes? He's right on the other side of the treeline!* Daniel grit his teeth together. *If that guy's giving the deputies tours of the Chariot, I'll flay him alive.*

The EMT studied Daniel for a moment and then returned to dressing his head wound he received from striking the rock he now rested against. A minute later, lights illuminated the forest and at the opening in the tree line, the Chariot appeared, angling in and hovering over an open clearing, landing with a bounce, the cabin door sliding open to reveal a cabin illuminated with red light. The EMT and paramedic stared slack jawed at the spectacle of the Chariot and looked back down at Daniel.

"Who are you guys?" exclaimed the paramedic.

"That's classified," replied Daniel, with a grin. "Thanks for the patch up."

Daniel clambered to his feet and with a wave of his hand, Leonard, Stephen, Josh and Chad marched off toward the Chariot. Joseph rose slowly and walked over to Daniel.

"You okay?" said Joseph, coming out of his daze. A look of shame crept over his face as he examined Daniel's mending gunshot wound.

"Yeah," replied Daniel, his eyes boring into Joseph's, not forgetting his breach of protocol. "I'll be good as new once the doctors at Andrews give me a onceover." Then added as an afterthought, "Thanks for the save."

"Hey," smiled Joseph, as though the whole mess of his transgression was forgotten, "don't mention it. You did me a solid with this job. I'd say we're square."

Joseph and Daniel stepped into the cabin to see Bradley and McCormack sitting in their seats.

"Thought we'd save you the trouble of having to pick us up," said McCormack with a grin.

"How sweet of you," scoffed Daniel with a weak grin.

"You okay?" asked McCormack, eyeing Daniel critically.

"I'd wish people would stop asking me that," muttered Daniel.

Daniel closed the cabin door on the snowy embankment and sat down in his seat with a sigh. Without even looking, Daniel reached up behind him and tapped the intercom icon to communicate with the cockpit.

"Pilot," called Daniel, "we're all in."

"Roger that," replied the pilot. "Andrews Airbase ETA three minutes."

Daniel leaned his head against the headrest of his chair and closed his eyes, listening to the sound of his pulse pound and throb between his ears as a euphoric feeling took over. He felt no pain. In fact, he couldn't feel his molars grinding together. He was in an interesting place and he mused over the sensations of his body as he sat perfectly still, interrupted by the jolts of speed from the transport and the buffeting of the wind sending tremors through the cabin. Like being rocked gingerly into unconsciousness, Daniel was asleep.

CHAPTER 17

TERROR ALERT

The next morning, Daniel woke to find his head throbbing and his stomach turning violently. It was such a contrast from his high the night before, he wondered if he was suffering from a hangover. The ache in his skull and nausea could easily have been side effects of sustaining a concussion. He had had concussions before—playing high school football, as well as suffering trauma from explosions during the war—but this felt different. Too acute. Too harsh. Maybe it was shock settling in. Whatever it was, it made Daniel reassess himself as he lay there in bed, preferring the comfort of his pillow to the violent change he felt when he rose.

He lay there for a few minutes breathing shallow and feeling his bandaged skull before letting his fingers work their way down to his abdomen. The wound on his stomach was raw but knitted. He ran his finger down the thick white line surrounded by raised raw skin marking where the bullet had penetrated his abdomen and sighed as he looked down at the sore. It seemed his body was at war with sepsis. Some pus had infected the wound, but the red rash seemed to surround it. The rash tingled and throbbed and seemed to move like tide against the wound. *What's happening to me?* he thought.

"It's the nanites," came the familiar voice of McCormack from the door.

"What?"

"The rash. You were wondering what it was."

"You've been reading my mind?" murmured Daniel, annoyed. "I didn't think that was possible since our little 'talk.'"

"You've been projecting your thoughts."

"I'll have to watch that."

"That would be wise."

In truth, Daniel already knew what the rash meant. He had felt the itching underneath his SPARTAN EVA battle armor during the war—a maddening need to scratch that made him jog in place on many occasions, letting the armor rub against the mending wound—and was glad that this time he could scratch the affected area without hindrance. McCormack leaned against the doorframe as if there were more to their conversation than his rash of nanites.

"So," opened Daniel, "is that the only reason why you've come?"

"No, not really."

"Is Boatman here?"

"In the office."

Daniel pursed his lips and a silent groan tried to climb up his throat to make itself audible.

"Has he come to hand me my walking papers?"

"Surprisingly no," said McCormack with a grin.

Daniel stared at him for a long moment, and then his curiosity burst from him.

"So what's he doing here?"

"I'll let him tell you."

"You want to give me a heads up?" scoffed Daniel, his annoyance clearly visible on his cheeks. "I want to know what I'm walking into."

"It's part good, part bad," said McCormack, grinning. "You'll have to sit through the bad to get to the good."

"Not too cryptic."

"I don't like speaking for other people."

"So I see."

"Come on. He's waiting. And Lawrence hates to wait."

"Got it."

With that, McCormack turned and left Daniel sitting up in his bed. Daniel swung his legs out of bed and tested his footing on the prickly carpet. The wound pulled as he stood up, pulling tight like fresh stitching threatening to come undone. He pulled on his shirt gingerly and buttoned it up over the wound, then dragged his pants on, pulling a little when he felt the pinch in his abdomen. He slipped his shoes on and exited the bedroom quickly, hoping to leave the pain and discomfort behind him, but it followed anyway.

When he entered his office, it was to find Boatman standing there with his phone in hand talking with his back to the door.

"I understand DHS's contribution to the Task Force. Yes...And if you had allowed us overriding clearance to the elevators, perhaps my team could have set up a tighter net, cordoning off all possibility of escape. Don't put this on me. You don't want to see me when I'm put to task...

Alright, then…Have your men dealt with. I want this to be the end of it. There are many uses for the Task Force as they get their feet wet…My team will be ready."

With that, Boatman closed his phone and turned to face Daniel.

"Ah," exclaimed Boatman, "speak of the devil."

"I take it that was about last night?"

"Apparently you made some enemies last night with DHS's Security and Special Tactics Departments. No big loss. The chances of you running in their circles will be minimal. And I surveyed the security footage. Grenades seem to be your team's weakness."

"So it would seem," scoffed Daniel. "I've been meaning to talk to you about that-"

"Yes, JUNCOs," said Boatman as though he were reading Daniel's thoughts. "Easy enough to supply. I'll see you're fitted with them, soon enough."

"So what's the problem?"

"Well, I believe you know the problem," answered Boatman. "You broke protocol last night. The failure to apprehend both suspects was a bit of dirt in the eye, but the breach last night in arresting a normal human gang…that is something I believe we must discuss."

"We did the right thing," defended Daniel.

"No," answered Boatman. "You did the 'cop thing.' Something that no longer applies to you."

"They were taking fire," defended Daniel. "There were casualties."

"Yes," answered Boatman, as though coming to the point. "You were one of them." Daniel was silent. It was as if Boatman punched him in the gut, leaving him winded. "I've given you a long leash. Apparently too long. You fail to abide by simple protocols like, say, not directly entering into the fray. That's a job for the Task Force. Not its leader."

"What did you expect me to do? I wasn't going to sit there while my team went in there blind."

"So you all went in blind," concluded Boatman.

"We had cover."

"Yes," cut off Boatman. Daniel sat there fighting the urge to scratch the rash on his stomach. If they were nanites on his exposed skin, he would only be disrupting them from doing their job sealing the wound and fighting infection. Boatman continued as though Daniel's discomfort was a minor issue. "K-9 units in the north woods, deputies to the west and Feds to the south with a river running south and cutting between the Feds and the woods. I surveyed the footage. You marched straight into them. They opened fire and everything nearly went to hell if it wasn't for Joseph Little Bird. Are you still insistent that Giordano is capable of being employed by this Task Force as a long distance energy projector? Because I don't see that in your actions or his."

"What's the problem?"

"Why did you push him out of the way of the bullet?"

"Instinct."

"Instinct…Your instinct was to protect your teammate…I can see that. But Giordano is a weapon that needs to be used. His expense in training states that he should be employed, would you not agree?"

"It won't happen again."

"You won't save him again?"

Daniel blinked at Boatman, exasperated.

"What do you want me to say?"

"I want to hear what you have to say."

"Stephen is a cocky hothead whose talent can be beneficial to the team when he's ready."

"So he's not ready?" implied Boatman.

"He's only just begun to taste combat with his new reaching ability," concluded Daniel. "He's unsure of himself, and that's a liability to the team."

"So you want to bench him."

"No." contradicted Daniel, "I want him employed. But I want him wearing armor and ready for long distance combat. That's why he was trained. I don't want him getting killed without having the chance to fire back. And I expected Stephen to recover and return fire. Joseph just robbed him his chance to battle test himself."

"So Joseph is the problem?" concluded Boatman.

Daniel sat still for a long moment and then nodded.

"Joseph needs a talk about working with a team and not going it alone. And listening to superiors in the field."

"I've already spoken with Little Bird. Joseph is a tracker. He was probing the field to find the suspects and report back."

"But he didn't report back. He-"

"Saved your life. And Giordano's."

"Don't turn this around. He could have just as easily covered us by entering the woods with the rest of us. He doesn't work well with the team yet. That will have to be addressed."

"And it will," concluded Boatman, then added, "By you."

"I didn't have any intention on passing this off," replied Daniel.

"Good," chimed Boatman, as though the matter were resolved. "Now, your little Maryland escapade will be written up as a bit of good ink for our Department. Right now, we are still in the *men in black* phase, so the press won't get much detail. Just enough to know that something's stirring in the government, but no specifics."

"I understand."

"Get your house in order. I want press I can capitalize off of."

"Yes, sir."

"Let's adjourn, then. I can see you have plenty of work to accomplish between Giordano and Little Bird."

"Right away."

With that, Boatman stalked out of the room and was gone. Daniel had no suspicion that he would actually stay long enough to interact with the team—He was a busy man, and taking the time to sit down and talk with the men was a matter for Daniel to attend to. In a way, Daniel was grateful he was leaving the task to him. *Too many chiefs* meant confusion in the ranks, let alone *not enough Indians*.

As it was, Boatman made his silent assurance that Daniel's path would go unhindered, despite his transgressions the night before. As far as Boatman was concerned, the bullet wound was enough to keep him on course. How wrong he was.

Daniel walked down the hall and found the team congregating in the kitchen over breakfast. Joseph, who seemed to sense something was wrong, looked apprehensively at Daniel as he entered the kitchen.

"Joseph, a word."

"Right," murmured Joseph with a nervous look in his eye.

The others at the table did little to reassure him, giving him reprimanding glares as he rose to follow Daniel out of the kitchen.

"Let's take a walk," said Daniel. He led Joseph down the stairs where he stepped at a light brisk pace, while Joseph plodded nervously behind him. Finally, he came to a dead stop at the final step in the lobby, stopping Daniel with a nervous grip on his shoulder, before he could round on him to speak.

"Look," stammered Joseph, "if this is about last night, I just wanted to say I overreacted by taking that guy on the trip."

"This has nothing to do with Chris Young," assured Daniel.

Joseph looked perplexed.

"Oh."

"What it has everything to do with is your actions in the woods."

Joseph blinked.

"My actions in the woods?"

"Look," said Daniel, "I need people who can be a part of a team, and act accordingly. No *gung-ho, man-apart* bullshit."

Joseph swallowed.

"…Okay."

"You *going off on your own* is not how we do things. It's how someone can get hurt, or worse."

"But I was just scouting a bit-"

"You disappeared into the woods and didn't wait for the team."

"Yeah, but-"

"You were so focused on what was in front of us you didn't take into consideration we could have been walking into a trap and flanked."

"But it wasn't a trap-"

"You didn't know that. You left the team high and dry without backup."

"I didn't leave you without backup," retorted Joseph, but Daniel cut him off.

"How can you back us up when you're in front of us?"

Stymied, Joseph stood there like he got punched in the gut. Daniel tried not to feel too much pity for him— he needed to hear it—but still, he was starting to feel as though he were taking on Boatman's personality in this argument, with Joseph squirming with no real ground to stand on.

"Hey," he stammered. "I saved your life!"

"You didn't save me," answered Daniel coldly. "You nearly got Stephen Giordano killed. The bullet was meant for him."

"So you're blaming me for the actions of the suspect?" clarified Joseph, infuriated.

"I'm telling you if you want to stay on the team you'll treat the remainder of your stay like an exemplary soldier. Going through the door with the team, covering their backs and not breaking off from the group without a plan that the group has agreed upon."

Joseph mulled it over blank faced.

"I didn't know…"

"And that's why I'm telling you, now." replied Daniel. "If this was a matter of you disregarding the team's safety to play hero or to gain the glory you would have not made it past breakfast, this morning. But I know your head was in the right place, so I'm telling you how it is. No more going it alone. You're a tracker? Cool. We'll have use for you. But you don't disappear until I order you to. Is that understood?"

"Yes, sir."

"Good." concluded Daniel, relieved. The last vestiges of Boatman's infuriating personality draining out of him, he saw Joseph utterly defeated and knew he had just shaken his confidence in himself. Daniel sighed. "You need some time to think about things?"

"No."

"Good," concluded Daniel. "Get back upstairs and re-join the team."

"Thank you, sir."

Daniel nodded and Joseph pensively stepped away from him as though in fear Daniel might summon him back to fire him at any moment.

The truth was, Joseph really liked his job and had a lot to contribute. He was strong and tough, he was smart, he could teleport and he was a tracker. These were useful assets for the team. All he needed to do was learn to fit into the team, and everything else would work itself out, Daniel had no doubts.

Where Daniel *did* have doubts was in Stephen Giordano's ability to be a part of the team. His instinct to push him out of the way of the bullet had told him he was not ready. Stephen stood so still when Chris jumped out of the shadow—like a rod had been shoved straight up his spine—it was clear he would not react in time to prevent the gunfire. Still, it was not entirely Stephen's fault. Daniel had pushed Stephen to be the perfect long-range weapon, and perhaps pushed too hard to get him up to snuff, putting him in the field before he was ready. Stephen was a thirty-something kid. As mature as he looked, there was something off in his manner, like an adolescent struggling against a parent. For better or worse, Daniel realized he had inherited the role of parent to a rebellious kid.

Slowly, Daniel made his way back up the stairs to the flat and found Stephen sitting in front of the television flicking through channels. He still looked like he had been punched in the stomach. Daniel could not blame him. Near death experiences were seldom easy to overcome.

"Stephen. I'd like a word."

Stephen rolled his eyes and turned to look at Daniel with all the defiance of an adolescent.

"Here we go."

"What?" demanded Daniel.

"You're going to cut me," said Stephen, "aren't you?"

"No."

"Then what?"

"I think you need time to train in the GhettoFab."

"Why," demanded Stephen, "because of what happened last night?"

"Yeah."

"What do you think happened out there?"

"Look, it happens to the best of us."

Stephen stood up, every muscle coiled as he glared at Daniel.

"What happens to the best of you?"

"Look," said Daniel calmly. "You froze. It's as simple as that."

"Oh, I froze?"

"You need more training with your new ability. My fault was in letting you train in that box for as long as I did. It took you out of the fight. Putting you into one last night was a mistake."

"So you think I can't handle myself?" challenged Stephen, his tone harsh and cutting.

"Can you?" demanded Daniel.

"I can do anything you can do." spat Stephen. "And I didn't need your ass pushing me out of the way. I had it under control."

"Sure you did. Just go to the GhettoFab. Run the course and prepare yourself for long distance combat."

"Whatever." scoffed Stephen and then he went to his room to change into his workout gear. Daniel was pleased that he was still sure enough about himself that he could run the course. Behind him Josh stirred.

"What about me?" offered Josh, nervously.

"You feel you need training?" asked Daniel, somewhat pleased that Josh had spoken up.

"To tell you the truth," began Josh, "last night kinda freaked me out. I could use a run at the course."

"Gear up," nodded Daniel.

Josh nodded and raced to his room to change. Daniel stood there in the flat pleased with the morning's talks and the fact that no one walked. McCormack rounded the corner from the hallway and leaned against the wall.

"Got everything in hand?" asked McCormack.

"Of course I do," said Daniel.

"Glad to hear," responded McCormack, studying Daniel curiously.

"You got anything to say?" demanded Daniel.

"Just that Boatman was right," replied McCormack. "You can't be going through the door with us. It's just not safe for a normal human."

"Again, with the normal human." scoffed Daniel. "Look, I can handle myself. But the team, with the exception of Leonard and Chad is full of individuals."

McCormack pressed that point, glowering at Daniel, taking his words as an affront to his professionalism.

"So you're including me as an individual?" challenged McCormack.

"Your powers mark you and Bradley as individuals," answered Daniel. "and you don't follow the team plan when it counts."

"What's that supposed to mean?" demanded McCormack.

"It means," replied Daniel, "why did you leave the strike team to meet up with us at the security room?"

"Leonard had the strike team in position," answered McCormack with a wave of his hand, "and I trusted him not to fumble the ball."

"Don't put this on him," snapped Daniel. "You abandoned your position."

"So now we're looking at me?" snapped McCormack.

"Your ability is immune to grenades," snapped Daniel. "You would have been the only person who could have contained Olsen Cadiff and prevented him from escaping."

"I sensed Athena and came to back you up. It was perfectly acceptable-"

"We had Kalinowski just fine."

"So now we're going to second guess every step we made?"

"I'm not second guessing my decisions. I'm calling you out on your lack of team compatibility."

"So what now, you going to bench me?"

"I should. But you're the team's most powerful member. I need you to follow orders, and not float around like you know best. It's the GhettoFab all over again. You disappeared to fight a Special on your own without communicating with the team. In the interim, Bradley was nearly killed."

"You're putting that on me?" blinked McCormack, his temper flaring. Daniel felt a chill down his spine as McCormack's aura flared into a physical force between them. Ignoring this he pressed his point.

"Why shouldn't I?" for the first time, Daniel was surprised to find McCormack speechless. "If I'm going to lead this team I need my orders followed, and I need the communications to keep coming. It was like groping in the dark at the GhettoFab."

"And you're just telling me about this now?"

"This is my first time seeing us interact in the field. In practice, it doesn't work because some of the members of the Task Force haven't grasped the old concept of there not being an 'I' in team!"

"So I'm not a team player?" challenged McCormack, his aura flaring again.

"I'm sure you think you are," answered Daniel dismissively.

"What do you want me to say?" demanded McCormack.

"That you'll treat every mission like the Maryland mission," answered Daniel. "You follow orders and keep the communications line open."

"I can do that," acquiesced McCormack, his eyes still boring into Daniel's. "Just make the orders good ones."

"You don't get to pick which orders are acceptable enough to follow. Just follow them."

"Fine," spat McCormack.

"Fine," answered Daniel, insisting on having the last word.

McCormack turned and walked into his office, slamming the door behind him. Daniel sighed and shook his head. *Well, that went well...* he thought. And then he walked down the hallway to his office, collapsing into his seat behind the computer and rubbed the itch on his abdomen. Daniel's eyes wandered the office, taking in the Spartan room with a lazy expression on his face when his computer blinked and scrolled with information.

//TERROR ALERT\\-FBI intel suggests imminent terrorist attack on landmark under US sovereignty. Perceived attack to occur at high profile target, suggesting White House, Pentagon or Hall of Congress situated around President. Evacuation Order 7 has been issued. All agencies should be on high alert, and contact DHS for orders.\\

Daniel sat upright in his seat, his heartbeat thumping in his throat. He reached over to pick up his phone to dial Boatman's cell phone when the phone rang. Daniel picked up on the first ring.

"I was just calling you."

"Did you get the email?" asked Boatman, lazily.

"The terror alert?" said Daniel, demanding Boatman to spell it out for him.

"That would be the one." answered Boatman, his voice bored.

"You want to deploy us on a terror alert?" clarified Daniel.

"That would be the reason I was calling," replied Boatman, "yes."

"What about the whole not getting involved in normal human scenarios?"

"Since you breached protocol last night and made a spectacle, I could stand for a more contained spectacle to

employ the team in. Plus your savvy with other departments can be put to use."

"How contained?" said Daniel, insisting on clarification.

"Let's just say you'll get none of the glory on this one.
This is my olive branch to the heads of DHS. Apparently
they want to see you work for them."

"Don't we work for DHS?"

"Not officially. Your team is more off the books than
that. But considering the little flap you hit last night, and
I don't lay blame on you or your team, the powers that be
have taken notice and not in a favorable light. They wish to
scrutinize you under their thumb for a while. I can see no
reason to not allow them their moment of examination of
the team, so I'm ordering you in."

"So basically we're going to be gofers to the teams who
got embarrassed by our failure to make an arrest, last night."

"Quite succinctly, yes."

"If you order me in, I won't refuse. But I want to go on
record as saying I really don't want to do this."

"So noted. And so ordered."

"Yes sir. Wheels up within the hour."

"Oh, that won't be necessary."

"Why not?"

"I've arranged for your arrival via SUV caravan. Since
it's a terror alert, the airspace has been closed tightly. For
the moment, I cannot override the protocols for flying
through DC airspace."

"Lawrence," chided Daniel, "are you getting old on
me?"

"This is no laughing matter," snapped Boatman, the
edge in his voice leaving little room to argue or negotiate.
"Get it together, son."

"Yes, sir."

"Have the team ready in five minutes."

"Attire?"

"Look official."

"Suits it is."

Daniel walked down the hall to Leonard's room.

"What's up?" said Leonard grimly eyeing Daniel's face.

"Rally the men," ordered Daniel. "Full suits and shoul-dered side arms."

"What's going on?"

"Terror alert," answered Daniel. "We're going to be sta-tioned around D.C. under DHS oversight."

Leonard's eyes widened and his lips pulled into a pout, sensing the coming interagency conflict.

"This should be interesting," said Leonard.

"Tell me about it," muttered Daniel, and he turned and marched to his room to change while Leonard darted down the hall pounding on doors, spreading the news.

Within five minutes, the team had gathered in the flat dressed in full suit and ties. Stephen and Josh were the only ones absent. Leonard turned and grew rigid in Daniel's presence, his face a dark smirk.

"Sir," said Leonard, "team almost all accounted for."

"It's okay," answered Daniel. "Stephen and Josh will be redirected to the base of operations and we'll meet up when we arrive. Boatman wants us *all* on the ground."

"Are we really going to be put to task by the same peo-ple we dealt with last night?"

"I wouldn't be surprised to see Agent King, today, let's put it that way."

"This is going to suck," muttered Leonard.

"Suck it up," demanded Daniel. "I need you at your best today. I've got a feeling it's going to be a long one."

The team looked at Daniel with a sense of dread grow-ing and flashing across their expressions. After yesterday's mishap with the escape of two suspects at DHS headquar-ters, they did not want to encounter agents from Homeland Security or the Bureau any time soon—especially when they were still not fully trained and cohesive as a team. Their dread was shattered by the sound of a horn blaring and the chirp of a police siren.

"Let's get downstairs and get this over with," said Daniel, quickly turning and heading toward the stairs. The rest of the team followed silently behind him, taking the stairs down to the lobby to greet the SUV caravan.

The SUVs pulled up in front of a line of SUVs and Metro PD SWAT vans outside the Washington Mall with uniforms swarming the plaza. Daniel stepped out of the SUV into the chill wind and surveyed the ordered chaos of mass mobilization without a clear target. Nothing had changed since Homeland Security's inception. It was still ordered chaos. Hundreds of voices ordered and reordered procedure over the radios as Daniel led the team through the mess of Metro PD until he found the calm of the storm. A lone man standing smugly in the center of the maelstrom of bodies, completely at ease with himself. Agent King looked up with a grin of vindication at the sight of Daniel, and gestured him over.

"Agent Rooke," sneered King, "Glad you could make it."

"I'm under the understanding you requested our services?"

"That I did," lorded King, "That I did. We have a terror alert, you might have heard, and we need men evacuating public places of civilians. I think that is right up your alley."

Daniel sensed some menial task to humiliate his team and grit his teeth.

"Actually, it's nowhere close," growled Daniel. "We were under the understanding our role would be closer to Congress or the White House. That would be the best place for us. At high-risk targets. The President is speaking at the world leaders dinner taking place on the USS Olympus. That would be a good place for us."

"You would think so, would you? No." sneered King, savoring the moment with Daniel firmly beneath his heel—reveling in the expression on his face. "No, I need you here assisting Metro PD in the evacuation process. You see, we need traffic officers to direct cars away from the Mall and out of harm's way. That's what you are here for."

"Traffic duties?" scoffed Daniel. "Forgive me, but that would be underutilizing our resources which should be going on good intelligence instead of puff rumors."

"Be that as it may," snapped King, as if Daniel were under his employ. "That is where I'm placing you. You have a problem with that, Rooke? Because after last night's cluster-fuck, I sorely doubt your superiors can be very happy with you. And my understanding is you need a *gleaming* report from me to keep your Department solvent. You would like to keep your little Task Force working another few days, would you?"

Daniel resisted the urge to strangle King on the spot and thought it through rationally. A little goose-stepping could go a long way toward healing the rift between SITF and the other agencies. Daniel sighed and eyed King, who could barely contain his glee.

"Traffic duty?"

"That's why you're here."

"Fine, I'll mobilize my men to Independence Avenue, Madison Drive and Jefferson Drive to oversee Metro and get our hands dirty."

"Actually, you'll be working *for* Metro. I have better things to do than oversee you. Perform your duties to Metro's satisfaction, and maybe you'll have a job tomorrow."

With that, King turned and signaled a Metro officer with a lot of stars on his shoulders and scrambled eggs filling his left breast and presented him with some flair.

"Chief Swann, this is your traffic assistance you called for. I hear they are quite adept at traffic control. Put them to work between 4th and 14th and between Constitution and Independence."

Chief Swann walked up and glared at Daniel grimly.

"You are?"

"Agent Rooke." said Daniel, and gestured over his right shoulder. "This is my team."

Chief Swann studied Daniel and the SITF team grimly before turning back to Daniel.

"I don't know who you pissed off to draw this card, but don't be a problem for me. I need traffic moving and not stopping. We're already clogged, and evacuation of this magnitude is going to stress the streets. Move like you've got a purpose and don't stop until I come get you."

"Understood." replied Daniel. "However we can assist you we will, but if we get called in, we're going to evac quick."

Chief Swann shook his head and an amused chuckle escaped his lips.

"There won't be any call," said Swann, grimly. "From my understanding, you're in the doghouse. Which means you're mine. There will be no rescue for you." Chief Swann snapped his fingers and two uniformed officers brought a box over and set it on the ground next to the Chief, then began rummaging through it, pulling out neon-green mesh vests with reflecting tape on it, keeping the wearer visible to traffic. Swann handed one to Daniel and pulled a thick stack out of the box. "I need you to put on these vests and man the intersections. That's the closest to the glory as you're going to get. Do we understand each other?"

"I hear you fine."

Chief Swann pushed the stack of vests into Daniel's arms who fumbled to keep hold of them.

"Then don't let me stop you."

With that, Chief Swann walked away leaving Daniel standing there with the vests in his arms.

"Alright men," announced Daniel. "You heard the man. Each of you gets a vest. Put 'em on and no complaining."

Each of them took a vest and scowled as they slid it on over their suits. Daniel slid his on and sighed. As he expected, wearing the uniform vest over a black suit looked hideous, and the embarrassment rose in him like he had been ordered to appear in public naked, which for a split second, he preferred to this assignment. Daniel summoned all his character to remain professional, studied his men— who by the looks of them felt as foolish as he did in the vests—and sighed.

"We're splitting up. McCormack, I want you at Constitution and 4th, Bradley, I want you at Constitution and 14th. Leonard, I want you at Independence and 4th, and I want Joseph at Independence and 14th. Stephen, you'll be at Madison and 14th and Josh will be at Madison and 4th. Chad, I want you at Jefferson and 14th and I'll be on Jefferson and 4th dealing with the mess over there."

"Yes sir," muttered the team.

"Don't let me keep you," dismissed Daniel.

SITF mobilized to their assigned street corners and Daniel took the *walk of shame* to his position at Jefferson and 4th.

Unlike the rest of his team, Daniel had pulled traffic duty before, and though he did not care for it much, he quickly took the tone of a traffic cop, blowing his whistle and directing traffic out of the district. It required a keen eye and a stern handling but traffic soon bowed to his wishes and responded to his movements and gestures as he shoved the cars down side streets and avenues until traffic was moving smoothly.

All in all, it took Daniel the better part of an hour before traffic lightened up enough for him to notice the rest of the traffic cops standing on the street corners chatting with each other as though the job was no longer their responsibility.

Daniel gestured to the men and women but was thoroughly ignored by them as they went back to their conversations, leaving him standing there feeling foolish. Just then, a limousine pulled up alongside Daniel.

"You can't stop here," shouted Daniel to the driver. "I'm going to need you to make a right and proceed down 3rd Street out of the area."

The driver thumbed back toward the rear of the car and began to roll forward. As the rear door came into view, the window rolled down. Daniel cautiously leaned toward the window, his right hand sliding over his holster. What he did not expect to see was Lawrence Boatman smiling up at him.

"Daniel, my boy!" chimed the blueblood voice Daniel knew full well. "Are you having fun out here in this damnable weather?"

"Give me a break, Lawrence."

"Would you like a break?"

"What have you got?"

"Step inside my parlor."

Daniel did not need to be told twice. With a quick hop he disappeared into the limousine and the door slammed shut behind him.

"So," began Boatman, "I see that Homeland Security is using you to the best of your ability."

"Funny," answered Daniel moodily, "Honestly, I want to break my foot off in Agent King's ass."

"There will be time for that, I assure you. As for now, would you like to know where we're going?"

"Not as much as I'd like to know my team is pulled off this bullshit assignment."

"That is up to you."

"Up to me?" blinked Daniel. "I thought this was all about getting the agencies to see us as amiable."

"Oh, I could give a damn how they see us. Once our official duties start they'll be lining up to us with hat in hand to have us solve their problems for them. No. This was a test to see how you handle your peers."

"A what?"

"A test. To see if you would stand firm, bend or break. And you, my dear Daniel, bent."

"I'm here because you said it would be a good idea to work with them to smooth over the start we had with them last night."

"And it was. But honestly, the fact that you allowed yourself to fall under Metro authority…" Boatman clicked his tongue against his teeth in reproach. "I honestly would have thought I'd find you back at the Post."

"Well if there's a way to be of assistance in a national crisis, I thought it best to take some small part in it."

"But your part could be expansively larger. You do see it, don't you?"

"I see it. It's getting invited to the party that's the trick."

"You weren't invited last night. You made your way in and flashed your credentials and the sea parted for you. That is what I wish to see."

"They're not going to fold for the credentials twice, Lawrence."

Boatman sat back with a wild gleam in his eyes as a Cheshire grin stretched his face.

"Oh, but they will. You'll see."

"I'll want the team together for this."

"Call them."

Daniel tapped his earpiece.

"SITF come in?"

The radio cracked to life and Daniel was entertained to a menagerie of sounds and voices over the din of traffic. "McCormack, here." said McCormack, "Bradley Overman, standing by." said Bradley. "Are we done here yet?" demanded Stephen "This is bullshit." Leonard clicked on the line: "That's a negative on the language, Giordano."

Finally Josh's voice clicked on the line sounding desperately bored: "I haven't seen a car since I got here!"

"All units report to…" suddenly Daniel was aware he had no idea where they were going. "Where are we going?"

"I have SUVs driving to their location as we speak."

"Team, stand ready for pick up. This party's over."

"Are we heading back to the Post?" said Stephen, hopefully.

"Negative," replied Daniel. "We're going to where the action is."

"Roger that." answered McCormack. "Confirmed." said Bradley. "It's about time!" exclaimed Stephen. "Can the chatter, Giordano!" barked Leonard. "I'll go wake up Joseph." said Josh. Daniel grimaced at the thought that Joseph decided to take a nap when he should have been working, but decided to put a pin in that and wait for later to deal with him.

"Alright," said Daniel. "The team's ready for pick up."

"I'm sure the team's been ready for pick up since they were dropped off."

"I'm sure."

The limousine slowed and Boatman's eyes lit up.

"Here we are."

Daniel looked outside the window and saw a big rig and trailer with the letters DHS Mobile Station on the side. Boatman opened the door.

"Are you ready, Daniel?"

Daniel looked out at the DHS Mobile Station with some unease. The beat cop in him was nervous. Back in New York, he would never think about approaching this truck. It was for his superiors to enter, and even they did not do so without some trepidation. But that was another life. In this one, he was the head of a government team indirectly funded by Homeland Security. Whether they liked it or not, he had a place at their table. And it was now clear Boatman was ensuring they knew him and knew he was untouchable.

Daniel swallowed his concerns and stepped out of the limousine following behind Boatman as he parted the agents with his very presence. Not once did Boatman pull his credentials. He just walked with the authority of a general. Which he was...retired. Boatman took the steps of the trailer and the agents walking back and forth on the steps made way for him. Daniel had to smile—the way Boatman could walk in anywhere and command respect—this was a talent he would have to learn.

Inside the trailer, high ranking agents stood around a map of Washington D.C. highlighting areas that have been evacuated and illuminating sections of the map that were considered high profile for a terrorist attack. Agent King was there, receiving orders and explaining his accomplishments in the hours preceding this meeting. Boatman stepped up toward them and every eye trailed up to him, their conversations and orders silenced in his presence. Boatman turned away facing the coffee dispenser, and filled his cup, helping himself to the cream and sugar. Agent King turned to face him.

"Excuse me," demanded King.

"I'll be done in a minute." said Boatman, not turning to acknowledge King. "I'm afraid you'll have to wait your turn."

"This is a Homeland Security mobile command center," growled King, "not a Starbucks. You'll have to leave." And with a snap of his fingers, "Agent!"

Two agents stepped forward at King's behest and approached Boatman. Daniel turned to face them, reaching for his credentials, and resting his palm on his side arm. The two agents stood perfectly rigid. Boatman continued stirring his coffee as though nothing out of the ordinary were taking place. Boatman turned and stood straight with a carefree smile and eyes that dared King to challenge him.

"And I am afraid you don't have the authority to remove me."

"Who are you?" demanded King, the others at the table studying Boatman as a credible threat to their careers remained silent, letting King do all the talking. Boatman turned to King and smiled.

"My manners," said Boatman, almost forgetfully, and he produced his identification holding it within inches of King's face so King would have to go cross-eyed to read the ID badge. "Lawrence Boatman." A chill crept through the room and the silent agents surrounding the desk instantly straightened and grew statue-like. The *man in black* himself had entered the room. All were keenly aware their jobs really were in the palm of his hands. King was the only one oblivious to the change in the room. With a turn of his head, Boatman drew attention to Daniel for the first time, who stood with his back to them facing the other two agents like a gunslinger with his identification in one hand and the palm of his other hand on the grip of his pistol. "I believe you're familiar with my Agent Rooke?" For the first time, King recognized Daniel was there, and his jaw set. Boatman took this as an acknowledgement and smiled. "Excellent."

"What is the meaning of this?" demanded King.

"The meaning of this is you are in a heap of trouble, Agent King." snapped Boatman, eyeing King critically. "I leased my team to you to secure the capitol from terrorist threats…something they have familiarity with. Instead, you put them on traffic duty. Tell me it is not so."

King turned to look for a helping hand from his superiors behind the desk and found only dismissive glances and noncommittal expressions. Realizing he had no support, King's face turned beet red as he began to fathom the dangerous waters he found himself in and he stammered his response to Boatman.

"I placed your team where they were needed-"

"No," snapped Boatman. "You placed them where you could embarrass them."

"Sir," stammered King, vainly trying to grasp hold of the situation and turn it to his advantage. "This is not the place or time to discuss this matter."

"Oh, you're quite right. It should have never become an issue to be brought up. But here we are." Boatman's eyes bored into King who squirmed under the critical glare, as though the eyes would glow red hot and burn into his skull. It was as if Boatman had condemned King to his own personal hell through the mere intensity of his gaze and the others behind the desk turned away, averting their eyes from the vampiric intensity of the stare. Finally, before King could do more than shudder, Boatman looked away from him and bored into the men behind the desk. "Now, what is the situation? Brief me."

Instantly the men behind the desk jerked forward and rifled through their notebooks for data to offer and appease the god of darkness. A quick-witted agent behind the desk quickly stepped forward pointing to the locations on the map that had been highlighted red and blue.

"We have security at the White House and the Pentagon, and we have just closed off the Mall with a tight cordon."

"As well as your security detail at St. Elizabeths," said Boatman. "It seems you've closed off the areas that would be juicy targets. Now, what about the USS Olympus?"

The agents blinked at each other nervously, but the agent in charge leaned forward and placed his hand casually on the map with a show of security before the stare of Boatman.

"We have complete operational control of the space station, and all in attendance have passed through rigorous security check points to the point of cavity search."

"I have no doubt you've been thorough in searching the guests. What about diplomatic cases?"

The agents traded blank expressions, as though some threat had eluded them.

"Sir?" stammered the agent in charge.

Boatman sighed.

"Bombs can be hidden in cases that are not usually searched, am I not correct?"

"No, you're quite correct." conceded the agent in charge, looking down at the map for something to stare at. With a sweep of his hand, the map slid away from the screen and he flicked his finger at another icon, opening a window to the security feed from the USS Olympus. He studied the screen for a long moment before looking up at Boatman. "I can put you in touch with our chief of security aboard the Olympus, if you'd like."

"That would be wonderful."

The agent in charge looked over at King who tried his best to fade into the wall.

"See Mr. Boatman has everything he needs." said the agent in charge. "No screw ups, King."

"Yes, sir," replied King, not at all enthusiastic about his new job.

"So glad we can work together, Agent King." said Boatman, as though enjoying a good meal. His smile was warm though his eyes were dead and bored into King's. "Mind you, how you act in the next half hour will reflect on the remainder of your employment with the Federal Bureau of Information. Your DHS status will not protect you from me. I hope you're up to the task."

"Yes sir," gasped King, his eyes wide with fear and a lingering streak of pride burning the back of his neck.

"Daniel, will work with you."

King stopped dead and turned questioning to Boatman, his voice fragile and distant.

"Daniel?"

"Agent Rooke," clarified Boatman.

"Ah," grimaced King with dismay. "...yes sir."

"Carry on."

King shot Daniel a malevolent glance that faded quickly as he rushed to the front of the trailer where the viewscreen illuminated with a man talking rapid fire with a starlit background. The chief officer aboard the Olympus was hard pressed to keep orders flowing to the security details working with the event staff and behind the scenes.

King handed Daniel an earpiece and then picked up the other and held it over his ear. Daniel scoffed and flicked the speakers on and the chief officer's dialogue was pumped into the trailer: "...Sensor sweep of the shuttle bay reports no detectable threat...Sending in personnel for visual sweep... Confirmed. You have twenty AB's to search and I need that sweep completed within twenty minutes. I want that bay cleared ASAP...Roger that. We should be complete with time to spare...Security detail, report...All clear on the observation deck. All guests seated for the dinner... Snipers in position....Confirmed. Good hunting...Roger that... Airlock Sentry checking in. All Airlocks accounted for and covered on both sides...Confirmed. Report any intrusions at your positions as they appear...Confirmed...Sensor Com, what's your status?...Nothing on Delta or EDAR. The skies are clear...What about neighboring vessels?...I'm reading clear on all autonomous vessels in the region, and clear chatter from all manned craft in geosynch. No trajectories veering in our direction. All static. We're in the eye of the storm...Confirmed. Keep me posted on the status of the neighboring craft...Will do...I'm getting a heat reading on a vessel within our security perimeter...Say again?...

Unknown heat signature emanating from neighboring satellite…Can you zero in on the vessel?…Stand by. Heat signature coming off of USS Elysium…What is their status?… Patching through to the Elysium, stand by…"

Daniel turned to see the Secret Service agents watching the dinner speeches on the window reserved for the USS Olympus. The Olympus has a large clear nanocrystal dome covering two football field lengths where the congregation of who's who in politics, and world leaders as well as musicians and Hollywood A-listers listened to the President speak.

Boatman floated over and stood behind Daniel and King, ignoring the Olympus window completely as he listened to the chatter between the Olympus and the Elysium: "This is the Olympus, Elysium, reply…This is the Elysium. How can we be of service, Olympus?…Elysium, we're detecting a heat signature from within your ship. What's your status?….Checking. All looks clear on our onboard sensors, are you sure about your readings?…Elysium, our readings show a rapid increase in reactor output and heat signatures register you have a fire onboard your vessel…I'll move our fire teams to sweep the B level…I'm showing fires spreading to the airlocks…Stand by…Olympus, we have reports of fires on B level. Status of Reactor unknown. It's weird, our boards are green shipwide. Our firefighting detail is reporting casualties. Requesting emergency assistance… Confirmed, Elysium. Putting Emergency Assistance teams on alert…Feeling slight tremors. Tremors building in intensity…Confirmed, My resources are spread thin, I'm calling for additional teams from other ships in geosynch. Stand by for emergency assistance teams to dock…The board is green! This shouldn't be happening! We're blind up here! I'm sending additional teams down to combat the fire and stand ready at the airlocks…It's alright, you're doing fine. Just keep your com open and prepare to be boarded…Hurry!

The tremors are getting worse!...I'm sending my first team in now and I have reports from five other vessels that they will change course and send AB's as well. Stay calm and keep the information coming...Yes, sir! We're getting reports that the fires are melting the walls. Radiation sweeps show the reactors are leaking...All intercepting vessels, we've got a radiation leak, dress accordingly...This is the Intrepid. Reactor leak confirmed. We'll wear our hazmat gear for this party. Keep us informed about that reactor... Roger that, Intrepid. Rads are climbing in the reactor but is still contained by the blast shields...Confirmed. Docking in three minutes...Elysium, you have a team docking ETA three minutes. Have your teams ready to greet and direct as they arrive...Confirmed, Olympus...

"Monitor Elysium's internal chatter," commanded Boatman.

"Sir?" stammered King.

"Just do it!" snapped Boatman.

King opened another window and broadcast the radio activity from inside the Elysium into the trailer:

"...The blast doors are melting! We need coolant pumped into that room!...at those temperatures the fire retardant will be broken down and consumed before it can be any use...Negative! Negative! The chemicals will break down into a flammable material! Do not release the fire retardant!...What do you expect us to do?...Fall back to the next blast door and seal it!...Negative! I've got men on the floor...That's an order! Fall back and seal it!...All units fall back to the secondary blast door point, ASAP! I've been ordered to seal the doors!...Seal it now!...My men are still in there!...They're wearing their RAD armor! They'll survive! Seal the doors now!...Sealing doors...Blast Doors sealed. I just sealed seventeen men and women in there...Stand by for further orders...Yes sir...Engineering, come in?... [screaming cracked in on the open com line. Horrible wails of agony]... Engineering, please respond...Engineering, here! We're under attack- [cries of agony followed by silence]... Engineering, say again! Come in, Engineering!... [Static]...Get me Tech! I want my ship back! Get me my shipwide sensors online, now!...Working on it! We'll be up in fifty seconds!...What's wrong with my shipwide?... It's a hack! Someone's overridden eyes and ears shipwide and put them in Engineering. We've tracked the command overrides. They're moving toward airlocks behind the blast shields. They're sealed in!...What are we dealing with?... We have intruders onboard, sir. It's the only explanation... Intruder alert! Security, armor up and meet me at B deck! Set weapons to full auto. I want these intruders down before they can do any more damage to my ship!...Security team mobilizing to B deck...Wait for me at the blast doors!...Yes sir!...Ramirez! You have the helm...Release blast doors... Blast doors open!...The fire has melted through the blast door at the far end of the hall...Man down! Man down!... We've got bodies all over the place! Seventeen total... They're gone!...Security team, activate gravity boots!... Gravity boots on!...Tech, do we have control?...Yes sir! Control has been restored...open airlocks on B deck. Get these damned flames out of here! Security teams, stand fast!...We lost Malcolm!...Malcolm's wearing his armor, his armor will activate its homing beacon as soon as he clears the Elysium. Stand ready!...Fire's out! Repeat, fire's out! Open blast shield 32B...Blast shield is wedged where it's melted. It's expanded and warped. Release coolant to Blast shield 32B...Cut off the coolant. That should do it. Security team, move in...Activate winvid...I've got movement up ahead...We're taking fire! We're taking fire!... Command, give me security countermeasures in hallway 11 on B deck...Security countermeasures deployed...Security team, move forward...We've got activity on the observation deck! Repeat, observation deck is compromised...

How did they get behind us?...They're using the emergency access ladders! Owens, open that EA hatch, take a team and advance. I'll take the rest of the team to Engineering... Security team to Captain...Go ahead...We found the invaders. They're taking position. Request order to fire...Fire! Take them down!...We're taking casualties! They're working on something in the center of the observation deck! I can't make out what it is...Take them down, and investigate!...Confirmed! Moving in!...Owens is down! Taking fire...Take down those intruders!...Can't get close! They're firing weapons we've never come across before! They appear to be built into their suits!...I don't want to hear excuses, I want results! Take them out!...They're gone! The shooting stopped! The observation deck's empty!...Get to whatever they were working on! Move!...Reaching target...What do you see?...Oh God! Sir, it's a [explosion and scream followed by static]...What was that?! Security team, report! Com, what was that tremor?...Sir, I'm getting energy fluctuations from Engineering!...What's that?... [explosion and static]

On the window display, a look at the Elysium burning, the observation deck shattered and venting atmosphere into space while a secondary explosion flared out of the side of the ship. The Elysium tilted and burned sending debris out to in all directions.

Daniel blinked at the screen as a feeling of dread climbed up his spine.

"How many souls were on the Elysium?" demanded Daniel. When no one responded he grabbed King around the collar and yanked him toward him. "How many people?!"

"I don't know," replied King, still too shocked by what he had just seen to register more than a little hostility toward Daniel.

Daniel quickly released King and turned to Boatman, who stood there watching him expectantly. This however

442

was only for a second, when all eyes steered toward the Olympus window.

On the other window, the live feed of the Olympus Convention dinner was interrupted as the cameras panned away from the President to view the plume of fire extending outward silently in space. Debris hurled through space— large chunks of metal tumbling toward the observation deck—growing larger as it threatened the envoys. Soon the sounds of hysteria filled the observation deck as the approaching pieces of the Elysium spun closer toward the Olympus.

"Tactical! Arm cannons and target that flack! Fire!"

The cannons fired as beams of light superheated and melted the incoming flack to smaller pellets that super cooled in the void and pelted the clear crystal of the observation deck. The cannons continued to inundate the area with fire, still, some pieces crept through the maelstrom of concentrated fire only to roll on unhindered as the cannons spun and swiveled looking for the unimpeded shot. A larger chunk tumbled and rolled closer to the observation deck, threatening to impact with it with disastrous results, inspiring the frenzy of the dinner guests to stampede their way toward the exits leading down from the seemingly naked platform they stood on. Over the din of the mob came the assertive voice of the deck commander calling over the shipwide band: "All hands brace for impact!"

The patrons and dinner guests went wild as hundreds of people forced themselves into an access hatch meant for no more than three bodies at a time. The result was the trampling of the elderly and the less sure of foot as the mob stormed the access hatch into the belly of the ship—all the while, the crowd still on the deck pressed with all their might against the wall of flesh to fit them into the hole and make room for them—crushing the people who waited in terror for their turn through the hatch. The camera trailed back and forth from the carnage on the deck to the rolling space debris approaching the clear crystal dome that encircled the observation deck. Finally, the camera became stationary and slumped slightly to the side as the cameraman abandoned his post to join the mob down below. The camera watched, going in and out of focus as it followed the large chunk of the Elysium rolled closer and closer until finally it collided with the crystal dome with a horrifying crash, shaking the observation deck, the vibrations extending throughout the ship. The last thing they saw before the camera fell over was the spiderweb fingering its way across the dome.

"Bad Strike! Bad Strike! The observation deck is compromised. Evacuate the observation deck and get them below!...We need to seal it!...We have half the leaders from the free world on the deck without access to EVA armor! Get them below deck, now!...Yes sir!"

Daniel turned away from the video feed and made his way toward the door. Outside, his SITF team stood anxious for orders. Boatman appeared at his side.

"Where will you go, Daniel?"

"To the Olympus. Our first priority is the evacuation of the world leaders. We'll catch a ride from there to the Elysium."

Boatman simply nodded.

"Proceed," said Boatman, quietly.

"Thank you, sir." Daniel turned and exited the mobile command center.

Outside, grim and disgusted, the SITF team stood apart from the bustle of the agents around them, clearly viewed a plague on the career of anyone who so much as talked to them. Daniel stepped into the mid afternoon light and immediately demanded their attention with the clear severity in his eyes.

"SITF team!" commanded Daniel, his voice hard. "We've got a situation and we've been called in to play."

McCormack and Bradley nodded their encouragement to Daniel and Leonard stood at attention. Giordano high fived Joseph who grinned hungrily, while Josh watched warily as Daniel clicked on his cellular phone and dialed the Flight Office at Andrews Air Base.

"Flight Deck," clicked the voice over the line.

"This is SITF agent in charge Daniel Rooke. I need the Chariot on emergency airlift immediately. Meet me at the Constitution Gardens."

"Inside D.C. airspace?"

"DHS has got bigger fish to fry. Get the pilot in the cockpit now! Drag that son of a bitch if you have to! Touch down at Constitution Gardens in five minutes. And get me an AB-4 on the tarmac ready for rendezvous with the USS Olympus. Have it stocked for seven soldiers with extra-environmental tactical armor and side arms. You have the specs we need on file, so I want armors that fit. Get it done. I need to be on that space station ASAP."

Daniel approached Constitution Gardens and stood on the lawn with the rest of his team looking off into the northeast. Leonard came to his side, and Daniel looked to his right and left and saw the entire team take equal footing next to him waiting impatiently studying the horizon. All the faces he met were hard but there was a sense of peace in every face. Now they would be put to good use. Now they would stand for a cause. Now they would prove themselves. In the distance, the Reflecting Pool glittered with the light of the afternoon sun.

Thirteen minutes later, off on the horizon, the Chariot sped to the rendezvous point. Daniel was too focused on the mission unfolding before him to be bothered with his inept pilot's timeliness. He had bigger concerns. How was he going to get on board the Elysium? What would he find there? But most doggedly in his mind was the feeling of grim nostalgia as a hundred battlefields replayed in his memory. This would be Daniel's first time in space since the war. As the Chariot touched down with a bounce in Constitution Gardens, Daniel swallowed hard. *And so it begins...*